Cheater

Cheater

KAREN ROSE

HEADLINE

First published in the USA in 2024 by
BERKLEY
An imprint of Penguin Random House LLC.

First published in Great Britain in 2024 by
HEADLINE PUBLISHING GROUP

1

Cataloguing in Publication Data is available from the British Library

Hardback ISBN 978 1 4722 9690 0
Trade Paperback ISBN 978 1 4722 9691 7

Typeset in 9.88/12.85pt Palatino LT Std by Jouve (UK), Milton Keynes

Printed and bound in Great Britain by Clays Ltd, Elcograf S.p.A.

HEADLINE PUBLISHING GROUP
An Hachette UK Company
Carmelite House
50 Victoria Embankment
London EC4Y 0DZ

www.headline.co.uk
www.hachette.co.uk

To JoCarol Jones. Love you, my friend.

And, as always, to my sweet Martin.
You've been my heart for forty-two years.
I love you so very much.

Prologue

Carmel Valley, California
Saturday, 22 October, 2.15 P.M.

Homicide detective Kit McKittrick opened the barn door, making sure it made noise as she did so. She was more accustomed to slipping into the barn unseen and unheard so that she could be alone when life became too loud and frenzied. The barn had been her escape since she'd stumbled upon it as a terrified twelve-year-old runaway.

With Wren.

Her heart gave a familiar painful squeeze at the thought of the sister she'd lost sixteen years ago. They hadn't known it at twelve, but they'd stumbled into far more than a barn. They'd stumbled into salvation, in the form of Harlan and Betsy McKittrick, who'd given them warmth, security, and so much love.

Wren was long gone, taken from them by a killer who hadn't been found. *Not yet.* Kit still searched because Wren deserved justice. *As do we.* She and Harlan and Betsy had gone on because they'd had to. They'd lived. But they'd never forgotten the girl who'd brightened their lives.

Normally Kit came to the McKittrick barn to think and to remember Wren.

Today, however, she had a different mission. She entered, making sure she was loud enough to be heard. She didn't want to sneak up on the teenager who'd entered the foster care system after finding her mother's murdered body. The girl had endured enough pain and trauma and fear for a lifetime. Everyone at McKittrick House was always careful not to startle Rita.

1

Kit slid the door closed behind her, muffling the sound of the birthday party going on outside. The yard was full of McKittrick fosters, those who'd passed through and aged out and those who were still officially in the system and under Harlan and Betsy's care. They gathered for birthdays and holidays and Sunday dinners. They were a family. A huge, wonderful family. Rita was one of them now, but they all knew how overwhelming they could be when gathered en masse. It wasn't the first time someone had fled a celebration and it wouldn't be the last.

Kit would check on Rita, then leave her alone if she so wished. Cocking her head, Kit listened and, sure enough, heard the sound of quiet sobbing coming from the stall that was never occupied by any of the farm's resident animals.

Kit wasn't the only one who escaped here to be alone. The stall was her adoptive father's unofficial workshop, where Harlan McKittrick came to create art with his carving knife and a block of wood.

Opening the stall door, Kit found Margarita Mendoza huddled in the corner. Rita sat on a hay bale, her knees drawn up to her chest, arms wrapped around her legs. Her head was down, her face hidden by sandy blond hair that was streaked with purple and pink and blue.

'Hey,' Kit said. 'We went to cut your birthday cake and realized that nobody had seen you in a while.'

The family's initial reaction had been to panic at Rita's absence, as she'd been abducted six months before. She'd been brought home safe and sound, but Rita's disappearance had reminded them far too much of Wren's. Today, however, they'd suspected that the teenager had simply wanted a little quiet. Still, Kit needed to report that Rita was safe, so she texted Harlan. *Found her, Pop. In the barn.*

Harlan's reply was quick and heartfelt. *Thank God. Do you need me?*

Kit smiled. She'd always need Harlan and Betsy, but this was about Rita. *Give me five minutes, then wander in. She'll need you.* She slipped her phone into her pocket and studied the now-fourteen-year-old foster child. Rita hadn't moved, but she hadn't told Kit to leave, either.

2

'You want me to stay or go?' Kit asked.

Rita shrugged thin shoulders and Kit took that as assent. Sitting next to Rita on the hay bale, Kit ran a hand over the girl's hair the same way Harlan had always done to Kit's when she was upset.

'I'm sorry,' Rita whispered. 'I spoiled the party.'

'You spoiled absolutely nothing. I used to come and hide in here during parties, too.'

'Not on your own birthday.'

'You'd be wrong about that. I spent my fourteenth birthday in here, too.'

Rita lifted her head enough to peer through her hair. 'You did?'

'I did. I can prove it, too.' Kit eased to her knees and brushed hay from the edge of the barn wall, smiling sadly when she saw the names carved into the wood. She and Wren had been officially under Harlan and Betsy's care by then, their days of running away a thing of the past. 'It's not a pretty carving like Pop makes, but it's still here.' They'd both been fourteen. Her sister's fifteenth birthday had been her last.

Rita scooted to the edge of the hay bale and looked where Kit was pointing, her eyes growing wide. '"Wren McK, fourteen, and Katherine Matthews, fourteen."' She met Kit's gaze, the girl's dark eyes red and swollen. 'You went by Katherine then?'

'I did. Only Pop called me Kit back then. Never Katherine.'

'Why not?'

'I don't know. I've never asked.' Although she'd wanted to know, too. 'I figured if he had a reason, he'd have offered it up.'

'Your name was Matthews. But Wren was a McKittrick?'

'She was. They'd offered to adopt both of us. Wren said yes, and I said no.'

Rita seemed to tense. 'Why did you say no?'

Kit thought this question might have been part of what had driven Rita to hide in the barn. Harlan had shared that they'd asked Rita if she wanted to be adopted the week before and she'd stared at them like a deer in the headlights before bolting to her bedroom. They hadn't mentioned it again, hoping she'd approach them to talk about it after she'd had a chance to consider it.

'I didn't think that the McKittricks were real,' Kit said. 'I'd been in ten different foster homes by then, and I didn't think this would last, me living here. Them being so nice. I guess I didn't want to get my hopes up because I figured they'd get tired of me and make me leave.' She stroked Rita's hair again. 'But they never did.'

'Were you mad at Wren because she said yes?'

'No, never. Wren was everything sweet and kind and good. I figured she deserved a good place like this. I'd done . . . Well, I'd done some things that I wasn't too proud of when I was being moved from foster home to foster home. I figured that when the McKittricks found out, I'd be tossed back into the system.'

Kit thought that Rita would ask what she'd done, but she didn't. The girl dropped her gaze back to the carved names and traced them with her fingertip.

'When did you let them adopt you?' Rita whispered.

'A year after Wren died. I realized one day that Harlan and Betsy *were* real and that they were going to love me even when I was a disagreeable brat. I think I finally got tired of being angry and mad.' She chuckled. 'They waited me out. Out-stubborned me.'

Kit returned to the hay bale, wishing she'd covered it with a blanket first, because the hay was pricking her through her jeans. How Harlan sat here, carving his little wooden figures for hours on end, was a mystery.

Rita didn't look up, continuing to trace the carved names with her finger. 'Did they ever find out? About the things you did?'

'Yes. I came clean before the adoption was finalized. I figured I'd give them one more chance to change their minds before we signed on the dotted line, but they already knew. They'd always known.' Her eyes stung, remembering. 'They loved me anyway.'

They sat quietly for a few minutes. Kit could be patient and Rita was worth it.

'Do you still miss Wren?' Rita finally whispered, her question tentative.

Kit's throat tightened. 'Every single day,' she whispered back.

Rita's shoulders heaved in another sob. 'I miss my mom.'

'Oh, baby, I know you do.' Kit rubbed Rita's back gently. 'How

4

could you not? I felt guilty, you know? After Wren died, I didn't want a sixteenth birthday party, but Pop convinced me that Wren would be happy if I had one. That celebrating birthdays was part of going on after her death. But I came in here right afterward and cried because the guilt really hit me hard. Wren was dead and I was eating cake and opening presents.'

Rita said something that sounded like *It's not fair*, but she was crying too hard for Kit to be sure.

Kit sat there, stroking Rita's hair. 'It's not fair that they're gone, Rita. Not your mom or my sister. But they are and we have to go on. We have to live. We have to make them proud of us. Although I think you've already made your mom proud. You make me proud of you, too.'

Rita covered her face with her hands, her body shaking as she cried. 'I didn't do anything good. Not like you. You're a cop. You help people. You get justice for people like me and my mom.'

'I wasn't a cop when I was fourteen. I wasn't good then. I wasn't kind. I was too scared of being hurt to be kind. But you do good every day, Rita. You're smart and funny. But most important, you're kind. To people, to animals, to everyone.' Rita just shook her head, so Kit tried a different tack, saving the pep talk for when the girl was better able to listen. 'From what you've told me about your mom, she would have wanted you to have the best life. Wouldn't she?'

Rita nodded. Her face was still hidden behind her hands, but her tears had slowed. 'She always said that.'

'Well, that's what you're going to have. Pop and Mom and I and all the others out there are going to make sure of it. You're going to have a good life, Rita. But that doesn't mean you'll stop missing your mom. And if you don't want to join the party, nobody will be mad. You can stay out here as long as you want to.'

'I don't want to hurt their feelings.'

'See? You're kind. But they really will understand. It's days like this that you miss the one you loved the most. They all know that.'

The girl was quiet for another full minute before sighing. 'Did Mom and Pop McK tell you they offered to adopt me?'

'Yes. They said you kind of freaked a little.'

Rita's laugh was shaky. 'Yeah, that's fair. I was rude.'

'You were taken by surprise. No shame in that.'

Rita dropped her hands to her lap. 'Do you think I should let them?'

'That's not my decision to make.'

Rita rolled her eyes. 'I didn't ask you to decide. I asked what you thought. Then *I'll* decide.'

Kit's lips twitched. God, the girl reminded her of herself at fourteen. 'Then, yes. I do. Your mom was amazing, I know, but after her, you won't find better parents than Harlan and Betsy. And adoption gives you a sense of permanence. Of truly belonging forever. Five stars, would totally recommend.'

'I knew you'd say that. Dr Sam said the same thing.'

Kit sucked in a breath, caught off guard.

Dr Sam.

Sam Reeves, psychologist with a heart of gold. The man Kit had been avoiding for six months. He was a good, kind man and he liked her.

Which terrified her.

'Oh?' Kit managed. 'When did you talk to him?'

Rita's mouth curved slightly, as if she'd been expecting Kit's reaction, the little stinker. 'Last week after I freaked out about the adoption thing. I called Dr Carlisle, my normal therapist, but she was on vacation. Dr Sam was her backup. He helped. I was ready to tell Mom and Pop yes on the adoption, but then I ran from my party and . . .' She shrugged.

'You thought they'd change their minds? Honey, if they didn't change their minds about me, they'll never change their minds about you. Trust me.'

'Okay. I will. Trust you, I mean.' Rita stood resolutely, brushing the tears from her face and the hay from her jeans. 'I'm going to have cake. Then I'm going to say yes to adoption. Then I'm gonna have a life.' She opened the stall door, then paused, looking over her shoulder. 'Dr Sam is really nice, Kit, and he asks about you every time I see him. You should date him. Five stars, would totally recommend.'

6

Then she was gone, leaving Kit staring after her.

The clearing of a throat had Kit looking up into the eyes of her father. 'She's right, you know,' Harlan said lightly.

'Leave it, Pop.' She was not discussing her love life – or lack thereof – with Harlan McKittrick. 'Were you standing outside the whole time?'

He shrugged. 'You told me to give you five minutes, so I only heard the last part of what you told her. It was good advice, Kitty-Cat. Thank you.' He extended a hand, pulling her to her feet. 'Let's have some cake.'

Kit took a last look at the names carved into the wall. Wren McKittrick and Katherine Matthews. 'I miss her, Pop. Wren.'

Harlan kissed the top of her head. 'So do I. But she's watching, Kit. And she's proud of you. And you were wrong about something. You *were* kind back then. You were scared and kept people at arm's length to keep from being hurt, but you were not unkind. I'll never forget the night I discovered two little runaway girls in my barn, huddled under a scratchy saddle blanket, trying to get warm. You jumped to your feet and put yourself in front of Wren, your little fists raised, ready to fight.'

Kit smiled at the memory. 'You were so tall, and I was so scared.'

'But you were going to protect Wren. You always put her first, Kit. Always.'

Kit's smile faded. 'I didn't protect her when she needed it most.' When Wren had been snatched off the street by a killer who'd left her body in a dumpster, like she was trash. 'I was supposed to keep her safe and I didn't.' And that would haunt her forever.

'Would you hold Rita responsible for her mother's death?' Harlan demanded.

'Of course not. She's just a—'

Harlan's brows lifted. 'A child? Like you were back then?'

Kit narrowed her eyes, but she had to respect how neatly he'd maneuvered her. 'Fine. Point made.'

He smiled down at her. 'Rita thinks she wants to be a cop.'

Kit sucked in a breath. 'I thought she wanted to be a veterinarian.'

'Nope. She wants to be just like you.'

Kit shook her head. 'That's too much responsibility.'

Harlan chuckled. 'Live with it, girl. And maybe consider the example you're setting when you hide from nice men who want to date you because you think they deserve better, when they couldn't get any better than you.'

'Pop,' she growled in warning.

'I'm done meddling,' he said. 'I promise. You want some cake?'

He might actually be done meddling, at least for now. But he'd meddle again because he loved her, and she'd always cherished his interference. Except for this. Maybe because he was right. 'Yeah. Let's get some cake before the others eat it all.'

One

Shady Oaks Retirement Village
Scripps Ranch, San Diego, California
Monday, 7 November, 11.20 A.M.

Kit McKittrick allowed herself a moment to feel pity as she stood over the body of the elderly man lying dead on his apartment floor in the Shady Oaks Retirement Village. Then she squared her shoulders and proceeded to do her job.

The mood in the dead man's living room was subdued. The ME was examining the body while CSU took photos and Latent dusted for prints, but there was little of the normal scene-of-the-crime chatter to which Kit had become accustomed in the four and a half years she'd been in Homicide.

Everyone spoke in hushed whispers, like they were in church. Because it kind of felt like they were. Haunting melancholy music from a single piano was coming from the speaker mounted on the victim's living room wall. The music wasn't loud, but it was overwhelming nonetheless. Kit wanted to turn it off, because the music was so sad that it made her chest hurt and her eyes burn.

But neither the speaker nor its volume controls had been dusted for prints, so she couldn't touch it yet. Until then, she could only square her shoulders, ignore the music, and focus on getting justice for Mr Franklin Delano Flynn.

The cause of death of the eighty-five-year-old white male was most likely the butcher knife still embedded in his chest. But she'd learned long ago not to assume. Still, a butcher knife to the chest was never good. It was a long wound, the gash in the man's white

9

button-up shirt extending from his sternum to his navel. Whoever had killed him had to have had a lot of strength to create such a wound.

The victim had been dead long enough for his blood to dry, both the blood that had soaked the front of his shirt and the blood that had pooled on the floor around his torso.

His eyes, filmy in death, stared sightlessly up at the ceiling. His arms lay at his sides, his hands slightly curved. Not quite flat, but not quite fists, either. It wasn't a natural pose for the victim of a homicide who'd fallen after being stabbed. She wondered if his killer had repositioned his arms.

Mr Flynn had been a hardy man, broad-shouldered, tall, and still muscular. *Not in bad shape for eighty-five,* she thought. He wore dark trousers, the pockets turned out, as if he'd been searched.

His shoes were black oxfords, buffed to such a shine that she could nearly see her own reflection. She wondered if he'd come home, surprising his attacker, or if he'd welcomed his killer into his home.

His living room had been ransacked, books knocked off shelves, knickknacks strewn on the floor. The sofa cushions had been slashed open, foam stuffing on the floor as well. The man's bedroom was in a similar state. The drawers in the kitchen had been opened and emptied, their contents dumped on the counters. Flour and sugar containers had been dumped on the kitchen's tiled floor. Someone had been looking for something and had left a terrible mess.

Kit wondered if they'd found what they'd been looking for. She wondered if Mr Flynn had fought back.

Kit crouched on the victim's right side, leaning in so that she could better examine his hands. The knuckles of his right hand were scraped and bruised, but his fingernails were what caught her attention. They were mostly gone, clipped way past the quick, down into the nail bed.

That he'd fought back was a decent assumption, then. His killer hadn't wanted any evidence to be found under the man's nails.

'Time of death?' Kit asked the ME, who knelt on the other side of the body.

Dr Alicia Batra glanced up, a slight frown creasing her brow.

'Less than twenty-four hours, according to the first responder, who talked to the facility director. The residents in this part of the building live independently, just like in any other apartment, except that they have to pull a cord every morning by ten a.m.' She pointed over her shoulder to a cord on the wall in the breakfast nook. 'If they don't pull it by ten, the staff assumes they need help and comes in to check. The victim supposedly pulled the cord yesterday at ten, but not today. When the staff checked in on him, they found his body.'

Supposedly? 'The first responders told Connor that the victim was found by one of the nurses,' Kit said, her partner, Connor Robinson, having arrived at the scene an hour before. He'd already reviewed the crime scene and was somewhere downstairs, making sure the witnesses were properly situated in separate rooms while they awaited questioning.

'A nursing assistant,' Alicia corrected. 'She's downstairs with Connor. He said you had something personal to do this morning, but he didn't say what. Is everything okay?'

Kit appreciated that Connor had been discreet with the details of her morning meeting, but Alicia was a friend and this was happy news. 'We were at social services with Rita. She's decided she wants to be adopted and Mom and Pop took her in to start the process. She asked me to go with her, too.'

Which had filled Kit with a lot of affection and more than a little pride. She'd known most of the foster kids to go through McKittrick House since she'd landed there nineteen years ago, but Rita was special. They had a bond.

Alicia's smile was brilliant. 'I'm so happy!'

Kit smiled back. 'Me too. I asked Connor to keep it under his hat because we didn't want any media attention, what with Rita's mom's murder case coming to court soon, but that didn't include keeping it from you.'

Alicia's brows rose. 'How's it working out with Connor?'

'Pretty good. We're getting used to each other.' Connor Robinson was Kit's new partner of six months. At thirty-two, he was a year older than Kit, although he'd been a detective for only eighteen months to her four and a half years. He was something of an over-grown frat boy who spoke before he thought, although he was improving. There were times that he could be incredibly insightful and kind. 'I still miss Baz, though.'

'Of course you do. He was your first partner in the homicide department, after all.'

'We worked together for four years, and I've known him four times that long.' Baz Constantine had been the detective who'd investigated the murder of Kit's sister, sixteen years before. As an angry fifteen-year-old, Kit had assumed the man hadn't cared about finding Wren's killer, but she'd soon learned that he cared far too much. He'd encouraged her as she'd grown from that angry teen into a responsible adult, helping her realize her goal of becoming a homicide detective.

She understood why Baz had retired after having a heart attack, though that didn't make her miss him any less. But wishing he were here wasn't getting justice for Mr Franklin Delano Flynn.

'Why did you say the victim "supposedly" pulled the cord at ten a.m. yesterday?' Kit asked.

'Because rigor has fully passed. I would have thought he'd still be in the final stages of resolution, given his musculature. But he *is* elderly, so we'll see what we see when I get him on the table.'

'Can you lift his left hand?'

Alicia did so, and Kit frowned. The fingernails on his left hand had also been clipped to the nail bed, but there was also a strip of pale skin on his ring finger where a ring had been. 'He was married. I'll need to find out where his wife is.'

'Husband,' a man said behind her. Kit looked around to see CSU's Sergeant Ryland holding a photo encased in an evidence bag. 'All the photos were out of their frames, the glass shattered. This one was lying on top of the pile, so I grabbed it for you to check out.'

'Thank you.' Kit, hands already gloved, reached for the photo, snapping a picture of it with her phone in case she needed it later. In the photo, the victim and another man stood side by side, the victim's right arm around the other man's waist. They wore black suits and brilliant smiles, and each man had his left hand extended, showing off their shiny gold wedding bands. The iconic door of San Francisco City Hall was in the background.

'He's considerably younger in this photo than he is now,' she said, frowning at the feeling of déjà vu that she got from the picture. 'At least ten or twenty years. Any idea of when it was taken?'

'Not yet,' Ryland said. 'But there'll be a record of the marriage.'

So they had a gay man stabbed to death in his own apartment, the place ransacked. They'd have to at least consider the possibility that this had been a hate crime.

She started to hand the photo back, but a memory was struggling to the surface of her mind, so she refocused on the taller of the two men – Mr Franklin Delano Flynn.

'What's wrong?' Ryland asked.

Her frown deepened. 'I have the feeling that I've seen this man before.' She darted a quick glance at the victim's ashen face as he lay dead on his living room floor, then looked back at the wedding photo. Yes, she'd definitely seen him before.

'Where did you see him?' Ryland asked.

Kit stared hard at the picture, mentally sifting through all the faces and places in her mind, but nothing was clicking. 'Can I see the rest of the photos?'

Ryland handed over a stack. 'These are the ones we've bagged so far.'

Kit examined each one. They were mostly photos of the deceased with his husband, taken in faraway places – Cairo, Rome, Paris. A few featured another couple, a woman and a man, and there were a few with two other women, both elderly.

Nothing here helped. Until she got to the bottom of the stack. Here was a much younger Franklin Delano Flynn, holding up a mug of beer, a somewhat reluctant smile on his face.

'This,' she said softly. 'This place. Look at the walls, the pictures.'

Ryland looked over her shoulder, sucking in a surprised breath. 'That's Julio's.'

Yes, it was. Kit knew this place well. Knew the faces in every photo that hung on its walls. She'd been studying them since the first time she'd entered its battered wooden doors.

The first time . . . And then the memory snapped into place. '*Oh.* I was twenty-one and Baz took me to Julio's for a birthday drink, because I was finally legal.'

'The cop bar,' Alicia murmured. 'I've never been there.'

'It's a dive,' Kit said with a fond smile, 'but we love it. I remember the day because Baz told me to change out of my uniform – I was still in the Coast Guard then – before he picked me up, because we were going to the bar. I was so excited, because I'd heard so much about it.' She studied the victim's face in the photo thoughtfully. 'This man was there. Baz introduced us.'

'He was a cop?' Ryland asked, his eyes going wide.

'He must've been.' Kit drew in a sharp breath, because now she remembered it all. 'Oh my God. Not just a cop, Ryland. He'd been a homicide lieutenant, retired for twenty years by that point. I remember being tongue-tied.'

'*You* were tongue-tied?' Alicia asked, surprised. 'No way.'

'In the presence of greatness like this man? Oh yeah. Baz was, too. This guy had been the homicide lieutenant when Baz was still a rookie. Baz talked to him at the bar sometimes. Said he was open and helpful, really encouraging to young cops. Baz considered him something between a mentor and a hero. Baz was so excited when he saw him that day. The man hadn't been at Julio's since his retirement. When Baz introduced us, I got chills. I'd read articles about him and he was a kick-ass detective before he was made lieutenant. But his name wasn't Flynn. It was Wilson. Frank Wilson.'

'Frank Wilson?' Ryland exclaimed. 'I've heard of him from some of the old-timers. This is him?'

'I believe so,' Kit murmured. 'I wonder if he changed his name after he married the other man in this photo.' She gave the photo back to Ryland. 'This could be another high-profile case.'

Ryland sighed. 'I was thinking we were about due. It's been, what? Six months?'

Six months since they'd stopped one of San Diego's deadliest serial killers, throwing their entire homicide department into disarray. They were finally getting their acts together again and now they had a dead, high-ranking retired cop. 'Yep. I guess we are due.'

'Should I expect your lieutenant to breathe down my neck again?' he asked.

'Probably.' Lieutenant Navarro had recently returned from personal leave and was chomping at the bit for something big to do. 'Was there anything missing from the bedroom?'

'Possibly a computer,' Ryland said. 'The router and Ethernet cable are still there, but the desk is empty. There's a dust-free space the size of a laptop, so that one was stolen is a reasonable guess. The bedroom is in the same state as the rest of the apartment – photos, papers, books all over the place. It'll take us a while to get through it all, but we'll be as quick as we can.'

'Okay. I need to find Connor and we'll get started. First thing we need to do is inform Navarro.' Their lieutenant would take care of informing the hierarchy. She cast a glance at the speaker on the victim's living room wall. 'At least I'll get away from the music.'

'Why?' Alicia asked. 'It's beautiful.'

Yes, it was. It was also too damn sad. 'I'll find out what CD he's listening to and if it was his norm,' Kit said, evading Alicia's question because she didn't like to talk about things like feelings on the job. She suppressed a shudder at the thought.

'There's no CD player, Kit,' Ryland said. 'Just an old-fashioned stereo. I'm still looking for where the music is coming from.'

Even more reason to get out of here. 'Let me know when you find it. See you guys later.'

Kit left the apartment, nodding to the officer guarding the door. 'Do you know where the common room is?' Because that was where Connor had told her to meet him.

'Yes, Detective. Go down the elevator to the ground floor, turn left, and it's at the opposite side of the building from the lobby. Most of the residents on this floor are in the common room. They were asked to stay out of our way, so they gathered there.'

She glanced at his badge. 'Thank you, Officer Stern. I appreciate it.'

'Yes, ma'am.'

Kit ducked under the crime scene tape and took the elevator down as the officer had directed. And was surprised to still hear the music. A different tune, but the same melancholy piano.

It was faint when she exited the elevator on the ground floor but grew increasingly louder as she made her way to the common room. Again, her chest tightened. She'd gone to church enough in her youth to recognize the melody now being played. ' "Amazing Grace," ' she murmured.

Suddenly she was transported back to the small church where they'd said goodbye to Wren. They'd played that song at her sister's funeral, sixteen years before. She remembered the numbness, the feeling of being outside her own body. She remembered the tears. Not her own, of course. Not then. Not in front of everyone. Kit hadn't cried until hours later. She and her foster father, Harlan McKittrick, had both waited until the rest of the house had been asleep, both taking refuge in the barn, not knowing the other would be there. It had been the first time she'd seen her foster father cry.

The sight had shaken her. And had changed her life.

It had been the moment when the wall she'd built around her heart had begun to crumble. The moment when she'd started to let herself believe that Harlan and his wife Betsy could really love her.

I need to go home. I need to see them. Even though she'd seen them only an hour ago at Rita's meeting. Even though she'd been home nearly every Sunday for the last six months, hearing the music left her feeling vulnerable. Left her feeling like she was fifteen years old again and grieving.

But you're not. You're thirty-one and standing here with your hand on the doorknob like some kind of zombie. Move it, McKittrick.

Kit swallowed hard and drew a deep breath before she opened the common room door, pausing in the open doorway to the large, well-lit room. And realized that the music wasn't coming from a radio or a CD player. It was coming from a baby grand piano. A pianist sat with his back to her, his hands moving gracefully over the keyboard.

She gave herself a shake, trying to clear her mind of the music and the memories. *Pay attention.* There were about a dozen folding chairs on the right, filled with senior citizens. Most looked like she felt right now – numb and vulnerable. Some cried quietly. Some had closed their eyes. All appeared to be in shock.

Well, having one of your own stabbed with a butcher knife will do that.

The first thing she had to do was silence that music. Otherwise, she wouldn't be able to think.

'Kit, wait!'

Kit turned to see her partner hurrying her way. 'Give me a second, Connor. I have things to tell you, but I need some quiet.' She stepped into the common room. 'Excuse me?' she called to the pianist. 'Sir, can you take a break?'

'Kit, *wait*,' Connor hissed in her ear, grabbing her arm, but her eyes were fixed on the pianist.

She had a single moment to think that the man's dark hair and strong back looked familiar before he turned and met her gaze. She sucked in a startled breath as she met the vivid green eyes of the man she'd been avoiding for the past six months.

Dr Sam Reeves.

'I tried to warn you,' Connor whispered. 'Dammit.'

Dammit was right. Their new criminal psychologist was the one man who'd snuck under her guard, the one man she'd pushed away. He was also the one man she wanted even after trying for months to convince herself that she didn't.

He was the one man who deserved a whole lot more than she had to give.

He approached warily, his eyes swollen and bloodshot behind his Clark Kent glasses because he'd been crying. Finally, he stopped in front of them. Connor let go of her arm and Kit felt it hang heavily from her shoulder. She wanted to say something, but her tongue was not cooperating. Neither was her brain.

'Hello, Kit,' Sam murmured. 'I'm so glad you're here.'

Shady Oaks Retirement Village
Scripps Ranch, San Diego, California
Monday, 7 November, 11.45 A.M.

Kit's here. Sam had figured she would be when he'd seen Connor Robinson talking to the facility director and some of the residents. Sam had been bracing himself for her arrival, but he hadn't braced nearly enough.

She looked as flummoxed as he felt.

He'd surprised her, Sam thought wearily. And not in a good way. He'd been so careful to stay out of her way for the past six months, ever since she'd told him that there was nothing between them to pursue. That they couldn't even just be friends.

He'd been patiently waiting for her to get over her fear. To give him a chance. To give them a chance. Because she was worth waiting for.

And then today, he'd shown up at Shady Oaks for his normal volunteer session to find the facility in an uproar. Part of him had hoped a different pair of detectives would show up, but a bigger part of him was glad it was Kit. She'd make sure Frankie's killer was brought to justice.

'What are you doing here?' Kit demanded in a whisper that clearly conveyed her displeasure.

'I've volunteered here for four years,' he said quietly. 'I play the piano for the residents at least once a month. I was scheduled this morning for arts and crafts hour.' All of which he'd already told Connor.

Sam hadn't liked Kit's partner at first, but he and Connor had developed a solid professional working relationship. Which was good, because Kit refused to work with Sam.

She wasn't obvious about it, of course. She never stomped her foot or told her boss she wanted another profiler. She simply sent Connor to Sam's office whenever they needed a profile on a killer. Which had happened only twice since Sam had begun working with San Diego PD's homicide unit. Kit and Connor were usually able to figure things out without his assistance.

The other homicide detectives, along with his private practice, kept him busy. Unfortunately, not busy enough, because he still had time to think about Kit. But he'd promised himself he wouldn't push her.

And then Frankie had been murdered. Sam couldn't believe it.

He swallowed hard, still numb with the shock. 'I got here and everyone was crying. The director asked me to play for the residents who'd gathered in the common room while the police did their job. So I did.'

Her expression softened, making him wonder how bad he looked from the all the crying he'd done that morning. 'You knew the deceased?' she asked.

Sam nodded. 'I did. Frankie was a good man.'

'I'm so sorry, Dr Reeves.'

He managed to control his wince, even though her use of his title was like a slap to the face. Once upon a time, she'd called him Sam. That was before she'd gotten scared and run.

'Thank you, Detective. I have appointments this afternoon, so I'll be heading back to my office soon. If you need any assistance or have any questions about Frankie, please don't hesitate to ask. I want whoever killed him punished.'

'So do we. Dr Reeves, do you know where we can find his husband?'

Sam blinked, startled by the question. 'Ryan passed away a few months before I started volunteering here. I never met him. Frankie didn't talk about him often, but I do know that they'd been together for more than forty years when Ryan died. They got married when same-sex marriage was legalized in California back in 2008, in that period before Proposition 8 made it illegal. Frankie didn't talk much about feelings, but I know that he loved his husband. They ran an antique store together for years.'

It was only because he was watching her face so carefully that Sam saw her surprise. It was quickly erased, replaced with professional curiosity.

'An antique store?' she asked. 'Where was this?'

'San Francisco.'

'Thank you. Do you know who his friends here were?'

That was an easy question, because Frankie hadn't had that

many real friends. 'Benjamin Dreyfus and Georgia Shearer. They were his main companions. He didn't socialize much. He seemed to be grumpy, but he really just liked to be alone.'

Connor Robinson spoke up for the first time. 'I have Mr Dreyfus and Ms Shearer set up in the visitation rooms, Kit. We should be getting back to them. Mr Dreyfus didn't look well.'

Sam didn't expect that Benny would be handling this well. 'Benny's health is fragile. Physically and mentally.' He hesitated, wanting to warn them so that they'd be careful with Benny but uncomfortable sharing the man's personal information.

Kit leaned in, lowering her voice. 'What is it? You look like you want to tell us something.'

'Just . . . be gentle with him. Like I said, he's fragile, and any murder would have upset him. Frankie's murder will devastate him.'

'They were close?' Connor asked.

'Best friends. They're related by marriage. Ryan was the brother of Benny's late wife, Martha. Benny and Frankie have been friends for decades.'

'We'll be careful,' Kit promised. It was her turn to hesitate, and Sam wondered what was going through her very intelligent brain. But she only smiled – her professional smile, not the real one that had made him feel ten feet tall, and he felt the loss. 'Thank you, Dr Reeves. We'll be sure to contact you if we have any questions.'

And then she walked away from him. Again. It should have hurt more than it did, but Sam was already hurting over Frankie. Maybe her dismissal would hurt later.

Connor stood out of the way as she started down the hallway toward the family visitation rooms, turning to Sam with an expression of regret. 'I'm really sorry about the loss of your friend. I'll be in touch soon.' He gave him a nod then followed his partner, leaving Sam standing alone.

A feeling he'd gotten used to.

With a sigh, he headed back to the piano to gather his things, but was stopped by a tiny, electric-blue-haired lady pushing her blinged-out walker. Her normally jubilant smile was absent, her heavy makeup tear-streaked.

'Will you come back, Dr Sam? Before next month? We're gonna need you here.'

'Of course, Miss Eloise,' he said gently. 'I'll try to come back tomorrow, if Miss Evans says it's okay.' The director most likely would ask him before he inquired. Sam had been around even longer than she had and knew all the residents well.

'Thank you,' Eloise said, her eyes filling with tears. 'Who would do such a thing, Sammy? Frankie was kind of a jerk, but he didn't need killing.'

'Miss Eloise. Just because he reported you for cheating at cribbage doesn't mean he was a jerk. You *were* cheating.'

She made a pouty face. 'Nobody else even noticed. I'm that good.'

'At cheating or at cribbage?' Sam said, his lips curving.

'Both, Sammy. Both. Frankie was here even longer than me.' Her tears returned. 'Now Benny and I are the old-timers here.'

Sam gathered her in a gentle hug. 'I'm awfully glad you're here.'

'Will they catch who did it?'

He let her go, lifting her chin with his fingertip. 'Did you see the lady I was just talking to? She's Detective McKittrick and she works homicides. She's very, very good, and if anyone can find Frankie's killer, she can. You can take that to the bank, ma'am.'

'Thank you, Sammy. You're a good boy.'

'I try.'

He'd gathered his belongings and was signing out at the front desk when Shady Oaks's director, Faye Evans, hurried out of her office. She lifted her hand, delaying his exit.

'Dr Reeves? Can I have a moment?'

'Just one. I have to get back for appointments.'

'It's quick.' She took him aside and lowered her voice. 'Will you play at Frankie's funeral? He would have liked that.'

'Of course. Tell me the date and time as soon as you know it and I'll rearrange my schedule. His funeral might not happen for a while, though, given the circumstances. The ME will have to release his body.' She flinched and too late Sam remembered that she'd seen Frankie's body. The grapevine had been buzzing and everyone knew that Frankie had been stabbed with a butcher knife. 'I'm sorry.'

She shook her head. 'No need. It's just that I've never had a murder in any of my facilities before. Lots of death. I can deal with ordinary death, but I'm not equipped to deal with murder.'

'Have you informed Frankie's family? Does he have family?'

Frankie had only talked to him about his late husband Ryan. Never any brothers or sisters or anyone else.

Her lips pressed together. 'Yes. He has a son who told me to handle his funeral arrangements however I wanted to. He won't be coming.'

Sam stared at the woman in shock. Frankie had a son? Who wasn't coming to his funeral? 'What? Why?'

'I don't know, but they weren't on good terms. So I'm planning the service. I thought I'd ask Georgia to give his eulogy. I don't think Benny's able to anymore.'

Because Benny was in the early stages of dementia and sometimes got confused. 'Benny might surprise you, but Georgia is still a good choice. Tell her that I'll help her if she needs me to. I have to go now. I can't be late for my sessions.'

'Thank you, Dr Reeves. You made this morning a little more bearable with your music. Have a good day, and we'll see you soon.'

'Oh – if it's all right, I told Miss Eloise I'd try to come tomorrow.'

Miss Evans smiled fondly. 'We can't disappoint Miss Eloise. See you then.'

Sam frowned as he walked to his vehicle. Frankie's son wouldn't be coming to his funeral? What the ever-loving hell?

And why hadn't Frankie mentioned having a son?

Clearly Sam hadn't known the man as well as he thought he had.

And now he was dead. *Dammit, Frankie. I miss you already.*

Sam slid into the driver's seat, then simply sat and stared out the windshield for a moment. Then he pulled out his phone and texted to a number he hadn't used in six months, hoping Kit hadn't blocked him.

Sam Reeves here. Spoke to the director on my way out. Frankie has a son who is refusing to participate in his funeral. Bad blood between them. Was news to me. Thought you should know.

He was about to hit send when his phone buzzed, startling him. For a brief moment, he hoped that it might be Kit, but . . . no.

'Miss Evans,' he answered, hoping nothing else had happened.

'Dr Reeves, I know you're in a hurry, but it's Benny Dreyfus. I just checked in on him and he's extremely agitated. Can you spare us a few more minutes of your time?'

'I can stay for another half hour.' He'd skip lunch if he had to. It was Benny, after all, and Sam couldn't imagine what the man was going through. Benny and Frankie had been as close as brothers, friends for so long. To have seen that knife . . . 'I'll be right back in.'

'Thank you.'

Two

Shady Oaks Retirement Village
Scripps Ranch, San Diego, California
Monday, 7 November, 12.05 P.M.

'I'm sorry,' Connor said quietly as he and Kit left the common room. They were heading toward a closed door, in front of which stood a uniformed officer.

'It's fine,' she murmured. Even though it wasn't. Seeing Sam Reeves again was like a kick in the gut, intensifying the vulnerability she'd been feeling at the memory of Wren's funeral. She hadn't known Sam could play the piano like that. But of course he did it well. The man did everything well. 'I knew he volunteered with the elderly. I just didn't expect that he'd be doing it here.'

'I can handle any interviews we need to have with him. He and I get along pretty well. I don't mind.'

Kit made herself smile at her partner, because it was sweet of him to offer. Lately, Connor was sweet more often than he was abrasive. Which was a pleasant change from when they'd first been assigned as partners six months before. Still, avoiding Sam as a consultant was one thing. Avoiding him as a potential witness was something else, and she couldn't allow herself to do that. 'Let's play it by ear. Who's in this room?'

'Benjamin Dreyfus. Goes by Benny. He saw the body.' Connor stepped closer to the officer and lowered his voice. 'Is he any better? What's been going on in there?'

'He's quieter than he was before. He got very agitated when we first put him in the room,' the officer explained to Kit. 'Kept

24

shouting that he needed to see Frankie, that he needed to save Frankie. One of the nurses is in there with him now. She seems to be calming him down.'

'How did he see the body?' Kit asked.

'One of the nursing assistants discovered Mr Flynn,' Connor said. 'She'd come up to check on him because he hadn't pulled the "I'm okay" cord in his apartment, and she saw the victim with the knife sticking out of his chest. She screamed, which brought the other residents on the floor running. Benny lives in the apartment next to the victim's and he was first in Mr Flynn's doorway. The nursing assistant tried to shield Mr Flynn from view, but . . .' He shrugged. 'She felt bad about screaming, but she'd never seen the victim of a murder before. She's young, only eighteen. She's in the third interview room down. The room in the middle is Georgia Shearer, one of the other residents who was close to Mr Flynn. She also saw the body. She's much more lucid than Mr Dreyfus, but not very chatty.'

Kit regarded the three closed doors. 'Where is the facility director?'

'Faye Evans is in her office,' the officer said, pointing toward the building's lobby. 'She was the one who called 911. The nursing assistant called her as soon as she saw the body.'

Connor pointed to the third door. 'Evans asked if we could start with the nursing assistant, so that she could go home and pull herself together. Evans said she'd need the assistant back for the night shift because she's already called in nurses who currently aren't on duty and she'll be shorthanded tonight. But she didn't think the young woman was capable of providing adequate care at the moment.'

'All that's fine, but I need to talk to you for a minute.' She drew Connor down the hall so that they could have some privacy. 'I think the victim is a retired homicide lieutenant. Frank Wilson.'

Connor's eyes widened. 'Are you sure? His name is Flynn.'

'Mostly sure. I only met him once. Baz introduced us. He must have changed his name when he married.'

Connor shook his head. 'Wow. This is going to be a mess, isn't it?

Was that why you were surprised when Sam said that the victim had worked with his husband in an antique store?'

'Exactly. He must not have told Sam that he'd been a cop and now I'm wondering if anyone else knew – and why he didn't mention it.'

Connor blew out a breath. 'Have you told Navarro?'

'Not yet. Let's do it now. The victim retired thirty years ago, but Navarro's been around that long. He might have known him, and I don't want him to hear this from someone else. Is there an empty room we can use?'

Connor pointed to the fourth door down. 'There.' He closed the door behind them once they were in the room, and Kit dialed their lieutenant.

'I think our victim is a retired cop,' Kit said once Navarro had answered. 'Frank Wilson.'

There was a beat of silence. 'What did you say?'

Kit repeated it, then sighed. 'I'm not certain. I recognized him from the photos in his apartment. He married in 2008 and that's when I think he changed his name to Flynn.' She texted him the picture she'd taken of the wedding photograph and waited a few seconds for him to receive it. 'Is this him?'

'Fucking hell,' Navarro said quietly. 'It is. SDPD didn't know he'd remarried. We didn't know he was gay. At least I didn't, and that's not the kind of thing that stays a secret around here.'

Kit exchanged a glance with Connor, who shrugged. 'Yes, sir,' she said, because she wasn't sure what else to say. She knew her boss well enough to know that he wasn't homophobic, but she didn't want to speculate as to what he was feeling or why.

Navarro cleared his throat. 'What are your next steps?'

'Talking to key witnesses first, sir,' Connor said. 'I asked the site director for the surveillance footage from the floor of his apartment. Hopefully we'll get an ID from the cameras.'

'Good. What the hell was Frank doing in a retirement home?'

'He was eighty-five, sir,' Kit said. 'I guess he retired here.'

'But none of us knew he was back in San Diego. Last I heard, he'd moved up north. Right after his retirement. San Francisco, I think. I saw him at Julio's once about ten years ago. Word had spread that he was visiting, so I took a few hours' break to see him again. He was important to my career in my early days. I'd hoped he'd come back to town, that he might even consult with SDPD, but he said he had other plans. Why didn't he tell us he was moving into Shady Oaks?' He sighed. 'Normally, I'd wait until after the autopsy to share the news upstairs, but this will get out and I can't blindside the brass. They'll want to give Frank a police funeral with an honor guard.'

'Yes, sir,' Kit murmured. 'We didn't want you to be blindsided, either.'

'Thank you. Keep me updated. Frank Wilson was an institution around here.'

'We will. Goodbye, sir.' Kit ended the call and exhaled. That hadn't been as bad as she'd expected. 'Let's get to work.'

At least it was quiet now. She wasn't sure how much longer she could have withstood that music. Even now her chest felt tight and she pushed the feeling away, following Connor into the room next door.

The nursing assistant was a young woman with dark brown hair and a pale, tear-streaked face. She immediately sat up straighter when Kit and Connor entered the room, her expression becoming guilty.

Well, this should be interesting.

Shady Oaks Retirement Village
Scripps Ranch, San Diego, California
Monday, 7 November, 12.15 P.M.

'We've reserved these three rooms for the police to conduct their interviews,' Miss Evans explained as she walked Sam through the corridor just past her office. A police officer stood guard between the first and second doors, looking over his shoulder with obvious worry.

That would be the room where Benny was waiting. Sam could hear the old man's terrified voice and it twisted his heart. *Poor Benny.*

Sam caught sight of Connor Robinson entering the third of the visitation rooms. 'Who's in that room?' he asked Miss Evans.

'Devon Jones.'

Because she'd found Frankie's body, poor kid. That meant that Georgia Shearer was in the room adjacent. Sam's heart broke for her, as well. After Benny, Georgia had been closest to Frankie. Their acerbic personalities had suited each other.

Sam made a mental note to pay extra attention to Miss Georgia in the coming days. She liked to put up a Teflon front, but the old woman felt things deeply.

Georgia was kind of like Kit, at least in that respect.

The thought of Kit reminded Sam that he hadn't sent the text he'd been writing when Evans had called him, so he pulled out his phone and hit send. Pushing the thought of his homicide detective from his mind, he turned to the director, who was still talking about Devon Jones.

'I asked the detectives to start with her,' Miss Evans was saying, 'so that she can go home and compose herself. We need to get Benny calm as quickly as possible, because they'll never be able to interview him in this state.' She glanced back toward her office nervously. 'Do you need me for this?'

'No,' Sam said, mostly because he didn't and partially because there was something about Faye Evans that made him twitchy. In the role for about a year, she was so purely admin focused that she didn't take the time Sam thought she needed to spend making connections with the residents. The last director had been a very detail-oriented administrator, yet she'd still known every resident and had taken the time to make sure they were all okay. Sam had liked her so much more than he did Miss Evans, but the board of directors hadn't asked him before hiring the woman, and he was only a volunteer.

He added a smile to soften his *no*, because Evans was frowning at him. 'I know you're busy,' he said gently. 'I've got this. Don't worry.'

'Excuse me,' the officer said when Sam reached for the door. 'No one is supposed to go in there.'

'This is Dr Reeves, a psychologist,' Evans said, more haughtily than she needed to.

Sam lifted his hand, hoping Miss Evans would be quiet. 'I consult with the SDPD. I'm their profiler.'

The cop frowned. 'I thought you were the piano player.'

Sam smiled at him. 'Purely on a volunteer basis. Counseling and consulting is my day job. If you want to call Lieutenant Navarro of the homicide division, he can clear me.' He turned to Miss Evans. 'I'll handle this. You don't need to wait.'

She didn't need to be told again, hurrying back to her office.

Sam pulled his ID from his wallet, along with his cell phone. 'I have Lieutenant Navarro's number, if you'd like to call him. If you could do it quickly, I'd appreciate it. Benny's not well.' He could hear Benny's voice growing louder and more agitated behind the door. 'He has a bad heart. If I could get in there, I might be able to calm him.'

The cop called SDPD from his own cell phone and asked to be transferred to the homicide lieutenant, studying Sam all the while.

Smart guy. Sam didn't blame him for being careful.

The cop explained the situation, listened for a moment, then thanked Navarro before ending the call. 'Dr Reeves, Lieutenant Navarro has given you free access to the entire facility. I'm sorry, but I had to be sure.'

'I'm glad you did,' Sam said sincerely. Then he braced himself and opened the door.

Benny Dreyfus was . . . unraveling. His eyes were wild and his normally perfectly straight bow tie was askew. His hands were clenched into pummeling fists, his target the nurse who stood against the wall, her own hands raised placatingly.

Nurse Roxanne was as tall as Benny and probably weighed twenty to thirty percent more than Benny did. The old man had lost so much weight recently. A strong wind would blow him over. He couldn't be doing much damage to Roxanne, but she still winced with every blow.

Benny needed to be stopped. Roxanne wasn't restraining him, probably for fear of hurting him. His skin bruised so easily now. Sam would have to calm him down or they'd end up sedating him again.

Enraged, Benny continued pounding on Roxanne, his words coming out in shrill bursts, his shoulders heaving with angry sobs. 'Shouldn't have . . . listened,' he shouted between huffs. 'My . . . fault.'

'Benny,' Sam said softly, and Benny threw him a haunted look before returning his attention to the nurse, resuming his attack on Roxanne.

The nurse continued to hold very still, avoiding any escalation.

'Benny, can we talk?' Sam stepped forward, holding out his hands. 'Please?'

When he got close enough, Sam gingerly gripped one of Benny's wrists, taking care not to hurt him. He squeezed ever so lightly, tugging Benny's fist away from the nurse. 'Benny, you're hurting her.'

Indecision clouded Benny's expression. 'No.'

'Yes,' Sam whispered. 'Let her go.' He tugged a little harder. 'Come to me. I'm here.'

Benny hesitated for only a moment, then sagged into Sam's arms. 'He's gone, Sam. He's gone.'

Feeling Benny's sorrow, Sam tightened his arms around the older man in an embrace, rubbing his back. 'I know, Benny. I'm so sorry.'

'My fault, Sammy,' Benny cried, now pounding Sam's chest – hard enough to bruise, but Sam could take it. 'All my fault.'

Sam met the nurse's eyes over Benny's shoulder. She was on her phone, having dialed as soon as Benny had moved into Sam's arms. It sounded like she was talking with one of the doctors, explaining the situation and asking if she could give Benny a sedative. The doctor must have approved, because she ended the call, pocketed her phone, and drew out a small bottle and a syringe.

Sam knew the woman from his visits. She often stayed with the residents while he played for them, occasionally requesting songs for herself. Her favorite was an old country song, 'Smoky Mountain Rain.' She took such good care of the elderly residents, so Sam had learned the song especially for her.

Roxanne shook her head sadly. 'I keep telling him that it's not his fault.'

'She lies!' Benny cried. 'It *is* my fault.'

Roxanne stiffened, still shaking her head. 'It's not, Benny. It's not your fault.' She came up behind them, syringe in one hand and an alcohol wipe in the other.

Sam continued rubbing Benny's back, tightening his arms around the old man as Roxanne quickly administered the injection.

Sobbing in Sam's arms, Benny didn't even seem to notice. 'It is. It is. It is.' He chanted the words before mumbling, 'I didn't listen to him. He was wrong.'

Sam frowned. 'Frankie was wrong? About what?'

'He's been saying that ever since I got him down here,' Roxanne explained patiently. 'I don't know what he means.'

Benny pounded a fist against Sam's chest, but far more weakly now. He was quickly winding down. 'I didn't listen. Nobody listened.'

'Listen to what, Benny?' Sam asked, keeping his voice calm. He guided Benny to a comfortable chair and lowered him into it before kneeling in front of him. 'I'm here, Benny. I'm listening.'

Benny looked so heartbroken that Sam's chest constricted painfully. 'Frankie was my friend.'

'I know. He was your brother.'

New tears filled Benny's rheumy eyes. 'I loved him. You have to believe me.'

'Oh, I do. I believe you.'

Benny's lips trembled. 'But I said awful things.'

'You couldn't, Benny. You don't say awful things to anyone.'

It was true. Benny was the kindest and gentlest of them all. He always had a cheerful word – unless he was caught in one of his anger episodes. They were coming more frequently these days. It was devastating to watch, especially since Benny could often remember the things he'd said and done during the episode. Watching him process his own guilt was even worse than the episode itself.

'I told him he was a fool.' Benny's lips drooped. 'But the fool . . . was me.' His eyelids lowered, as if they were too heavy to keep propped open. 'He . . . loved me.'

'He did,' Sam agreed. 'So much. And he knew that you didn't mean any of it. He knew you couldn't control when you got angry.'

It was part of the vascular dementia that had come on after Benny's recent stroke. Dementia was an insidious disease, robbing people of their memories, their personality. Their dignity. Benny would have to go to the memory ward eventually, but his disease hadn't progressed enough for that yet. For now, he'd remain in the apartment he'd lived in for more than ten years. But without Frankie living next door.

This could be enough to speed his decline. It hurt to think about.

Sam took a moment to straighten Benny's crooked bow tie, knowing the older man would hate it being imperfect. Benny's yarmulke was still very straight. Sam had never seen Benny without it.

Benny shook his head, lifting a hand to fretfully rub at his temple. 'I meant it.'

Okay. 'What did Frankie say that you didn't listen to?'

Benny blinked blearily. 'I told him that he was jealous of me.'

Sam had to physically quell his frown. 'Why was Frankie jealous of you?'

Benny's mouth firmed in what appeared to be frustration. 'He *wasn't*. He was *right*.'

Sam drew a steadying breath, trying to piece together the puzzle of words. 'Frankie was wrong, but he turned out to be right?'

'*Yes,*' Benny said, slumping in relief. '*Yes.*'

'What did he say?' Sam asked, injecting some urgency into his voice.

'That I was naive. And lonely.'

Sam couldn't imagine Frankie telling Benny that he was naive. Benny was, actually – and had been even before the dementia – but no one mentioned it. Everyone loved him too much to ridicule him.

He'd been a scientist and a professor. An absentminded one. It was part of his charm, because even when Benny was absentminded and naive, he had the sweetest soul.

'Were you lonely?'

Benny swallowed hard. 'I miss Martha.'

Sam let out a breath that hurt. 'I know.' Martha had been Benny's

32

wife of more than fifty years, having died only a year ago. She'd been the one to make all the family decisions, leaving Benny to his books. The man loved his books and always carried one with him. Sometimes they were physics books, sometimes books about coins. Every now and then he'd have a paperback romance in his pocket. He was unapologetically a fan of love.

He didn't have a book now, though. His hands were empty, his clenched fists relaxing as his blinks grew slower.

The sedative was kicking in.

'Benny, why did Frankie say you were naive?' Sam asked softly, because he thought Kit and Connor might need to know. That the two had argued right before Frankie's violent death might be a critical clue.

'I believed,' Benny said, his words growing slurred. 'Believed a lie. Was so stupid. Now he's dead. My fault.'

Sam gripped Benny's hands. 'Not your fault, my friend. Not ever your fault.'

Benny's chin dropped to his chest, but his tears continued to flow. 'I'm sorry,' he wailed plaintively. 'I didn't mean to.' He lifted his head slowly and with apparent difficulty to look at Roxanne, his frustration muted by the sedative, but still there. 'I didn't listen,' he insisted.

'I know.' Roxanne gently picked up his wrist and began taking his pulse. When she was finished, she placed his hand on the arm of the chair with the same gentleness. 'It wasn't your fault, Benny,' she whispered. 'I promise.'

Benny's head lolled back and a soft snore escaped his open mouth.

'What are you going to do now?' Sam asked her quietly, rising to his feet.

She brushed a lock of Benny's hair from his forehead, the movement both practiced and tender. 'Call for someone to help me get him into the nursing ward. We're going to want to watch his heart for a while, until we're sure that he's okay. What he saw today would be stressful for anyone. But with Mr Benny's heart condition . . .'

33

'It could kill him,' Sam said grimly, 'if he gets too wound up.' It had nearly happened before, more than once.

'That's what we have to make sure doesn't happen. Thank you, Dr Reeves. I'm glad it was you who came to help me. I needed someone to help me distract him.'

'Are you okay? He hit you pretty hard.'

Wincing, she rubbed between her collarbones. 'I'm okay, but I did not know that he had that much strength. He certainly doesn't look it.'

Sam shrugged. 'When he's having an episode . . .'

Roxanne patted his arm. 'I know. It's my job to know. I'll be fine. I'm more worried about him.'

It was Sam's turn to wince when he checked the time. 'I have to go. I have sessions soon and I'm going to be late.'

'You go ahead. I'll take it from here. Thank you, Dr Reeves.'

He took one last look at Benny. 'He's a good man. The kindest.'

'I know. He didn't mean to hurt anyone. He never does.'

'I'll come back and see him tomorrow. Will you tell him that when he wakes up?'

'Of course.'

Sam took a step back, then turned for the door. When he left, he spoke to the officer. 'He's asleep now. They'll take him to the nursing ward for observation.'

The officer frowned. 'The detectives never got to talk to him.'

'They can when he wakes up. He wouldn't have been a good witness in that state, anyway. Have a good afternoon, or as good as you can under these circumstances. I have to run.'

And Sam did, literally, jogging through Shady Oaks until he was outdoors and continuing until he reached his RAV4. He'd had this one for six months, his old vehicle having been damaged beyond repair. But this new RAV4 was the same color as his old SUV. Sam liked consistency.

For the second time in less than an hour, Sam slid behind the wheel and checked his phone. No word from Kit. He was tempted to text her again, to tell her about his conversation with Benny Dreyfus, but he could do that later.

Kit wasn't going to be happy about the delay in interviewing Benny. But Kit didn't get everything she wanted. *Neither of us does.*

With a sigh, Sam tossed his phone to the passenger seat and headed toward downtown. His clients needed him and he had to be ready to listen.

Shady Oaks Retirement Village
Scripps Ranch, San Diego, California
Monday, 7 November, 12.15 P.M.

Devon Jones set her cell phone on the table when Kit and Connor entered the interview room. She folded her hands, her guilty expression as bright as a neon sign. 'I wasn't talking to anyone about what I saw,' she blurted out. 'I swear. I was watching videos. Cats in boxes.'

Lordy, she *was* young. Kit didn't think she looked even eighteen. Was that the source of the girl's guilty expression? Watching cats in boxes? *Honey, this world is gonna chew you up and spit you out.* On the surface, it didn't seem possible that she could be involved in Mr Flynn's death. But if she was, Kit would see justice done, no matter how young the woman was.

Taking a seat at the table, Kit smiled, hoping to put the woman at ease. 'I'm Detective McKittrick and this is my partner, Detective Robinson. What's your name?'

'Devon Jones.'

'How old are you?' she asked gently.

'Eighteen, ma'am. Last week.'

Connor's brows went up. 'How long have you worked here?'

'A year, almost. You only have to be sixteen,' she added defensively. 'I got my CNA right out of high school. I did a dual enrollment program when I was a senior.' She looked between them, visibly tensing. 'Sorry. That wasn't what you asked.'

'It's okay,' Kit soothed. 'Why cats in boxes?'

Devon smiled shyly. 'They're cute and they make me feel better when I've had a rotten day. Today was . . .'

'A rotten day,' Kit murmured. 'Tell us what happened.'

'I got a call from Miss Evans that Mr Frankie hadn't pulled his cord, so I went to his place. I knocked, but there was no answer, so I opened the door with my master key.' She swallowed audibly. 'I saw him lying there. With the knife in his chest.' New tears began to roll down her cheeks. 'I never saw anything like that before.'

'It's okay to be upset,' Connor said, giving her a tissue. 'Did you know Mr Frankie well?'

Devon wiped her eyes. 'No, but I don't think anyone really did except Mr Benny, Miss Georgia, and Miss Eloise. He didn't get involved in group activities, and he wasn't on my list to visit every day. He was independent.'

'Independent?' Connor asked.

'Yes, sir. He didn't have assistance. Nobody helped him with bathing or meds or anything like that. I didn't see him that often, to be honest. He kept to himself. But he was always nice to me when we passed in the hallway. A little growly, maybe, but nice. He'd always ask about my little girl, and he'd smile at the photos I showed him. He always remembered her name.'

'What is her name?' Kit asked, trying to get the young woman to relax even more. The question about her child seemed to do the trick.

'Mila. She's two. That's why I got my CNA right out of high school. I needed to support us. I'm . . . a single mom. My mom helps, but she's strapped for cash, too.' She closed her eyes. 'Sorry again. I ramble when I'm nervous.'

'It's fine,' Kit assured her. 'So you saw Mr Frankie's body. Then what happened?'

Devon cast an embarrassed look at Connor before turning to Kit. 'Like I told Detective Robinson, I screamed. I was . . . shocked. I've found residents dead before, but never like that. I'm sorry.'

'It's a natural reaction,' Connor said, gentleness in his tone. 'Don't be embarrassed.'

'Miss Evans wasn't happy. I disrupted a lot of residents when I screamed. Especially Mr Benny.' Devon's lips trembled. 'I hope she's not still mad. I can't lose this job.'

Kit couldn't tell her everything would be all right, because she didn't know if that was true. 'What happened after you screamed?'

'A few of the residents rushed out to see what was wrong. Mr Benny and Miss Georgia got there first because they live in the apartments on either side of him and they'd just come back up from breakfast. He's at the end of the hall, you know. It's one of the nicer apartments. But of course you know that. I'm sorry.' She took a deep breath, visibly trying to compose herself. 'I closed the door so that they couldn't see, but I was too late. Mr Benny started screaming and Miss Georgia had to push him back into his apartment. I called Miss Evans and waited by the door until she came. One of the nurses came with her and stayed with Mr Benny. The policemen came a few minutes later and one of them brought me down here. I didn't do anything wrong. I swear it.'

Kit really wanted to believe her because she was so earnest, but the best criminals often were. 'Which nurse came with the director?'

'Roxanne. She's good with Benny and got him to calm down for a while.'

'She's in with Mr Dreyfus now,' Connor told Kit, then turned to Devon. 'I'm curious about the way this place works. You mentioned independent residents. What are the other groups?'

'Miss Evans could describe it better, of course, but this is a continuing care facility. A senior citizen can come here to live before they need help, and then we can add on services as they need them. Everyone can get housekeeping and a dining plan. The food's good, too.' Devon did seem to like working here. 'They start out like Mr Frankie, living like they would in any other apartment. Then, as they get older or have medical issues, we help them. Making sure they take their meds or bathing them or whatever. And if they get sick or fall, we've got a nursing home wing. When they're better, they come back to their apartments. And there is another area for memory care. Those are the patients with Alzheimer's or other kinds of dementia.'

'I think you explained it very well,' Connor said warmly.

'Thank you. After you saw Mr Frankie's body, did you enter his apartment?'

Devon shook her head hard. 'Oh no, sir. I did not. I watch cop shows on TV. That's why I closed the door. I didn't want anyone rushing in and trampling the crime scene. One of my feet might have crossed into his residence, but I yanked it back really fast. I promise.'

'Thank you, Miss Jones.' Kit gave her a business card and Connor did the same. 'We've written our cell numbers on the back. If you think of anything or hear anything, please call one of us. I'll provide Miss Evans with a list of counselors, in case you need to talk to a therapist. You might not need one, but please consider it – what you experienced could shake anyone up.'

Devon slipped their cards into her pocket. 'Thank you, but if I need a therapist, I'll probably call Dr Sam. He was the one playing the piano this morning. He said I could always ask if I needed help.'

Once again, Kit felt sucker-punched at the sound of Sam's name, but the feeling was quickly overshadowed by annoyance. 'He talked to you already about Mr Frankie?' she asked, trying to keep her tone casual.

Devon's eyes widened, so Kit evidently hadn't been successful. 'No, ma'am. But he's here at least once a month with the residents, and we talk sometimes. My little girl was pretty sick a few months back and I was a nervous wreck. He's got a soothing way about him and . . .' She shrugged. 'He helped. He must be sad himself, though. He was friends with Mr Frankie. They had lunch together whenever he'd come to play for the residents. Mr Frankie once said that Dr Sam was like the grandson he'd never had.'

'Did Mr Frankie have any enemies?' Kit asked, a little surprised that Sam hadn't mentioned how close they'd been. But he had been in a hurry. *And I was not . . . kind to him.* She'd follow up with him later.

'I don't know, ma'am. I don't think so, but somebody killed him, so he had to have had at least one.'

True enough, Kit thought. 'You're free to go. But please don't talk about what you saw, especially to the press.'

'I won't. I liked Mr Frankie. I want you to arrest whoever did this to him.'

Connor stood and held the door open for the young nursing assistant. 'Miss Evans asked that you see her when we were finished. I think she's going to let you go home for the day,' he added quickly, when Devon became alarmed. 'Take care.'

Devon hurried away and Kit took a moment to check her phone. She'd felt it buzz with an incoming text as they were talking to the young woman.

She stared at the screen for a long moment, déjà vu hitting her like a rock.

'What's wrong?' Connor asked.

'Nothing. It's just a text from Dr Reeves.' He always started his texts out the same way. *Sam Reeves here.* Like she didn't recognize his number from memory. Clearing her throat, she read his message. '"Sam Reeves here. Spoke to the director on my way out. Frankie has a son who is refusing to participate in his funeral. Bad blood between them. Was news to me but thought you should know."'

It took her back six months, to when Sam had provided critical information as they'd pursued a serial killer. He'd gleaned details from witnesses who were too afraid to speak to SDPD. They couldn't have solved the case without him.

'Well,' Connor said after a beat of silence. 'Given his proven track record at getting witnesses to talk, maybe we should interview Miss Evans next for more on Flynn's son.'

Kit shook her head, something inside her chafing at Sam's involvement. It was probably immature and petty, but she couldn't rein it in. Not when she still felt so raw inside. 'We'll get to her. Let's talk to the victim's friends first.'

'Okay,' Connor said with a vexed look that indicated it was not okay and that they'd probably talk about this later.

Kit wanted to sigh.

They'd reentered the hall when Connor stopped midstride, pulling his phone from his pocket. With a frown, he showed Kit his screen.

The call was coming from somewhere inside Shady Oaks.

Connor hit accept and put the phone on speaker. 'This is Detective Robinson.'

'Detective, this is Miss Evans. Can you come to my office, please?' Her tone sounded very stressed. 'Right away. It's important.'

'My partner and I will be right there.' Connor ended the call and smirked at Kit. 'Guess we're seeing her next after all.'

Three

The director of Shady Oaks appeared to be visibly shaken when Kit and Connor approached her open door. Faye Evans was in her midfifties, her silver hair cut in a bob. She was dressed casually, but her stance was anything but. She stood at the window, her head bowed and her body tense.

Connor knocked on the door and the woman spun around, fear flickering in her eyes when she saw them. The fear was quickly hidden behind a professional mask, but it had been there. It could simply have been due to one of her clients having been murdered with a butcher knife. Or it could have been something more.

'Detective Robinson.' The woman sat behind her desk and gestured to the two guest chairs.

'Miss Evans, this is my partner, Detective McKittrick,' Connor said as he and Kit took their seats. 'She's been reviewing the crime scene.'

Evans folded her hands on her desk and drew a breath. 'I might as well just say it. The camera on Mr Flynn's floor was disconnected.'

Well, shit. 'How do you know this, ma'am?' Kit asked, because this was far too convenient to be an accident.

'I tried to look at the security footage this morning, right after the first officers arrived, but the feed was blank. Like gray static. I thought I'd done something wrong. It's a brand-new system and more complicated than I'm used to. But our IT guy just called to tell

41

me that he'd checked the system remotely and there was no camera connection at all. He couldn't tell how long it had been down. He's coming in to check it out.'

'We need his name and contact information,' Connor said. 'We'll talk with him when he comes in. Do you normally watch the feeds, Miss Evans?'

'Yes, sometimes, but usually not the third-floor cameras. Nearly all the residents there live independently. I tend to focus on the areas where we have residents who exhibit exit-seeking behaviors.'

Kit had heard of this before. 'You mean those who wander off or try to escape?'

'Exactly. It's especially a problem in the memory care wing, which is why we have security there – to keep those patients safe. Even so, someone manages to get out every now and then. So I watch when I have a break, along with the security personnel. I checked the feeds from all the other cameras, and the rest are working just fine.' She turned her computer monitor so that they could see the four-by-two display. All cameras were functional. She tapped a few keys on her keyboard and the array changed, several of the blocks a solid, staticky gray. 'The floors in the independent living wing are always calm and quiet, so we only view the footage if there's a problem.'

'Who has access to the surveillance system?' Kit asked.

'Our IT guy, Archie Adler. He works full time, but mostly at night. He's putting himself through school during the day, which is why he's not here at the moment. He's a nice young man. Only twenty-five, but incredibly responsible.'

That remains to be seen. 'We'll talk to him when he gets here. Does anyone else have access?'

'I do and so does my director of security, Kent Crawford.'

'We'll interview him as well,' Connor said. 'Does your assistant have access? Lily Watson?'

Evans shook her head with affectionate exasperation. 'I inherited Lily and I'm keeping her on only until she retires next month. She doesn't do computers. At all. Archie and I do all the things I'd normally ask her to do. My life will be much easier once she retires and I've hired a new assistant.'

Kit and Connor had met the assistant on their way in, and Kit found Evans's assessment of her assistant's skills to be believable. The woman's desk blotter was a big calendar that was literally covered in scribbles and white-out. Kit would bet that the assistant never used scheduling software.

'Where is the security system housed?' Kit asked.

Miss Evans pointed to the door behind her. 'In there. I have a key, as does Archie. The head of security has a master key. No one else has a key.'

Kit fired off a quick text to Ryland, asking him to send a CSU tech to process the server room, then opened her secure notes app. 'Have you been in there this morning?'

'Yes. When Mr Flynn's body was found, the police took over that entire floor upstairs. I came back to my desk and checked the cameras. When I saw that the feed in that hallway wasn't working, I went into the server room to see if the camera was on. It didn't appear to be. I checked the other camera feeds and saw that they were functioning. That's when I closed the door and called Archie.'

'Where is your head of security?' Connor asked. 'Kent Crawford.'

'He's not here today. He messaged me that he was sick on Friday and today, as well. I can call him and ask if he can come in, if I need to.'

That the only person with a master key was out sick was also far too convenient. 'Give us his address,' Connor said, and from the tone of his voice, it seemed he was thinking the same thing. 'We'll go to him.'

'And his master key?' Kit asked. 'Where is that kept?'

Miss Evans looked a bit uncomfortable. 'He keeps it with him. Look, I know what you're thinking, but he's a decorated army veteran. He's been working here for nearly ten years with no complaints.'

'Yes, ma'am,' Kit said mildly, because things didn't look so good for Mr Crawford.

'What can you tell us about Mr Flynn's family?' Connor asked, abruptly changing the subject.

Miss Evans grimaced. 'Mr Flynn has one son, Gerald, but he and Mr Flynn were estranged and, apparently, have been for decades. I informed him of Mr Flynn's passing, that he was killed, and he said he didn't care. He said that the only call he wanted to take was from his father's lawyer with regard to the reading of Mr Flynn's will.'

Connor frowned. 'I asked you not to inform the next of kin. That's our job, ma'am.'

Evans's cheeks flushed, whether from anger or embarrassment, Kit wasn't sure. 'I'd already done it,' the director confessed. 'I wasn't thinking that I was supposed to leave that to the police. I'm used to informing the next of kin when one of our residents passes and . . .' She exhaled. 'I've never had a murder at any facility I've managed, and I was shaken. I'm sorry.'

Well, there was nothing to be done about it now.

Connor's nod was curt. 'Please do not have further communication with the deceased's family.'

'I won't,' Evans promised.

Kit hoped they could trust her discretion. She also wondered what had happened to cause the father-and-son estrangement but needed another question answered first. 'There was an inheritance?'

'Oh yes. Mr Flynn was a very wealthy man.'

That was a surprise. Usually, retired cops were not even remotely wealthy. Money was often a motive for murder, though, and stabbing was an intimate, personal crime.

The kind of crime an angry, estranged son might commit.

'From what I understand, the money came from his late husband,' Miss Evans went on to explain. 'Mr Ryan Flynn was a software designer. He sold one of his programs for millions of dollars back in the nineties during the rise of the dot-coms. Apparently, he invested well and he and Mr Frankie were able to realize a dream. They owned an antique shop in San Francisco for years until they came here to live. Mr Ryan died about four and a half years ago, leaving his entire estate to Mr Frankie.' She lifted a hand. 'And no, I don't know the exact amount. But the rumor mill – and his son's interest in his will – indicates that it was quite a lot.'

So quite a lot of motive.

Kit glanced at her phone, reviewing the list she'd made of all the people they needed to talk to. There were the victim's friends, Benny and Georgia, who still waited in interview rooms. Then Archie Adler, the IT guy; Kent Crawford, the head of security; Lily Watson, the assistant; and Gerald, the victim's son.

She wondered if Navarro had known about the son. He'd said that they hadn't known that Frank had *re*married. 'What about Mr Flynn's ex-wife? Is she still living?'

Miss Evans shrugged. 'I'm sorry, but I don't know. I didn't know that he was married before Mr Ryan. Mr Frankie never spoke of a previous marriage and I never asked. All I know is that there are no other names listed in his file as a next of kin.'

Kit added locating the ex-wife to her growing to-do list.

'What about the medical records of your residents?' Connor asked. 'You said that the surveillance camera system is located in the server room behind you. Where are the medical records kept?'

'Not on the premises. We use a vendor who maintains their own servers and our data to ensure that our systems are government compliant. The only systems stored on our own servers' – she pointed to the server room behind her – 'are the security and sur-veillance system, internal email, and personnel records. We don't even manage the payroll. We have a service that does that, too. Do you think we had a security breach?'

'Perhaps,' Connor said. 'We'll need to examine your server to see how the camera was tampered with. That means we'll be shutting the server down until Forensics is finished.'

Evans's mouth dropped open and Kit thought she saw true fear flicker in the woman's eyes before she covered it with outrage. 'You can't just take our server! We need it to function!'

'You actually don't,' Connor countered calmly. 'You've just told us that all the patient files, the payroll, everything urgent is done on the servers of provider companies. Your patients' care and your employees' pay can continue without interruption.'

Evans's cheeks flushed with angry color. 'This is absurd,' she blustered. 'I'm going to involve our attorneys. They'll be speaking with your supervisor.'

'His name is Lieutenant Navarro,' Kit said helpfully. 'Two *R*s.'

Evans scowled and said nothing.

'We'll also need a list of all your staff, volunteers, and anyone who has access to the facility,' Kit added.

Evans narrowed her eyes. 'That's all on the server.'

Connor smiled, but it wasn't friendly. 'I trust you'll help us find the appropriate information on the server,' he said, his tone silky with an unspoken threat that was subtle yet very clear. 'Since this is a murder investigation, I'm sure you'll want to be cooperative.'

Evans swallowed hard, her expression visibly resetting into the professional mask she'd been wearing before Connor had dropped his server bomb. 'Of course. We want to catch Mr Frankie's killer. You can count on our full cooperation.'

'Thank you,' Kit said sincerely, privately amused that Connor had taken on the role of bad cop. He didn't play it often, but when he did, he did it well. 'You mentioned internal email on your private server?'

'Yes. It's mostly for personnel issues, announcements, and the planning of social events. We have a lot of social events here at Shady Oaks.'

And they'd need to look at those, too, Kit thought. They needed to find when the victim crossed paths with his killer. 'Can you tell us when Mr Frankie left the compound? Did he still drive?'

'He had a car and drove himself wherever he wanted to go. Records of the dates and times that he left the grounds are kept in the surveillance system. Every resident has to use their key card to get in and out of the doors.'

Connor glanced at Kit. 'I hope those records haven't been scrubbed as well.'

Kit nodded grimly. 'How many entrances are there?' *Please say there's just the front door by the receptionist's desk.* But she knew they wouldn't get that lucky.

'There are fifteen exterior doors that cover the nursing ward, the memory ward, the main lobby, and the residences. All require a key card for entry. Visitors have to sign in at the front desk, but residents have been known to sneak someone in.' Evans shrugged. 'We don't encourage this and there are fines if anyone's caught doing it. But some of our residents have families that are very involved in monitoring their daily lives. The residents find it chafing, seeing as how they've been independent throughout their lives. So they sneak around.'

'But Mr Frankie didn't have that kind of family,' Kit murmured.

'No, he didn't.'

'Is Mr Frankie's vehicle still in the parking lot?' Connor asked.

The victim's pockets had been turned out, like he'd been searched and robbed, so it was likely that his keys were gone. The obvious search of his apartment pointed to a robbery of some kind.

'I don't know,' Evans said. 'Vehicle registration information is kept on the server as part of the security system. It also tracks the coming and going of the cars. We have a gated lot for residents. Each car has a UPC-style sticker that triggers the gate to lift. We track resident movements that way. Not actively, but if they don't come back when they're expected, we can put out a silver alert.'

So if more than just the camera feed was compromised, they'd lose a lot of important information. *Dammit.* They needed to track down both the head of security and the IT guy as quickly as possible.

But first, they needed to know who might have wanted to kill Frankie Flynn.

Kit settled her gaze on the director. 'Miss Evans, where were you between ten a.m. on Sunday and ten a.m. this morning?'

Evans didn't look upset by the question. 'My mother is in a continuing care center in Temecula. I was with her all weekend and drove home this morning. I can give you the name of the hotel where I stayed and the contact at my mother's facility. They can verify my whereabouts.'

'Why isn't your mother here?' Connor asked.

'My mother moved into continuing care five years before I started working at Shady Oaks. She likes where she is and it's less than a two-hour drive, so I visit on the weekends.'

'That makes sense,' Connor said mildly, then gave Kit a questioning glance.

She nodded. They were done here for now. 'We're going to talk to the victim's friends now. While we're doing that, can you compile a list of all the personnel and volunteers from memory? And will the front desk have a guestbook that visitors have to sign? We'll need that, too.'

'Of course,' Evans said. 'I'll see that it's done. And, um, Detectives? Mr Benny – that's Benjamin Dreyfus – is . . . fragile. He had a stroke last year, which has triggered vascular dementia. He's in the early stages, and most of the time he's okay. I only share this because he may not be able to answer your questions. One of his symptoms is short-term memory loss. He also becomes very emotional when he's stressed.'

'Like when seeing his friend dead, with a butcher knife in his chest,' Kit said bluntly, and Miss Evans flinched, horror flickering in her eyes.

'Yes, Detective,' she whispered, her voice cracking. 'Like that.'

Kit always felt bad, springing statements like that on those who'd found a body, but she'd needed to see that the director's reactions were genuine, especially with the woman's resistance to relinquishing their server. Kit thought that Evans was hiding something, but it could have simply been a desire to protect her employees' privacy. Her horror at the memory of Flynn's body seemed genuine. *I guess we'll see.*

Kit softened her tone. 'We can provide recommendations for counselors who specialize in treating victims of crime. That includes anyone who's witnessed the body. Mr Flynn's was a brutal murder, Miss Evans. It's okay to ask for help.'

The woman nodded. 'Thank you. I'll take your recommendations, but to be honest, I'll probably just talk to Dr Reeves – he was the man playing the piano this morning. He's a psychologist who works with victims of crime.'

Kit forced her lips to curve, because . . . Sam. *Again.* But the man was definitely worthy of trust. 'He's a good choice. Thank you for your assistance, ma'am. We'll be in touch.'

Evans rose with them, her body language screaming that she had something else to share. 'Um . . . You should know something else about Benny because he might tell you himself, and I don't want you to get the wrong idea. When I got up to Mr Frankie's room, Mr Benny was . . . wild. He kept screaming that this was all his fault.'

Stunned, Kit glanced at Connor to find his eyes as wide as hers. 'Why didn't you lead with this?' Kit demanded.

'Because Benny couldn't have done this. He and Frankie were best friends.'

But stabbing was an intimate crime.

Evans shook her head. 'I can see what you're thinking, but Benny's not violent. He couldn't hurt a fly. Plus, he's far too frail to have wielded that knife.'

Kit wanted to snarl at the woman. They likely wouldn't have believed that Mr Dreyfus had killed his friend, but they certainly would have interviewed him first. They may have wasted valuable time. The victim's best friend could very well know something important – like why Mr Flynn was dead or who'd wanted him that way.

Rarely did the person saying 'It's my fault' actually murder the victim.

I always say that Wren's murder was my fault. Kit had learned at an early age that grief and guilt went hand in hand.

So she drew a breath and said in a calm voice, 'Thank you. We'll interview Mr Benny right now.'

Evans twisted her hands together. 'You'll be gentle with him?'

Kit wanted to roll her eyes. *No, we're going to rough the old man up.* But she held her sarcasm back, nodding instead. 'Of course we will.'

Shady Oaks Retirement Village
Scripps Ranch, San Diego, California
Monday, 7 November, 1.30 P.M.

Kit and Connor approached the cop on guard outside the three interview rooms – only one of which still had a closed door.

'What happened to Benny Dreyfus?' Connor asked.

But before the officer could answer, a harsh voice from behind them said, 'They had to take him to the nursing ward because you took too damn long.'

Both Kit and Connor turned to the source of the explanation, finding an elderly woman standing in the doorway that had been closed a moment before. Her sour face frowning, she rested her gnarled hands on the handles of a baby stroller, in which sat a very small dog. At least the dog seemed happy to see them.

Kit glanced back into the empty room where Benjamin Dreyfus had been waiting. She and Connor *had* made them wait a long time, and the old man had been highly agitated.

We should have talked to him first. Dammit.

'Why did they take him?' Connor demanded.

The old woman shrugged. 'Nurse Roxanne waited for you for as long as she could, but he was getting . . .' Her shoulders slumped as she sighed wearily. 'He was stressed and lashing out, so she gave him a sedative and they put him in a room in the nursing ward – just until you let us go back to our apartments. Then they'll put him in his own bed. Roxanne said they want him to wake up somewhere familiar. He's not going to be able to talk to you all for a while. He was asleep when they moved him.'

Kit frowned. 'When we walked by this room on our way to see Miss Evans, it was quiet.'

'He was asleep by then, I suppose. But he'd been swinging his fists and cursing and . . .' The woman swallowed hard. 'I haven't seen him like that in a long time. I couldn't get through to him, nor could Nurse Roxanne. Miss Evans had to call Sam back in.'

Kit snapped her mouth closed. *What the hell?*

'Sam?' Connor asked. 'You mean Dr Reeves?'

'Yes, sir,' the officer on guard said. 'I wasn't going to let him in, but he suggested I call Lieutenant Navarro, who said he was free to talk to anyone in the facility.'

'I see,' Kit managed. 'How long ago was this?'

'He was in there when you two got the call from the site director,' the officer said. 'He left when you were in her office.'

'I see,' Kit said again. 'Of course, whatever our boss says goes, but could you inform us next time?' She hated to be surprised.

'Yes, ma'am. Will do.'

'If you're finished with your little pissing match,' the woman said crisply, 'could you talk to me so that I can go?'

'I'm sorry, ma'am,' Kit said. 'This has been a shock for all of you.'

'Yes,' the old woman said, not appearing to be mollified in the least. 'It has been.'

Connor cocked his head. 'When was the last time Mr Dreyfus became that agitated?'

'When his wife died. He nearly gave himself a heart attack that day. I think they were afraid of that today, which was why they had to get him quiet.'

'He has a heart condition?' Connor asked.

The old woman narrowed her eyes. 'Not your business.'

Which was likely a yes.

'You're Georgia Shearer, ma'am?' Kit asked.

'Yes,' Georgia said with a tilt of her chin. 'Are you finally ready to talk to me?'

Kit ignored Georgia's snark and gestured to the open doorway where she'd been waiting. 'Yes, ma'am. After you.'

'I'm going to double-check that Mr Dreyfus is asleep,' Connor murmured to Kit. 'Be right back.'

Georgia's sneer was glacial. 'I can hear you. I'm not deaf, nor am I a liar.' She gripped the stroller and pushed the dog back into the room.

'Never said you were, ma'am,' Kit said to her back, following her inside and closing the door behind them. 'I'm Detective McKittrick. My partner is Detective Robinson.'

Georgia's gaze sharpened. 'I've heard of you. Not him. Just you. Bagged yourself a serial killer last spring.'

'Yes, ma'am. But it wasn't just me. Team effort, and all that.'

Georgia rolled her eyes. 'Whatever. Tell me, Detective, what are you doing to find out who killed Frankie?'

'We're following procedure, ma'am. That's all I can say.'

51

Georgia rolled her eyes again. 'Ask your questions. I haven't got all day.'

'I'll wait for my partner to return, if that's okay.' She pointed to the Chihuahua in the baby stroller. The dog wore a rust-colored vest with a matching bow tie. 'Who's your friend?'

Georgia's expression softened. 'Marmaduke. He thinks he's a Great Dane.'

Kit chuckled. 'Does he bite?'

'Sometimes. If he doesn't like you.'

Kit decided to take the risk on the off chance that petting Marmaduke would calm Georgia's angry demeanor. They needed information.

Kit held out her hand for the dog to sniff, then gave him a friendly scratch behind the ears. 'How many residents have pets here?'

'Some. Some people get another when the animals pass, some don't.'

'Did Frankie Flynn have a dog?'

'No. Not anymore.'

'And Benny?'

'Nope. But he always has a treat for Marmaduke.'

Kit dug into her pocket and brought out a large dog biscuit. 'I have a dog. A standard poodle named Snickerdoodle. I carry treats everywhere I go. Can Marmaduke have a piece?'

Georgia gave her a cutting look. 'You can't bribe me through my dog, but if you want to give him a treat, be my guest.'

Biting back a smirk, Kit broke off a piece and offered it to the Chihuahua, who took it gently. 'Good boy.'

Behind them, the door opened and closed. Connor slid into the seat beside her. 'He's out for at least a few hours.'

Dammit. 'Thanks for checking.' She took her phone from her pocket and opened the secure notes app. 'How well did you know Mr Flynn?'

'Well enough to know that he used to be a cop.'

Wondering why this was the first detail the woman willingly offered, Kit feigned surprise. 'I thought he owned an antique store with his late husband.'

Georgia's expression indicated that she didn't believe Kit's surprise was genuine. *Sharp old lady.* 'He did that, too. But you already knew he was a cop.'

Kit didn't confirm or deny. 'Was it common knowledge?'

'No.'

'Did he tell you?' Kit asked.

'Yes.' The woman grimaced. 'Well, not voluntarily. I was helping him clean out his closet after the death of his husband and I found a photo of him in his uniform. He was very young in that photo. I asked him about it, but he was upset that I'd seen it, so I let it go. Much later, we discussed it. He told me that he'd been a homicide lieutenant, but he'd walked away from the job when he turned fifty-five.'

'Why did you tell us this?' Connor asked.

'Because I figured if you knew he was a cop, you'd work harder to solve his murder.'

Again, Kit didn't confirm or deny. 'Did he tell you why he walked away from the force?' Because Navarro and the brass would probably want to know.

Her expression softened. 'For Ryan. They'd met in the late seventies. Ryan was out, but Frankie wasn't. He couldn't have been. Not as a cop. Not back then.'

'No,' Kit agreed quietly, hating that it was true.

Georgia absently petted Marmaduke. 'Frankie told me that he'd promised Ryan that he'd retire as soon as he hit fifty-five, no matter what position he'd attained. And he did. Moved away, helped Ryan start his dream business, and married him as soon as it was legal.'

'He changed his name when he married Ryan,' Connor commented.

'You'll find that he actually changed it legally years earlier. It was part of the break with his old life. Said he owed Ryan that much for putting up with him being in the closet for fifteen years.'

'Do you know why he returned to San Diego?' Kit asked.

'And when?' Connor added.

'It was for Ryan.' Georgia sighed. 'I miss Ryan. And now . . .'

Tears gathering in her eyes, she swallowed hard and whispered, 'I'll have to learn how to miss Frankie, too.'

Kit and Connor waited silently as the older woman visibly pulled herself together. Neither told her that they were sorry for her loss. Kit didn't think the woman wanted to hear it and it seemed Connor was of the same mind.

'Apologies,' Georgia said briskly. 'Ryan's sister Martha was Benny's wife. Martha was losing her eyesight, and she and Benny decided that continuing care would be best for them. They sold everything and moved in here about . . . maybe ten years ago. She and Ryan were close, so Ryan and Frankie followed them here. Frankie said that he always thought that his previous life – that's what he called his career in SDPD – would catch up to him, but none of his old colleagues ever tracked him down here. He wasn't ashamed of his years as a cop, but he was resentful of the depart-ment. He said that he would have moved in with Ryan years earlier if he hadn't been afraid of repercussions amongst his colleagues. He'd offered to leave before he retired, but Ryan didn't want him to walk away from his full pension. They weren't rich then. Ryan was just a computer programmer. So Frankie stayed with SDPD. When Ryan died, I think Frankie wanted to leave Shady Oaks, but Martha and Benny were still here. So once again, Frankie stayed. Frankie didn't say much, but he was deeply loyal to the people he loved.'

'What about his son?' Kit asked.

Georgia scowled. 'Frankie tried so hard with that boy. Well, he's no boy. He's got to be in his midfifties by now. I never met Gerald, but I know Frankie wanted a relationship with him. By the time I met him, though, he'd given up. Frankie, I mean. To my know-ledge, they hadn't seen each other in twenty or thirty years. Maybe more.'

'What about his ex-wife?' Connor asked.

'Sharon. He spoke of her, though infrequently. Always with fondness. I don't think they had an acrimonious divorce.'

'Do you know of anyone who would have wanted Frankie dead?' Connor asked.

Georgia hesitated for the briefest of moments. 'No.'

But she knew something, Kit was certain. 'Ma'am, if you know anything, please tell us.'

'I don't know anything concrete. Something was bothering him in the last week or two, but I don't know what. We didn't have that kind of relationship. We were friends. He played a mean game of bridge and a better-than-average game of cribbage, but he didn't share everything with me.'

'Would he have told Benny?' Connor asked.

'No.'

The finality of the reply had Kit's suspicions rising. 'Benny said that Frankie's death was all his fault.'

Georgia glared. 'Benny is confused. Do *not* upset him any further. He had a bad heart before his stroke. It's only gotten worse since. If you upset him, you could kill him.'

'We don't aim to upset Mr Dreyfus,' Kit said, 'but if we're going to solve Mr Flynn's murder, we need to have all the facts.'

Georgia shook her head. 'I don't know anything that will help you.'

'But you do know something,' Kit pressed.

Georgia stared her straight in the eye. 'No. I do not. If I did, I'd tell you, so stop asking me.'

Well. Okay, then. 'When was the last time you saw Mr Flynn?'

'Saturday evening, after sundown. It was Eloise's birthday party and Frankie came. They were friends, even though Eloise cheats at every card game she ever plays and Frankie called her on it. Eloise and Benny were partners in cribbage and bridge, and Frankie and I were partners.'

'Mr Dreyfus can still play bridge?' Connor asked.

'Benny's in the early stages of dementia,' Georgia said quietly. 'He forgets where he puts things and forgets to take his medications and occasionally will forget a person he's recently met, but not only does he remember how to play bridge, he could probably build a particle accelerator out of common household materials. He was a physics professor at UC San Diego for twenty-five years. When he retired, he and Martha moved to San Francisco to live near Frankie and Ryan.'

55

'Why didn't they go to a continuing care facility in San Francisco?' Kit asked, because Navarro would want to know. 'Why did they come back to San Diego?'

'Benny and Martha have grandchildren and great-grandchildren here in San Diego. The grandchildren are all grown now, but most of them live close by and bring their babies to visit. Someone needs to tell them about Frankie.'

'We'll check Mr Dreyfus's next-of-kin list,' Kit promised. 'Thank you.'

'Mr Flynn died sometime yesterday after ten a.m.,' Connor said, getting them back on track. 'That leaves Saturday night and Sunday unaccounted for. Do you know where he was?'

'Not for sure. He took a walk every morning and sometimes on weekends he went home.'

Kit blinked. 'Home? I thought he lived here.'

Georgia's mouth curved sadly. 'He did, but he and Ryan kept their home in San Francisco. Frankie would go back occasionally to sit with Ryan's things and just . . . be.'

'They didn't rent it out?' Connor asked.

'Not that I know of.'

'You're sure you don't know of anyone who'd want to kill him?' Kit pressed.

'No. I do not.'

Kit still didn't completely believe the woman. 'We may have more questions for you as we learn more.'

'I figured you would.' Georgia rose, appearing to be calm, but her grip on the baby stroller handles was white-knuckle tight. 'If I might be excused, I'm going to sit with Benny if they'll allow me to.'

Kit and Connor rose along with her.

'We're very sorry for your loss, ma'am,' Connor said softly, once again surprising Kit with his gentleness. 'Thank you for waiting to speak with us.'

Georgia gave him a curt nod. 'Just see that you find who did it. Frankie was a little grouchy sometimes, but you couldn't find a kinder, nicer, smarter man. He'd give you the shirt off his back, and sometimes did.' One side of her mouth lifted. 'I'd be surprised if there's much money left for the son. Frankie was big into giving to charities and he already told me that Ryan had wanted their house sold and for the proceeds to go to shelters for LGBTQ youth. Frankie hadn't had the heart to sell it yet, but he planned to. He won't have completely forgotten Gerald in his will, but the estate will be much smaller than Gerald thinks it is.'

And if Gerald had found this out? Another motive for murder.

'Thank you,' Kit said. 'We'll be speaking to him very soon. And, ma'am, we understand you saw Mr Flynn's body, too. If you're in need of counseling, we can recommend someone.'

Georgia shook her head. 'I'll just call Dr Sam. But thank you.'

Kit waited until she was gone before slowly exhaling. Sam. *Again.*

Connor looked . . . not smug, exactly, but he was smirking. 'They really love Sam here. Because he's a nice guy.'

Kit ground her teeth. 'Let's call Navarro with our report.'

Connor nodded soberly. 'Whatever you say.'

They were silent until they'd exited the facility and were in their department sedan. Kit called Navarro and together she and Connor brought him up to speed.

Navarro sighed. 'I hate to say this, but I get why Frank left the force. Even in the nineties when he retired, it wouldn't have been easy for him to be out.'

'No, sir,' Kit said. 'I think we should have someone seal up his house in San Francisco. We can go through it to see if there's anything that might lead us to his killer.'

'Good idea.' There was the sound of keys clacking and then Navarro whistled. 'Holy shit. His house is in Russian Hill. It's got to be worth six or seven million, at least. And it was just sitting there *empty*?'

'According to Miss Shearer,' Connor confirmed.

'What about the best friend?' Navarro asked. 'Benjamin Dreyfus? I get that you can't question him yet, but what was your impression? Is he capable of killing Frank?'

'Not physically,' Connor said. 'I met him when I first arrived this morning and he's nearly ninety years old and in bad health. He's also only about five-eight and very thin. I don't think he'd have the strength to . . . well, to cut the victim the way he was. The son is a possibility and we'll contact him right away, but after him, we want to talk to Kent Crawford, the head of security. It's no coincidence that the cameras outside the victim's apartment were disconnected.'

'I agree. I'll keep the brass up-to-date, and—' He cut himself off. 'Wait a minute. Did you say Kent Crawford?'

Kit and Connor shared a look of dread. 'Yes,' Kit said. 'Why?'

'Because he's dead. I'm looking at the initial report right now. He was found in a motel room this morning by the housekeeping staff. Ate his gun. Looked like he'd been there at least a day. Maybe two.'

Kit huffed out a breath. 'Well, shit.'

Four

San Diego, California
Monday, 7 November, 3.00 P.M.

Sam ushered his two o'clock appointment to the door. 'Good session, Mrs Gibson. I'll see you next week.'

Whether it actually had been a good session, Sam couldn't truthfully say. His mind had been occupied with thoughts of Frankie Flynn. And Kit McKittrick. He'd been a piss-poor therapist this afternoon, and his clients deserved a hell of a lot more than he'd given them.

Luckily Mrs Gibson always used her hour to talk through her issues, and Sam rarely had to say a word. Today had been no different.

Mrs Gibson, a petite woman in her fifties, looked up at him with her usual smile, and Sam felt a wave of relief. He hadn't screwed up too badly. 'Thank you, Dr Reeves. Today really helped. I'll see you next week.'

He stood in the doorway until she'd reached their receptionist in the outer office, then started to close his door but stopped when a familiar voice called his name.

'Sam?' Vivian Carlisle was limping down the hallway, tightly gripping her cane. She'd been in a car accident six months ago, and while the cast had come off her broken leg, she was still in considerable pain.

He opened the door wide to let her in, helping her to one of his client chairs.

She'd been in great shape before her accident, one of the fittest seniors he'd ever met. She was somewhere between a well-preserved midsixties to a remarkably well-preserved midseventies, but he would never, ever ask.

'Thank you,' she murmured, then stared up at him. 'Sit down, Sam. You're giving me a crick in my neck on top of this stupid leg of mine.'

He sat dutifully. He owed much to this woman. She'd been his mentor for years, first as a grad student then after he'd come to work in her practice, but even more important, she was his friend.

'I'm sorry about your friend,' she said quietly.

He wasn't surprised that she'd heard. He'd mentioned Frankie's murder to Angeline, their receptionist, when he'd returned, telling her to alert him if either McKittrick or Robinson called for information. They hadn't called. That really hadn't surprised him, either. Especially that Kit hadn't called.

'Angeline told you.'

She nodded. 'She was worried about you. Said you looked pale. Which you do. Tell me what happened.'

Sam shrugged. 'I really don't know much. My friend Frankie was stabbed sometime after yesterday at ten a.m. One of the nursing assistants found him with a butcher knife in his chest. I was on the schedule this morning to play for the residents and . . . Well. Everything was in an uproar, so I stuck around until the detectives arrived. I helped calm one of the residents who'd seen the body, then I left to do my sessions. That's all I know.'

But it really wasn't all he knew, and it must have been written all over his face, because Vivian tilted her head to study him.

'Which detectives arrived?'

Sam felt his cheeks heat but kept his gaze level. Vivian knew him too well. She knew how he felt about Kit McKittrick. She knew Kit's rejection six months ago had stung. But he was all right. He really was. 'McKittrick and Robinson.'

'Well, at least we know they'll get to the bottom of things,' she murmured. 'Tell me about your friend. He was a resident of Shady Oaks?'

'He was.' Sam swallowed. *Was.* Damn, he hated that word. 'One of the first residents I met.' One side of his mouth tipped up as he remembered. 'It was in an art class four years ago, like this morning's class was supposed to have been. I'd asked the residents for requests and they all named the old standards. You know, Sinatra or Dean Martin. Frankie sat there, all silent, looking like the grumpiest of old men, arms crossed. I singled him out for a request and he raised a brow and I knew a dare was coming.'

Vivian smiled. 'A musical dare? What did he request?'

Sam smirked. 'Iron Maiden. "The Number of the Beast." '

Vivian choked on a surprised laugh. 'No way.'

'Oh yes. So I launched into it. With gusto.'

Her eyes widened. 'You can play Iron Maiden? On the piano?'

'Oh sure. I'd learned that song to torment my classical piano teacher back in middle school. Turned out she was a metal fan, too, so it didn't get the reaction I'd hoped for. I was a very disappointed twelve-year-old boy that day.'

'So what did Frankie do?'

'For a second he just stared at me, then he threw his head back and laughed while flipping me the bird.' Sam smiled, remembering. 'Everyone in the room went silent and turned to stare at him, mouths open. I got the impression that he didn't laugh like that often, and later learned that was the case. His husband had died a few months before, and he hadn't smiled since.' He drew a breath. 'His sister-in-law and her husband Benny came up to me afterward and thanked me. Told me about Ryan's passing and how Frankie had been inconsolable. They were crying.' He cleared his throat. 'I cried too, then.'

Vivian's smile was sweet. 'And you became friends?'

'Yeah, we did. We talked every time I went to play. My own grandfather had passed away and I missed him. Frankie reminded me of him. Turned out they even shared first and middle names. Franklin Delano. My grandpa was called Del. Frankie kind of took me under his wing. I'd just broken up with my old girlfriend and . . . well, we were both lonely, I guess. He loved Siggy. Used to growl at me when I'd leave him at home. Frankie growled, not Siggy.'

Vivian chuckled, then sighed. 'What else do you know? Did he have any enemies?'

'Not that I knew of. But I guess I didn't know him as well as I thought. I found out today that he has a son. A son that despises him, apparently. Enough not to want to be involved with his funeral, only the reading of his will.'

'Frankie had money?'

'Yeah. He told me once that his husband had made a "shitload of cash" – his words, not mine – when he sold some kind of software. We talked sometimes about what he should do with the money. Charities he could give it to. He gave away a lot. But never once did he mention a son.'

'That hurts you.'

Sam shrugged uncomfortably. 'Yeah. But I'm sure he had his reasons. Who knows, maybe the son was from a previous marriage and hated him for being gay or for leaving his mother. We see that from time to time in clients.'

'We do,' she agreed. 'And what else?'

'Why do you think there's more?'

'Because I know you. You've got that groove just here.' She pointed to her forehead. 'Talk to me, Sam. You'll feel better afterward.'

He would. He always did. 'There was something going on with McKittrick. She asked me where his husband was and I told her that Ryan had died and that they'd been together for a long time, that they'd run an antique store together before their retirement. She . . . tensed. Just a tiny reaction.'

But Sam had been watching her carefully. The fact had startled her.

'Why would that make her tense?'

'I don't know.'

'Did you ask her?'

Sam laughed bitterly. 'No. I didn't.'

Vivian sighed again. 'So she wasn't happy to see you, I take it.'

'No, not at all.'

'Well,' Vivian said briskly. 'Why do you *think* it would make her tense?'

Sam looked away, concentrating on that moment when Kit's blue eyes had flickered before she'd yanked down the iron curtain over her expression.

'It was almost like she was surprised because she knew some-thing different.'

And now Sam really wanted to know what that something dif-ferent was.

'You could ask her partner,' Vivian suggested cautiously.

'I could.' But he really wanted to hear it from Kit. Asking Connor Robinson felt like . . . cheating, somehow. 'Or I could ask one of Frankie's friends at Shady Oaks.' He gave Vivian an assess-ing look. 'You just transformed some of my grief into curiosity. Well done.'

She gave him her best impression of innocence. 'I have no idea what you're talking about. We're just chatting.' She held out her hand. 'Help an old woman up. I'm done for the day, so I'm going home early.'

He pulled her to her feet, then patted her back when she gave him a motherly hug. 'Thank you,' he murmured, then pulled away. 'I'll need to rearrange my schedule for the next few days so that I can support the residents. I promised I'd be back tomorrow for a little while. The music helps them.'

She smiled up at him. 'I think it's you who helps them, Sam. The music is a nice freebie. Let me know if I can take any of your cases.' She started for the door, then paused, her smile brightening. 'I have a message for you. Rita Mendoza says to tell you that she's "taking the plunge."' She used air quotes.

His heart immediately lightened. 'She's going for the adoption?'

'She is. She and the McKittricks met with the social worker this morning. She said that Kit was there and to thank you for suggest-ing she include her. Kit helped.' Vivian lifted her eyebrows. 'She also said to tell you that she's "working on Kit."'

Sam's cheeks heated a second time. 'She oughtn't do that.' It wasn't fair to Kit. Besides, Sam wanted Kit to want him on her own, not because she'd been worn down to accept him.

'Well, Rita's fourteen and thinks both you and Kit walk on water. Have a good evening, Sam.'

'You too.' He closed the door behind her, then sat at his desk and forced his mind back to his session with Mrs Gibson long enough to complete his notes. Then he stared at his phone, wishing he could call Kit and ask what she'd learned about Frankie's killer.

Wishing he could call Kit, period. But he couldn't. He'd promised himself that he wouldn't pursue her. That when she came to him – if she came to him – it would be her decision alone.

But he wanted to know why she'd seemed startled at Frankie running an antique store. And he wanted to know about Frankie's son.

Had Frankie been married before Ryan? To a woman perhaps? Or was the son adopted? Adoption would have been unlikely given Frankie's current age, as single men hadn't been allowed to adopt back then. But it wasn't impossible.

He did a quick Google search on Frankie Flynn, but only the articles about his murder came up. He searched a free person-finding database, only to come up with an address in San Francisco. Which couldn't be right. Shady Oaks had been Frankie's permanent address.

When he googled the address itself, he was doubly sure it couldn't be right. It was a super-ritzy house in one of the wealthiest neighborhoods in the Bay Area.

His glance fell to his phone once again. He really wanted to know about Frankie's life before Shady Oaks, but he couldn't ask Benny. It would upset him too much. Plus, he was probably still asleep.

So he dialed the main number and asked for Georgia Shearer. Georgia might know, but he couldn't come right out and ask. She was a crusty old lady and was sometimes tight-lipped if she thought you wanted to gossip.

But this wasn't gossip. Was it?

He winced at the thought. *Maybe.* He was reaching for the end button to hang up when Georgia's voice came on the line. She sounded so tired and Sam felt guilty anew.

'Hello?'

'Miss Georgia, this is Sam Reeves.'

She blew out a sigh of relief. 'I'm glad it's you. I've had dozens of calls from reporters today, asking about Frankie. I asked the front desk to screen incoming calls.'

'They must have recognized my caller ID. How are you, Miss Georgia?'

'I'm okay. Rattled and tired. It'll sink in about Frankie later. It always does.'

'It always does?'

'This isn't my first rodeo, Sam. I'm eighty-two years old. I've seen just about everyone I know die. Some have been harder than others. Some hit fast and some take a while to sink in. I think Frankie will take a while, just because of the circumstances.'

The circumstances. Frankie getting stabbed to death with a butcher knife. 'You saw him.'

A hard swallow, audible over the phone. 'Yes. I did. Everyone keeps telling me to go to sleep, but I can't. I'm afraid I'll see it again.'

He wished he had a good suggestion, but it was a fair worry. 'I'm sorry, Georgia.'

'I know,' she said quietly. 'You loved him, too.'

'I did. Miss Evans asked me to play at his service. She said you might do the eulogy.'

'I'm sitting here right now, trying to write it. I may ask for your help.'

'You know you've got it. Anything you need. If you need to talk about what you saw or even just talk about Frankie.' He hesitated, then decided to ask. 'Miss Georgia, Miss Evans also said that Frankie had a son who wasn't coming to his funeral.'

Georgia sniffed. 'Brat.'

Sam blinked. 'Me?'

'Of course not. I'm talking about Gerald. Frankie loved him so much, but they were estranged. I think Frankie had all but given up on healing whatever rift was between them. Now it's too late.'

' "It's too late" are some of the saddest words.' Sam wasn't going to be hurt that Georgia knew about Frankie's son. He was not. Except that he was. A little. 'Frankie never mentioned him. Was his last name Flynn?'

Georgia sighed. 'No. Frankie's last name was Wilson before he married Ryan. And Frankie didn't talk about Gerald to anyone, really, so don't be hurt, Sam. It was painful for Frankie and I don't know why they were estranged, although I suspected it had something to do with Frankie being gay. I wish I could fix it, but it's not my battle. Nor is it yours.'

Sam took the warning for what it was: *Stay out of it.* 'You're right, ma'am. And I know that family dynamics aren't always what they seem to be on the surface.'

'No, they aren't. Would you mind if we talked later? I need to get back to Benny. He was in the nursing ward all afternoon.'

'Is he awake now?'

'I don't know. I was with him most of the afternoon, because I didn't want him to wake up alone in a strange place. I think they're moving him to his room soon.'

'You'll call if there's anything I can do.'

'Of course,' she said warmly. Or what passed as warmth for Georgia. Most people would think her tone gruff and prickly, but Georgia had a soft heart under her armadillo exterior.

They ended the call and Sam lifted his gaze from his phone to his computer screen. Frankie had been a Wilson before marrying Ryan Flynn.

Sam opened a new browser window and typed *Franklin Delano Wilson*.

Then stared in shock at the long list of links that came up.

And the photos.

Frankie had been younger in them – thirty years younger.

Frankie had been wearing a uniform.

Frankie had been a cop.

And not just any cop. A homicide lieutenant.

This was what Kit had known. *This* was why the antique store had been a surprise.

Frankie used to be a cop. And now he was dead. Murdered.

Chills ran over Sam's skin. He would have sworn that Frankie had no enemies, but that opinion had just radically changed.

Cops made enemies. Had one of them plunged a butcher knife into Frankie's chest? If so, then who? And why? Why thirty freaking years later?

He started to dial Connor's phone, then stopped himself. Those two were good detectives. They'd be calling him soon enough for information, so he'd wait. It would probably be Connor, because Kit had cut him off.

And Sam would have to be okay with that.

National City, San Diego, California
Monday, 7 November, 3.00 P.M.

'I thought it seemed off,' Detective Marshall said when Kit and Connor arrived at the motel room in which security head Kent Crawford's body had been found. 'We were called at about eight thirty this morning when housekeeping entered the room. The victim had put the "Do Not Disturb" sign on his door, but housekeeping smelled "something funky." She knocked and when he didn't answer, she went in and found him. Apparently he's not the first dead body she's discovered in this place.'

Kevin Marshall was new to the homicide division, one of two detectives brought in to replace the two detectives who'd retired six months ago. Somewhere in his midforties, he'd spent the last ten years in the narcotics division, earning a reputation as a solid, ethical, and intelligent cop. Kit liked him.

'What made it seem off to you?' Connor asked him as Kit took in the room.

It was a generic room in a cheap motel, located off one of the old roads that used to be well traveled before the highway was built. The room was threadbare but clean. Well, except where bits of the victim had been blown by the bullet exiting his skull. That was always nasty.

The walls were a dingy beige, the chair in the corner old, the vinyl torn. There was a pair of athletic shoes tucked neatly under the chair.

The body had been found on the bed, now soaked with the victim's blood and brains. The body had already been taken to the morgue.

There was an open suitcase on the luggage rack, its contents jumbled, and a golf bag with a full complement of clubs in the corner. A glance into the bathroom revealed a towel on the floor and a tooth-brush and a disposable razor on the sink.

She could smell the stench of death, but it wasn't all that strong. Of course, the body had already been taken away, but the odor of a rotting body took a while to dissipate. The housekeeper must have had a very sensitive nose.

'To start with, nobody heard a shot,' Marshall said. 'There was no suppressor on the gun found in the victim's hand, but it can take one.'

'You think someone took the suppressor with them?' Kit asked.

'I think it's possible.' Marshall showed them photos of the body on his phone. 'Also, he's holding the gun in his left hand, but he was right-handed.' He pointed to the golf clubs. 'Right-handed clubs. I checked. He could have been an ambidextrous shooter, but it made me pause.' He shrugged. 'Plus, I read all about that staged suicide that was really murder six months ago. I didn't want to be fooled.'

'Smart,' Connor said with a sigh.

Kit smiled wryly, saying nothing. She'd suspected that death six months ago had been a staged suicide, but her superiors had been anxious to believe the man had taken his own life. They'd had a good reason, but it had sucked when the truth had been discovered.

It would be a long time before any of the homicide detectives dismissed a case as suicide before doing a thorough study of the evidence.

'I left Forensics to process the scene,' Marshall went on, 'and went to notify next of kin – his wife, Denise Crawford. She said that he was golfing in Palm Springs with friends. He left Friday in the early afternoon and was supposed to be gone for four days. I haven't checked with the friends yet, but in my experience, when a man lies to his wife about his whereabouts and is then found in a motel ten miles from his own home, that spells affair.'

'Makes sense,' Kit said. 'How did the wife seem?'

'I didn't tell her that I thought he'd been murdered. I only said he'd been found with what appeared to be a self-inflicted gunshot wound. I figured I'd wait for CSU to process the scene before I shared the murder angle. She was shocked that he'd killed himself. Then angry when I asked why he'd checked into the motel so close to their home. She'd suspected he'd been having an affair but had been telling herself that she was overreacting. Said she'd even packed his bag for him for this trip.'

Kit winced. 'Ouch. Poor woman.'

'Yeah. She had several choice names for her husband. She gave me the names of the friends he was supposed to have been with, as well as the name of his employer.'

'Shady Oaks,' Connor said.

Marshall nodded. 'I hadn't heard that there was a murder there this morning when I turned in my initial report to the lieutenant, or I would have called you directly. So I guess it's your case now.'

He didn't seem upset by this, fortunately.

'Most likely,' Kit agreed. 'The victim here was the director of security at the retirement facility and one of the few people with a key to the room housing the security camera controls. The cameras were conveniently not working in the hallway where the murder took place.'

'Then, yeah. Your case, and you're welcome to it. My partner is slogging through the financials of the suspect on our highest-priority case, and I've got a ton of interviews to do. I'll forward all the photos I took to your email. You've got my initial report?'

Kit pointed to her phone. 'Read it on the way over here. Before you go, did you ask the ME to do any specific toxicology tests?'

'Just the normal. You think he was using?'

Kit swiped to the first page of Marshall's report. 'He was a big man. Five-ten, two hundred pounds. Faye Evans, the director at Shady Oaks, said he was an army vet, so he probably knew how to defend himself. Since we're thinking this was not suicide, that means someone put the gun into his mouth. If he was conscious, he would have fought. But you noted that there were no defensive wounds or signs of a struggle.'

'You think his killer drugged him, then set it up to look like a suicide,' Marshall said.

69

'It's been done before.' Kit sent a quick email to the ME, request-ing a full tox screen, especially for sedatives. 'Did the ME give an estimated time of death?'

'Rigor had passed, so thirty-six to forty-eight hours. Can't be any more than three days because that's when he checked in – on Friday.'

'When he called in sick to work,' Connor observed.

Kit nodded. 'Let's hope whatever his killer used – if he did drug the victim – has a half-life greater than two to three days, or it'll be gone.' She scanned Marshall's initial report once more. 'Oh. The manager said that the victim had initially reserved the room for only one night, but that he'd extended the stay online for an add-itional two weeks. So his killer could have changed the checkout date without talking to the front desk.'

'Assuming his killer had access to his online account,' Marshall said. 'If he brought a laptop with him here, it's gone now. So's his cell phone.'

'His killer wanted the victim to remain undiscovered for as long as possible,' Connor said. 'Cameras?'

Marshall made a face. 'I requested the footage. The manager said the surveillance system's been broken for years. I don't think he wants to be able to provide the police with evidence. I saw two drug deals going down in the parking lot while I was waiting on Foren-sics to arrive.'

'Once a narcotics cop,' Kit said with a smile. 'You arrest them?'

Marshall's lips twitched. 'The uniformed officers did. I might have directed them to the bust. But as for surveillance tapes from this hotel, I wouldn't hold my breath. I was on my way to canvass the neighboring businesses for surveillance footage when I got the call from the lieutenant to meet you here.'

'We'll handle it,' Connor said. 'Did the vic's wife have an alibi?'

'She was visiting her parents in Bakersfield up until last night. She has receipts from a gas station, and her parents vouched for her whereabouts. I mean, an alibi from parents is a little shaky, but she says they had a barbecue over the weekend and lots of neighbors saw her there. That's not in the initial report. Just got that info an hour ago.'

Kit noted it. 'We'll check the wife out, too. I want to know who he was having an affair with and who knew he'd be here.'

Marshall smiled. 'Good hunting. You have any more questions for me?'

'Yeah,' Connor said. 'Where's his car?'

'Not in this parking lot. I haven't had a chance to check for GPS location. His wife said he drove a year-old Beemer, six series.'

'Pricey,' Kit mused. 'Wonder how much he made at Shady Oaks.'

Marshall nodded. 'Good question. Anything else?'

Connor checked his notes. 'Nothing right now. Kit?'

'Me either. We'll call if we do.'

When Marshall was gone, Connor gave Kit a cautious look. 'If we want to know more about his affair, we should ask the friends he was supposed to be golfing with and his coworkers at Shady Oaks.' He paused and Kit grimaced, knowing what was coming next. 'We should also talk to Sam. He observes things. People tell him stuff. He might know details about Kent Crawford that nobody else noticed or will be willing to tell us.'

'You're right.' She went into the bathroom to search. 'Toothbrush and razor, but no shaving cream. No toothpaste, either. His shaving kit is here, but it's empty. Huh. No little soaps or shampoos.'

'His killer took them. Maybe to wash off the blood.'

Because there would have been spatter. A lot of spatter. If the killer had put the gun in Kent Crawford's hand, they'd been close enough to be wearing that spatter.

'We'll ask Forensics to check the shower trap.'

'Gross,' Connor muttered. 'This doesn't look like the kind of place that routinely cleans the drains. Can you even imagine what's piled up in there?'

'Unfortunately, I can.' She crossed the room to the luggage rack, tugging on a pair of gloves before checking the contents of his suitcase. 'There's only two changes of clothes in this bag. One golf shirt, one dress shirt, and two pairs of shorts. But no nice shoes or slacks to go with the dress shirt. If he expected to be gone for four days, why doesn't he have more clothes? Did his killer take his clothes, too?'

'All good questions,' Connor said. 'And why make the original reservation here for only one night? Unless he actually did plan to catch up with his friends after spending the night with whoever he was having the affair with.'

'We should chat with his friends. You up for a trip to Palm Springs?'

Connor gave her a knowing look. 'Yes, but after we talk to Sam. I'll believe what he has to say over friends who might be prepared to lie for the victim. Especially if they knew he was cheating on the wife.'

Kit sighed. 'Let's go pay a visit to Dr Sam.'

San Diego, California
Monday, 7 November, 4.15 P.M.

Sam was locking his desk when he heard a knock at the door. He turned, expecting Angeline with a copy of his revised schedule, but stopped short when he saw Kit and Connor waiting in the doorway.

Kit clearly did not want to be here. Connor simply looked resigned.

He took a steadying breath. 'Detectives. What can I do for you?'

'Can we sit down?' Connor asked.

Sam gestured at the sofa in his therapy area. 'Please.' He sat in the chair as he did during most therapy sessions. It made him feel more in control.

He needed control right now. The sight of Kit McKittrick, here in his space, had his heart thundering all out of rhythm. Drawing a breath, he tried to relax.

'How can I help you?' he asked, hearing the stiffness in his voice.

Kit's expression softened slightly. 'Kent Crawford is dead.'

Sam stared at her, the words not immediately registering. Then they did and he fumbled for words. 'You mean Shady Oaks's head of security? That Kent Crawford?'

She nodded. 'His body was found in a motel room this morning. He'd been dead at least a couple days.'

'Oh my God.' That Kit and Connor were investigating meant it had been a homicide. Two murdered bodies found in the same day couldn't be a coincidence. Kent's death had to be connected to Frankie's. 'When?'

'Two days ago,' she replied. 'Maybe three.'

'How?'

'Gunshot wound. It was supposed to look like a suicide,' Connor said quietly.

Sam closed his eyes, trying to take that in. *Kent is dead. Just like Frankie.* 'Do faked suicides happen often? Or only when I'm involved?' Because the last case he'd worked with Kit had featured a faked suicide.

Kit sighed. 'More often than we probably know. How well did you know Mr Crawford?'

Sam blinked hard, then scrubbed his hands over his face and concentrated. Kit was here when she'd avoided him for six months. This was important. 'Not all that well. I didn't spend much time with him.'

'On purpose?' Kit asked. 'Or your paths didn't cross?'

Sam blew out a breath. 'Both. But I didn't really trust him. Neither did Frankie.'

Connor tilted his head. 'Why not?'

Sam shrugged. 'Little things. Kent was kind of a blowhard. He liked to brag about his athletic prowess. How he played college football and could have gone pro if he hadn't decided to join the military and "serve his country." ' Sam used air quotes. 'He was always talking about having served his country. And I suppose he did, but I've known a lot of people who served and didn't bring it up in every conversation.'

'He was a braggart,' Connor said. 'What else?'

Sam hesitated, unsure if he should share what he and Frankie had suspected. He didn't know if it was true, and if it wasn't, it could hurt Crawford's widow.

'Sam?' Kit murmured.

Sam jerked his gaze to hers. She hadn't called him by his first name in a long time. But she hadn't intended to. He could see the blush on her cheeks. And the surprise in her eyes before she looked away.

He shifted his gaze to Connor. 'Frankie thought that Kent was cheating on his wife. That was something Frankie couldn't condone – and neither could I. Knowing that made us mistrust his judgment on other things.'

'Like?' Connor pressed.

'Like the security system he had installed. It was so complicated that the night guards had trouble using it, which resulted in two patients in the memory wing leaving the grounds unattended in the past six months. Frankie thought the security system was too expensive, that it was a waste of money. Especially since it didn't work well. Frankie suspected that there was some palm-greasing going on.'

Both Kit and Connor looked surprised at this. 'How did Frankie know what it cost?'

Sam shrugged. 'He asked the installers. People told Frankie things.'

'Is Shady Oaks having financial problems?' Kit asked.

'Not that I know of. Frankie was irritated more on principle. Any money spent on expensive, unnecessary things was money that wasn't being invested on behalf of the residents. Frankie traveled when Ryan was alive, but generally he was careful with money. He expected Shady Oaks to be careful with the residents' money, too. They pay in for life and need the funds to be available for their care when they need it.'

'Did Mr Flynn tell anyone what he suspected?' Kit asked. 'Other than you?'

'He tried to tell Miss Evans, but the director said he was clearly out of his element. That he should stick to antiques.' Sam's lips curved sadly. 'Finding out he was a cop makes Frankie's suspicions about Kent make a lot more sense.'

Connor's eyes had widened. 'How did you know Mr Flynn was a cop?'

Kit was looking at him again, gaze shrewd. 'Did you know before today?'

74

'No, I didn't know. I called Georgia and asked if she knew about Frankie's son, and she told me his name was Gerald and that Frank had been a Wilson before marrying Ryan. So I googled Frank Wilson. I was . . . well, stunned. I had no idea that Frankie was a cop. You knew, though.'

Both detectives nodded.

'I met him ten years ago,' Kit said. 'Just briefly. Only long enough to shake his hand. Frank Wilson was a legend in the department. None of us knew he'd changed his name to Flynn.'

'I never knew he was a cop.' Sam looked Kit in the eye. 'I would have told you.'

'I know you would have,' Kit said, her expression softer. 'I shouldn't have even asked that. If it makes you feel better, I don't think many people at Shady Oaks knew.'

'I was thinking that his killer might have been one of his old cases. But now that Kent's dead, I don't guess that's a strong possibility.'

'Not off the table, though,' Kit said. 'Let's go back to Kent Crawford cheating on his wife. Did either you or Mr Flynn suspect who the other woman might have been?'

'I didn't know. If Frankie did, he didn't tell me. It's clear that there were a lot of things he didn't tell me.'

'What made you and Mr Flynn suspect infidelity?' Connor asked.

'Again, a lot of little things. His wife would stop by Shady Oaks thinking he was there when he'd taken a long lunch or left early. Once she came at ten a.m., when I was playing piano for the residents' dance class. She waited until the class was over and asked me if I'd seen Kent. I had to tell her no and I could see that she suspected something. Her eyes filled with tears and I wished I could say something to comfort her, but . . .' He shrugged again.

Kit's eyes narrowed. 'Did she confide in you?'

'If she did, I couldn't tell you.'

Kit sighed. 'She did.'

Yes, she did.

'Was it in a professional capacity?' Connor asked.

Yes, it was. She'd shown up on his therapy schedule, wanting

75

advice. And it had been so very awkward. 'Again, I can't tell you what was discussed in private, but I noticed other things. Mrs Crawford's skin is very pale. Her makeup is always flawless, and her lipstick is never bright or bold. Always light pinks. But I saw bright red lipstick stains on Kent's shirts a few times. More than once, Kent came back from one of his long lunches smelling like perfume. It wasn't Mrs Crawford's perfume because she said she was allergic to strong scents and never used them.'

'When was this?' Connor asked.

'The perfume was maybe six, eight months ago, but that stopped. He still takes the long lunches, though, and I've seen a lipstick stain on the collar of his shirt as recently as a month ago. Not bright red anymore. This one was more of a burgundy wine color, but I only got a glimpse. It definitely wasn't light pink. He'd whisk off to his office to change his shirt right away, as soon as he came back from lunch. Maybe he wasn't seeing the same woman. I don't know.'

'So Kent Crawford wasn't a straight shooter like Miss Evans would have had us believe,' Kit said thoughtfully. 'Do you think there was anything between Mr Crawford and Miss Evans?'

Sam blinked. 'I don't know. I never got the impression that they particularly liked each other, but it is possible, I suppose. She respected him. Was always singing his praises to prospective residents.' He exhaled. 'I guess she's going to have to hire someone new.'

'Is there anything else you can think of?' Kit asked. 'Any irregularities or strange behaviors at Shady Oaks – either the staff or the residents?'

'Oh, there are a lot of irregularities. *Lots* of affairs among the residents. Yes, I know,' he said when both detectives winced. 'Sex among the retirement set is off the charts. There have been a few catfights among the ladies – it's always the ladies fighting over the men. When I first started volunteering, there was a hair-pulling fight in the dining hall when one of the ladies was caught stepping out with a married man. His wife had to be pulled off the "Jezebel" – her word, not mine – and ended up grabbing the other woman's hair right off her head. It was a wig, so there was no pain involved, but it was a sight, I must say. Both those women have since passed, as has the cheating husband. Now Miss Eloise is the major femme fatale of Shady Oaks. She's usually the first to stake a claim on any new male resident, but there haven't been any fights in a while. But I don't think that's what you're referring to.'

Kit looked pained. 'No, but now I'm visualizing that woman holding the Jezebel's wig.' She gave her head a little shake. 'Mr Flynn was married to a woman before he married Ryan. Did he ever speak of her?'

'Not to me. Only of Ryan. He was devoted to him.' He sighed quietly. 'To his memory, anyway. Now they're together again. So there is that.'

Sadness shadowed Kit's face. 'I suppose so,' she murmured.

Sam remembered how her voice had broken when she'd talked about the victims on their previous case and wondered if she felt so deeply for every victim. He suspected that she did, but that she'd never admit to it.

He wanted to take her hand, wanted to give her comfort, but she'd made her wishes clear. 'I wish I could help you, but he never spoke about his life before Ryan. All I know is what I read online this afternoon.'

'Thank you,' Kit said, and then her gaze sharpened. 'We hear you talked to Benny Dreyfus today, too.'

Sam sighed, knowing that this had been coming. 'I did. Miss Evans asked me to calm him down so that he could speak to you. But he was past the point of calm. He had to be sedated.'

'Did he say anything to you?' Connor asked. 'Even if it didn't seem related, we'd like to know what he said.'

Sam shook his head. 'It was related, but it didn't make much sense. He was rambling. And angry, taking it out on Nurse Roxanne. He was hitting her hard. I distracted him so that she could call his doctor and confirm giving him a sedative. Benny was so wound up that he didn't even realize she'd given him a shot. Have you spoken to Roxanne?'

'Not yet,' Kit said. 'But we will ASAP. Can you remember Mr Dreyfus's actual words?'

Sam closed his eyes, replaying the chaotic scene in the visitation room. 'He said it was all his fault, that he should have listened to Frankie. But that Frankie was wrong.'

'About what?' Kit asked quietly.

Sam opened his eyes to meet hers and had to remind himself to focus. He could stare into those blue eyes of hers all day. Which made him feel pathetic, given that she didn't feel the same way. 'I don't know. I tried to make sense of it. Later he said that Frankie had been right, so I tried to clarify. I asked if he meant that Frankie was wrong at first, then right? And Benny said yes. He said that he'd been angry with Frankie because Frankie said that he was naive and lonely. I asked if that was true, and Benny said that he missed Martha – she was his wife for more than fifty years. He also said that he'd believed lies. But he wasn't specific. I thought he might be ready to give me more, but then he fell asleep.'

'So we know that there was disagreement between Mr Flynn and Mr Dreyfus,' Kit said.

Sam frowned. 'Benny didn't kill Frankie. Even if he was strong enough emotionally – which he wasn't – he was too weak physically.'

'You said that he was hurting Nurse Roxanne,' Kit pointed out, but he could tell that she didn't believe that Benny was guilty of murder.

'Yes, but she wasn't fighting back. She was just taking it. She had her hands up, protecting herself, when I came in, but she let Benny take out his anger on her. It wasn't hard to make him stop. I just gently pulled his fists away from her and hugged him. He collapsed against me right away. He didn't kill Frankie.'

'We don't think so, either,' Connor said. 'But we will go back and talk to Benny when he wakes up. Perhaps, if you're available, you can join us? If you can keep him calm without sedation, that would be a big help.'

Sam didn't miss Kit's slight tensing. On some level, she didn't want him involved, but she wasn't going to say anything to the contrary. At this point, he couldn't let himself care that she didn't want him around. This was about getting justice for Frankie while protecting Benny.

'I'd be happy to help.'

Kit smiled tightly. 'Thank you,' she said, rising to her feet and heading for the door. 'We'll call if we have more questions.'

Connor followed her, giving Sam a grateful smile. 'You've filled in a bit more of the picture. Thanks, man.'

'You're welcome.' Sam stood by his chair, watching them go, his heart already heavy. She was leaving again.

But she did call me Sam.

He frowned at himself. *And you are not going to pin any hopes on that.*

'Let me know when I can call Mrs Crawford to give her my condolences. I don't want to impede your investigation, but I know she has to be hurting. In spite of his cheating, she loved Kent – or at least she did once upon a time.'

'I will,' Connor said, because Kit was already at the elevator, her gaze fixed on the shiny steel doors.

Five

San Diego, California
Monday, 7 November, 5.10 P.M.

Kit waited until she and Connor were back in the department sedan before breaking the silence. Settling into the passenger seat, she fastened her seat belt. Partly because it was the law and partly because Connor drove like he was on a NASCAR track. 'That wasn't a total waste of time.'

Connor laughed. 'High praise, coming from you.' He guided the car into traffic, sighing when they immediately hit a rush-hour snarl. 'We're going to be stuck here forever.'

'Stop whining.' Kit opened the secure notes app on her phone. 'So Mr Dreyfus knew something, but we still don't know what. Whatever it was, it had caused friction between Flynn and Dreyfus. We still need to know what Flynn and Dreyfus were upset with each other about, but we'll put that on hold until Dreyfus wakes up. Also, Kent Crawford was almost definitely having an affair. Let's focus on that. If Sam and Mr Flynn both noticed that Crawford was sleeping around, there's a chance that others did, too. Someone knew he was in that motel room. Either his killer knew he was meeting a woman or they simply followed him, but we need to find out who knew. And if we can find out who his affair partner was, that person might have seen something useful.'

'What're the chances that Crawford's and Flynn's deaths are unrelated?'

'Small,' Kit said. 'Really small.'

'Agreed. Especially since the cameras on Flynn's floor were out. Crawford would have known how to disable them.'

'We need to find out if he had his laptop with him. If it was possible to disable the cameras remotely, it's possible that his killer either broke into Crawford's laptop or forced Crawford to do it himself.'

'At least we know that Crawford didn't kill Flynn. He was already dead when someone stuck a knife into the old man.'

Kit nodded. 'His killer needed the cameras off, so he—'

'Or she,' Connor interrupted.

'Or she,' Kit agreed, 'took out the cameras, either met or followed Crawford to his motel room, took out Mr Crawford, then . . . what? Waited a day to kill Mr Flynn with a butcher knife? That seems odd to me.'

Connor frowned. 'Yeah, me too.'

'We need to find out where the butcher knife came from.'

'It was a chef's knife,' Connor said. 'Smaller than a butcher knife. And it was a Wüsthof.'

Kit blinked at him. She knew damn well the difference between a chef's knife and a butcher knife, but she had no idea what a Wüsthof was. 'A what?'

Connor smirked. 'A damn pricey knife.'

'How pricey?'

'A hundred, two hundred.'

'For a set?' Kit asked cautiously, because Connor came from family money. He was constantly surprising her with what he paid for things.

'For one knife.'

Her mouth fell open. 'Holy shit.'

Connor laughed. 'Do you even own a knife set, Kit?'

'Sure. I got it at Walmart. The whole set was less than thirty bucks and that included the block *and* a sharpener.'

'Well, anyone who actually uses their knives tends to pay a little more than thirty bucks.'

'So says Mr Moneybags. Mom doesn't have pricey knives.' And Betsy McKittrick cooked amazing meals, thank you very much.

Connor's smirk grew. 'Sure she does. Not Wüsthofs, but the next grade down. Your sister bought them for her.'

Kit narrowed her eyes. 'How do you know that?'

'Because I wanted to get your mother a thank-you gift for taking my mother meals when she was sick last month. I thought Betsy might like a nice set of knives, but Akiko said she'd gotten them for her for Christmas a few years ago.'

Kit scowled. 'I got Mom a fuzzy robe and bunny slippers. Now I feel bad.'

Connor's smirk faded to a kind smile. 'I'm sure she loves them. Your mother would be happy with a box of Kraft mac and cheese if you gave it to her.'

'Yeah, well.' Kit wrote *Wüsthof knife* in her secure notes app. 'I checked Mr Flynn's kitchen. He didn't have a knife set, so the killer may have either taken it with him or . . . maybe brought it with him. Or her.'

'Probably him,' Connor conceded. 'Whoever sliced Flynn up had a lot of strength. I'm not sure a woman could have done it.' He held up his hand. 'And before you go all "I am woman, hear me roar," it's a question of leverage. Flynn was tall, well over six feet. He had defensive wounds, so he fought back. Whoever wielded that knife had to have been able to overpower him and be tall enough to hold the knife at an angle to make that wound.'

'That's probably true,' Kit grumbled. 'And, for the record, I've never said "I am woman, hear me roar." '

'So noted. The knife does bother me, though.'

'Because Flynn's killer might have brought it with him?'

Connor nodded. 'Exactly. That doesn't seem like a weapon you'd just casually carry around. It's more like one that you'd grab out of a knife block in a fit of anger, but I didn't see a place on Flynn's kitchen counter where a knife block might have been sitting. He had a bunch of knives in his kitchen drawer, but not the same brand. It's possible he kept the one Wüsthof knife, but if the killer brought it with him, then Flynn's murder was planned.'

'Something was planned,' Kit pointed out. 'They turned off the cameras.'

'Yes, but we don't know if it was the murder or simply a burglary that Flynn discovered in progress and the murder was unplanned. We need to know if the Wüsthof came from somewhere else.'

Kit glanced in the side mirror, stiffening when she saw a familiar figure approaching them on the sidewalk. Sam Reeves had left his office and was walking home. His shoulders were hunched, his head down. He looked tired.

He looked sad.

Her chest tightened painfully, hating the thought that someone as kind as Sam Reeves was hurting. She wanted to make him feel better, but she didn't know how. Not without raising his hopes for something more. Because that would be too cruel.

'Kit?'

She looked over at Connor, who was watching her with a frown. 'Sorry. Yes, you're right. The knife doesn't fit the circumstances of the crime.'

Connor checked the rearview mirror, then sighed. 'Sam. He looks wrecked.'

'He really cared for Mr Flynn,' Kit said quietly.

Connor shrugged. 'That too.'

Kit shot Connor a harsh glare, hearing the censure in her partner's tone. It wasn't the first time Connor had criticized her avoidance of the psychologist. The two had become friends over the past six months. 'Stop.'

He sighed. 'Your reasons are your own, Kit, but Sam Reeves is a nice guy. Several women in the department would grab him up in a heartbeat.'

They can have him was on the tip of her tongue, but she was taken aback at her intense flare of jealousy at the thought. She was forced to admit, at least to herself, that giving him up wasn't what she wanted. But it was what he needed.

'I hope he finds someone to make him happy,' she said quietly. Which she really did want. It was the whole reason she'd told Sam Reeves 'no' six months before. He might be sad now, but she was sparing him a shitload of heartbreak later. Abruptly, she changed the subject. 'We need to ask Georgia Shearer or Benny Dreyfus if

Mr Flynn had a Wüsthof, and if he didn't, do a search of the kitchens at Shady Oaks and find out if anyone's missing a pricey knife.'

'We also need to find out if the gun that killed Kent Crawford was his or if his killer brought it with him.'

Kit added it to her list, mostly so that she wouldn't look for Sam Reeves in the side mirror, because he was coming closer. She exhaled quietly when he walked by them without seeing them. Thankfully, Connor kept his mouth shut. She'd halfway expected him to roll down the windows so that he and Sam could chat.

Back to work, McKittrick.

'We also need to talk to the IT guy.' She checked the notes she'd taken that morning. 'Archie Adler. He could tell that the camera was disconnected by checking remotely. We need to make sure that Crawford also had that capability – and that he could control them as well, not only see their active status. Even cheap home security systems can be controlled remotely, so Shady Oaks's system must have the capability, especially if it's as fancy as Sam said.'

'What about Miss Evans?' Connor asked. 'Involved?'

'Oh, she's definitely a person of interest. I didn't completely believe her this morning.'

'Neither did I. She knew about the cameras being out well before she told us. Probably even before I arrived, since that was the first thing she'd checked.'

'She also wasn't keen on our taking over her computer server.'

'No, she wasn't. Have you heard from Ryland on any of the evidence that CSU gathered?'

Kit checked her email. 'Not yet.' Then she noticed the time. 'Damn. It's almost five thirty. I have to meet the family for dinner at six. It's a celebration for Rita because she started adoption proceedings today.'

'Where do you need to go?'

'Mateo's Place a few blocks over. You wanna join us?'

'I'd really like to, but I have a date. I'll drop you off.' He changed lanes abruptly, earning him blaring horns from the cars he narrowly missed hitting.

'What about Crawford's friends in Palm Springs?' he asked, seeming oblivious to the angry drivers behind them.

'They might not be there any longer. If they heard about Crawford, they might have cut their golf trip short. I'll check with Mrs Crawford after dinner to see if she told them. If not, we can leave early in the morning and catch them before they tee off. I want to know who the other woman was.'

'It could be a number of women. It didn't need to be an actual relationship. Crawford might have hired prostitutes. The motel where he died was the type hookers like to use.'

'True. But even that would be useful information. If the golf bros are already on their way home, we can talk to them tomorrow. I'm not missing this dinner.'

Connor smiled. 'Look at you, putting your family first. Go, Kit.'

Kit might have been annoyed, but he was right. Work–life balance was not her strong suit. 'At the rate we're moving, I won't get to the restaurant on time. I can walk it. I need some time to think about this case anyway. I'll text you when I find out whether we're going to Palm Springs. Have a nice date.' Kit hopped out, crossed to the sidewalk, and set off toward Mateo's at a fast walk.

That she was following in Sam Reeves's path was merely a coincidence.

San Diego, California
Monday, 7 November, 5.40 P.M.

Kit murmured apologies to the people she stepped around as she hurried down the street. She didn't need to hurry. She knew that. She had plenty of time to get to Mateo's.

She was hurrying because she hoped she'd catch up to Sam Reeves.

And . . . there he was. He'd stopped on the corner and was talking to two teenage girls. The girls were sneering up at him, but Sam wore his usual kind smile.

The girls looked to be about fifteen or sixteen. And, as Kit approached, she realized why Sam had stopped. The girls weren't dressed for the weather. It had been a warm day, but the sun was going down and it was becoming chilly. The teens wore holey jeans and tank tops. One of them was visibly shivering. They had a hungry look, like they hadn't eaten in far too long.

Kit knew that look. She'd worn that same look, fake sneer and all. That was before the McKittricks, of course.

One of the girls, the shorter of the two, had long red hair. Just like Wren's. She was about the age Wren had been when she'd been murdered. Kit's feet moved forward of their own accord, bringing her close enough to hear them.

Sam had reached into the breast pocket of his suit jacket and brought out a thin stack of what looked like coupons. '. . . help you,' he was saying.

The taller of the girls narrowed her eyes. 'This can't be legit.'

'Nothing's free,' the other added softly.

'This place is,' Sam said with quiet sincerity. 'It's called New Horizons and it's a shelter for runaway teenagers.'

The taller girl lifted her chin defiantly and Kit was dragged back nearly twenty years. She'd held herself that exact same way when Harlan McKittrick had discovered her and Wren hiding in his barn.

'We're not runaways,' the girl insisted. 'We have families.'

Sam smiled. 'Then take the vouchers anyway. You can get a hot meal and rest for a few hours before you start for home.'

The girl took the vouchers, still suspicious. 'How do we know you aren't part of some freaky group who'll trap us and sell us?' Tall asked.

He lifted one shoulder. 'You don't. But I'm not. I volunteer for the shelter.'

'He's telling the truth,' Kit said, and all three turned to stare at her. 'He's a nice guy and New Horizons is a nice place. They'll take care of you.'

Tall stepped between Kit and the other girl. 'You're his partner. You're trying to trick us.'

Sam's eyes had widened. 'What are you doing here, De— Kit?'

Tall's eyes narrowed once more. 'What kind of name is DeKit?'

Sam had stopped just short of calling her 'detective' because that would have sent the girls running faster than anything else.

'It's Dutch,' Kit said, and Sam cleared his throat, probably choking back a laugh. 'Look, ladies. I'm going to be straight with you because I have a family dinner to get to. This guy is Dr Sam Reeves and he's legit. I'm a cop, but I'm not out to get you for anything. I can show you my badge if it helps you believe him.'

Tall held out her hand. 'Give it to me.'

Kit laughed. 'No. But I will hold it out so you can examine it.'

Tall leaned forward to study it closely. 'What kind of cop are you?'

'Homicide. And Dr Sam works with us. Helps us catch the bad guys. But in his spare time, he volunteers with New Horizons, just like he said.' She sighed. 'I know what you're thinking, but there *are* good people in this world who will help you.' The girls were hesitant, fear still obvious in their eyes, so Kit made a decision. 'If you don't believe me, come with me to the restaurant where my family is having dinner. You can ask them. And you can have a meal there, on me. If you're still nervous at the end of the meal, you're free to go. But New Horizons will give you a safe place to sleep either way.'

'Why?' the shorter girl asked, her voice trembling. 'Why are you pretending to be so nice?'

'I'm not nice. I'm snarky and selfish. But I'm also not pretending.' Kit pocketed her badge. 'I was a runaway when I was a little younger than you are now. The restaurant where I'm going will be filled with former runaways. Today, we're a family because of our mom and dad. They fostered, then adopted us. We're celebrating another adoption tonight. She's your age. She'll tell you true.' Kit drew a breath and told them the real reason she'd gotten involved. 'Plus, I don't want you guys on the street tonight. My sister was killed on these streets when she was fifteen. I'll do a lot to keep even one more kid from dying on the street. I'll even be nice.'

Sam's green eyes had gone soft. Grateful. And full of respect, not pity.

Dammit.

The two girls shared a long glance, and then the shorter one nodded. Tall squared her shoulders. 'I'm Jane and she's . . . Janey.'

87

The shorter one rolled her eyes. 'Janey? Really?'

Tall – Jane – elbowed her. 'Hush.'

Kit's lips twitched. 'Come on. You can follow behind us. That way if you change your minds you can bolt, and we won't be the wiser.'

'Right,' Jane muttered. 'I bet you have eyes in the back of your head.'

Kit chuckled. 'Maybe I do. Come on. It's getting late and I promised my mom I'd be on time for once.' She set off walking, Sam falling into step beside her. 'Rita's having an adoption dinner. You want to come?'

'She asked me already. I declined.'

Kit glanced up at him, surprised. 'Why? She really likes you.'

His smile was back to being sad. 'Because I didn't think you'd want me there.'

Kit sucked in a breath. 'Ouch.'

Sam shrugged. 'Was I right?'

'Probably,' she muttered. 'I'm sorry.'

'It's okay. It's your family. You need to feel comfortable with them and I make you uncomfortable.'

'Why?' Jane asked from behind them. 'Why does he make you uncomfortable, *DeKit*? Or should I say "Detective Kit"?'

'She's smart,' Kit said to Sam, then looked over her shoulder. Jane and Janey were still following them, but their fear had returned full force. So Kit was honest, because if they didn't trust her and Sam, they wouldn't go to New Horizons. 'Because he likes me and I told him no. He's respected every boundary I've set.'

Jane's gaze flicked from Kit to Sam, then back to Kit. 'Then why did you tell him no if he's such a nice guy?'

Sam cleared his throat. 'She *is* smart, DeKit.'

Kit hesitated, because this wasn't a conversation she wanted to have with anyone, much less with two teenagers she'd never met before. But the girls balanced on the balls of their feet, poised to run, so Kit bit the bullet. 'Because *I'm* not nice,' she said, hating that her eyes burned. 'I'm driven and selfish with my time. I work a lot. He needs someone nicer than me.'

'You're scared,' Janey said meekly.

'She's smart, too,' Sam muttered.

Cheeks burning, Kit stopped walking, turning to face the teens. Janey took an anxious step back and Jane, fists clenched, put herself between Janey and Kit.

So much like I was. The memory of her fear that night as she glared up at Harlan McKittrick, her fists clenched, came back to her in a rush. Harlan had been honest with her. That night and every single day of her life thereafter.

So she'd pay it forward to these girls. Anything to keep them off the street.

'You're right,' Kit said quietly. 'I am scared. Dr Sam's nice. Far nicer than me. He deserves not to be hurt, and I don't want to hurt him.' She stiffened, done with the conversation. 'Are you two coming to dinner or not?'

The two girls looked at each other again. 'Yes,' the shorter girl all but whispered. 'Because I think you *are* nice. If you weren't, you wouldn't worry about hurting him.'

Kit scowled. 'Come on. We're late.' She turned on her heel and started walking. If they followed her, so be it. She'd done her best.

'And me?' Sam asked as he kept pace with her. 'Should I come, too?'

She kept her eyes forward. 'It would mean a lot to Rita.'

'And you?'

Her throat thickened. 'Sam. Please.'

'Fine, but Janey hit the nail on the head. Thanks, Janey.'

Kit glanced at Sam. He was smiling at Janey over his shoulder.

'Also,' Sam added, lowering his voice, 'you're making choices for me. You wouldn't like it if I did that to you. Just think about that.'

Kit did think about that. She thought about it all the way to Mateo's. Sam was right. *But so am I.*

Have dinner. Tell Rita you love her, then get the hell back to work.

Because work was safe.

Kit pointed to the sign for Mateo's restaurant. 'It's a legit place. We have a private room in the back. I won't force you to come with us, but if you decide to take off, go to New Horizons. Please.'

Jane studied her shrewdly. 'Okay. We'll come with you.'

'If your parents say it's okay that we crash your party,' Janey added like she didn't care, but there was a glimmer of hope in her eyes.

Kit understood that, too. 'They will.' Both girls held their breath but followed them into the noisy restaurant, hand in hand.

Kit swallowed hard, remembering clutching Wren's hand the same way.

'You okay?' Sam murmured.

She nodded. 'Memories.'

'Thought so. You did a good thing, Kit.'

Her name on his lips sent a shiver down her spine. 'Let's find the party.'

The private room wasn't much quieter than the main dining room. Harlan McKittrick loomed over everyone, tall and broad-shouldered. He was strength personified and Kit loved him with her whole heart.

'Kitty-Cat!' he called, crossing the room in a few long strides. 'And Sam. I'm so glad you came.'

Sam shook Harlan's offered hand. 'Thank you, sir.'

Harlan shook his head. 'We've talked about the "sir," Sam. Cut it out.' He folded Kit into a rib-crushing hug and kissed the top of her head before letting her go. 'Who have we here?'

'This is Jane and Janey,' Kit said with a straight face. 'We met them on the way.'

Jane still looked ready to run as Harlan smiled warmly. 'Welcome. We're so glad you came. Come and meet Rita and Mrs McK.'

'Dr Sam!' Rita came running, giving Sam a hug. 'I didn't think you were coming.'

'I changed my mind,' Sam said mildly.

Rita gave Kit a too-knowing grin. 'Thanks, Kit.' She turned to the girls. 'Hi, I'm Rita. I'm glad you're here. Come meet my new mom.'

She led them away, chattering merrily.

'She's come so far in a short time,' Sam said quietly.

'She has,' Harlan said proudly. 'Team effort. Mostly Rita, though.

She knows what she wants and isn't afraid to go after it. She said she's channeling her "inner Kit." '

Sam chuckled. 'I like it.'

Kit wanted to run away but forced her feet to stay put. 'Hey, Pop. Did the present arrive?'

'It did.' Harlan pointed to a table with a few wrapped gifts. 'It's behind the table.'

'What is it?' Sam asked.

'A bike,' Kit said. 'She's been saving for her own bicycle for a few months, and we knew which one she wanted, so we all chipped in. One of those wrapped presents is a helmet.'

Sam's eyes grew shiny. 'She's gonna love it.'

'I know,' Harlan said, sighing happily. 'What's with Jane and Janey?'

'Sam found them on a street corner,' Kit said. 'They didn't want to go to New Horizons, but I didn't want them on the street.'

'No,' Harlan murmured, a shadow passing over his face.

None of them had ever gotten over losing Wren, who'd gone to the movies with some friends and was walking to the bus stop when she'd been taken. Her body had been found in a dumpster five days later.

I should have gone with her. But Kit had hated socializing. She'd hated everyone and everything back then. Everyone but Wren. And Mom and Pop. She hadn't realized that at the time, though. That had come later.

'Not your fault,' Sam whispered.

Kit's nod was shaky. 'Right. Anyway, Sam met the girls on the corner, and I just wanted them safe.'

Harlan's smile was full of pride. 'Well done, Kitty-Cat. I'm going to see if Mateo needs any help serving the food. I'll be back. You two can . . . talk.'

Kit wanted to roll her eyes. Her brother had servers and cooks and all the staff he needed. Harlan was matchmaking again, giving her and Sam some alone time.

'He's not very subtle, is he?' Sam asked, amused.

'No, he's not.' She sighed, dropping her head. 'Sam . . .'

'I get it, Kit. I promised myself that I wouldn't rush you and I wouldn't try to make you feel guilty. So I'm going to have a quick conversation with your mom, give my congratulations to Rita, and then I'll head out.'

He started to move away, but she grabbed his arm. She stared at her hand for a moment, stunned. She hadn't expected she'd do that. She glanced up, saw Sam watching her, his expression gone carefully blank.

She retracted her hand, drawing a deep breath. 'Stay,' she murmured. 'My family really likes you.' *So do I.*

Dammit.

His expression didn't change and she found herself wishing it would. She wanted those kind eyes smiling at her. But she wasn't being fair to either of them, so she took a step back.

'Okay,' he said. 'I'll stay. Then later, you can tell me how I can help you and Connor on your case.'

Kit managed a smile, but it felt false. 'Thank you.'

She watched him cross to her mother, who gave her a quizzical look before dragging Sam close for a hug.

Betsy McKittrick gave the best hugs.

'You okay, kid?'

Kit spun around, relief nearly buckling her knees. 'Baz.'

Her former partner was watching her as carefully as everyone else in the room seemed to be. 'Rita asked Marian and me to come.'

Baz and his wife Marian had been a big part of Rita's life over the past six months. Marian had tutored Rita, helping her catch up on the content she'd missed while bouncing around the foster system before coming to the McKittricks. Now Marian settled herself next to Jane and Janey.

Kit had to smile. 'Jane and Janey don't stand a chance. Between Marian and Mom, they're going to be mothered.'

Baz chuckled. 'Jane and Janey? Really?'

'No. Sam found them this evening, and those are the names they gave us. Jane is the leader. She hasn't decided if she trusts us, so she's leaving them an out.'

'Sounds like someone I used to know.'

Kit nodded, because Baz had known her since she was fifteen years old and so angry over Wren's murder. 'Yep.'

'So . . . you got Frank Wilson's case.'

It didn't surprise her that Baz had already heard. She imagined it was all over San Diego PD by this point. Baz was retired, but he stuck close to the gossip mill.

'Frank Flynn,' she corrected. 'He changed his name.'

Baz nodded soberly. 'I heard that. I also heard that he married a man after he and Sharon split up. Dammit. I wish he'd been free to be out.'

Baz wouldn't have blinked at a cop sharing about their sexuality, but not every cop was like Baz. Sad but true.

'I know. I think he had a happy life with his husband, though. They ran an antique store in San Francisco until ten years ago when he and Ryan came back to San Diego to live at Shady Oaks with Ryan's sister and brother-in-law.'

'I asked around. He only went to Julio's Bar once after he retired. That was the day I introduced him to you. I introduced him as Frank Wilson and he didn't correct me. Didn't give me his new married name although he'd changed it nearly fifteen years before.' He shrugged. 'I dug into his background a little after hearing the news. I guess he still didn't trust us, even ten years ago. You know, SDPD in general.'

Unfortunately, that made sense. 'I checked his records at Shady Oaks. He and his husband Ryan moved into the retirement home the day after we saw him.'

'We saw him on your twenty-first birthday. Easy date to remember.'

'Exactly. Do you know why he picked that day to go to Julio's?'

Baz shrugged. 'Nope. I asked around and nobody was having an anniversary or promotion. Maybe he just wanted to experience it one more time. Julio's, the atmosphere.'

They might never know why, and that made Kit sad. 'And he never went back to Julio's?'

'Not that anyone remembers. Shock waves are crashing around

SDPD, kid. You pulled another big case. Have the brass started demanding updates?'

'Probably, but Navarro is shielding us from all that for now. We have a second murder that appears to be related.'

'The head of security at Shady Oaks.' Baz shrugged again. 'Cops have been calling me all day, pumping me for information. They think you tell me everything.'

'I do. I just haven't yet. Connor and I are still trying to get the facts straight.'

'Could this be related to one of Frank's old cases?'

'I mean, it's certainly possible. Especially if Kent Crawford was forced into disabling the camera so that Frank's killer could get to him. Whoever tossed Frank's apartment was looking for something and may have brought the knife with them. Who can I talk to to find out if there's anyone who might have wanted revenge for Frank putting them behind bars?'

'Henry Whitfield lives in La Mesa, and he was Frank's partner for years. He might be a tough nut to crack, though. He isn't the most open-minded guy.'

Great. 'Hopefully he'll want justice for Frank.'

'Hopefully. I heard that Frank had some money.'

Kit thought of the house in Russian Hill. 'Quite a lot of money. Why?'

'Have you checked his bank accounts?'

'We froze the account that was linked to his Shady Oaks expenses. If there are others, we haven't found them yet. His killer could have been searching for account information, I suppose. Did you know that Frank had a son?'

Baz tilted his head, thinking. 'Yes. And no. I never met the son, but I went to the ceremony when Frank retired thirty years ago. There was an empty seat in the front row, and I remember someone saying that he'd saved it for his boy, but he never showed up.'

'They're apparently estranged.'

'And there's a lot of money involved. I hate to think the son could have done it, but we both know that money is a great motivator.'

Kit sighed. 'Yeah.'

'You know I'm here if you want to bounce any ideas off me, right?'

She smiled up at him. A heart attack had forced his decision to retire, but Baz still helped her however he could. 'I know. Thank you.'

'Anytime, kid. You make me proud.'

'Stop,' she protested.

They were quiet for a long minute, then Baz asked, 'Are you happy, Kit?'

'Yes,' she answered, startled. 'Why?'

His gaze moved to rest on Sam Reeves, who sat between Betsy and Rita. Rita was all smiles, still chatting with Jane and Janey, who seemed to have relaxed – at least a little. Sam was talking to Betsy, but his green eyes were fixed on Kit.

Baz hummed low in his throat. 'Don't shortchange yourself. That's all.'

'I'll call you soon,' she said, ripping her attention away from Sam Reeves and steering them back to work. Back to safe ground. 'I might need to drive to Palm Springs tomorrow.'

'The golf buddies.'

Kit laughed, relieving a tiny bit of the stress. 'Why are you even asking me questions? You already know everything.'

'Because I miss you, kid.'

She gave in to the need and rested her head on his shoulder. 'Same.'

The doors opened and Mateo and his staff carried in large trays of food. The party had begun.

'Let's go eat,' Baz said. 'I'm going to sneak food that's bad for me and you're not going to tell Marian. That's my price for my help.'

'I'm not covering for you with Marian. She terrifies me.'

Baz beamed. 'She's an amazing woman, isn't she?'

Yes, she was. Kit had long admired the relationship Baz had with his wife. Had secretly wished for the same.

You could have that. He's looking at you right now.

Sam wouldn't rush her, of that she was certain. How long would he wait, though? How long could she expect him to?

95

One of those women that Connor had mentioned might snap him up while she . . .

While I cower in fear.

I need to do something. But what?

The answer didn't make her proud. Because for now, she was going to focus on getting justice for Frankie Flynn. Then she'd have to see what happened next.

San Diego, California
Monday, 7 November, 8.10 P.M.

'Hey,' Kit said, setting a covered plate and a plastic fork on the ME's desk. 'I got here as soon as I could.'

Alicia Batra grabbed the plate of Rita's celebration cake and dug in, closing her eyes with a blissed-out look on her face. 'I'm so hungry. I missed lunch. Did somebody close a homicide?'

'I wish.' By department tradition, whenever a homicide was solved, one of the detectives – whoever was next on the list – brought in baked goods. Normally Kit brought in cupcakes from her favorite bakery when it was her turn. Sometimes Betsy sent in goodies and those were always demolished before lunch. 'I was at a family dinner for Rita. Mom made the cake.'

Alicia smiled. 'The adoption. That's so nice. Tell Rita I said congratulations. Your folks, too. I hope you didn't leave too early.'

'Nah. Dinner was wrapping up.' And not looking at Sam Reeves had become exhausting. *You're a coward.*

'Good.' Alicia licked the fork and set the half-eaten cake aside. 'I missed lunch because I was strongly encouraged to get these two autopsies done ASAP.'

Kit felt a twinge of guilt for taking off the time for Rita's dinner, then quashed it. The case was still here. Frankie Flynn and Kent Crawford were still dead. Rita, however, had needed her support tonight.

'What did you find? You said it was important.'

'Pull up a chair. I have some photos to show you.'

Kit did, fighting her impatience. 'What?'

'Should we wait for Connor?'

'No. He said to go ahead. He's taken his date up to LA for a concert and can't get back to the city for several hours. So spill.'

'The tox results aren't in yet, but I do have preliminary stomach contents. Mr Flynn's last meal was still mostly undigested. He had some kind of poultry dish.'

'I'll check with CSU to find out if anything like that was found in his trash or drain. There wasn't anything like it in his fridge, though. I checked. How long would you say it had been between his last meal and his death?'

'Zero to three hours. Probably closer to an hour. I sent samples to the lab and they'll be able to tell you exactly what was in the meal. Again, the lab results will be able to tell you more.'

Kit noted the details. 'Thanks. What else? Because you could have told me this on the phone.'

Alicia's smile was sharp. 'Mr Flynn wasn't killed with that butcher knife.'

Kit's eyes widened. 'Then what did kill him?'

'Another blade. A sharper one. Whoever did this was very good. But I'm better.' Alicia opened a series of photos. 'Look here, at this cut. Look at where it stops.' She enlarged the picture on her screen and Kit squinted.

'It looks like it stops, then starts again.'

'Exactly. But what I think we're really looking at is two different blades. This top part – only a few millimeters – was made by a thinner, sharper blade. Then it becomes a thicker wound.'

Kit frowned. 'Someone sliced him twice?'

'Yes and no. I think he was killed with the thinner blade. Then someone took a great deal of care to go over that first slice with another knife. That's the one they left in his chest.'

Kit leaned closer to study the photo. 'But why?'

'I dunno. That's your area, not mine. But you don't have the murder weapon.'

'Well, shit. That's a good enough reason, I suppose. We'd be chasing our tails looking for whoever owned that uber-expensive Wüsthof knife and not the real murder weapon. Do you know what kind of blade the thinner one was?'

'A stiletto or something similar that was long and wicked sharp. But I can't tell you more than that.'

'How long after the first cut was the second made?'

Alicia nodded approvingly. 'Good question. Not long. Minutes to a few hours.'

'Long enough for someone to find a Wüsthof knife in Mr Flynn's kitchen drawer or to go fetch one if they didn't bring it with them.'

'I'd say so.'

Kit sat back in her chair, thinking. 'Connor and I wondered about the knife. It didn't match any of Mr Flynn's other knives, but he could have bought that one nice knife. Did you know they cost a hundred to two hundred apiece?'

Alicia chuckled. 'Yes, Kit. My wife has a set and she guards them zealously. I once used one of her Wüsthofs to cut open a box and I thought she'd divorce me on the spot.'

'The horror,' Kit deadpanned. 'Okay, so whoever killed Mr Flynn went to a lot of trouble to make us think that they used a butcher knife. They took their stiletto knife with them, so now I'm wondering why. Was it to throw us off the trail, or did they have an attachment to their knife? Or was the knife singular to them in some way?'

Alicia shrugged and went back to eating her cake. 'That's your job.'

'That it is. Do you have anything more on Mr Flynn?'

'Nope, but I do have something you're gonna love on Mr Crawford.' Alicia opened another photo file and Kit flinched.

'God, Alicia, dick pics? Really?'

'A special dick pic. This is Mr Crawford.'

Kit made a face. 'That's something I'll never unsee. Why are you showing it to me?'

'Because of this.' Again Alicia enlarged the photo and pointed. 'Right here.'

Kit leaned in . . . then grinned. 'Lipstick? Wine-colored lipstick?'

'Or a deep purple. I've sent samples of it off to the lab as well. You look like this sounds familiar.'

'Oh yeah. Sam Reeves said he saw lipstick stains that color on Mr Crawford's shirt as recently as a month ago.'

'This is a little more personal than his shirt,' Alicia said dryly.

Kit huffed a laugh. 'Yeah, it is. This means he was with someone shortly before he was killed. I need to find her.'

'Or him,' Alicia said.

'Or him,' Kit agreed. 'Connor and I think he was having an affair with someone. He wasn't with his wife. Or at least the wife says so. We're checking out her alibi.'

'It looks like he tried to wipe the lipstick off. This bit was kind of . . . hiding. I nearly missed it. If he was having an affair, he probably wouldn't have wanted his wife to know. But don't limit your search to women.'

Kit nodded, appreciating the criticism, because Alicia was right, just as Connor had been. Jumping to conclusions about gender simply wasn't good detective work. 'I won't. Connor thinks Flynn's killer was male, based on the angle of the wound, because Flynn was very tall. But that would only be true if they made that cut when Flynn was standing.' She rose and paced the length of Alicia's small office. 'What if Flynn came home, surprised an intruder, and they whipped out a blade to stab him?'

'After a struggle. There were defensive wounds on Mr Flynn's hands.'

'And the killer took his fingernails down to the nail bed,' Kit recalled. 'So they struggle and the killer pulls the stiletto on Flynn—' She frowned. 'Can you tell if the original cut came from top down or bottom up?'

'Top down.'

'So they plunged the stiletto into Flynn's sternum and dragged it down. Still took a lot of strength.'

'Yes, it would have. But the original wound wasn't as long as the one made by the knife left in his body. That second cut could have been made when he was lying on the floor.'

'Because he'd been stabbed already. He did seem . . . posed. Now we need to find out where the butcher knife came from. And where Flynn's killer stashed the stiletto. Thank you, Alicia.'

Alicia scraped the plate with the fork, licking away the remaining crumbs. 'You're welcome. Thank you for the cake. Call me tomorrow around noon. I should have some of the tox results by then.'

'Will do.' Kit's mind was filling with to-do lists. It was going to be a long evening.

Six

Kit knocked on the Crawfords' front door, wishing that she'd come to interview the widow sooner. But they'd been pulled in too many directions.

I'm here now. That was what was important.

The door was opened by a woman with brown hair and eyes that looked tired. But resolute.

'Mrs Crawford?' Kit asked. Denise Crawford was forty-five years old according to her driver's license, but she looked ten years older. The marriage license that Kit had pulled showed that Denise and Kent had been married for fifteen years. No kids.

'Yes. Are you Detective McKittrick? Detective Marshall said you'd be stopping by.'

'I am. May I come in?'

'Of course.' Denise led her into the kitchen, gesturing to a set of stools in front of an island counter. 'Please have a seat. I've just made coffee. Would you like some?'

'No, ma'am, but thank you for offering. I've had a lot of coffee today.'

It wasn't true, but until they could validate Denise Crawford's alibi, she was technically still a suspect. Kit sat on one of the stools, while the woman poured herself a cup of coffee that smelled so good that Kit nearly changed her mind.

Finally Denise turned, cradling the cup in both hands. 'It wasn't suicide.' It was a statement, not a question.

'How do you know?'

'Because you're a homicide detective. I read up about you while I was waiting. You close a lot of cases.'

'I do my best. And I'll do my best for your husband.'

Denise chuckled bitterly. 'Yeah, well. He wasn't much of a husband, to be honest. I didn't want him dead, just out of my life. I'd asked for a divorce and he'd said no. But I was going to file anyway. Whoever killed him saved me a lot of trouble, because it was going to be a nasty process.'

That was interesting. 'Do you know of anyone who did want your husband dead?'

Denise eased onto a stool on the other side of the island, sipping her coffee, her hands slightly shaking. 'I've thought of nothing else all day. Look, my husband was a blowhard. None of my friends liked him because he always thought he knew everything. My family hated him because he's been . . . impatient with me. My illness.'

Kit's brows went up. 'May I ask what illness?'

'I have lupus. I have good days and bad days. I didn't have it when we got married, and back then I was "fun." Now not so much. I tire easily. Kent didn't like that we had to cancel our plans when I had a bad day. He didn't like that I prepared foods that were less likely to cause flare-ups. He kept throwing statistics at me about the number of people who go into remission, like I was slacking because I hadn't. My family has wanted me to divorce Kent for a long time.'

'So why did you pick now to initiate a divorce?'

'I didn't in the past because it takes a lot of energy to meet with attorneys, and on bad days, I simply don't have the energy to spare. And partly because I kept hoping he'd . . . I don't know. Grow up? Fix himself? I loved him once. I'd hoped I could love him again. But about six months ago I started to suspect he was cheating. That was the final straw. My dad found an attorney for me to meet with. That's what I was doing this weekend. Talking to a lawyer and planning my divorce.'

'I see.' And Kit did see. Kent Crawford was an asshole. 'I know you told Detective Marshall earlier, but would you mind telling me where you were between midnight and eight a.m. on Saturday?'

'Sleeping in my parents' house.' She slid off the stool and picked up a folder from the counter next to her knife block – which, Kit noticed, still contained all of its knives.

Denise took a piece of paper from the folder and pushed it across the island to Kit before retaking her seat. 'I made a list of my family's names and contact information. You can ask them. I went to bed about eleven on Friday night and got up at seven. My folks have an alarm system with cameras and they're happy to give you copies of the video. I didn't leave the house.'

Kit took the information with a murmured *Thank you*. She'd check into it, but she believed this woman. 'What made you think he was having an affair?'

Denise's cheeks flushed with embarrassment. 'Um . . . he used to be really mean when I didn't feel like sex, but then he stopped asking. Which was about the same time he started spending a lot of weekends at work when he hadn't before. And he'd started coming home smelling like another woman's perfume.'

'Did you recognize the scent?'

'No. I tried at first, and then I just didn't care. I was mostly grateful that he was leaving me alone. Now I'm wondering if he was having affairs before that and hid them better. I don't think he cared anymore, either.'

'Then why was he so opposed to a divorce?'

'I don't know. He wasn't Catholic or even religious at all. My family thinks he got pleasure from hurting me.'

What a guy. 'Do you have any suspicions on who he was having an affair with?'

'No. For a while I thought he was having an affair with his boss, Faye Evans, but now I don't think so. She's not his type. She's too old. Hell, according to Kent, *I'm* too old, and Evans has got at least ten years on me.'

Yep, a real asshole. 'Would he have confided in anyone? Maybe the friends he was going golfing with?'

Another bitter chuckle. 'Sure, you can ask them. I think they've been covering for him. For how long, I don't know. Kent says how much they like him, but he's a freeloader. They might just be getting tired of paying his way all the time. They stay in fancy hotels in Vegas and Palm Springs, and they play the really expensive courses. I googled how much one of those hotels cost and I hit the roof. Even the cheapest rooms are more than we can afford. Kent said that his friends pay for his room and greens fees. He just has to buy his food. Now that I know where he was found this morning, I'm wondering if he ever actually went golfing with them or if he was just using it as an excuse to meet women ten miles away.'

'Do you know his friends?'

'No, never met them. I have their names – Dave, Pete, and Garrett – but they've never visited. I've talked to Pete on the phone. He's one of Kent's emergency contacts. Every time I called Pete to ask if Kent was okay because he hadn't called, Pete said Kent was fine and he'd have him call me. Kent always did and was always impatient with me for worrying. Kent knew them from the army. Saved their lives once, or so he said. Who knows if that's even true? I'm reevaluating everything right now.'

'I can understand that. Have you contacted his friends to tell them about your husband's death?'

'No. Like I said, I don't really know them. Or trust them.'

Good. Kit might be able to catch them unaware and see their reaction to the news. 'We'll need to go through his financials and search his things. Do we have your permission to do so?'

Denise handed Kit the entire folder she'd brought over from the counter earlier. 'All our bank statements for the last year. I downloaded them from our bank's website and printed them out for you. If you need records further back than a year, I can get those for you tomorrow. There are credit card statements in there, too. And his pay stubs from this year. Mine too. I have nothing to hide.' She grimaced. 'I don't have the energy to do anything I'm ashamed of.'

Kit smiled gently. 'Thank you for this. Detective Marshall mentioned that you told him you'd packed Kent's suitcase. What was he carrying?'

Denise blinked, as if she hadn't expected the question. 'Oh. Okay.

He was supposed to be gone four days, so I packed five or six pairs of underwear, same with socks. Four pairs of ugly golfing pants. Six golf shirts, two nice sets of slacks, three dress shirts.'

So someone had stolen most of the contents of Crawford's suitcase, just as Kit had thought. 'Shoes?'

'He was wearing his Nikes when he left the house. I packed his golf shoes and a pair of dress shoes. Why?'

'Because most of those items were no longer in his suitcase. What about electronics? I assume he had his cell phone with him.'

'His work phone and his personal. I can give you access to our Verizon account and you can see what calls were made from his personal cell. You'll have to talk to Shady Oaks about the work phone.'

Kit made herself a note to ask. 'Laptop? Tablet?'

'Both.'

'Toiletries?'

'Only his toothbrush, toothpaste, a razor, and shaving cream. He liked to use the shampoos provided by the hotels where they stayed.'

'Thank you. You wouldn't happen to have the serial number of his laptop, would you?'

Denise's smile was tight. 'Of course. I bought it for him. The receipt and registration information are in that folder.'

Wow. 'What about his gun? I'm sorry, ma'am,' she added when Denise flinched.

'No, no, it's fine. I just have been visualizing him getting shot all day, whether it was by his own hand or someone else's. I didn't love him anymore, but I didn't want him dead. I especially didn't want him to suffer.'

Kit remembered the photos of the body. 'I don't think he did.'

'That's good. He had a SIG Sauer M17. Said it was what he'd used in the army, so he bought one for himself when he was discharged. Was . . . was that the gun he was found with?'

'Yes, ma'am. Do you know if he owned a silencer?'

'Um . . . no. I mean, I don't know. That would be disturbing, if he did. You can check his gun safe.'

'Do you own a gun, ma'am?'

'Yes. I'm home alone when Kent works late.' She sighed. 'Worked late. Plus the weekends that he went away with his friends. I still practice at the range, but not as much as I used to. Not enough energy for that, either. My gun hasn't been fired in maybe a year. You can check that, too.'

This woman was being extremely cooperative. *Maybe too coopera-tive.* 'Ma'am, I have to say that you're one of the most organized and open family members I've met.'

Denise smiled sardonically. 'I need you to prove he was murdered, Detective. If he did take his own life, I get no life insurance and I need that. Kent didn't make a lot of money, but I make even less because I can't work full time. And now I'm going to have to get my own health insurance because we got ours through Shady Oaks.'

Ah. That made sense. 'Did Mr Crawford have a will?'

'Yes. The house and bank accounts go to the surviving spouse.' She swallowed hard. 'He always thought it would be him. That I'd die first. Said so on multiple occasions.'

Kit really hated this guy. 'I have only a few more questions, Mrs Crawford. His car. It's a very expensive model. How did he afford it?'

She shrugged. 'He said one of his army buddies gave it to him.'

Kit's eyes widened. 'They *gave* him a brand-new BMW 6-Series sedan? That's a nice gift.'

'I thought so, too. When I pressed Kent, he got angry, so I backed off. The car was his. My car was ours,' she added dryly. 'Because he figured he could sell it when I met my maker. It's a ten-year-old Toyota Sienna minivan. They "hold their value for resale." ' She used air quotes. 'Kent was a real piece of work.'

'Got it.' Kit had to bite her tongue to keep from agreeing with the woman, reviewing her notes instead. *Oh, right. Left- or right-handed shooter?* 'Did you practice shooting with your husband?'

'Yes. He taught me how to shoot, but that was years ago.'

'Do you happen to know which hand he used to shoot?'

Denise winced again. 'His right. Why?'

'Are you certain?'

'Yes. He used to shoot with both hands and was very proud of that fact, but he broke a finger on his left hand a few years ago and

106

it didn't heal right. Since then, he could only shoot right-handed. He made a big deal about it.'

Kit nodded. 'Thank you. Can I look at his belongings?'

'Help yourself, Detective. If you don't mind, I'm going to stay down here. I'm too tired to climb the stairs.'

'Yes, ma'am,' Kit said gently, because Denise did look exhausted. 'Did he have a home office?'

'No. He kept all his work at work.'

'Did he do work from his personal laptop that you'd bought for him?'

'I don't know. He usually checked his stocks and such. One of his friends is a financial advisor and he gave Kent stock tips. Kent said he gave his friend better stock tips, but that was Kent.'

'I heard he played football in college.'

Denise rolled her eyes. 'Everybody that ever met him – even on a bus – knew that he played football in college. Glory days, you know.'

'Thank you so much. I really appreciate you taking the time to talk with me. I'm going to take a quick look around upstairs right now and I'll probably bring my partner back with me tomorrow. Two sets of eyes.'

'I'm going to sit in my easy chair. I might fall asleep, so if I do, please lock up before you go.'

Kit followed her into the living room, just in case she became unsteady and started to fall. But Denise made it to what looked to be a very comfortable chair, sighing wearily as she sank into it.

Kit hurried up the stairs, taking in the pictures on the walls. Football, football, football. Lots of pics of Kent in his college ball uniform. A few of him in his army uniform. In one, he stood shoulder to shoulder with three other men. These would be his friends. Dave, Pete, and Garrett.

She opened the folder and rifled through the contents. Denise had applied sticky-note-style tabs, marking the documents.

'Bank statements,' she murmured. 'Pay stubs. Phone records.'

Ah, here it is. Army Buddies. Full names and addresses. One lived in Portland, one in Seattle, and one in LA. Denise had included a copy of the photo on the wall, identifying each man. She'd even made a list of every trip the four had taken, with dates and locations. They were in Palm Springs this weekend at the Silver Palm Resort.

Kit searched the Crawfords' bedroom but found nothing of interest. Nothing hidden under the socks, nor in the pockets of the coats and trousers hanging neatly in the closet. There was a gun safe, which was locked, but no fireproof safe for documents.

It was surprisingly sterile for a couple who'd been married for as long as the Crawfords had been. Kit found no collections, no jar of pocket change, no loose cuff links. None of the things she usually found lying around when someone died unexpectedly.

Denise might have removed them.

Or Kent might have had another hiding place.

Putting everything back as she'd found it, she checked the bathroom medicine cabinet to see if Crawford had any prescription medications. Like sedatives.

But she found nothing. If he'd been drugged so that his killer could more easily stage a suicide, then the killer had brought their own pills.

The only room in the house that had any personality at all was Denise's sewing room. There were fabrics in bright colors and unfinished projects draped over chairs. The sewing machine had a layer of dust, though. Kit didn't think Denise had been up here recently, which was sad.

She went back downstairs to find Denise asleep in her chair, her afghan having slid to the floor. Kit covered her, then checked the doors to make sure everything was locked up before letting herself out.

Rarely did Kit feel zero compassion for a murder victim, but she thought Kent Crawford might be one of those cases.

Getting back into her car, she googled the Palm Springs hotel, then placed a call to the reception desk.

'Silver Palm Resort. How can I help you?' a dapper-sounding man asked.

'My name is Detective McKittrick and I'm with San Diego Homicide. I'm currently investigating a murder in which the victim was supposed to have checked into your hotel on Saturday.'

'Oh my,' the man said. 'How awful.'

'Yes. I'd like to talk to his friends who are also staying there. Just to see if they have any pertinent information. They're not suspects. I need to know when they're checking out.' Because they'd be returning home to three different cities and it would be far easier to talk to them in Palm Springs. 'One of the party is David Jenkins.'

'Oh, Mr Jenkins. He checks out tomorrow, ma'am. But he and his party have an eight o'clock tee time.'

'Thank you so very much. Have a nice evening.'

Kit ended the call with a grimace. It was at least two and a half hours to Palm Springs with no traffic. They'd need to leave well before dawn. Connor wasn't going to be excited about that.

She called Connor's cell, hoping that he was on his way back from LA by now.

He answered on the first ring. 'Hey, Kit. You're on speaker.'

He was still with his date, then. Kit hoped this girlfriend would last longer than the others had. Usually Connor messed up his relationships in the first month, but he'd been dating this woman for at least two months now, so there was reason for optimism. 'Call me when you're free. I learned quite a bit tonight.'

'Hi, Kit,' a woman's voice called.

'Hi, CeCe.' Kit liked CeCe. She was a kindergarten teacher with a sweet smile and an even sweeter disposition. She'd gentled Connor. 'How was the concert?'

'Not bad. How was your family dinner?' CeCe asked.

'Really nice.' CeCe had met Rita a month ago when Connor had brought her to a McKittrick Sunday dinner. 'Rita was happy.'

'I'm glad you took the time,' she said warmly. 'You deserved the break. I see how hard you both work. I'm glad you had time with your people.'

'Me too. You guys be safe. Connor, call me when you get home. We have to get an early start tomorrow.'

'Palm Springs?'

'Yep. Arrival by seven.'

'In the morning?'

Kit chuckled at the predictable horror in his voice. 'Yep. Call me.

Set every alarm you own. Don't make me come over to your place and wake you up again.'

CeCe laughed. 'I'll set my alarm, Kit. He'll be awake.'

'Oh man,' Connor complained, then sighed. 'Fine. Talk to you soon.'

Kit ended the call, then checked the time. Her father would still be up, and she needed them to keep her dog overnight. She'd taken her poodle Snickerdoodle to McKittrick House for Sunday dinner and left her there with Rita. Rita had been needier lately, which wasn't a bad thing. It meant she was finally comfortable enough with them to allow her vulnerability to show.

Kit knew all about that.

She dialed her dad, number one on her favorites list. 'Hey, Pop.'

'Kitty-Cat. How are you?'

'I'm good.' Out of habit she reached into her pocket for the good-luck charm she never left home without. It was a figurine of a bird sitting on the head of a cat, and Harlan had carved it six months before. It was perfect for her, of course. She was the cat and Wren was the bird. Nobody knew her as well as Harlan and Betsy Mc-Kittrick. 'I need to get an early start tomorrow. Like four a.m. early. I need to get home and get some sleep. Can you keep Snick another night?'

'Of course. She's already asleep on Rita's bed. Drive safely.'

'I will. Pop, what happened with Jane and Janey?'

'They're at New Horizons for now.'

'For now? They gonna run?'

'I don't think so. We're going to try to get foster custody.'

Kit wasn't at all surprised, but relief still hit her hard. 'Thank you, Pop.'

'Thank Sam. He suggested it, even though he knew Betsy and I were already thinking it. He said he'd make a formal recommendation with social services.'

Kit's chest tightened with feelings she did not want to have for Sam Reeves. 'Still, you'll be the ones saving them.'

'It's what we do, Kitty-Cat.'

'I know. Love you.'

He swallowed hard because she didn't say it often. Not often enough, anyway. 'I love you, too, Kit,' he said gruffly. 'Call me when you're back tomorrow so I know you're safe.'

'I will. Night, Pop.' She ended the call and let out a contented sigh.

Palm Springs, California
Tuesday, 8 November, 7.10 A.M.

'Wake up, Connor.' Kit reached over the department sedan's console to shake Connor's shoulder. 'We're here.'

'Fucking hell,' he muttered, stretching his neck until it popped. 'Hate falling asleep in a car. Why didn't you wake me up?'

'You looked like you needed the sleep,' Kit said.

'You were the one who went back to work last night,' he said. 'I should have driven.'

'You can drive back because I'll be crashing by then.'

Unable to sleep after her visit with Denise Crawford, Kit had returned to the office to do background checks on all the parties involved in the case. No one had raised any real red flags. Yet.

One name hadn't raised any flags at all because it didn't seem to exist – Gerald Wilson, Frankie Flynn's only son, didn't have a driver's license or a social security card. She'd texted Baz for help when she'd stopped for coffee. Her former partner had promised to do some digging with Frankie's old SDPD colleagues.

She'd had no trouble finding Kent Crawford's three army buddies. Their background checks looked pretty clean, aside from lying for Kent to his wife.

Kit hoped she and Connor would find them at breakfast so that they could assess the reactions of the three men to Kent's murder. And she definitely wanted to find out which one of them had given Kent a brand-new BMW.

She parked the car in front of the hotel, flashing her badge at the valet. 'We won't be long. Please don't touch the car.'

The valet frowned. 'Yes, ma'am. But we're going to get busy in about an hour. I'll need this space for the guests checking out.'

'We'll try to be done by then,' Connor promised.

111

The hotel lobby was as decadent and overwhelming as she'd anticipated. Everything was marble and gold, with imposing chandeliers casting sparkling reflections on the glossy floor. One whole wall was a plate glass window, with a view of the lush grass of the tidy golf course. The uniforms worn by the busboys were nicer than the clothing Kit wore. Not a wrinkle in sight. There was a polish to the place that screamed that it was a cut way above the normal hotel.

Connor, however, navigated it with ease. He'd come from money and, in situations like this, it showed.

'I've been here before,' he told her. 'With my folks when I was still in high school. It's been a while and I'd forgotten the name of the place, but I recognize the lobby. The dining room should be that way.'

She followed, noting the personnel behind the desk watching them. Connor looked like he fit in here, but Kit knew that she did not. Trying not to stare, she matched Connor's longer stride.

'Do you see them?' he asked when they paused at the entrance to the dining room.

Kit scanned the crowd, ignoring the hostess who asked if they'd like to be seated. Connor told her they were meeting their party inside, injecting the right amount of haughty confidence in his voice, and the hostess became solicitous.

Baz would have barged right in, probably making a scene. So Connor was good to have along.

I still miss Baz.

'Ah. I see them.' The photo Denise had provided made the identification easy. Pete, Dave, and Garrett were an accountant, a financial advisor, and a marketing manager, respectively. 'Over by the window.'

Connor smiled tightly when they reached the table – just in time, as the men were signing their breakfast bills. 'Gentlemen, we're sorry to bother you, but it's urgent that we speak to you. I'm Detective Robinson of the San Diego PD. This is my partner, Detective McKittrick. Can we go somewhere less public?'

One of the men, Pete, paled. 'Is this about Kent? He never showed up and didn't answer his cell phone. Is he all right?'

Kit leaned in, dropping her voice. 'We'll answer your questions as best we can, but not here.'

The three frowned at one another but rose as one. 'We can go to my suite,' Dave said. 'It's a quick elevator ride.'

To their credit, the three didn't pepper Kit and Connor with questions, waiting until they'd reached the penthouse suite, which was the nicest hotel room Kit had ever seen.

'So tell us,' Garrett demanded. 'Where's Kent?'

'He's dead,' Kit said, keeping her tone gentle, but watching the three men carefully.

Garrett dropped into a chair while Pete and Dave stared at them.

'Dead?' Pete whispered. 'How? When?'

'Where and why?' Dave added, his jaw clenched. 'I'm guessing you don't know who yet, which is why you're here.'

'We believe it was intended to look like a suicide,' Connor said. 'But there is evidence of foul play.'

'Did Mr Crawford mention any issues he might have had with anyone?' Kit asked. 'Anyone that might want to hurt him?'

'Just his wife,' Garrett muttered. 'What?' he snapped at his friends when they glared at him. 'She suspected.'

'Suspected what?' Kit pressed.

Garrett shoved his fingers through his hair. 'That he was having an affair.'

'You three knew?' Connor asked.

Each man shrugged and Garrett sighed. 'Kent was always looking for the perfect woman,' he said with a little too much sincerity. 'We kept telling him that his wife was good for him, but he didn't listen.'

That, Kit thought, was a lie. She'd bet a week's pay that these men all covered for one another. Connor's glance said that he agreed.

'Do you know who he was seeing?' Connor asked.

'No,' all three said in unison.

'We don't live in San Diego,' Garrett added. 'I live in Seattle, Dave's in Portland, and Pete lives in LA. We get together a few times a year, either here or in Vegas. It's guy time.'

Kit thought about the luxury car Kent Crawford had driven. The car that one or more of his friends had given him. The car that was still missing, probably in a chop shop by now. 'This is an expensive resort. Do each of you pay your own way?'

She knew that they'd paid for Kent, but she wanted to hear them say it.

'Of course,' Dave said, a bit smugly. 'We can all afford it.'

Pete shrugged, looking uncomfortable. 'Well, maybe not this level of accommodation. Dave, Garrett, and Kent do a good bit better than I do as an accountant, but I usually use my credit card points for upgrades. What exactly are you asking, Detective?'

Kent Crawford made more money than his accountant friend? That didn't seem possible, because Mrs Crawford had disclosed her husband's salary. And what about the friends paying Kent's way? 'I'm asking how Mr Crawford was able to afford this kind of trip a few times a year on his salary as the head of security at a retirement center.'

The three men looked at one another with puzzled frowns. 'Retirement center?' Dave asked. 'That's not right. Kent worked for Delta Technologies. They're a defense contractor hired by Coronado. Kent made as much money as I do.' The man faltered as he searched Kit and Connor's faces. 'Didn't he?'

Connor cleared his throat. 'No, sir. He did not.'

'Holy shit,' Dave whispered. 'He *lied* to us?'

Oh boy. Did he ever.

Garrett laughed bitterly. 'He lied to Denise about his affairs. Why are we so surprised that he'd lie to us, too?'

'What about his BMW?' Kit asked. 'His wife is under the impression that you gave it to him.'

All three men gaped at her.

Pete opened his mouth and closed it before managing to speak. 'He said *what*?'

'He told his wife that the BMW was a gift from one of you.'

'It wasn't,' Garrett insisted. 'He bought it himself.'

Dave was shaking his head. 'If he didn't work for Delta Tech, where did he get the cash that he threw around when we had our golf trips? Where did he get the money for that car?'

'That's a good question, sir,' Kit said. 'If you have any answers, we'd be happy to hear them. Somebody killed your friend. Knowing that he was spending well above his means opens up an entirely new avenue of investigation.'

All three shook their heads. 'I don't know,' Pete said. 'But he had a black AmEx card and he flashed it around plenty. Paid for things we never asked him to cover. Greens fees, cart rentals . . . He was the big man, carrying around a wad of cash.' He took the chair next to Garrett, his expression one of stunned despair. 'Why? Why did he lie about that?'

Connor smoothed his tie, a gesture that Kit had learned meant that he was processing. Kit didn't blame him, because this was so very different than what they'd been expecting. 'Did he mention his affair to you?' Connor asked. 'Maybe not a name, but anything that could help us find this woman?'

'Or man,' Kit added.

'Not a man,' Dave insisted. 'I'm gay and Kent never had any problem with me, but he was straight as an arrow. I've known him for twenty years and he always went for the ladies.'

'He liked them . . . experienced,' Garrett offered.

'Like sex workers?' Kit asked.

Garrett winced. 'Not that I knew of, but he liked when a woman picked him up in the bar. The last time we met up in Vegas, he left with a different woman every night.'

Dave's eyes widened. 'He did? How did I not know this?'

'Because you were out clubbing,' Garrett shot back. '*You* came back with a different man every night.'

'*I'm* not married,' Dave said defensively. 'Stop slut-shaming me.'

Kit waved her hand. 'Gentlemen. Let's focus. Did you know that Mr Crawford told his wife that he was meeting you for a four-day weekend? The day before you arrived here, he checked into the motel where he was found.'

Once again, Garrett looked uncomfortable. 'I knew. I was his alibi. If Denise called me asking for him, I agreed to tell her that he was in the bathroom or otherwise busy. He usually tacked on an extra day either before or after our trips for some alone time. I never asked with whom.'

Dave sighed. 'Hell, Garrett.'

'I wish I hadn't done it,' Garrett said. 'But . . . he begged. Insisted, actually. Said he needed space from her. Said I owed him.'

Pete rolled his eyes. 'Not this again. Kent saved our asses in the sandbox once. Never let us forget it.'

'I see,' Kit murmured. *Yeah, Crawford was a total douchebag.* 'So he did actually spend the arranged golf trips with you?'

All three nodded. 'He never missed a trip,' Pete said.

At least he told his wife a partial truth, she thought. 'Did he describe this woman to you, Garrett?'

Garrett shook his head. 'No. I'm sorry. If I knew, I'd tell you.'

She believed him. Mostly. 'Okay. Thank you for your time, gentlemen. If you think of anything else that can help us, we'd appreciate it.'

'Wait,' Connor said. 'Let's go back to Mr Crawford's black AmEx card. Do any of you remember where he last used the card?'

That was a good question, because Crawford's wallet had been stolen from his motel room and his wife hadn't mentioned a black AmEx.

Kit searched her memory for black card details. They were highly exclusive and cardholders had to have a *lot* of money in the bank. Not in real estate or other assets, but cold hard cash. Connor would remember exactly how much but she thought it was somewhere around a million bucks.

Where had Kent Crawford gotten that much money? Because his joint checking account with Denise had only about eight hundred dollars and their savings was only about five grand.

Kit assumed an illegal enterprise. Had Frankie Flynn found out? Was that why he was dead? Except Crawford had died at least a day *before* Flynn, so that didn't make sense.

'He bought dinner for the four of us at that fancy steak house in Vegas this past Easter,' Pete said. 'Dinner was about two hundred a person and we had wine. I couldn't afford it, but Kent insisted it was his treat.'

Garrett nodded. 'The tab was at least eleven hundred bucks. It was Good Friday, I remember. He used the card to pay his hotel bill at the MGM, too. Why?'

'Because we'd like to find the bank account that he used to pay that card,' Kit said honestly. 'His wife didn't know anything about it and it's not linked to any of the accounts I uncovered. That money trail might lead to his killer.'

'I can get that for you,' Dave said wearily. 'I managed his personal investments. He had an account offshore. Started modestly at about a hundred grand about ten years ago. He's added a fair bit every year, and I've grown it for him.'

Wow. Kit half wished she could ask Dave to manage her money. *Ha-fucking-ha.* Like there was any to manage.

'So now it's large enough that he can get a black AmEx card?' Connor asked.

Dave sighed. 'Yes. Detectives, you'll need a warrant, but I'll get all the information together so that when the paperwork goes through, I can hand over the account details right away. I can't just give it to you. I hope you understand.'

Dammit. Kit had hoped he wouldn't make them get a warrant. But at least they knew what to ask for. And the connection to a former homicide lieutenant's murder would expedite the paperwork.

'Thank you,' she said. 'We appreciate your help, and we are very sorry for your loss.'

'Safe travels home,' Connor added.

'Same to you, Detectives,' Pete said. 'I still can't believe Kent lied to us like that. At least now I know why he didn't want me to be his accountant. You could manage his money with enough distance, Dave, but I would have had access to his earning statements. I would have known he couldn't afford what he was spending. I'll admit that it hurt my feelings when he outright refused to hire my firm but used yours. Now I think I dodged a bullet.'

'Yeah,' Dave agreed. 'You did.'

As Kit and Connor left the room, all three men sagged wearily, the truth of their loss starting to sink in.

'Crawford's got layers,' Connor said once they were back in the department sedan.

'Like an onion,' Kit said sourly. 'Stinks as bad as one, too. None of this makes sense. Crawford died on Saturday morning and Flynn died sometime between Sunday at ten and Monday at ten. Crawford couldn't have killed Flynn personally.'

'No,' Connor agreed. 'I wonder if Mr Flynn's friends knew if he suspected that Crawford was dirty.'

'Let's go ask them. Benny should have woken up from his sedative last night. Hopefully he'll be having a better day today. And if he doesn't know, hopefully Georgia will.'

'You sleep, Kit. I'll get us back home and we can dig into what Frankie Flynn knew.'

'Thank you. I need to check my phone first, though. Baz was doing some legwork for me.'

Connor steered them away from the hotel and toward the interstate. 'What legwork?'

'Finding Gerald Wilson.' She was pleased to see a text from her old partner. *Call me.* Hopefully that meant he had something.

'Why didn't you get the man's number from Faye Evans?'

'That was going to be my next step if Baz came up dry. I didn't realize that Gerald didn't exist until late last night, and there was no one at the Shady Oaks office.'

She dialed Baz's number and he picked up on the first ring. 'Hey, kiddo.'

'Hey, Baz. I've got you on speaker and Connor is here. What do you have?'

'Hey, Connor.' Baz sighed. 'You couldn't find Gerald because he was legally adopted by his stepfather when he was sixteen years old. Changed his name to White.'

Kit wondered once again what had happened between Frankie Flynn and his son. 'Oh. Then I can look for him myself. Thanks, Baz.'

'There's more. I found him for you. Called Frank's old partner, the one I told you about last night. He said that Frank's ex-wife, Sharon, is in a hospice. I'll email you the details. Frank's old partner said that he's visited Sharon and that Gerald is always there at his mother's side.'

'Oh.' Kit exhaled. 'Thank you, Baz.'

'You're welcome. Makes me feel useful.'

'Retirement getting old?' Connor asked.

'Not old, but sometimes a little . . . slow. I'd come back as a part-time consultant, but my wife would not be happy with me. And she's waited a long time for my undivided attention. Speaking of, we've got breakfast plans this morning. We're meeting some old friends. Be careful, you two.'

'We will,' Kit promised. 'Have a good breakfast.' She ended the call and immediately called Navarro to share the information they'd gathered, from Kent Crawford's hidden income to Gerald's location.

'I'll send someone to the hospice to get Gerald's alibi,' Navarro said. 'And I'll get a warrant started for Crawford's banking. Where are you headed next?'

'Back to Shady Oaks,' Connor said. 'We need to talk to Benny Dreyfus. I want to know what he and Flynn argued about and what Flynn said that Dreyfus didn't listen to.'

'Keep me updated, and don't speed too much, Connor.'

Kit ended the call with a snort. 'He's got your number.'

'I'm a good driver,' Connor insisted, but he eased off on the gas pedal. 'Go to sleep, Kit. I promise I'll get us back in one piece.'

Seven

Shady Oaks Retirement Village
Scripps Ranch, San Diego, California
Tuesday, 8 November, 10.45 A.M.

Kit ended the call with their lieutenant as Connor pulled up to the entrance of Shady Oaks. She'd been napping when Navarro had called, but the sound of his voice had had her instantly alert. And good thing, too, because her boss had come through in a big way. 'Navarro says we should have signed search warrants for Kent Crawford's house, financial records, and his car by one or two o'clock. They still haven't found Crawford's car, though. Navarro's got uniforms out checking all the area garages and chop shops.'

'His killer might not have taken the car,' Connor said. 'If it was parked in one spot in that neighborhood for a few days, some car thieves could have grabbed it.'

'I know, but I'm hoping that Crawford left something in the car to explain where all that money came from.'

Connor put the department sedan in park, then turned to face her. 'He started investing with Dave ten years ago.'

'Same time that he started working at Shady Oaks. I thought of that. A hundred grand is a lot of money, though. If he'd stolen that much right away, surely someone would have missed it.'

'Maybe. Or maybe he had help back then. Maybe he still does.'

'You're thinking about Miss Evans being uncomfortable when we said we'd have to examine the contents of her in-house server. She wasn't there ten years ago, but we can find out who was. I still

120

don't know how he could find a hundred thousand to steal. From where?'

Connor shrugged. 'I mean, it's a ritzy place. They're on fifteen acres of prime real estate out here.'

'True. I meant to find out how much it costs to live here.'

'Depends on the plan and the kind of living quarters you get,' he said. 'I asked my mom about it, because she's been looking into arrangements for my grandparents. They're in their late seventies. You can get a plan that covers everything you need until you die, one that covers only the basics and everything else is à la carte, or a plan in the middle. There are entrance fees and then additional monthly fees. The entrance fee for the everything-you-need plan at Shady Oaks starts at a hundred grand and goes up to a million.'

Kit gasped. 'Dollars?'

Connor chuckled. 'Yep. The monthly fees are anywhere from fifteen hundred to seventy-five hundred.'

'A month,' Kit said, stunned.

'Yep.'

'Wow. I think we'll be taking care of Mom and Pop on the farm.'

'They're lucky to have so many of you. Some seniors only have each other or maybe one or two adult children. Some are all alone.'

'We're lucky to have Mom and Pop,' Kit said quietly. 'I don't think there's a foster among us that doesn't owe their life to Harlan and Betsy McKittrick. I know I do.'

Kit returned her focus to the retirement facility. She'd known the location was expensive, but she'd had no idea how much money was actually involved. 'There are three hundred residents at Shady Oaks. Even at the lowest prices, that is a hell of a lot of cash coming in.'

'Skimming could be very lucrative.'

Kit lifted a brow. 'I wonder where Miss Evans keeps the books.'

Connor grinned. 'I hope it's on the server. Evans said they outsourced their payroll, but she never mentioned who did the bookkeeping.'

Kit nodded once. 'Good point. Let's find out. But let's be sneaky. We don't want Evans to know that we're looking at the books, just in case she's in on it. If the books aren't on the server we seized, she could conveniently lose or change them.'

Connor got out of the car and stretched, groaning. 'I never used to mind long drives, but my bones are really yelling at me right now.'

'Mine too. Let's stop in Evans's office, then visit Benny and Georgia. My bet is that they'll be together.'

Connor held open the door and Kit walked through.

Then stopped short, because piano music was filtering through the closed doors of the common room, just as it had been yesterday.

Sam was here.

'He said he'd be back,' Kit murmured, almost to herself.

Connor sighed. 'It's sad music again. I thought he'd be playing something peppier to cheer the residents up.'

' "Amazing Grace." ' Again. *Dammit*. Why did she always have to walk in on that song?

Connor tilted his head. 'What bothers you about that hymn? You looked like this yesterday when I was trying to warn you that Sam was here.'

'They played it at Wren's funeral.'

Connor's face fell. 'Oh, Kit. I'm sorry.'

She waved his sympathy away because her eyes were burning. 'It was a long time ago, but music takes you back.'

'It does. I can question Benny if you need to go.'

Kit smiled at him gratefully. 'Thank you, but no. I'm okay. At least we're not dealing with dead teenagers this time.' Not like they had six months before.

'Small mercies.' He pointed to the office door. 'After you.'

But Miss Evans wasn't in the office. A uniformed officer was, however. Kit recognized him from the day before. He'd been standing guard outside Frankie Flynn's apartment.

'Officer Stern, right?' she asked.

The officer nodded. 'Detectives.'

'What's going on?' Connor asked. 'I thought CSU took the server to the lab.'

'They did. I was assigned to watch this room while the lab guys did their thing.'

'Did CSU find something suspicious?' Kit asked.

Stern shrugged. 'I don't know, ma'am. I'm here to make sure nobody makes off with any paperwork. Not everything was stored digitally. These drawers are filled with paper copies of patient financial info and personnel records.'

'Good to know,' Kit said. 'We should expand the warrant to include the physical files.'

Stern looked curious but, to his credit, asked no questions.

'Where is Miss Evans?' Connor asked.

Stern sighed softly. 'They had a death this morning. Benny, the man who my partner was watching yesterday? He had a heart attack during the night.'

Fucking hell. We'll never get to talk to him now.

Then Kit flinched. That this was her first thought made her feel dirty. *Have some compassion.*

She'd never met the man, but it was clear to see how much Benny Dreyfus had been loved by his fellow residents. 'Poor Georgia.'

Stern nodded sadly. 'She found him just after eight. Called 911.'

That sounded odd. 'She didn't call Miss Evans or the nurse?'

'No, ma'am. I was here on duty by then and all hell broke loose when the medics showed up. Someone must have called Miss Evans, because she rushed in around eight thirty. She was crying.'

'For Benny or for Crawford?' Connor whispered to Kit.

Kit nodded, wondering the same. 'Officer Stern, where is Mr Dreyfus's body now?'

'I don't know, ma'am. The funeral home arrived a few minutes ago. They came in through the back.' He pointed at the security monitors. Sure enough, there was a hearse parked at the service door.

Connor huffed out a frustrated breath. 'I don't mean to be crass, but we can't talk to him now.'

Which was terribly convenient, she thought, hating that the notion had to be considered. 'Let's see what's happening.'

Luckily Sam was no longer playing 'Amazing Grace' when she and Connor went back into the main hall. Kit could breathe again.

But Connor paused as they passed the closed common room doors. 'Oh,' he whispered.

Kit turned to find him looking uncharacteristically sad. 'What's wrong?'

' "I'll Be Seeing You." ' He pursed his lips hard. 'My mom's folks are still alive, but my dad's parents are gone. This was their song. They loved Sinatra's version. Damn, Sam plays it just like they loved to hear it.'

Kit opened the door just enough to let the music escape. And to peek in on Sam. He was hunched over the keyboard, his shoulders bowed, occasionally shaking. Like he was crying. But his hands flowed over the keys, never missing a note.

Dammit, Sam. Kit wanted to go to him, to give him comfort because he'd cared about Benny, too. But she couldn't. She was working.

I'm always working.

A tiny old lady stood beside him. Her hair was blue and her walker was studded with dozens of colorful, shiny rhinestones. Her hands were gnarled, but her fingernails were painted scarlet. She patted Sam's shoulder with one of those gnarled hands and Kit had to slowly release the breath she was holding.

Someone was taking care of him, at least. He finished the song, reaching up to pat the lady's hand, his gentleness obvious. Then he rolled into another hymn.

Kit pulled the door closed. 'Let's find the funeral director before he takes Benny's body.' She started for the elevator, remembering the way from the day before.

'You're going to want an autopsy?' Connor asked grimly.

'Yes. Don't you?'

'He had a bad heart, Kit.'

'I know,' she murmured.

'His family might not want an autopsy.'

Kit sighed as she pushed the elevator button. 'I'm going to insist. I'll be the bad cop.'

'Not a bad cop,' Connor said quietly. 'You're a good cop. This whole situation just sucks.'

'It does. They might blame us, the family. For putting Benny under stress yesterday.' It hadn't been their fault, of course. She knew that. But Sam's songs had her off center.

'If anyone's to blame, it's whoever put a butcher knife in Frankie Flynn's chest. And Frankie and Benny were related by marriage. If Benny's family loved Mr Flynn like he did, hopefully they'll want to find who killed him and will cooperate with us.'

Kit certainly hoped so.

Shady Oaks Retirement Village
Scripps Ranch, San Diego, California
Tuesday, 8 November, 11.10 A.M.

Sam clenched his jaw, breathing deeply through his nose. His heart hurt. So did his eyes because, once again, he'd arrived to find the facility in tears. He'd started crying, too.

Benny was gone. *Dammit*. He'd been such a relentlessly kind old man.

Frankie had been stoic and bold. He'd always known exactly where he was going and what he'd do when he got there. He hadn't spoken much, but when he did, people listened. Benny, on the other hand, had been soft-spoken, absentminded even before the dementia had set in. He'd been a stereotypical professor, glasses perched on the end of his nose. But his yarmulke had always been centered, his bow tie tied just right.

Except for yesterday. Sam hated that his last memory of Benny would be him in an episode.

This place wasn't going to be the same without the two of them.

And now Sam was playing 'I'll Be Seeing You' because it had been Benny's favorite. Not always. Not until his wife had died. Afterward . . . there hadn't been a single time that Sam had sat at the piano that Benny hadn't requested the old Sinatra tune. Benny would sing along and Frankie and Georgia would put their arms around him.

Goddammit.

Sam gave in, letting a little sob shake him. Then nearly lost it completely when Miss Eloise patted his shoulder. He'd known she was there, but her gesture of comfort shattered him. He managed to finish that piece and move on to the next, but Eloise put one of her arthritic hands over his, stilling his fingers on the keys.

He looked up at her, blinking to clear his eyes.

'You're a good boy, Sammy,' she said with a sweet smile, her own eyes red. 'That lady detective was just here.'

Sam twisted to look at the door. There was no one there. 'When?'

'Just now. Now, I know I'm almost blind, but these Coke-bottle lenses of mine still work well enough. She was watching you. I could see her face. She looked like she wanted to hug you.'

The thought made Sam's heart beat faster. 'She did?'

Miss Eloise patted his cheek. 'Take a break, Sammy. Go see if she needs anything.'

'No, ma'am. She won't want me around when she's working.' *Or when she's not.* She'd run the night before. As soon as Rita's adoption dinner had finished, Kit had given the teenager a hug and fled, claiming that she had to work.

'Nonsense. I know what I saw. Go.' Eloise lifted brows that she'd dyed blue to match her hair. 'Or I'll start to sing. Not an empty promise.'

Sam laughed, a broken sound. 'Okay, Miss Eloise. You twisted my arm.'

Eloise sobered. 'Georgia will need you.'

Sam nodded, taking another deep breath. 'I know. I'll be back, okay?' He dropped a kiss on her cheek, making her grin lopsidedly. 'Thank you.'

'Tell that detective that she might have competition,' Eloise said, fluffing her blue hair.

'I will.' He pulled the fallboard over the keys and stacked his music. He never really used it because he knew the songs by heart, but sometimes the residents liked to read the lyrics over his shoulder. 'I'll be back soon.'

Sam had expected it to be somberly quiet when he exited the elevator on the upper floor, but ardent arguing met his ears.

He recognized one of the voices. Vanessa, Benny's granddaughter. She was a nice woman, about Sam's age, who visited Benny often, usually bringing Benny's great-grandchildren. But she sounded angry at the moment.

'He had a heart attack, Detective,' Vanessa shouted. 'There is no need for an autopsy. He wouldn't have wanted that. We're Jewish.'

Benny's apartment door was open, so Sam went in. Two dark-suited men that Sam didn't know stood in the living room with a gurney. One of them grimaced. 'We're from the funeral home. The cops and the family are in the bedroom, disagreeing.'

Sam gave them a tight smile before pausing in the bedroom doorway. There were too many people in Benny's small room. Kit and Connor were there, along with Vanessa and her husband. Vanessa's mother Carla sat at the side of the bed, quietly crying, holding her father's hand, cold by now.

Miss Evans stood off to the side, looking like she wanted to bash some heads. Probably Kit's and Connor's.

Georgia stood sentry on the other side of Benny's bed, unmoving. She resembled a statue, her expression grim. Except for her eyes, which were devastated and red-rimmed.

Benny lay on his bed, his skin now gray. He wasn't wearing a bow tie or a yarmulke now and never would again. Sam's chest tightened and it hurt to breathe.

I'm so sorry, Benny.

'It was natural causes, Detective McKittrick,' Miss Evans said. 'He had a documented heart condition. He was eighty-nine years old. Why are you upsetting the family?'

Kit exhaled, her expression professional, her voice calm. 'I'm sorry. I really am. But two people connected with Shady Oaks have been murdered in the last seventy-two hours, and one of them was Benny's closest friend and confidant. We need to be sure Mr Dreyfus died of natural causes.'

Vanessa's eyes filled with tears. 'My grandfather would not have wanted this. Miss Evans, isn't there something we can do?'

The director hesitated. 'You can file an appeal.'

'We don't need to,' Carla said with quiet authority. 'My father signed documents to ensure no autopsy would be done. The original is in his safe-deposit box. I have a copy right here.' She drew a sheet of paper from her purse and handed it to Miss Evans. 'His Certificate of Religious Belief. Signed and notarized – long before the dementia began, Detective. You may not autopsy him.'

'It's legal, Detective,' Miss Evans said, sounding relieved that the argument was settled.

Kit rubbed her forehead, looking suddenly weary. 'Miss Evans, I'd like a moment with the family, please. Alone.' Miss Evans opened her mouth to object, but Kit held up a hand. 'Please, Miss Evans.'

Miss Evans shot Kit an icy glare. 'Of course, Detective. I'll be downstairs in my office.' She turned, her eyes widening when she saw Sam. 'Dr Reeves. Why are you here?'

'I thought the family might need me.'

Vanessa smiled weakly. 'Thank you, Dr Sam. I'd like him to stay, Detective.'

Kit nodded. 'If that would make you more comfortable. Dr Reeves, can you first escort Miss Evans and the two men from the funeral home into the corridor outside Mr Dreyfus's apartment?'

Sam did as she asked, Miss Evans's displeasure evident to everyone. The two men from the funeral home took the gurney out into the corridor. 'Just wait here,' Sam told them, then shut the front door and returned to the bedroom.

'Come in and close the door, Dr Reeves,' Kit requested. She glanced down at Benny's body, her gaze lingering on his face. When she lifted her eyes, they were filled with genuine sadness. 'First, I am very sorry for your loss. I never met Mr Dreyfus, but I've heard so many lovely things about him. Second, I want to respect your traditions and religious beliefs. I truly do.'

'But?' Vanessa said acidly.

'But,' Kit said calmly, 'Mr Flynn is dead, and he was clearly murdered.'

Vanessa's face fell. 'I know. Uncle Frankie was a good man. He didn't deserve to die that way.'

'I agree,' Kit said. 'Were you aware that the head of security was also killed, about three days ago?'

They nodded. 'But that has nothing to do with my father,' Carla said, her chin lifting.

'Maybe you're right,' Kit said softly. 'But what if you're wrong? Yesterday, Mr Dreyfus was heard saying that Mr Flynn's death was all his fault. Now, give me a minute,' she hurried on because Vanessa's eyes flashed fire and Carla looked ready to shout. 'I don't believe for a moment that Mr Dreyfus killed him. People say "it's all my fault" all the time, for a variety of reasons.' She hesitated, then shrugged. 'My sister was murdered when we were fifteen, and I blamed myself, like I could have stopped it if I'd been with her.'

Sam's chest hurt anew. *Oh, Kit.*

Both Vanessa and her mother were listening now, so Kit went on.

'Mr Dreyfus had some reason for expressing feelings of responsibility. He may have known something. He might not have even known that he knew it. We didn't have the opportunity to talk to him yesterday. And this morning, he's dead. So, again, what if you're wrong? What if Mr Dreyfus's death *is* connected? Wouldn't you want whoever hurt him punished?'

Both women hesitated. Then Vanessa's husband spoke up. 'What do you think, Georgia? You spent the most time with him.'

Georgia blinked, surprised. 'Um . . . Well, I think the detective has a point, but I know that Benny wouldn't have wanted an invasive autopsy.'

Kit tensed, poised to argue her point.

Sam broke in, knowing that Benny's family wasn't going to budge on their own. Kit and Connor could appeal Benny's Certificate of Religious Beliefs, but that would take time and Frankie's killer was still out there. 'Detective, is there any way to get the information you need without . . .' He winced. 'Cutting him?'

Kit smiled at him gratefully. 'Yes, Dr Reeves, there is. This is what I propose. Let the medical examiner draw some blood. We can test it, holding Mr Dreyfus's remains in the meantime. If something looks suspicious, we can proceed.'

Benny's family still looked unwilling, so Sam pressed forward. 'I've read that in situations like this, a rabbi has been known to attend the procedure to ensure the remains are . . . you know. Respected. Put back the way that they were. Can you promise that, Detective, if a full autopsy is required?'

Kit's shoulders relaxed. 'Yes, Dr Reeves. We can. I'll personally make sure of it.'

'We might be willing to do that,' Carla said slowly.

'Thank you,' Connor said. 'We do ask that you refrain from discussing this with anyone. Not the press, not the administrative staff, the nurses, not anyone.'

Georgia, Carla, Vanessa, and her husband all gaped.

'*What?*' Georgia demanded. 'Are you saying the *staff* was involved?'

'No, ma'am,' Connor said firmly, his tone managing to calm the drama before it exploded. 'But one of the staff is dead, and Mr Flynn was killed the very next day. Something connects them and until we find out what it is, it's our responsibility to keep this investigation as private as possible. I'd like to suggest that I ride with the mortuary representatives, transporting Mr Dreyfus's remains to the county morgue. Nothing more invasive will be done until the blood tests come back. That will take a few days, though, and I'm aware that you'd ordinarily want the burial to occur within twenty-four hours.'

Carla gazed down at her father's face, sorrow etched into hers. 'He'd want to help catch whoever killed Frankie. I know that. I still believe his heart simply failed, but let's follow this through. At least with the blood tests. We have family and friends all over the country that will want to attend the funeral. All of them won't be able to get here until Thursday or Friday. We wouldn't do the funeral on Friday anyway, because of the Sabbath. Saturday either. So you have until Sunday, Detective. That's all the time I can give you.'

Kit opened her mouth, then closed it, hesitating before finally nodding. 'I'll get those blood tests ordered right away. For now, behave as if the funeral home took his body and . . .' She smiled dryly. 'You can even gloat about how you got the cops to back down.'

Vanessa's lips twitched. 'Grandfather would love that. He looked like a nerd, but he was a real rebel.'

Carla turned to fully face Kit and Connor. 'You know that Frankie was once a homicide detective, yes?'

Kit nodded. 'Yes. I met him once, many years ago. Before I was a cop. I recognized him yesterday morning.'

'And,' Connor added, 'Mr Flynn was greatly respected.'

Carla frowned. 'Not all that respected. He couldn't come out while he was a cop.'

'I know,' Kit murmured. 'I hate that that was the case for him.'

Carla studied Kit's face, then Connor's. 'All right. Let's proceed as you've suggested. If you'll respect my father like you seem to respect Frankie, we'll have no quarrel with you.'

'Thank you,' Connor said.

Kit nodded. 'Yes, thank you. I know this is hard, on every possible level. I'm sorry that our conversation started badly.'

Carla patted Kit's hand. 'You're young, child. You'll learn.'

Kit nodded. 'I hope so. We'll keep you apprised. Miss Shearer, can I have a word with you? I'd like to get your statement about what happened from the time we left yesterday until you found Mr Dreyfus's body.'

Georgia nodded. 'Of course.'

Connor left the room to get the mortuary representatives, and Kit stepped away to give the grieving family privacy at Mr Dreyfus's bedside, turning her attention to Sam. 'Thank you, Dr Reeves,' she murmured.

Sam shrugged, his cheeks heating. 'I didn't do anything.'

'You came to help. And, speaking of helping, my father said I should also thank you for getting Jane and Janey to go to New Horizons and recommending they be placed with them.'

Sam truly smiled for the first time since hearing of Benny's death. 'They're really Tiffany and Emma, and they're afraid to go into the system. But your folks may have them convinced that McKittrick House is safe.'

Kit's smile bloomed. 'That's good. They're lucky young ladies that you stopped to help them. Miss Shearer, I'll wait for you in the hall. We can talk in your apartment, if that's okay. I'll tell the men from the mortuary to come back.'

Her smile loosened the tightness in Sam's chest, and he felt like he was finally able to breathe again. *Something's changed with Kit. For the better.*

'Dr Sam?' Georgia asked cagily. 'What was that about?'

Sam just shook his head. 'I need to get back downstairs. I'll be in the common room if anyone needs me.'

Shady Oaks Retirement Village
Scripps Ranch, San Diego, California
Tuesday, 8 November, 11.35 A.M.

Kit followed Georgia Shearer into her apartment and shut the door. 'I'm so sorry, ma'am,' she said quietly as the older woman slowly lowered herself into an overstuffed chair upholstered with cabbage roses.

Georgia had been as straight-backed as a soldier in Benny's room. Now she seemed to fold in on herself. Her voice was still strong and strident, though. 'Thank you, Detective. What's this about the staff? We deserve to know.'

Kit sat on the sofa closest to Georgia. Little Marmaduke was curled up on the center cushion, so Kit scratched behind his ears. 'I don't know, and that's the honest truth. All I know is that Kent Crawford was found dead in a cheap motel room yesterday morning, a gunshot wound to his head.'

Georgia grimaced. 'Messy. How do you know Kent was murdered? Maybe he shot himself in the head.'

'There were enough inconsistencies at the scene that we're considering foul play at this time.'

'Like?'

'Like, he was holding the gun in his left hand, but he was right-handed.'

Georgia frowned. 'There had to have been more, Detective. That detail alone seems flimsy.'

'There was, but I can't share details yet. Did you talk to Mr Crawford often?'

'Not unless I had to. I didn't like him. He was . . . I don't know. Self-important, maybe. He'd roar up in that car of his and strut into the building like he was cock of the walk.'

'So a narcissistic braggart.'

'Pretty much.'

Kit opened her secure notes app. 'Cock of the walk. I haven't heard that phrase in a long time.'

'I haven't used it in a long time. Where did you hear it?'

'One of the foster homes I lived in had a resident grandma who didn't want to be there any more than we did. She was the foster mother's mother, I think. She used to say it about her son-in-law.'

'Was he a cock of the walk?'

'Oh yeah. Not one of my favorite memories. He treated the grandma like he treated us. So . . . not good.'

'So you grew up in foster care.'

Kit nodded. 'Yes, ma'am.' Then waited to see where Georgia would go with the observation.

'You have a reputation as a closer for SDPD.'

'I try.'

'I read up on you when you left here yesterday.'

'I read up on you, too,' Kit said blandly. Georgia Shearer's background check had been extremely boring reading.

'I guess you did. Or you tried. Not much out there on me.'

'There really isn't. You were a paralegal for thirty years. Your record is squeaky clean. You don't even have a parking ticket.'

'Helps that I never learned to drive,' Georgia said dryly, and then she sighed. 'Frankie and Ryan were foster parents when they lived in San Francisco.'

Kit frowned. 'I didn't know that.'

Georgia looked pleased. 'I surprised the detective. Go me.'

Kit choked back a laugh. 'Yes, ma'am. What's this about?'

'A few of their former foster kids came to visit over the years. It was so nice when that happened. Ryan would hug them and cry, and Frankie would light up like the sun. Their fosters were always so happy to see them. It was clear that Frankie and Ryan had provided a loving home.'

'If you've been in the system for a long time, you know the good homes from the bad ones. And if the bad homes were really bad, it makes you appreciate the good ones even more.'

'You had a good one.'

'At the end, yes. The McKittricks adopted me out of the system even though I was rather prickly. In the beginning, though, I had some bad experiences. Do you think one of Frankie and Ryan's foster children is involved in Frankie's death?'

'Oh no. Nothing like that. I was remembering one of the times that Frankie had a foster son visit. This was only a few months ago, so Ryan was long gone. The young man brought his husband and their baby.' Georgia's eyes welled up and she dashed at the tears impatiently. 'They'd named their son Ryan Franklin.'

'That's lovely,' Kit murmured, her own eyes stinging. If she ever had a child, it would bear either Harlan's or Betsy's name.

And *that* was a thought she hadn't had before. Having a child?

No. Not happening. I'd be a terrible mother.

Sam, on the other hand, would be a wonderful dad. Just one more reason they could never work, even if Kit wanted it. Which she didn't.

At least she shouldn't.

'It was lovely,' Georgia agreed. 'We were all having lunch and chatting in the dining room when Crawford came in.'

Kit felt suddenly cold. 'What happened?'

'Nothing right then, except that Crawford kind of sneered at them. Muttered something I couldn't hear, but Frankie heard it and it made him angry, even though he tried not to let it show. Later, when the visitors were gone, Frankie went to Crawford's office. I followed him and listened at the door.' She shrugged. 'I was afraid Frankie would say something he couldn't take back. He was a good man, but he had a bit of a temper.'

'Did he say anything he couldn't take back?'

'No. It never got that far. Frankie told Crawford he'd been out of line and that he'd report him to the director if Crawford "ever said that homophobic shit again." Exact words. Crawford laughed. Said that Frankie needed to remember his place, that he wasn't a lieutenant anymore and that here, at Shady Oaks, Crawford was in charge.'

Oh. 'Crawford knew that Mr Flynn had been a cop.'

'He did. I don't know if it's important, but Frankie started watching Crawford after that. He noticed things that I didn't, like lipstick

134

on his shirt collar. He thought Crawford was having an affair.' Georgia studied Kit's face. 'But you knew that already.'

'Dr Reeves told us that Mr Flynn suspected Crawford was cheating on his wife. Do you think Mr Flynn suspected anything else about Mr Crawford?'

Georgia crossed her arms over her chest. 'Like he was stealing from Shady Oaks?'

Kit blinked. 'Yeah. Like that.'

'If he had proof, I don't know what it was. I think if Frankie had had proof, he wouldn't have kept it a secret. He did not like Crawford.'

'Why didn't you tell us this yesterday?'

'I didn't trust you yesterday.'

Kit lifted her brows. 'Do you trust me now?'

'Yes. I read about you, like I said. Also, Sam trusts you. I saw that just now in Benny's room.' She hesitated. 'If I'd told you and you'd gone after Crawford, he would have known that either Benny or I had told you. And it couldn't have been Benny because you never got the chance to talk to him.'

'I wish I had,' Kit said quietly. 'A man who engendered so much love must have been special.'

Georgia wiped away another tear. 'He was.'

'Miss Shearer, were you afraid that Crawford would take action against you? Abusive action?'

'I didn't know what would happen, but I still have to live here after you all go home, and I don't have Frankie or Benny anymore. Of our little group, only Eloise and I are left.'

Kit had thought that Georgia had been hiding something yesterday. 'I understand. So you don't think Frankie had any tangible proof against Crawford?'

'If he did, he sure didn't tell me, but Frankie was odd about things like that. He was protective, so he might have kept it from me for my safety. Also, Frankie didn't know I'd overheard their conversation because I slipped into an open meeting room when I heard Frankie come out of Crawford's office, and Frankie never mentioned it. But now Crawford is dead and you think it was a homicide, so . . .'

'Was Crawford chummy with any of the staff?'

'No. Like I said, cock of the walk. He thought he was better than the rest of us. I only talked to him when I had a security issue, like when my badge stopped working. That was only twice in the last six years that I've been here. He acted like I was stupid for demagnetizing the strip on the badge or something. Talked to me like I was a disobedient child. I just tried to stay out of his way. My life was less stressful that way.'

'Why did you say that Crawford might be stealing from Shady Oaks if Frankie never mentioned it?'

'Because I'm not stupid, Detective. Crawford drove an expensive car and lived in a nice neighborhood. He also went on golf trips a few times a year. Expensive places. He didn't make enough money here to pay for all that.'

'How do you know what he was making?' Georgia squirmed and Kit met her gaze directly. 'Miss Shearer?'

'I know how to find information,' Georgia said primly.

Kit leaned forward. 'I am *all* ears, Miss Shearer. Details, please.'

Georgia sighed. 'I heard Archie Adler talking about it.'

Kit frowned. 'The IT guy?' Whom they still hadn't met yet. *Step up the pace, McKittrick. You're behind.*

Shouldn't have gone to dinner last night.

But that wasn't true. She'd made time for family. And Rita had been so happy. *And don't forget Jane and Janey. You helped them, too.*

'Yes,' Georgia said. 'Archie mostly works remotely or at night. And I have insomnia.'

'You heard him talking one night?'

'Yes. He was in the dining room, drinking coffee and working on his laptop. He was on his phone with someone. Maybe a friend. They were talking about cars and Archie was lamenting that he needed a new one. He wanted something expensive but couldn't afford it. He said that he'd asked the director – this was two directors before Evans – for a company car like "that prick Crawford" had, but the director said nobody had a company car. Archie was wondering aloud how Crawford afforded it on his salary. His friend

136

must have asked if he was sure he had his salary right, because Archie said he was looking at it on his screen right then.'

'Did he know you were there, hearing this?'

Georgia shrugged again. 'Most of the admin staff ignore us. We're old so we're no threat. They think we're deaf and addled. And some of us are, but I'm not. Not yet.'

'You most definitely are not.'

Georgia smiled. 'Thank you, Detective.'

Kit smiled back. 'You're welcome. When was this?'

'Around two years ago? It was autumn and Benny's wife Martha was still alive. So, yes, two years ago.'

'Thank you. Do you think that Crawford was stealing from the facility?'

'He was getting it from somewhere, although I think he had investments. Archie told his friend on the phone that he'd asked Crawford about the car, who said his – expletive deleted – broker had made him rich. He used a homophobic slur that I won't repeat, but it starts with an *f* and ends with a *g*.'

Kit winced. Dave the financial advisor hadn't thought that Crawford had a problem with him. 'Good to know. So did Archie ever get a new car?'

Georgia blinked. 'I don't know. He must have gotten a new one or fixed the old one, because he gets to work, but I've never seen him driving. I only knew about Crawford's car because he made such a big deal of revving his engine when he passed us waiting at the shuttle stop.'

'Got it. So . . . Mr Dreyfus. What can you tell me about him?'

Georgia sighed. 'I stayed with him all day yesterday and into the evening, except for meal breaks. They moved him out of the nursing ward at about eight last night. They'd been monitoring his heart. I figured he was fine because they let him go back to his room.'

'Did he wake up?'

'Yes, but I was at dinner at the time. Nurse Roxanne said he woke up and was talking normally. No sign of slurring or memory loss. They had someone with him most of the night, but when the shift changed, I guess they thought he'd be okay on his own. Nobody was with him when I went in to get him for breakfast. I do that every morning. He didn't answer the door, so I used my key.'

'Key or key card?'

'Key card. Both Frankie and I had one for Benny's room. Crawford didn't want to give us one, but Benny's family filed a special request and threw their weight around. We worried about him and so did Carla and Vanessa. Once we got key cards, Frankie and I took turns checking on him. Devon Jones – she's the nursing assistant for our floor – she does a good job, but Benny's known us for years. Devon's only been here about a year and Benny sometimes forgets who she is.' She sighed again. 'He sometimes forgot. I have to get used to this new normal of past tense. I hate it.'

'I know,' Kit said quietly.

Georgia studied her for a moment. 'Yes, I suppose you do. Benny hadn't started coffee or anything, so I figured he was still asleep, but he didn't like to miss breakfast. He was an early riser. Usually up with the sun. I was surprised no one was in there with him, so I checked his bedroom.' She swallowed hard. 'He was cold. I checked for a pulse anyway.' She shook her head. 'Nothing.'

'I'm so sorry, Miss Shearer. I just need to ask a few more questions. Did you notice anything out of place?'

'No. His meds were on the bedside table, along with a bottle of water.'

'Was the water bottle opened?'

Georgia frowned as she thought. 'Yes. It was about half empty. His meds were in one of those seven-day pill minders. He hadn't taken this morning's, but he had taken last night's.'

'So he'd woken to do that.'

'Or the nurse woke him.'

'Who was with him last night?'

'I don't know. Roxanne was with him until I went to dinner, but I think her shift was over earlier than that. She stayed late because she was worried about him.'

'Okay, I'll talk to her, too. Do you know if anyone came into his room this morning?'

'I don't know, Detective. I took a sleeping pill last night because I didn't want to be awake at three a.m. when all the anxiety strikes.'

'Oh, I know all about the three a.m. anxiety strikes.'

Georgia smiled wearily. 'Detective, I appreciate that you're being thorough. I really do. But Benny's heart was bad. It was only a matter of time. I really think you're wasting your time investigating his death.'

Kit smiled gently. 'And I want you to be right. I want it *so much*. But I wouldn't be doing my job if I didn't check. Thank you, Miss Shearer. I appreciate everything you've told me. Do you still have my card in case you remember anything more?'

'I do.'

'Then I'll let you rest.'

Kit stood, wincing as her muscles complained. And she could feel a headache coming on. She patted her pants pockets, relieved to feel the outline of the small flat pillbox she used for ibuprofen.

'Miss Shearer, might I bother you for a glass of water?'

'Of course. Are you all right, Detective?'

'Just a headache.' She followed Georgia into the kitchen, emptying her pocket into her palm. A Swiss Army knife, half of a dog treat for her poodle Snickerdoodle, the pillbox, and the cat-bird carving Harlan had made for her. *For luck*, he'd said. She never left the house without it.

'Oh my,' Georgia said, peering at the carving. 'That's a beautiful figurine. What is it? A cat and a bird?'

Kit held it up so that the older woman could see it. 'My father made it for me. It's a good-luck charm.'

'It's exquisitely done. I don't know much about art and such, but Benny was a collector. He has some beautiful things.' She opened the cabinet door, frowning when she found no glasses. 'I haven't been in this kitchen for a week. I guess I forgot to unload the dishwasher. I hope I remembered to run it.' She opened the dishwasher, sighing in relief when she found it full, the contents clean. 'Here you go, Detective.'

Taking the offered glass, Kit turned for the sink.

Then froze.

On the counter, next to a mixer, sat a set of knives, the block bearing the brand's logo. Wüsthof. But one of the slots was empty. A big slot.

Georgia's butcher knife was missing.

Quickly, Kit looked back into the still-open dishwasher, hoping a knife would be in plain view, but there was no large knife.

Georgia followed Kit's gaze back to the counter, then gasped when she noticed the missing knife, her knees buckling. Kit gripped her arm gently, guiding her to a chair at the dinette.

'Sit, Miss Shearer. Breathe.'

'That knife in Frankie's chest . . .' Georgia covered her mouth, her skin so pale that Kit thought she might pass out. 'It was mine?'

'I don't know, ma'am.' *But probably yes.*

'I didn't kill him, Detective. I didn't.'

Kit patted her shoulder. 'We'll figure this out, Miss Shearer. For now, I'm going to call Miss Evans and have her send someone to check on you.'

'I'm not having a heart attack, Detective,' Georgia insisted. She was trying for haughty, but her voice trembled.

'Humor me, ma'am.' Kit called the office for assistance, then snapped a photo of the knife block and sent it to Connor.

Georgia Shearer's knife block.

Connor's reply was immediate. *WTF?!? She couldn't have done it.*

Agree. Going to call CSU. Learned stuff about Crawford. Will fill u in later.

We're on our way to the morgue. Will head back to you asap.

Kit sent a text to CSU's Sergeant Ryland, then sat next to Georgia. The older woman did not look good at all. Kit lightly gripped her wrist, frowning at the rapid pulse. 'Miss Shearer, nobody believes you did this. I don't think you could have even if you'd wanted to.'

The woman was normally full of snark, which made her seem stronger, but in reality, she was elderly and, at the moment, frail. There was no way she had the muscles or the height to have stabbed Frankie Flynn.

The first time anyway. That cut had taken a lot of strength. The second cut, the one made with the butcher knife, could have been done by someone of average strength, especially if fueled by fear and adrenaline.

Didn't have to be the same doer. But it most likely was.

Kit filled the glass with water and pressed it into Georgia's hand. 'Sip it.' Then she scooped Marmaduke from the sofa and placed him on Georgia's lap. The dog snuggled up close, Georgia's hand shaking as she petted him.

Georgia stared up at Kit, her eyes filled with horror. 'Who could have done this?'

'That's exactly what we're going to find out.'

Eight

Kit stood against Georgia's living room wall. Next to her was Miss Evans, who'd been wringing her hands since she'd arrived.

'This is terrible,' Evans whispered. Again. The words seemed to be the only ones the woman was capable of uttering at the moment.

Georgia sat at her dinette table, Marmaduke still cuddled in her lap. Nurse Roxanne had responded to the call for help, her manner calm and efficient despite her slightly swollen eyes. She'd apologized as she'd wiped away tears, saying that she'd only just heard about Benny Dreyfus's passing.

The man had been loved by everyone, it seemed. So far, the staff Kit had dealt with had reacted in a sadly resigned way. They'd expected his death for some time. That it had happened so close to the murder of Mr Flynn had many of them shaken, but Mr Dreyfus's death seemed to be the type that they were all used to.

Kit felt a twinge of doubt at requesting an autopsy but didn't change her mind. If his blood tests were clear, she'd release his body to the family for his burial. She really wanted to believe the man had passed peacefully in his sleep, but something hinky was going on at Shady Oaks, and if Mr Dreyfus's death *had* been due to foul play, she wanted the perpetrator punished.

'Your vitals are all good, Miss Georgia,' the nurse said, patting the elderly woman's arm. 'Hey, Marmaduke,' she added, giving the Chihuahua a scratch under his graying, grizzled chin. 'Miss

142

Georgia, Dr Tidwell ordered anti-anxiety medication. Do you want one?'

Georgia looked at the space where her knife block had been. It was empty now, CSU having picked it up. Shuddering, Georgia nodded.

Kit leaned closer to Miss Evans as the nurse gently led Georgia to her room. 'I'll need to know who had access to Miss Shearer's room.'

'Of course,' the director murmured. 'Anyone with a master key. I'll get you a list.'

'Today,' Kit insisted. Miss Evans had promised this yesterday but hadn't yet delivered.

'Of course,' Evans repeated. 'I'm sorry, Detective. I've been . . . scattered.'

'I also need the duty rosters for the last week. Including any last-minute changes.'

Miss Evans's expression became frosty. 'My staff had nothing to do with Mr Flynn's death.'

Kent Crawford was part of your staff, ma'am. And their deaths were connected. Kit was sure of it.

'Just following procedure, ma'am. We'll be able to conclude our investigation faster with your cooperation.'

The woman nodded stiffly. 'Yes, Detective.'

The nurse emerged from Georgia's bedroom, closing the door with a weary sigh. She crossed the room, stopping in front of Miss Evans.

'She'll rest now,' the nurse said. 'She's badly shaken, what with Mr Benny's death and now this knife business. But she's a strong woman. She'll be okay.'

Kit hoped so. She was starting to like Georgia Shearer. *She's who I'd like to be in fifty years.*

'Nurse Roxanne, yes?' Kit said. 'I'm Detective McKittrick. Can you give me a few moments of your time?'

Roxanne's lips thinned. 'I wish we'd had a few minutes of your time yesterday. I was with Mr Benny while he waited for you to get around to interrogating him. He was distraught and confused. You just left him there to suffer.'

Kit blinked, taken aback at the woman's overt hostility. 'I'm sorry, ma'am. I wasn't aware that Mr Dreyfus had a heart condition that needed special care. And we weren't going to interrogate him. We were going to interview him. There's a difference.'

Roxanne swallowed. 'I know and I'm sorry for being rude. But Mr Benny's last hours were not peaceful. He was so upset yesterday and he never really snapped back.'

Kit frowned. 'Miss Shearer was under the impression that he had spoken normally once he'd woken up. No slurring or lost memory.'

Roxanne's smile was wistful. 'That's true, but he wasn't himself. He was so upset about Mr Frankie. Kept saying that it was all his fault. He was calmer when he woke up, for sure, but he wasn't the same.'

'Why do you think he thought it was his fault?'

Roxanne narrowed her eyes. 'You're *not* suggesting that Mr Benny killed Mr Frankie.'

'No. Not at all.' Kit was certain of that, if nothing else. 'But he must have known something or felt like he did. Did he say anything yesterday while you were waiting for us?'

Roxanne shook her head regretfully. 'No, Detective. I think he believed that if he'd been there, Mr Frankie would be alive. I don't know how, but guilt doesn't always make sense.'

Kit wanted to sigh. She might never find out what Mr Dreyfus had meant. 'When did you last talk to Mr Dreyfus?'

'Around ten last night. I got him settled in his own bed and sat with him, monitoring his vitals until he went to sleep and my relief came on duty. I'd worked more than a full shift and we were still short staffed, so I crashed in the staff quarters. I think I was asleep as soon as my head hit the pillow. I was back on duty again at seven this morning.'

'Did you check on Mr Dreyfus this morning?'

'No. Nurse Trudy was on duty last night. I don't know if she stayed with him the whole time, but I doubt it.'

'She didn't,' Miss Evans said. 'We checked on him during the night, but like Nurse Roxanne said, we were short staffed. I had to rearrange schedules yesterday.'

Kit nodded. 'I remember you saying that. Is Nurse Trudy still on duty?'

Miss Evans nodded. 'She is. She's downstairs, checking on our assisted living residents today. I'll tell her that you wish to speak with her. Roxanne, can you cover for Trudy?'

'Of course.' Roxanne smoothed a hand over her hair, a vibrant mahogany color. 'Please let me know if I can be of any additional assistance, Detective. I haven't been here long, but I'd grown fond of both Mr Frankie and Mr Benny. Their passing will leave a hole in the fabric of this place, for sure.'

Kit turned to Miss Evans once Roxanne had left the apartment. 'How long has she been with you?'

Because Evans hadn't given them the employee roster, either. Evans hadn't actually given them anything that they'd asked for.

'She was assigned here for twelve weeks. She's a traveling nurse and we have her here for the rest of the week. Friday is her last day. I've offered to hire her full time because she's very good and we have a vacancy to fill, since one of our nurses retired recently. Roxanne told me today that she'd been considering my offer, but that the recent "drama" here has caused her to decline.'

'I'm going to check in with Nurse Trudy, and then I'd like to speak with your IT guy. Archie Adler. Is he here today?'

'Not at the moment. I can call him in, if you like.'

'That won't be necessary. You said he's a college student during the day? We'll find him.' She'd bring him in to the station to chat, because along with Crawford, he was the one with the most access and the most understanding of what had been described as an overly complicated system.

But first, she'd ask CSU what they'd learned from the Shady Oaks server so far. Hopefully they'd found something, because their list of questions was growing, but they had no answers.

Once she talked to CSU, she was going to interview all the nurses who'd had contact with Mr Dreyfus. Roxanne and Trudy were her priorities. She wanted to find out who was on duty at what times, though.

145

There were too many puzzle pieces floating around. She needed to either put them together or eliminate them.

She'd made it out into the hall when someone called her name. It was Vanessa, Mr Dreyfus's granddaughter. The woman wore a scowl and Kit prepared herself for another diatribe about her grandfather's autopsy.

'Yes, ma'am,' Kit said politely. 'How can I help you?'

'Can you come with me, please?'

Kit followed Vanessa into Mr Dreyfus's apartment warily. Carla, Mr Dreyfus's daughter, sat on the sofa in front of an open cabinet, her expression full of both dread and rage. 'What's happened?'

Carla pointed to the cabinet. 'My father's coin collection is missing.'

Kit peered into the cabinet, which was actually a very large – and empty – safe. 'What exactly is missing?'

'My father collected rare coins as did his father before him,' Carla said. 'Dad had his father's collection, too. I didn't want him to keep it here. It was too valuable. But it brought him such joy, especially since we lost my mother. I didn't want to deprive him of what little joy he had left.'

'The coins were kept in a small trunk with pullout drawers,' Vanessa said. 'Looked like a jewelry box. I've taken photos of the collection in its entirety for insurance purposes.'

Kit's head began to throb again. 'All right. Is it possible that Mr Dreyfus moved the collection somewhere else in the apartment? He was – forgive me – forgetful.'

Vanessa's husband came into the living room from Mr Dreyfus's bedroom. 'No, Detective. The collection is not here. I've checked the bedroom. We've checked everywhere.'

Conversation exploded then, with the three family members talking over one another.

Kit raised her hands like a traffic cop. 'Please. Stop.' The talking abruptly ceased, three pairs of panicked eyes shifting to her. 'When was the last time you saw it?'

Carla closed her eyes briefly. When she opened them, she appeared to have gathered her composure. 'Six days ago. I'd come to dry out the dehumidifier, which they also took. Detective, my father's collection was featured in magazines. It was a true treasure. Our family's legacy. My grandfather was able to hide some of their rarest coins in the lining of my father's coat when they fled Europe in 1939. We have to find them.'

'Okay,' Kit said, hoping she sounded calm. Because this just muddied the waters further. Had someone stolen Mr Dreyfus's collection? When? Had Frankie Flynn known? Was that why he was dead? Was that why Mr Dreyfus felt responsible? 'What was the value of the collection?'

Vanessa sank onto the sofa, next to her mother. 'Four million dollars.'

It was only her ten years as a cop that allowed Kit to keep her composure. *Four million dollars?* Which he'd kept in a cabinet in a freaking retirement home? *What the actual fuck?* She didn't think she'd ever understand rich people.

'I see,' she said, hearing how breathless she sounded.

Vanessa's husband sighed. 'I think we may be more amenable to your request for an autopsy, Detective.'

San Diego PD, San Diego, California
Tuesday, 8 November, 1.55 P.M.

Lieutenant Navarro pinched the bridge of his nose, his frustration all too apparent. 'So let me get this straight.'

Kit glanced at Connor, who grimaced. This really had become a highly visible shitshow, with one of the victims being one of their own.

Navarro's small office was crowded. The captain was there, along with CSU's Sergeant Ryland, ME Alicia Batra, Detective Bruce Goddard from the robbery unit, and one of the civilians from IT named Jeff Mansfield.

The assistant chief – the captain's boss – had even invited himself, having served under Flynn more than thirty years before.

So . . . no pressure.

And, of course, there was Dr Sam Reeves, whom Kit had

personally invited because Connor was right. Sam noticed things. And he had the ability to pour oil on troubled waters.

Hopefully they wouldn't need him for that during this meeting, but Kit wanted to be prepared.

Navarro got up to pace, then realized his office contained too many people for that, so he stood with his arms crossed over his chest. His face was more lined than it had been six months before, his hair a little grayer. But his focus was the same and Kit was grateful that he'd returned from his personal leave in time to preside over this case, because Navarro could manage the brass without them knowing he was doing so.

'We have three dead men,' Navarro said. 'Flynn, an obvious homicide; Crawford, a faked suicide; and Dreyfus, who may or may not have died from natural causes. Crawford might have been stealing from someone – maybe Shady Oaks, maybe somewhere else – and had an offshore bank account with a lot of cash that his salary doesn't support. And finally, we have a missing coin collection, worth four million dollars. And somehow there have been no cameras anywhere that have caught any of this, despite their incredibly intricate security system. Is that right, Detectives?'

'Mostly, sir,' Kit said. 'There is still no footage from the hallway outside Mr Flynn's apartment at the time of his murder, but we checked surveillance footage from the other on-site cameras.' It had been a quick search, to be honest, right before the meeting. They'd have to go back and review all the footage in more depth later, but they'd found at least one useful thing. 'We found someone leaving through a rear door with a box about the size of the missing coin trunk. This was at four fifteen a.m. on Saturday, three days ago.'

'Were you able to get an ID from the video?' Navarro asked impatiently.

'Not exactly, sir,' Kit said. 'His face is hidden by a cap. But the clothes the man was wearing fit the description of what was missing from Kent Crawford's suitcase, and he was about the same size as Crawford – five ten, maybe two hundred pounds.'

Sergeant Ryland frowned, puzzled. 'I thought Crawford was dead by four fifteen on Saturday morning.'

'Hard to say,' Alicia said. 'He died sometime Saturday, but I can't give you a specific TOD. My best estimate is between midnight and eight a.m.'

Navarro sighed. 'So Crawford could have stolen the coins from Shady Oaks, come back to the motel, gotten himself murdered, then . . . what? His killer stole the coins from there?'

'Maybe,' Kit said. 'We believe Crawford was stealing from someone. We're waiting on the warrants to be signed giving us access to his offshore account information, but at this point, his spending indicates more income than he was legitimately making at Shady Oaks. He could have been stealing from the residents all this time. He had the access with his master key. With Mr Dreyfus, he would have hit the mother lode.'

'Or,' Connor countered, 'he was partnering with his killer, turning off the cameras so someone else could steal the coins, then he became a loose end that his partner needed to snip.'

'Very possible,' Kit agreed. 'We don't know yet.'

'Frank Wilson must have figured it out,' the assistant chief murmured. 'That's what got him killed.'

'Again,' Kit said, 'very possible. We're partnering with Detective Goddard to trace the stolen coins. If we find the coins, we might find the thief, which might lead to the killer. Lots of mights, but right now, that's what we have.' She nodded in Goddard's direction. 'What are the odds we'll find them?'

Robbery Detective Bruce Goddard was in his early forties but looked fifteen years younger. His slow Southern drawl made him a real charmer with the ladies. Or so Kit had heard. She liked Goddard, but he was *not* her type.

Your type, her inner voice said slyly, *is sitting on the other side of the table wearing nerdy Clark Kent glasses.*

Which was true, but Kit still cursed that little voice while forcing herself to focus on Detective Goddard.

'Not great,' Goddard said. 'There was a single coin in the collection worth a cool million – a gold coin from the Roman era. It alone is enough to make the right collector go crazy with want. The remaining three mil is tied up in ten other coins, half of which are

149

antiquities from Greece, Rome, and the Middle East. They're worth about two million. The other half are early American coins and they're worth about a million all together.'

'For coins,' the captain murmured. 'Good God.'

'I know,' Goddard said with a rueful shrug. 'The thieves won't pawn the coins and they won't try to sell them on the legitimate market. These kinds of items tend to go to private auctions where the buyer might not care if the items are stolen. If they sell them within the continental United States, they can even deliver them in a car, bypassing any airport security. We're always monitoring online chatter for stolen artifacts and high-value collections, and we haven't seen anything about the coins, but we've doubled our coverage. And we're checking with our sources in the private auction industry. If they come up for sale, we might hear about it.'

'Odds don't sound good,' Navarro grumbled. 'What new information do we know about the homicides? Have we conclusively ruled that Crawford was not a suicide?'

'We know that he was definitely holding the gun in his nondominant hand,' Kit said. 'His wife confirmed that he fired with his right hand. He had a broken finger on his left hand that made pulling a trigger impossible. Dr Batra has confirmed that.'

'And he had benzodiazepines in his system,' Alicia added. 'He'd also ingested some alcohol. The combination of the benzos and booze would have knocked him out, making it easy for a killer to put the gun in his mouth.'

'He could have drugged himself,' Ryland added, 'but there was no evidence of any medication left in the room. Not even Tylenol. There were no bottles or baggies that he could have used to carry any meds. The gun was wiped clean except for one set of his prints. I don't know why he would have wiped his old prints if he was planning to kill himself. Plus, someone was in his room afterward because items are missing, like his laptop and cell phone.'

'Some of his clothes and two pairs of shoes were taken, too,' Kit added. 'He or whoever killed him was wearing them at four fifteen on Saturday morning when they stole the Dreyfus coins.'

'So we have at least two murders,' Connor said. 'Maybe three, if

Benny Dreyfus didn't die of a heart attack. Alicia, do you have the blood tests back yet?'

'No. Those will take at least until Thursday morning.' Alicia winced when everyone frowned at her. 'That's how long that test takes. I've moved it up to the front of the line. That's the best I can do. All we know is that Crawford couldn't have killed Flynn, because Crawford had already been dead for at least a day by the time Flynn was stabbed. Crawford died sometime on Saturday morning. We know Flynn was killed sometime after ten a.m. on Sunday because he'd pulled the cord Sunday morning. The exact time is hard to determine because the apartment was like an icebox. Someone had cranked the A/C down to sixty, so the body temp was affected. He'd completed rigor, though, so TOD had to have been close to ten a.m. on Sunday.'

'What else do we know about Frank's death?' the captain asked.

'He was killed by a stiletto blade,' Alicia said, 'then someone went over the original wound with a butcher knife to make it look like a different weapon was used.'

Sam Reeves gasped quietly and Kit wished she'd told him before the meeting. It wasn't fair to blindside him. She sent him an apologetic glance and he nodded numbly.

The two brass looked stunned. 'What?' they asked in unison. 'Why?'

'We're not sure why yet,' Kit said. 'But we know that the knife came from his next-door neighbor's knife block. Georgia Shearer doesn't know when the knife disappeared. She hadn't used her kitchen in several days, even before Mr Flynn was killed. And unless she's a lot stronger than she looks, she did not kill Mr Flynn.'

'We also know,' Alicia went on, 'that Mr Flynn had duck confit a few hours before he died. Could he have eaten it for breakfast or lunch on Sunday?'

Sam sat up straighter. 'Excuse me, Doctor. Did you say duck confit?'

The room turned to look at him. 'Yes,' Alicia said warily. 'Why?'

'Because that was dinner on Saturday. I was there. It was Miss Eloise's birthday and she'd invited me to her dinner party. The cook

151

made the duck because it's Eloise's favorite. Frankie attended the party, too.'

'Maybe he took leftovers to his room,' Kit said.

Sam shook his head. 'There wasn't anything left. There never is when Cook makes duck confit. I wanted a second helping and it was all gone. Everyone grumbled, except Frankie. He wasn't a huge duck fan. He only ate a little. It was a small private party, about twenty people. The rest of the residents had already had their dinner and the main kitchen was closed, and Frankie was irritated because he couldn't get anything else to eat downstairs.'

'What time was dinner?' Kit asked, her mind already building a new scenario. 'Did Mr Dreyfus observe the Sabbath?'

'He did,' Sam confirmed. 'Sunset was just before six, so we had dinner at six thirty. Normally dinner is at five, but Eloise wanted Benny to be able to join in. He couldn't eat until an hour after sunset, so he ate at seven, but Frankie ate with us at six thirty.'

The assistant chief shook his head. 'So if the duck was Frank's last meal, it means he was killed before eight thirty p.m. on Saturday, otherwise the food would have been completely digested. He wasn't killed Sunday after ten a.m., like we'd assumed. Dr Batra, are you sure that Crawford died between midnight and eight a.m. on Saturday?'

'Pretty sure, sir,' she said. 'It's still possible that Crawford killed Flynn, but not probable.'

The assistant chief sighed. 'That would have been too easy.'

'Wait,' Connor muttered. 'How did Mr Flynn pull the cord on Sunday morning if he was dead on Saturday evening?'

'*That* is a damn good question,' Kit said, crossing her arms over her chest. 'Alicia, you were a little doubtful at Mr Flynn's scene yesterday morning. You said something about expecting him to still have been in rigor.'

Alicia was nodding. 'Yes. I was surprised he'd completed rigor in twenty-four hours at his age. I mean, the room was cold, but not literally an icebox. If he died Saturday night, he would have been dead around thirty-eight hours. That makes the completion of rigor much more likely.'

Kit looked at Connor, then Sam. 'If this is true, if he died Saturday night, this means someone had opportunity and access to Mr Flynn's room to pull the cord for him on Sunday. He was found Monday morning.'

'And they took Miss Shearer's knife,' Navarro added. 'And stole Mr Dreyfus's coins. Whoever killed Frank had repeated and unfettered access.'

'The call's definitely coming from inside the house,' Connor said grimly.

Sam had grown pale. 'Is Miss Georgia in danger? Miss Eloise? Benny's gone and they were Frankie's only other friends. The ladies don't have family. No one is watching out for them. I'm going to stay at Shady Oaks with them.'

Of course he would. Sam Reeves was too kind for his own good.

'Let's come back around to that,' Kit said quietly.

Sam's chin lifted. 'You can't tell me not to.'

'No, I can't. And even if I could, you wouldn't listen anyway.' Making a note to request additional guards around the retirement facility, Kit turned her attention to Navarro. 'Now the mess in Mr Flynn's apartment makes sense. His killer was looking for something, and they gave themselves time by pulling the cord. Maybe evidence Mr Flynn had collected. What could that have been? Maybe proof he'd been gathering of Crawford's embezzling? And did his killer find what he was looking for?'

'All those destroyed photos,' Ryland murmured. 'And broken ceramic pieces. They emptied every canister and carton in the pantry and cut into the frozen meals.'

'What about Frank's car?' Navarro asked. 'Have we checked that? Maybe whatever the killer was looking for is there.'

'We found his car in Shady Oaks's lot,' Ryland said. 'It had been searched as well. The seats are a mess, all slashed. We examined it but didn't find anything.'

'So who within the Shady Oaks staff has unfettered access to the facility?' the captain asked. 'Who can get in and out of the exterior doors and into the residents' apartments?'

'Some of the nurses and nursing assistants have master door

keys,' Kit said, 'but I don't think they have unlimited access. Miss Evans does, as did Kent Crawford and Archie Adler, the IT guy, who we still haven't talked to. It could have even been someone in housekeeping or the main kitchen. We have to take a very close look at Mr Dreyfus and his coin collection. We don't know who knew about it.' She looked at Sam. 'Do we? Did you hear any of the staff talking about it?'

Sam shook his head. 'I visited Benny in his apartment a few times and I never knew there was four million dollars' worth of coins in his safe. Why didn't his family take them when he started to slip?'

Kit sighed. 'He'd lost his wife and was losing his memories. They didn't want to take anything more from him.'

Sam nodded sadly. 'I can see that. But still. Four *million* dollars? How was the safe locked? A key? A handprint? A combination?'

Smart question, Kit thought. Sam was good at asking smart questions.

'His daughter Carla said it used to be a combination dial lock,' she said, 'but they installed a safe with a biometric lock when he started to slip. She said she took the most valuable coins away at the beginning of his dementia, but he noticed and flipped out. He said that she was stealing his autonomy. So she upgraded the safe. I looked it up – the safe retails for twenty grand. Weighs about fourteen hundred pounds. And opens with a fingerprint *and* a combination. Carla said that if he forgot the combination, he'd call her and she'd come over.' She sighed. 'Benny's father's coins were in the collection. He'd smuggled them out of Germany in 1939. She said those were the super valuable Roman coins. Benny had added most of the early American coins.'

'I don't know who knew about them,' Sam said. 'If Georgia and Eloise knew, they never let on. The safe looked like a cabinet. It even matched the existing woodwork.'

'Carla had it custom made to do so.' Kit glanced across the room at the IT guy, who looked like he felt very out of place with the brass. 'But Georgia knew that Benny collected pretty things. We need to find out who else knew. Jeff, have you found anything on the servers we can use?'

Jeff cleared his throat nervously. 'I have a few things so far. First, everything on the server is buried under layers of encryption – much more than I'm used to seeing for normal personnel files – so it's been slow going even though we've put several people on it. But we have cracked the key-card logs and I have them right here on my screen. Your theory about the time of Mr Flynn's death makes sense.' He glanced at the screen of the laptop on the table in front of him. 'Someone using a master key card entered Mr Flynn's apartment at seven thirty-five on Saturday evening.'

Sam let out a slow breath, his shoulders slumped. 'Frankie left Eloise's birthday party right about that time. Like I said, he didn't like duck confit so he ate a little bit and went back to his apartment for a "real dinner." Maybe he surprised his intruder.'

Kit wished she could reach out and pat his hand. Or something. She hated seeing him so sad. 'Jeff, does the log show when someone exited?'

'No, just when they entered. But here's the thing. At seven fifty-five, so twenty minutes later, *Mr Flynn's* card was used to enter Miss Shearer's apartment.'

Kit nodded, understanding. 'That's when the killer got the Wüsthof knife from Georgia's kitchen. He must have stolen Mr Flynn's key card. Did he use it again to reenter Mr Flynn's apartment?'

'Yes, Detective, Mr Flynn's key card was used again two minutes later at seven fifty-seven, to reenter Flynn's apartment. And then he used Mr Flynn's key card again the next day at nine a.m. to enter his apartment a final time.'

'When he pulled the I'm-okay cord.' Connor leaned so that he could see Jeff's screen. 'Does that tell you who the master key card was issued to? The one he used when he first entered Flynn's apartment?'

Jeff nodded. 'That master key card belonged to Kent Crawford.'

Nine

The master key card used to break into Frankie Flynn's apartment on Saturday night had been Kent Crawford's? So many things about that didn't make sense to Kit.

'But Crawford had been dead for at least twelve hours by then,' she said, 'if he died between midnight and eight a.m. on Saturday.'

Navarro frowned. 'His killer must have stolen the key card along with his laptop and phone.'

Kit rubbed her forehead. She'd never taken any pain reliever for her headache and it was getting worse. 'Jeff, was that key card used at any other time?'

'It was used a lot, actually. Before Saturday, anyway. One of Crawford's responsibilities may have been opening doors for the residents if they locked themselves out. I would have overlooked that master card entry if I'd continued thinking that Mr Flynn died on Sunday afternoon. On Saturday it was used to enter Mr Flynn's apartment at seven thirty-five, but it had also been used earlier on Saturday, at four oh five a.m., to get into Mr Dreyfus's rooms.'

'When he stole the coins,' the assistant chief said. 'So the coins were stolen when Mr Dreyfus was still alive?'

Kit sighed. 'So it would seem. Someone had a lot of nerve.'

'Mr Dreyfus didn't notice they were gone?' Navarro asked.

Sam was quietly shaking his head. 'It was the Sabbath. He wouldn't have done anything like that on the Sabbath. Benny was very devout. It's unlikely that he would have looked on Saturday

156

evening because he'd have been tired from Eloise's party. He said he was going right to bed. I don't know if he checked the safe on Sunday, but I have to believe he would have made a ruckus if he'd found them gone.'

'When did the birthday party break up, Dr Reeves?' the captain asked.

'About eight thirty Saturday night,' Sam said. 'Georgia and Benny left together, and I escorted Miss Eloise to her apartment door. She hadn't brought her walker that night because the rhinestones didn't match her outfit, and she needed help. Eloise lives on the same floor as the others, but at the opposite end of the corridor. I was on their floor for only a few minutes with Eloise. Maybe from eight forty to eight forty-five. I didn't see anyone in the corridor, so Frankie's killer must have been gone by then.'

'So the killer was in Flynn's apartment for an hour or less,' Kit said, 'and that includes the time it took to kill him, then come back with the butcher knife. That doesn't seem long enough to create the mess we found.'

'Maybe he went back on Sunday to continue his search when he pulled the I'm-okay cord,' Connor suggested. 'Which is more than cold. I mean, searching the room while Mr Flynn was lying on the floor with a butcher knife in his chest.'

'This killer is a sociopath,' Sam said quietly. 'No compassion for Frankie or respect for his things. But there's also fear. He took a big risk coming back the next day. The residents have a later breakfast on Sunday, generally from eight to ten. That's the day many of them go to the store or play games in the common room, so they come to breakfast prepared for their day. Many of them don't go back upstairs, so the coast would have been clear. Seems like this killer knew their schedules pretty well.'

'Another reason to suspect staff,' Kit said. 'Can you give us a psych profile?'

Sam shrugged. 'A basic one. Male, although a female isn't out of the question. Very confident, intelligent. Good at planning. The camera had to have been disabled before he exited the elevator or came up the stairs early Saturday morning to steal the coins. I'm betting he used the stairs. He also had to have some upper body strength in order to . . .' He exhaled. 'To make that wound on Frankie's chest.'

'Maybe not as much strength as you think,' Alicia said. 'I believe the original wound was smaller, the one made with the stiletto blade. The one made with the butcher knife was made once the victim was lying on the floor.'

'True,' Sam acknowledged, 'but he had to have been strong enough to carry Benny from bed to the safe. Probably why the coins were stolen when Benny was still alive. Otherwise, how could he have opened the biometric lock? It required a fingerprint, didn't it?'

Detective Goddard nodded. 'I was thinking about that. Was there a wheelchair in the room?'

Kit nodded. 'There was. You think the killer moved Mr Dreyfus from the bed to the wheelchair, rolled him to the safe, then used his finger to open it?'

'You said a fingerprint and a combination code,' Navarro said.

'Yes,' Kit said, 'but if the killer knew the coins were there, he may have seen Mr Dreyfus open the safe. How come Mr Dreyfus didn't wake up when the killer used his finger to open the safe? Do you know if he was a light sleeper, Sam?'

'I don't, no, but Georgia might. He was sometimes given a sleeping pill at night, though. Helped control his night terrors. If he'd been dosed the night before, he would have slept through the thief stealing his coins.'

'That would explain how the fingerprint was activated,' Goddard said, 'but it still leaves the question of how the thief knew the combination.'

'Let's leave that for now,' the assistant chief said. 'I have a question about Frank. He was last seen on Saturday night, and his body wasn't discovered until Monday morning. Didn't his friends worry when they didn't see him all day on Sunday?'

'No,' Kit said. 'I talked to Miss Eloise this afternoon after Georgia was sedated. Eloise said that Mr Flynn would often drive up to San Francisco for the weekend to stay in the house he and Ryan had shared. He'd leave Friday, stay Saturday, then drive back through the night on Saturday and arrive for Sunday brunch. Maybe they thought he'd left Saturday night after the party.'

Navarro whistled. 'That's eight hours each way by car. I'd have trouble with that much driving, and Frank was eighty-five years old.'

'He was in amazing shape for his age.' Sam smiled sadly. 'And then if he wasn't going to San Francisco, he'd just hole up and be alone. On Saturdays, though, not on Sundays. Benny observed the Sabbath on Saturday and his family would usually pick him up on Friday before sunset so he could celebrate Shabbat with them, then bring him back on Saturday night. This past weekend was unusual because his family was out east at a bar mitzvah. That's why they weren't here until today. They traveled back yesterday. Frankie would make his San Francisco pilgrimage on the weekends so that he didn't lose time with Benny. He only stayed at Shady Oaks for Benny, otherwise he would have moved back to San Francisco a long time ago.'

'But Mr Flynn stayed this weekend for Miss Eloise's party?' Kit asked.

Sam nodded. 'Yes, he did. But he also stayed because Benny wasn't going to be with his family this weekend. Frankie wouldn't have left Benny alone that long. Frankie was loyal to his friends.'

'So if Mr Flynn's killer believed he'd planned a trip to San Francisco,' Detective Goddard said thoughtfully, 'then he wasn't expecting Flynn to be there on Saturday night, which was why he chose that night to search Flynn's room. Although if the staff knew he regularly made that drive, they wouldn't have expected him to pull the cord on Sunday, so why did the killer go to the trouble of returning?'

'Good question,' Navarro said. 'Dr Reeves, do the residents have to notify the office when they're leaving the building?'

'The independent living residents don't, not for little trips and if they have their own car. But on those San Francisco weekends, Frank would have to tell the office he'd be gone because he wouldn't be there to pull the cord. I think he'd send Miss Evans an email, letting her know. I don't think it was anything more formal than that.

But he wouldn't have sent one this past weekend, because he was staying in.'

Kit turned to the IT guy. 'Jeff, was there any kind of communication to staff concerning absent residents via the company email? Have you broken the encryption on that yet?'

'I can see the company emails and yes, Miss Evans sent out a daily message to the main staff with who would be out of the building. Recipients were . . .' Jeff tapped at his laptop keyboard. 'Kent Crawford, Evans's assistant Lily, and the head nurse, Janice Lenski.'

'Did you find anything unusual in the emails?' Connor asked.

Jeff hesitated. 'I think that Miss Evans and Mr Crawford were meeting each other outside of work.'

'So Miss Evans is Kent Crawford's mystery woman?' Connor said, his doubt clear. 'Really?'

Sam's brows went up. 'I did see them leave together a few times, but there didn't seem to be any intimacy between them. I'm not sure they even liked each other. They acted like siblings almost.' He tilted his head, considering. 'Or exes.'

Which Sam would know about, Kit thought. She'd met his ex earlier that year and had not been impressed. Sam was kinder to the woman than she deserved after she'd cheated on him. Kind, but stiff and formal around her, like he was walking through a minefield.

'I didn't say there was intimacy,' Jeff corrected. 'I said they were meeting each other. I've compiled a list of dates you should check based on their emails to each other. It's almost like the emails are written in a code. Things like "bring an umbrella" on days it was sunny and dry. I checked.'

'Then Evans may be connected,' Kit said. 'Can you send us the dates and messages, Jeff? We'll start looking at where the two of them were. I think Mrs Crawford will be very anxious to tell us where her husband was on those days. She needs us to prove her husband didn't commit suicide because she needs the insurance money.'

'We still need the warrant to get Crawford's bank information,' Connor said. 'Lieutenant, if you and the captain and assistant chief can help to expedite this, we could start following the money.'

'You'll have it in a few hours,' the assistant chief said, his jaw tight. 'The judge was waffling on just cause, but I think we've got enough now.'

'Thank you, sir,' Kit said respectfully. 'We've got a lot of things to do. First up is to find Archie Adler, the Shady Oaks IT guy. Miss Evans said that he was coming into Shady Oaks yesterday afternoon, but he never showed up. She says that she called him but only got his voice mail. We've sent uniforms to his apartment several times today, but he hasn't been home. His car wasn't in the lot, either.'

Kit hoped the guy hadn't run. He could be involved in anything from Crawford's embezzlement to any of the murders. That he'd effectively disappeared was not a good sign.

'Adler's fingers are all over the encryption,' Jeff said. 'If you can find a reason to make him cooperate, he could make my job easier and faster. I'll be able to get into the books and personnel files. That's where the encryption is the heaviest. I haven't been able to break through it. That makes me very suspicious, especially since they kept paper files of the same. I'm wondering if there are two sets of books. It doesn't seem smart to keep illegal activity on the work server, but if Miss Evans is involved, maybe they weren't worried about the wrong eyes seeing it.'

Kit nodded thoughtfully. 'I'm sure we can come up with something to make Mr Adler cooperate. Georgia Shearer overheard one side of a phone conversation between Adler and a friend. Adler had noticed that Crawford was driving a fancy car and said that Crawford had bragged about his investments. Adler knew how much Crawford made in salary and joked that he needed to hire Crawford's broker. If he'd kept poking, Adler might have found the embezzlement. If he did find it, he might be profiting from it somehow.'

The captain leaned forward. 'Have you looked into his finances?'

'Not deeply,' Kit admitted, wishing now that she'd looked harder. 'But maybe he learned from Crawford, who kept his money offshore. We'll find out.'

'Do that.' Navarro went to the whiteboard on the wall and drew a responsibility chart. 'McKittrick and Robinson, you're going to find Archie Adler. You're also going to find out where Crawford and Evans were on the days Jeff believes they were meeting. Detective Goddard, you're going to search for the missing coins. In that capacity, can you ask who at Shady Oaks knew they existed?'

Goddard hesitated. 'Someone closer to them might be able to get a better answer. Dr Reeves? You want to join me?'

'Oh yes,' Sam said coldly. 'I want whoever hurt Benny to go down. Because they're probably the same person who hurt Frankie.'

Navarro frowned. 'I feel like I should caution you about getting involved, Dr Reeves, but I realize it's way too late for that. Just . . . tread carefully, or I'll have to pull you.'

'Of course,' Sam said, but Kit recognized the determined look in his green eyes. He was a man on a mission now. She thought Navarro might be thinking the same thing.

She lifted her hand to divert Navarro's attention. 'Boss, we still need to search Mr Flynn's home in San Francisco. If he drove there recently, he might have hidden evidence there.'

'Good point.' Navarro wrote it down. 'Ryland, can you send up a CSU team?'

'As soon as we're done here,' Ryland promised.

'I'll make sure you have that warrant for Crawford's offshore account,' the assistant chief added.

Kit looked at Jeff. 'Can you send us the key-card logs along with those emails and dates?'

Jeff nodded. 'I'll send you a list of all key-card activity on all doors at the facility. I'll have it to you in a few hours. I made a copy of the Shady Oaks server, by the way. I had to return the original server to their server room because they still have to track key cards and access email and the security cameras. I put a program on the original server to alert me to any attempts at a connection, whether they be hackers or someone legitimately using the server-based systems.'

'We have camera and key-card logs for this morning?' Kit asked, relieved. She'd thought those had been lost without a working server. 'Who entered Benny Dreyfus's room during the night?'

Jeff looked it over. 'Quite a few people, but that made sense to me considering they were monitoring Mr Dreyfus's heart. Roxanne Beaton went in twice before ten p.m., then the head nurse, Janice Lenski, went in twice more at one and three a.m. Devon Jones went in at five a.m., then nobody went in until Georgia Shearer entered at eight oh five a.m.'

Kit stilled. 'Devon Jones? The nursing assistant? Are you sure?'

Jeff nodded warily. 'That's what the key-card log says.'

Sam frowned. 'That's impossible. Devon wouldn't hurt Benny.'

Kit hoped he was right, but she couldn't assume so. 'We'll track her finances and movements. She's a single mother with a toddler. She definitely needs cash.'

'What did the camera show?' Connor asked. 'We do have cameras now, don't we?'

'Yes, sir,' Jeff said quickly. 'I didn't check the feed, but I will as soon as we're finished.'

'Get back to me ASAP,' Navarro commanded. 'Anything else?'

Kit shared a glance with Sam. He was clearly vexed, but he'd said his piece and wouldn't push it. She gave him a small smile. 'We'll try to clear Devon quickly, Sam.'

'Thank you,' he murmured. 'I'd hate to see her reputation smeared over this. It sucks to be wrongly accused.'

Which Sam would know all too well, having been a suspect in a murder case six months before. Kit had never believed he was guilty, either. She trusted her gut, which was saying that Devon Jones was not guilty. But she'd dot her *i*'s and cross her *t*'s.

Connor lifted his hand. 'I have a question. If Crawford and Miss Evans were meeting, that suggests that she might be involved in his embezzling – if that's what he's been doing, and I think he has. I also think that he's been doing so for at least ten years, so I'm wondering about Evans's predecessor, if he or she knew. Who was that, Dr Reeves?'

'Selma Waite,' Sam said. 'She wasn't with Shady Oaks that long. She'd been a nurse at one of the local hospitals but had administrative experience. She was hired when the previous director retired. Both Kent Crawford and Archie Adler were hired by

Waite's predecessor, whose name was JoAnne Tremblay. Selma was director for only about eight months.'

'Did you trust her, Dr Reeves?' the captain asked.

Sam hesitated, then nodded slowly. 'I suppose so. She wasn't overly warm, but she took time to know each resident. She was very efficient with her time and with paperwork. She examined all expenditures. I once asked to have the piano tuned, and I had to fill out a stack of forms and she had to personally approve the expense. She was a real micromanager.'

Kit made a mental note to check out the facility's financial advisor, too. She wondered if any of the board members suspected anything was amiss, so she added that to the list, too. But for the moment she was focused on Sam, because he suddenly looked a little sick. 'What happened to her?'

Sam met her gaze. 'She fell down the stairs in her house. She had a broken neck.'

The room went quiet, then Navarro turned to Alicia. 'Dr Batra, can you look into the woman's autopsy records?'

'Of course. Selma Waite with an *e*, Dr Reeves?'

Sam nodded. 'Yes.'

'It's worth checking,' Navarro said. 'Something fishy is going on at that home, and if this woman saw it, she might have been killed to ensure her silence. What about the director before Waite? JoAnne Tremblay? You knew her, too?'

Sam nodded. 'She was the one who approved my volunteering. She was level. No drama. The facility functioned and she never seemed to sweat the details. I didn't know her well. I'm not even sure where she retired to.'

'We'll dig up the details,' Connor said. 'Do you know how Miss Evans was brought in? Did the facility's board of directors do an interview process, or did she know someone?'

'I don't know that,' Sam said. 'I'm sorry.'

Navarro shook his head, returning to the chart. 'Don't be. McKittrick and Robinson will find out and I'm going to put an unmarked car on Evans. I don't want her taking off if she is involved. Sergeant Ryland, I want you to go over Mr Dreyfus's room with a fine-toothed comb, especially around that empty safe. The thief might have left a hair or something. Dr Batra, please call us with the results of Mr Dreyfus's blood tests as soon as you know them. I think that's enough for now. Let's get started.'

Everyone got up to leave, but Sam stopped them with an urgent 'Wait.' All eyes turned to him. 'What about the residents? What about Georgia and Eloise? They were friends with both Benny and Frankie. Someone might think they know something, even if they don't. Will you give them protection?'

Navarro nodded. 'Officer Stern's been on-site since yesterday, so he's familiar with the main staff. We'll reassign him to security detail during the night on the floor where the women live and get another officer to stand watch in the office during Miss Evans's work hours. I don't want anything removed from the office, but the women might be in danger. We won't be able to do this long term, but we can budget additional personnel for a few nights.'

'Thank you,' Sam said, clearly relieved.

Navarro smiled. 'You're welcome. Now, everyone go. Get to work. McKittrick and Robinson, please stay.'

Connor's brows shot up. *What did we do?* he mouthed.

Kit shook her head. She had no idea.

'You didn't do anything wrong,' Navarro said after closing his office door. 'I just wanted to let you know that I personally drove to the hospice center where Frank's ex-wife is . . .' He sighed. 'You know.'

'Did you meet the son? Gerald White?'

'No, I didn't speak to Gerald. He was sound asleep on a cot in his mother's room. I did use his driver's license photo to confirm that he was Gerald White. His mother was also asleep and I didn't wake her, either. The nursing staff signed a statement saying that Gerald had been at his mother's side since Friday at noon. Before that, he was there ninety-five percent of the time. They said they'd make a schedule of exactly when he'd been there and send it to me. I think you can eliminate him from your suspect list.'

'Thanks, boss,' Kit said. 'At least we've got closure there. I didn't want to think that Mr Flynn's own son could kill him.'

'Now you know. Go. Find that Adler guy. Even if he's not guilty of anything, I want him to help IT break through the encryption on that server.'

Connor saluted. 'Will do.'

La Jolla, San Diego, California
Tuesday, 8 November, 3.25 P.M.

'Wow,' Kit said as Connor drove them into Mary Adler's neighborhood. Archie Adler's mother had begun renting this house less than two years ago. 'Her background check said that her last residence was a low-rent apartment. This is quite an upgrade.'

They'd already been to Archie Adler's apartment, but no one had answered once again. They were hopeful that his mother could help them locate her son.

Connor slowed to park at Mrs Adler's curb. 'She's a retired hairdresser. Divorced. Her husband hasn't been in the picture for years. I wonder where she got the cash to rent this place? Not to mention the brand-new Mercedes in the driveway. That model starts at eighty thou.'

'Maybe from her son,' Kit said grimly. She'd spent their drive time reviewing background checks of Archie and his mother. There was no evidence to indicate that Adler was involved in Crawford's scheme other than the fact that he also had access to Shady Oaks's camera system. Adler's access wasn't as broad as Crawford's – they'd learned from Jeff in IT that Adler could see the cameras remotely, but only Crawford could control them. Still, Kit hadn't ruled Adler out. 'The house is owned by a corporation that owns several homes in upscale neighborhoods and rents them out. It's a new company, incorporated only two years ago. The president is listed as Chadwick Redford. Owns a house nearby.'

'We could ask him who's paying the rent if we don't get anywhere with Mrs Adler,' Connor said.

'Sounds like a plan. How do we want to play this visit with Archie's mother? Are we just looking for Archie to answer questions? Do we tell her that he might be in danger? We want her to tell us where he is, not try to hide him.'

166

'The danger angle could work. I mean, *if* she likes him and wants to protect him.' Connor's tone turned hopeful. 'But if he's the family fuckup, she might be more than willing to throw him under our bus.'

'He's not the family fuckup according to her Facebook page.' Kit turned her tablet so that Connor could see Mrs Adler's page. 'She gushes about how proud she is of him, and there are photos of them having dinner together. Looks like a weekly event. I think Archie's a mama's boy.'

'But if we say that Archie's in danger, what's he in danger from? Kent Crawford's death was supposed to be a suicide and Benny's from a heart attack. Only Frankie's death is a known homicide. I don't want to give away that we suspect money shenanigans. She'll clam up fast then.'

'True.' Kit bit her lip, turning the possibilities around in her mind. 'What if we say that there were attempts to hack into Shady Oaks's computer system to get information on Frankie Flynn before his death, because he was known to be a wealthy man. That there have been attempts to get information on the other residents, all of whom had to have money, or they wouldn't be able to afford Shady Oaks to begin with. And that we're worried about Archie, because only he knows the passwords. That whoever killed Mr Flynn could be hunting the residents for their cash and Archie stands in their way?'

A Cheshire cat grin broke over Connor's face. 'You are very devious. I bow to you.'

'Thank you,' Kit said primly. 'I don't like the misrepresentation, but if Archie did steal money and she knows about it, she'll be on her guard. If she thinks Archie is innocent, she'll be angry if we suggest otherwise. This way, she can believe she's keeping him safe. And maybe he is innocent. If that's the case, whoever killed Kent Crawford could still be a danger to anyone associated with Shady Oaks.'

Including Sam. The thought rankled and Kit hoped the psychologist stuck close to Detective Goddard when they were asking about Mr Dreyfus's collection.

Together, they walked to the front door and Kit knocked. After a minute the door opened, revealing the woman pictured on Mary Adler's Facebook page. In her late forties, the woman was tanned and healthy looking. She wore a pristinely white tennis dress, and a diamond dangled from a tennis bracelet. She held a racket in one hand and an athletic bag in the other.

She eyed them with open suspicion. 'If you're selling something, that's illegal here.'

'No, ma'am,' Kit said, showing her badge. 'I'm Detective Mc-Kittrick and this is my partner, Detective Robinson. We'd like to speak to your son in relation to a case we're working.'

Mary's suspicion became obvious hostility. 'Why? My son's done nothing wrong.'

'A man was murdered in the retirement facility your son works in,' Connor said. 'Your son manages the computer servers and we've been trying to reach him to ask for help deciphering some of the security outages that led to the victim's death. He's the only one that seems to know how things work around there,' he finished with a self-deprecating smile.

Mary puffed up with pride. 'My Archie is a good man. And a smart one. He's been telling them that they need a security upgrade, but nobody ever listens until it's too late.'

That's interesting, Kit thought. Especially since the facility had just installed a complicated new security system.

'Do you know where we can find your son, Mrs Adler?' Kit asked. 'We've checked his apartment, but he's not there.'

'Oh, he'll be at the college. He's a grad student, you see.' More pride that seemed sincere. 'Archie's a hard worker. He goes to school during the daytime and works for the retirement center at night.' Mary smiled. 'And he still finds time for his mama.'

Kit made herself smile back because the woman seemed to expect it. 'That's really nice, Mrs Adler. Do you know where we should look for him at the college? It's a big place. Does he have an office?'

'Oh yes. Look in the computer science building. His office is on the fourth floor.' She glanced at her watch. 'Are we finished,

Detectives? I have a tennis date and I don't want to be late.' With a smile, she stepped outside and closed her front door, edging past them to go to her car. Waving, she drove away.

Connor's brows rose. 'I think we've been dismissed.'

'I think you're right. I also don't think we're going to find Archie at the college.'

'Then we'll drop by the Beachside Athletic Club afterward,' Connor said. 'We can kick up a public fuss, which will hopefully embarrass her into cooperating. She's new money. She won't want to be disrespected by the old-money members.'

'I'm so glad you know all this classist shit,' Kit said. 'How do you know which club she belongs to?'

'It was discreetly embroidered on the bag she was holding. It's a ritzy place. Hefty price tag and there's usually a waiting list to get in.'

Kit looked over her shoulder at him as they headed back to the department sedan. 'You're a member, aren't you?'

He shrugged. 'Legacy through my parents. I play squash there.'

She sighed as they got into the car. Sometimes she went whole days forgetting that Connor came from wealth. 'Of course you do.'

'Hey, don't knock it,' he said lightly. 'It's good exercise.'

She belted herself into the passenger seat. 'You any good?'

'Eh. Not bad. But it draws the ladies.'

'Even CeCe?'

He smiled, his expression softening. 'No, she's more into farmers markets and antiquing in places my folks wouldn't be caught dead in. I'm not telling my mom, but the gift CeCe gave her for her birthday came from a thrift store. Mom loved it and CeCe chuckled for days, so everyone won.'

'I like CeCe. She's good for you.'

He cast her a sideways glance as he started the car. 'I like Sam.'

'Connor.' But she felt her cheeks heat. 'Stop.'

His lips twitched. 'Okay. But you called him Sam during the meeting. Everyone else called him Dr Reeves.'

Kit blinked. She had. *Shit*. Had anyone else noticed? Had *Sam* noticed? 'Just drive to the college, okay?'

He chuckled. 'Whatever you say, Detective McKittrick.'

Ten

Shady Oaks Retirement Village
Scripps Ranch, San Diego, California
Tuesday, 8 November, 3.30 P.M.

'Whoa,' Detective Goddard said as he knelt to examine Benny's safe. 'Did McKittrick say it cost twenty grand?'

Sam nodded. 'She did. I had no idea it was even a safe.'

Goddard shook his head. 'Rich people, man. I thought I'd seen it all in this job and then I learn something new.'

Goddard was fortyish but still had a boyish face. Sam imagined he'd be able to blend in easily if he ever went undercover.

'How long have you been in the robbery division?'

Goddard looked up with a grin. 'Trying to get me to tell you how old I am?'

Sam made a face. 'Maybe.'

Goddard laughed. 'I'm forty-one. I was carded until I was thirty-five. My granddad is nearly eighty and doesn't have a single wrinkle, so I'm hoping I'll take after him.' He sat back on his heels with a sigh. 'I haven't investigated a robbery in a place like this. Nursing homes, yes, but this . . . This is a step above.'

'This is several steps above,' Sam said wryly. 'Most of the folks here are very nice. Every so often you get a resident who doesn't like anyone or anything, but by and large this is a good place. Benny was happy here.'

Goddard rose. 'And Frank Wilson?'

'Frankie Flynn wasn't unhappy. But his friends told me that when Ryan was still alive, he was different. More social. I mean,

170

Frankie was never going to win Mr Congeniality, but he apparently used to be freer.' Sam's eyes stung at the thought of Frankie bleeding out on his own living room floor. 'I hope he's free now.'

'I like to think so,' Goddard said gently. 'What was your relationship with him?'

'He was a friend. Had the same name as my grandfather who passed when I was in grad school. In a place like this, but not nearly as swanky. Still nice, though. I used to play for my grandfather and it made him happy. At peace.'

'Is that why you volunteer here?'

'Yes. I started out doing it for him, then ended up falling for all these old geezers. I've had to say goodbye to many of them over the past four years, but Frankie and Benny were special.'

'Tell me how they were related again?'

'Benny's wife Martha and Frankie's husband Ryan were siblings. They were family. And they drew Georgia and Eloise into that family.'

'Georgia Shearer, right? She's the retired paralegal. I read Mc-Kittrick's report,' he added when Sam raised his eyebrows in question. 'She was the only one here who knew that Frank was an ex-cop.'

'Crawford also knew. Georgia told me that as she was falling asleep this afternoon, after she realized it had been her knife she saw in Frankie's chest.'

'I did read that Crawford knew, too.' Goddard frowned. 'But McKittrick's latest report said that Miss Shearer was attended by a nurse. Roxanne Beaton.'

'She was, but Georgia asked me to sit with her instead. She'd just learned that SDPD suspected the staff and was nervous.'

'So Crawford knew Flynn was a cop?'

'Yep. Georgia didn't know how Crawford had found out, but she said that Frankie didn't like him.'

'Frank was one hell of a cop, according to all the articles I read. Smart and observant.'

Goddard had to be a freaking speed reader, Sam thought sourly. 'Georgia is also smart and observant. If she's awake now, we should ask her about the coins.'

'Then let's go.' Goddard started for the door. 'Did you see the photos that Mr Dreyfus's granddaughter took of his collection? It was amazing. A few of those coins . . . they must have been priceless to the family. My grandfather did some work in returning old art-work to owners that lost it during the war and he said it was one of the most rewarding things he'd ever done.'

'Your grandfather was a cop?'

'Fourth-generation cop here,' Goddard said, pointing at himself. 'My brother's a cop in Louisiana.'

'That's where you're from?'

'Yep. My blood runs blue. Rest assured, Dr Reeves, my team and I will do our very best to get your friend's collection back to his family.'

Sam was absurdly touched. 'Thank you.'

'So,' Goddard said with a casualness that put Sam on alert. 'What's the deal with you and McKittrick?'

'No deal,' Sam said, trying to smile as he opened the door from Benny's apartment into the outer corridor.

Goddard laughed. 'If I believed you, I'd be asking you how I could get her to go out with me. She's got a reputation.'

'What kind of reputation?' Sam suddenly felt like shoving God-dard against the wall and shaking him. Which was absurd.

'They call her "Detective No,"' Goddard said, chuckling. 'The look on your face, Doc. I'll keep my hands to myself. Promise.'

Sam's scowl intensified. In spite of his best intentions, he might actually like this man. 'She's free to do what she wishes.'

'If you say so.' Goddard pointed to the door directly across from them. 'Georgia Shearer.'

'Yes.' Sam gestured to the door on their left, at the tail end of the corridor. 'That was Frankie's apartment. He lived between them.' He knocked on Georgia's door lightly. 'Georgia,' he called. 'You awake?'

'Coming.'

The door swung open and Sam had to swallow a gasp. In just a few hours, Georgia had appeared to age years. Her shoulders were hunched, her face weary, her eyes full of . . . nothing.

Fear took hold of Sam's heart. 'Georgia?'

She waved them in. 'I'm okay, Sam. Just tired. Very tired.' She left them to close the door, sinking into her easy chair and closing her eyes. 'Who have you brought to see me?'

'My name is Detective Goddard, ma'am. I'm with the robbery division. I'm investigating the theft of Mr Dreyfus's coin collection.'

Georgia's lips trembled before she harshly pursed them. 'I hate those coins,' she hissed. 'I wish they'd never existed.'

'I can see your point, ma'am,' Goddard said, his tone respectful.

Georgia's tone was bitter. 'I don't care about the coins. Just . . . go away. Please.' She turned her face away, her eyes still closed, but a tear trickled down her cheek.

Goddard gave Sam an it's-your-turn look.

Sam pulled an ottoman close to where Georgia sat and took her hand. 'Oh, Georgia. I'm sorry. I should have explained better before we leapt into this. Goddard is working with McKittrick and Robinson. They believe the person who stole the coins probably killed Frankie. So we're here to find out who knew the coins were in Benny's apartment.'

Georgia's eyes flew open, snapping with fury. 'You think one of *us* did this? One of Benny's *friends*?'

Sam held on to her hand when she tried to yank it away. 'No. Absolutely not. Listen to me. *Please.* Think about this. If any of the residents or staff found out about the coins and . . . well, they're shiny and pretty, y'know? If it was a resident, maybe a relative came to see them. One who's not so nice. We know a few of those, don't we?'

She nodded cautiously and had stopped trying to yank her hand away. 'Yeah. Get to the point, Sam. I'm not going to live forever.'

Sam winced. 'Georgia. Please.'

Her expression softened. 'I'm sorry, Sam. That was uncalled for. I'm just so angry. But I shouldn't take it out on you. Never on you.'

Sam brought her hand to his lips and kissed it softly. 'You are one of my favorite people in the world, Georgia Shearer. I don't want to think of this world without you in it. So maybe save the biting sarcasm for next week?'

Her laugh was watery. 'Fine, fine. You want to know who knew about the coins? It's a short list, as far as I know. Even when he started to slip, Benny had a deep, instinctive drive to keep them hidden.'

'You knew,' Sam said.

Georgia flicked her free hand impatiently. 'Of course I did. So did Frankie. We've known for years. We were appalled that Benny's family let him keep them here, but . . . Carla was putty in Benny's hands. That woman loved her father so much. Always made Frankie a little sad to see them together.'

Because Frankie had a son who hated him. Sam had almost forgotten about Gerald Wilson. Or Gerald White, as Frankie's son had changed his name.

Georgia shrugged. 'Anyway, Carla always said they were Benny's coins, that he couldn't enjoy them if they were locked in a vault somewhere.'

Goddard sat on the sofa. 'So they bought him a vault here.'

Georgia nodded. 'They sure did. I was never poor, boys. I ended up selling my house to afford this place seven years ago – when I hit seventy-five. I'd bought it when the market was low and sold it for a rather indecent profit, more than enough to pay my entrance fee to Shady Oaks. I was nervous about relocating, but I met Frankie and Ryan and Benny and Martha on my first day here. They were my first friends and we stuck together till the end. Till *they* ended, anyway.'

Sam squeezed her hand and she smiled sadly.

'They had a wealth I could never imagine,' she went on. 'I mean, I had a reasonable amount of stuff and took vacations to faraway places, but I was never frivolous and I saved for those vacations. They did whatever they wanted. And then they started taking me along when they went on vacations. Let me tell you, the difference in level of accommodations was mind-blowing.'

Sam frowned. 'I thought Ryan and Frankie weren't rich until the nineties when Ryan sold his software program.'

'They weren't, but Benny's family has been wealthy since the sixties. Benny and Martha were generous to a fault and the money itself didn't really mean much to them. But Ryan and Frankie never forgot that they'd both been struggling middle-class before Ryan's windfall. Ryan and Frankie gave away so much money to charity. So did Benny and Martha. The money itself was just . . . stuff. I think Benny would have sold it all in a heartbeat. Everything except those coins. He'd sit and look at them. Sometimes he'd put gloves on and touch them, hold them to the light. And he wasn't seeing the coins. He was seeing his father and his grandfather.'

'His family's legacy,' Goddard said quietly. 'Family pride.'

Georgia nodded in approval. 'Quite right, Detective. Toward the end, when Benny's mind started to slip, those coins became a tether, holding him to reality. So we didn't say anything about him keeping a fortune in his apartment. We kept his secret as best we could, Frankie and I. When he was looking at the coins more recently, we'd make sure no one came into the apartment. We'd even shut the drapes, just in case. And then we'd breathe easier when he'd put them back in the safe.'

'Did Eloise know?' Sam asked.

'Yes, but she'd never tell. She helped keep the secret. She might seem flighty, Sam, but that woman is solid as a rock. Real rocks, not the rhinestones on her walker.'

Sam chuckled. 'I know. Miss Eloise is a treasure. So who else knew?'

'Janice, the head nurse. She'd sometimes respond when Benny needed assistance and the other nurses were occupied. She wasn't trying to snoop. At least I don't think so. But once Benny had the coins out and was walking down memory lane when she came in to administer his meds. He was lucid enough in that moment to know she'd seen them and that it wasn't a good thing. He told her they were commemorative coins.'

'Smart. They're usually inexpensive to collect,' Goddard told Sam. 'Some are valuable, but a lot of them are the kind of coins that kids might collect when they're just getting started. If Janice the nosy nurse googled them, she'd find out the average value was less than two hundred bucks a coin.'

'Exactly.' Georgia shrugged. 'I think she believed him. That was a year ago, and I think if she intended to steal them, she'd have done it already.' She hesitated, then sighed. 'I don't want to say this next one, because I think she's as innocent as a lamb. But Devon knew.'

Sam frowned. *No. No way.* But this, along with the fact that Devon's key card was the last one used before Benny's death, wasn't a good sign.

Goddard leaned forward. 'Devon Jones, the nursing assistant?'

'Yes. She helped Benny a lot at the end, bathing him, making sure he got his meds. She was in and out of his apartment all the time. She told me that she'd seen them, said that she knew they were valuable. "Worth at least a thousand dollars, ma'am,"' Georgia said in a shaky falsetto that wasn't a bad impression of the sweet teenager. 'I acted surprised. "That much? Oh my." But I don't think she bought my reaction. She's not stupid. Naive, maybe, but far from stupid.'

'And she's raising a child alone.' Sam felt physically ill at even the notion that sweet Devon could be involved. 'A child who gets sick a lot. The doctor bills from her daughter's last illness were in the tens of thousands of dollars.'

Georgia sighed again. 'Frankie paid her doctor bills.' She rolled her eyes. 'The child thinks that *I* paid them because I took one trip on the bus to see her and her daughter in the hospital, and Frankie wouldn't let me tell her the truth. The old fool,' she said affectionately. 'It was about two months ago that Devon found out about the coins. She and Benny became very close at the end. She'd sit with Benny and listen when he talked about his coins, his father and grandfather smuggling the best of the collection out of Germany. She'd sing to him when he became agitated, and it soothed him. She was good to him.'

'So Benny trusted Devon, but not Janice?' Goddard asked with a slight frown.

'I think Devon reminded him of one of his granddaughters.'

Goddard was still frowning. 'Do you think Devon knew how valuable the coins were?'

Georgia shrugged. 'Probably. It would have taken just a google to find the truth. But I can't believe she'd steal them. And she would never have killed Frankie. Never.'

176

'I agree,' Sam said firmly, wanting to wince at the overly positive sound of his own voice, as if he were trying to convince himself. Which was what he was certain Goddard was thinking as the man turned his frown on Sam. But there was no way Devon could be involved. No way. But . . . *Please, don't let her be involved.* 'Who else knew, Georgia?'

'I don't know. The other nurses spent time with him, but unless they saw him with the collection, there's no way they could have known.'

'Not true, ma'am,' Goddard said. 'There was a magazine article written about the coins. Mr Dreyfus's name is used, along with his father's name.'

Sam stared at him. 'Then anyone could have stolen them.'

Goddard shook his head. 'No, not just anyone. The article says they're kept in the vault at the family's bank. The average person would never dream that the collection resided in a retirement home. All it would take would be one staff member to ask Mr Dreyfus. And if he was having a bad day, was mentally weak and tired? He could have spilled it.'

'Then why are you asking me, young man?' Georgia snapped.

'He's *forty-one*, Georgia, not a *young man*,' Sam snapped back, then bit his own tongue. The man looked ten years younger than Sam. *When he's five years older than me. Probably Kit's type, too.*

Stop it.

'Sam?' Georgia asked, staring at him. 'Are you okay?'

'Sorry,' Sam said, shamefaced. 'I was out of line.'

Goddard was grinning again. He leaned toward Georgia conspiratorially. 'He's still mad that I said that I'd be interested in asking Kit McKittrick to go out with me.' He shot Sam an amused look. 'I said I'd keep my distance, Doc. I'm no liar or usurper.'

Georgia met Sam's gaze. 'She likes *you*, Sam.'

'Stop,' he said softly. Because it hurt to know it might never be true. 'Please?'

'I'm sorry.' Her regret was genuine. She turned to Goddard. 'So, Detective Babyface, where do we begin?' She straightened in the chair. 'I'm game to investigate.'

Goddard's cheeks dimpled, damn him. 'You're going to sit in your easy chair and let me do the investigating. If you hear anything, though, please pass it on. It's been a pleasure to meet you, Miss Shearer. And someday, I'd love to hear about *Leggett v. California.*'

Georgia's jaw dropped. 'What? How did you – ?'

'I do my homework, ma'am. Well, I've got a kick-ass clerk who does my homework. She's working to get her PI's license, so I throw her difficult searches every now and then.'

'What is *Leggett v. California*?' Sam asked, torn between curiosity and annoyance that Goddard knew something about Georgia that Sam didn't.

Georgia blushed, and Sam stared because he'd never seen her blush before.

'A case I worked on years ago,' she said.

'Forty-five years ago, to be precise,' Goddard said. 'She helped her boss at a very prestigious law firm get an innocent verdict for a very famous client who'd been accused of murder – John Leggett, who was an attorney himself. Georgia's boss was urging Leggett to take a plea, but Georgia put all the puzzle pieces together, doing a little investigating of her own. Leggett hired her after he was acquitted. Which is, I suspect, how you were able to buy your house when the market was good?'

Georgia ducked her head, looking more girlish than Sam had ever seen her. 'It was.'

'Aaaand,' Goddard went on teasingly, 'my clerk read a rumor that you and Mr Leggett were . . .' He wiggled his fingers and Georgia giggled.

The woman *giggled*.

Sam's lips curved at the sound. He wanted to be jealous of Goddard for making Georgia so happy, but he was too grateful. 'Georgia! You never told me.'

'Long time ago, Sam.'

'Well, we *will* talk about this. At length. Once I'm done helping Detective Babyface, I'm going home to pack a bag and get Siggy. Siggy and I are going to spend the night on your sofa.'

Georgia's eyes widened. 'Why?'

'Because I won't let anyone hurt you. McKittrick will find out who killed Frankie and we can all sleep again.'

Georgia's eyes filled. 'Thank you, Sammy. You're a good boy. Even though you're no babyface.'

Goddard laughed out loud and Sam couldn't blame him. Sam kissed Georgia's cheek. 'I'll see you later. You take another nap, okay? Call if you need me.'

'I think I'm rested up.' She did look better, rejuvenated compared to how she'd looked when she'd opened her door. 'I'm going to work on Frankie's eulogy.'

Sam waited until he and Goddard were out in the corridor before saying anything more. 'I want to send your clerk flowers. I've never heard Georgia Shearer giggle.'

Goddard chuckled. 'My clerk's allergic. Send her wine. I'm going to cry when she gets her PI license and leaves the department. So what's next, Doc?'

Sam sobered. 'I think we need to talk to Devon Jones. She's a sweet girl, only eighteen, and she works hard. She loves the old people. She comes off as doe-eyed and almost childlike, but she's got a sharp mind. Still, I can't see her stealing.'

'I hope you're right, then, Doc. Especially since she was the last person to see Benny Dreyfus alive.'

'Someone with her key card,' Sam insisted, gritting his teeth.

'I truly hope so,' Goddard said sincerely. 'Where can we find her?'

'She'll be in the nursing ward this time of day.' Sam led the way to the elevator. 'What about this article? Could someone have read it and targeted Benny? Even if they thought it was in a bank vault, the thief could have asked around and found out that it was here. It could have even been someone with the vault installation company. Why install a twenty-thousand-dollar vault if you don't have anything worth protecting?'

Goddard grinned. 'Look at you, Doc. Asking questions like a cop. I just sent my clerk a text asking her to check that out while you were talking with Georgia. But it's more likely that a staff member is involved. I know McKittrick has been running background checks on them. One of the staff might become abruptly richer, but by then the collection will be gone and the family's legacy with it. Let's find out who it is before that happens.'

'I really do think I like you,' Sam said, disgruntled, pressing the elevator button for the first floor.

Goddard snorted. 'I get that a lot. It's a terrible burden to carry, Sam.'

Sam laughed as the elevator doors slid open.

La Jolla, San Diego, California
Tuesday, 8 November, 4.05 P.M.

'You can park here,' Kit said, pointing to an empty space next to the university's computer science building.

Connor pulled the sedan into the space. 'I thought these spaces were reserved.'

'Only until four. Then they're up for grabs.' Kit got out of the car, looking around at the familiar landscape. 'I went here for my last two years.'

'I didn't know that,' Connor said. 'Where'd you go the first two years?'

'Did them online while I was in the Coast Guard. I attended the night school here, so I know about which parking places are free after hours.'

'Did you live at home?'

She smiled. 'I did. I'd missed Mom and Pop while I was a Coastie, so I came back until I finished school. Mom made sure I ate and Pop helped me with my math homework. And they needed help with the farm, so it all worked out. We can go in through here.' She led Connor to one of the entrances. 'For me, college was mainly a means to an end.'

'I enjoyed college, but I don't miss it,' Connor said. 'It was one big party, and I got a little tired of that by the time I was a senior.'

He'd gone to a fancy East Coast school and rarely spoke of it. Kit had the impression that something had happened to him there that had soured him on the university experience, but she figured he'd share when he was ready.

They found Archie Adler's office on the fourth floor as his mother had indicated, but Archie wasn't there. Which Kit had expected. Still, she was disappointed.

The sole occupant, a young man who looked to be in his midtwenties, stood when they knocked on the open door. 'Can I help you?'

'We'd like to speak to Archie Adler,' Connor said politely. 'Is he in?'

The man looked around the empty room, his sarcasm evident. 'No.'

Connor smiled, taking out his notebook with an exaggerated motion. 'We're San Diego PD. Detectives Robinson and McKittrick. Homicide division. And you are?'

The man's eyes widened, his gaze flicking to the open door where a sign said *A. Adler and D. Stanza*, listing the office hours for each. 'Um . . . Dominic Stanza.' His sarcasm was miraculously gone. 'How can I help you?'

'We're looking for Mr Adler,' Kit said. 'Have you seen him today?'

'No, Detective.'

Kit smiled in her best unfriendly way. 'Would you know where we can find him?'

'No. We just share space here. We're not . . . friends or anything. We don't share plans.'

He's lying. There was something in his manner that screamed it.

Acting on her gut, she chanced a reply. 'That's not what his mother said. She said you were good friends.'

Stanza swallowed. 'She's . . . out of the loop. We were friends, but not anymore. Not for months. He, um, tried to steal my girlfriend.'

'I see,' Kit said mildly. The man really was lying, but she didn't know why. It could be that he was simply covering for a friend, or he could know something. Like where Archie really was. 'That's unfortunate for us, because we'd really like to find him.' She gave Stanza her business card. 'Please contact us if you see him. His life may be in danger.'

181

Stanza paled. 'What? In danger? What kind of danger? From who?'

Connor gave the man one of his cards. 'Here's mine. We'd appreciate whatever help you can provide. And if you do see him, tell him that we want to keep him safe. Despite your differences over a woman, this isn't a game. People have died.'

Stanza's hands trembled as he clutched the business cards. 'If I see him, I'll tell him. But I won't see him. We don't hang out together.'

Kit pointed to the sign on the door with their office hours. 'He's supposed to be here now. When was the last time he was here for his normal office hours?'

Stanza closed his eyes for several seconds. When he opened them, he was visibly calmer. 'I saw him on Friday, here in the office. I think he called in sick yesterday. I hope you find him. He might be a girlfriend stealer, but I don't want him to get hurt.'

Not wanting him to get hurt might have been the only true statement to come out of the man's mouth. 'Thank you,' Kit said. 'We'll probably reach out again, so please keep your eyes and ears open.'

She backed out of the office and had started for the elevator when Connor touched her elbow. 'This way,' he said, pocketing his phone.

'Where are we going?' she whispered as she followed Connor down the hallway. A few of the office doors were open, but most were closed, a few sporting pictures of turkeys and other Thanksgiving decorations.

Kit had forgotten that Thanksgiving was only a few weeks away.

'To find Professor Chen. Adler is the TA for his class,' Connor said. 'How did you know to use Archie's mother to get to Stanza?'

'He was lying. I can usually tell. Growing up in foster care makes lie detection an important survival skill.'

Connor's jaw tightened. 'I'm sorry you had to learn that skill.'

She smiled at him. 'That was a long time ago. The McKittricks took me in and then I was safe.' Her sister hadn't been safe, but that had not been Harlan and Betsy's fault. Kit had always known that, even as she'd grieved Wren. 'But thank you all the same.'

Connor stopped, the nameplate on the closed door reading the professor's name. 'Here we are. I googled Adler's name plus "TA" and Chen's name came up. He teaches cryptography.'

Kit was intrigued. 'Including encryption systems?'

'Yep. It was one of those "rate your teacher" sites. For the record, the students really like Chen but think Adler is a pompous, stuck-up ass who acts like he's better than everyone.'

'Huh. Good to know.' Kit knocked on the door. 'He's probably gone for the day.'

'Not yet,' a mild voice said from behind them. They turned to find an older Asian man watching them carefully. 'I'm Professor Chen. It's good to know my students like me. You two, however, are not my students.'

'No, sir,' Connor said, showing his badge. 'Detectives Robinson and McKittrick. We're with—'

'Homicide,' Chen interrupted. 'I read the papers, Detectives. I remember the case you closed six months ago. That was good work.' He unlocked his office door and gestured them inside and into the two chairs in front of his desk. He took his own chair and folded his hands on his desk. 'How can I help you?'

'We're looking for Archie Adler,' Connor said. 'We understand he's your TA?'

'He is. For now.'

Kit watched the professor's face carefully. She saw truth and regret. 'Why for now? Is Archie graduating?'

'No. He was doing very well, but this year his work has slowed. I think he has outside distractions. Why are you looking for him? Has he done something wrong?'

Professor Chen didn't appear surprised at the notion.

'We need his help accessing the server at the facility where he works,' Kit said, choosing her words.

Chen tilted his head. 'You didn't answer my question, Detective. Has Archie done something wrong?'

'We don't know,' Kit answered honestly. 'We can't find him to ask. But there have been two deaths at his place of employment and we need information that we believe resides on the server. The encryption he's set up is pretty rigorous and we can't break through.'

'I see. Well, I am Archie's advisor and he's in my graduate encryption class. He's in danger of failing this semester.'

'Bad student?' Connor asked.

'No, on the contrary. Archie is one of the brightest students I've ever had the privilege to teach. His skills will surpass mine one day. But he doesn't come to class, and today he missed an important test. It counts as sixty percent of his grade. He's missed his office hours more and more often of late and his students are very unhappy. If he doesn't turn things around, I'll have no choice but to find another TA. I haven't seen him since Friday of last week.'

The activity on this case had started in the wee hours of Saturday with the theft of the coins. Crawford had been killed shortly thereafter. Kit hoped they wouldn't find Archie's body in a cheap motel somewhere, the victim of another 'suicide.'

'That's too bad,' Kit said. 'We really need his help, for one. But, even more importantly, he could be in danger. We need to find him.'

'I have his address.' He consulted his computer, then jotted the address on his notepad and slid it across the desk.

'We've been there,' Kit said. 'He isn't answering his door.'

Connor took the page from the notepad and put it in his pocket. 'Professor, did you teach him about encryption?'

'I did, yes. Why?'

'If our IT guys can't get through the encryption and we can't find Adler, would you be able to provide assistance?'

The professor shrugged. 'I might. Like I said, Archie is a very good pupil. If he set it up, even I might not be able to get through. But I'd be happy to try. I do hope you find him, though. He hasn't been reliable this year, but it hasn't always been so.'

'When did he begin to decline?' Connor asked.

Chen paused, his expression contemplative. 'Two years ago,' he finally replied. 'It was little things at first – leaving early or taking a long weekend when he wasn't scheduled for one. He always had an excuse. Most of the time it was that his mother was ill, but I called her once, looking for Archie, and told her that I hoped she was feeling better. She seemed startled to hear this and assured me that she'd been fine. I asked Archie about this and he was embarrassed. He said he'd only said that because it was a girlfriend situation and he didn't want everyone knowing about his business.'

Two years ago. Georgia Shearer had overheard Archie's phone conversation about getting money for a car around that time. A glance at Connor said that he'd come to the same conclusion.

'His whole personality began to change,' Chen went on. 'I've suspected drug abuse, but I've never seen him high. I know that his students are unhappy with him, but again, it wasn't always so. My students used to love Archie's class. Up until last year, his ratings were stellar. Now . . . I don't know of any student who'd sign up for his section again.'

'What about Dominic Stanza?' Kit asked. 'We got the impression that they'd had a falling-out?'

Chen sighed. 'Dominic covers for him. "He's been sick, Professor. His mom's sick, Professor. His car broke down again and he's stranded." So many excuses. Dominic is always here, and sometimes he covers Archie's classes, too. Maybe Dominic got tired of being walked on by Archie. Between us, I'm cutting Archie loose at the end of the semester. His grades alone are cause, but . . .' He sighed again. 'I hate when these things happen. When brilliant young minds become distracted.'

'Thank you for your candor, Professor,' Connor said. 'If we need to reach you about the encryption, what number should we call?'

Chen wrote on the back of one of his business cards and handed it to them. 'My cell phone number is on the back. Call me if you need me. Or if you find Archie. I am worried about him. I've known him for a long time. I hope he's okay.'

Kit took the card. 'We do, too, sir. Thank you for your time. We'll be in touch.'

They took their leave, returning the way they'd come and noticing as they passed Dominic Stanza's office that his door was closed and locked, even though the sign on his door said he had at least another hour of office time left.

'Stanza split,' Connor murmured. 'What do you want to bet that he's off telling Archie that we're looking for him?'

'Sucker bet,' Kit murmured back. 'Let's check Archie's apartment again.'

Eleven

Shady Oaks Retirement Village
Scripps Ranch, San Diego, California
Tuesday, 8 November, 4.10 P.M.

Sam's steps felt heavier the closer he came to the nursing ward where nursing assistant Devon Jones was on duty. 'I cannot believe she's involved in this,' he murmured.

'For your sake, I hope not,' Detective Goddard said gently. 'Maybe you should sit this one out, Doc. You're pretty close to this nursing assistant.'

Sam shook his head. 'I deal with criminals and liars nearly every day as a police profiler and I also counsel various offenders as a condition of their parole or probation, Detective. I'm pretty good at reading people, and Devon is not a criminal. She is a young, single mother, though, making it mostly on her own.'

'Vulnerable for someone greedy?' Goddard asked.

'Maybe.' Sam sighed. 'I didn't know that Frankie had paid for her daughter's doctor bills. I offered to help and she always said she had it taken care of.'

'Did everyone here know that Mr Flynn was wealthy?'

'If they'd been around more than five minutes,' Sam said wryly. 'This place is gossip central. It's one of the few vices most of the residents have left.'

'Where should we question the girl?'

Sam winced. 'Let's not *question* her, okay? Let's *interview* her instead.'

'Okay, fine.' To his credit, Goddard didn't sound impatient. 'Miss Shearer said that Devon was smart.'

'She is. She got pregnant when she was a junior in high school. The father ran away and sent a postcard from New York. So she had the baby, put in the work to graduate a year early, then took the CNA exam when she was seventeen. She's been here for a year and she's only eighteen.'

'Some forty-year-olds I know aren't that responsible.'

'I know.' They came to the nurses' desk in the nursing ward and Sam braced himself. Even if Devon was innocent, that they were asking her questions would quickly get around the facility. Tongues would wag and Sam regretted that the residents and staff would be openly speculating about Devon's involvement.

Let her be innocent. Please.

'Hi, Janice,' Sam said. 'We're looking for Devon. Can you page her to the desk?'

Janice's answering smile disappeared, her eyes narrowing. 'Why, Dr Sam?'

'I'm Detective Goddard, robbery division,' the man said before Sam could get any words out. 'We need to ask her some questions. Can you please call her?'

Sam met Janice's gaze. She was a good nurse and he liked her. 'Just to talk,' he said quietly.

Janice's lips pursed as she typed a command on her keyboard. 'I've paged her. She'll be here shortly. What's this about?' She frowned at Goddard. 'Robbery division? What's been stolen?' Then she sucked in a breath. 'Those damn coins. I knew they were trouble from the moment I saw them. Commemorative coins, my ass. They've been stolen?'

Goddard said nothing and Sam followed his lead.

Janice huffed, frustrated. 'Devon didn't steal them. You *know* this, Sam.'

'She had access to his room,' Sam said gently. 'We have to ask everyone who had access.'

Janice's chin lifted. 'Then ask me, too. I've tended to Benny for years.'

Sam smiled, because Janice was like a mama bear. The nurses and nursing assistants were her cubs. 'I know you have. So you didn't believe that they were commemorative coins?'

'I did at first, but then Devon told me otherwise. She'd looked up the coins he showed her and was worried that something so valuable might become a problem for Mr Benny. I spoke to the Dreyfus family about it, but they were stubborn. Said it was better for Benny if he had his things about him, and normally that's true. So if you're going to question her, best question me, too.'

'We will,' Goddard said and somehow made it sound like it wasn't a threat. 'Where were you between midnight and eight a.m. Saturday?'

'At Disneyland with my husband and grandchildren. I'm sure the hotel will remember me. I gave CPR to another guest when he keeled over with a heart attack.'

Goddard managed to look impressed, relieved, and disappointed all at once. Sam wasn't sure how the man did it.

'Thank you, Nurse,' Goddard said. 'To your knowledge, did anyone else know about the collection?'

'I informed Miss Evans, but no one else. If anyone else knew, I didn't hear about it. And I hear most things,' she added reluctantly. 'When Devon told me, it was in the privacy of my office, so no one could have overheard. When I told Miss Evans, it was the same. Door was closed, we spoke quietly, and no one could have overheard there, either. Devon is honest, Detective Goddard. She'd specially asked for the meeting with me. I absolutely refuse to believe she's involved. Does she need an attorney, Sam?'

'Not yet. If she does, I'll make sure she gets one.' He knew an excellent defense attorney, after all. His ex was a shark in the courtroom. And a cheater in the bedroom, but that was ancient history. Her infidelity didn't detract from her legal acumen in the least.

'When did Devon tell you about the collection, Nurse Janice?' Goddard asked.

'Two months ago. I informed Miss Evans right away.'

Devon came around the corner at a fast walk, abruptly stopping when she saw them. Fear took over her expression and Sam wanted nothing more than to soothe her. But he couldn't. Not yet.

'Devon,' he said quietly. 'This is Detective Goddard from the robbery division. We need to ask you a few questions.'

Her eyes widened, her fear intensifying. 'Robbery?' she whispered. 'I didn't steal anything.'

'They're just asking questions,' Janice said, giving Sam and Goddard a sharp look.

Devon's swallow was audible. 'Can I take my break now, Janice?'

Janice squeezed Devon's shoulder. 'No, you can take your break when you're finished. The interview with Detective Goddard isn't to come from your dinner break. Whose room were you in? I'll send someone in to cover for you.'

'Mrs Dodson. She's had a bad day.'

'I know,' Janice soothed, just like Sam wished he could. 'Go talk to Dr Reeves and the detective, and if you feel in any way uncomfortable, you call me. I will come and be your advocate. Okay?'

Devon nodded uncertainly. 'Yes, ma'am.' Bracing her shoulders, she turned to Sam. 'Where are we going?'

'Use my office,' Janice said. 'It's private.'

'Thank you,' Goddard said seriously, his previous charm gone.

Poor Devon was shaking when they closed the door to Janice's office. She sat on a chair, twisting her hands together. 'What's happened, Dr Sam?'

But he thought she knew. There was a resignation in her eyes that hurt his heart. 'Mr Benny's coins were stolen.'

She exhaled quietly. 'I didn't do it. I didn't steal anything.'

Sam sat in front of her, gently separating her hands so that she didn't hurt herself. 'Breathe, Devon. We just want to ask you a few questions.'

Tears filled her eyes as she pulled her hands free and turned to Goddard, her expression now resolute. 'I knew about the coins, Detective. I told Nurse Janice because I was afraid that having something that valuable in his apartment would cause problems.'

'How did you know about the coins?' Goddard asked.

'He was . . .' She frowned. 'Holding them when I came in one day.'

'Why did you hesitate?' Goddard asked.

'Because he wasn't really holding them. He was touching them like this.' She lightly brushed her fingers over her arm. 'It was a little creepy the first time I saw him doing it. It was like Gollum in *Lord of the Rings*. I half expected him to call the coins "his precious." But then I realized that he was remembering old times, so I asked him if he wanted to talk about them.'

'Them?' Goddard prodded.

'The people in his family. All the ones who are gone. That's what most of the residents and patients want to talk about. You know, their husband or wife who's already passed on, or their children.' She smiled sadly. 'They remember when their kids were small and are sad that time has passed. Some of the people here are the only ones left in their whole family and they're just . . . waiting. It breaks my heart. So I listen to them, and it seems to help. Makes them happy.'

Goddard cleared his throat. 'When did you first see Mr Dreyfus's collection?'

Devon puffed out her cheeks. 'A few months ago? He told me about his father and grandfather collecting the coins, how they'd smuggled them out of Germany before the war. He told me how his father had held him on his knee when he was a little boy and how he'd made him wear little gloves when he touched the coins. Mr Benny was wearing gloves that day and every day I saw him touching the coins. He had trouble remembering to take his medicine every day and sometimes thought he was a professor again, but he never forgot to wear the gloves.'

'Did you ever see him open the safe?' Goddard asked.

'No, sir. But he told me it needed a fingerprint and a code.'

Goddard nodded. 'Did he write the code down?'

'If he did, I never saw it. I don't think he did because when he'd forget it, he'd call his daughter or granddaughter. Carla or Vanessa.'

'Did his family come when he called?' Goddard asked.

Devon nodded. 'Always. Sometimes it would take a while and he'd get agitated, but I was able to calm him down.'

'How?' Sam asked, giving her an encouraging smile, ignoring the pointed look from Goddard. Because Devon did not do this thing. Sam was positive.

'His daughter would sing to him when he was agitated, so I asked her to teach me the song. "Mi Shebeirach." It's a Jewish song of healing. It's really beautiful. I'd sing it to Mr Benny when he got upset and it did help calm him. At least until someone in his family could arrive, then I'd leave.'

'And you never saw him open the safe?' Goddard asked, skepticism in his voice.

Devon held herself straighter. 'No, sir. I did not.'

Go you, Sam thought, proud of her.

'Devon, where were you between midnight and eight a.m. Saturday?' Goddard asked.

'Here. I was on duty. I worked a double that day.' She looked Goddard in the eye. 'I work for my money, Detective. I don't steal it. I was in the nursing ward all night. When I took my break, it was in the break room here. I signed out at seven thirty Saturday morning and was home by eight. My mom can vouch for my arrival time, as can two of her friends. Mom was watching my daughter that night and had a couple of her friends over for breakfast. I'm happy to give you their names. Dr Sam, should I offer to let him search my house?'

'Not yet. If it comes to that, we'll talk first, okay?'

Goddard made a noise that sounded like a soft growl. 'Dr Reeves.'

'She has an alibi. If she left the nursing ward, the cameras would have caught her going to her car and those cameras were functioning. How tall are you, Devon?'

Because the person leaving Shady Oaks with the box containing Benny's coins had been around five-ten.

'Five-two. Why?'

Sam gave Goddard a pointed look and the detective sighed. 'Fine,' he grumbled. 'She's too short to have been on the video. Miss Jones, where were you this morning between three and six a.m.?'

Devon's eyes flashed fire. 'I did *not* hurt Mr Benny.'

'I know,' Sam said softly. 'But McKittrick and Robinson will ask, so you might as well answer it now.'

She swallowed hard. 'I was in the emergency room with my daughter. Mila was running a fever. I'd just gotten her home and into bed when I had to come in here to start my shift. I work another double tonight.'

'Devon,' Sam said, concerned. 'You haven't slept all night and you're going to work a double?'

She shrugged. 'It's my life, Dr Sam. Mila still gets sick a lot. Don't tell Miss Georgia. I don't want her to feel like she has to pay my doctor bills again.' She looked Goddard straight in the eye. 'I have an unshakable alibi, Detective. The nurses in the ER will swear that I was there, and there were cameras everywhere around the hospital.'

'Thank you, Miss Jones,' Goddard said. 'I'm sorry I had to ask, and I hope your daughter gets better soon.'

'Thank you.' Devon was visibly trembling. 'I *need* this job.'

Goddard appeared subdued, but also respectful. 'I'll make sure everyone knows that you're not a suspect, if that will help.'

She nodded once. 'It would. Thank you.'

'You're welcome.' Goddard smiled at her, a much gentler smile than he'd turned on everyone else. 'Before you go, who else knew about the coins?'

'His friends, I suppose – Miss Georgia, Mr Frankie.' She looked uncomfortable. 'And Mr Crawford. He asked me about them. Said he'd read about them in a magazine and asked if I knew about them.'

Goddard leaned in. 'What did you tell him?'

'I told him that I knew of no such thing.' She started to wring her hands again. 'I lied to him. I should have told Janice. I know that I should have, but . . . Mr Crawford made me . . . nervous. He watched me, watched a lot of the nurses and nursing assistants. I avoided him whenever I could.'

Sam breathed through the abrupt surge of anger. 'Did he touch you?'

'No, sir. Most of us know to stay out of his way and not to let him get us alone.'

'When was this?' Goddard asked.

Devon stared at her clenched hands. 'A week ago. I should have said something. Mr Benny's family might have finally taken his collection somewhere safer and Mr Frankie might still be alive.' She looked up, her eyes filled with tears. 'Mr Frankie found out, didn't he? Because he used to be a cop. It's all over the center now. Everyone knows he used to be a homicide lieutenant. He had to have found out about someone planning to steal Mr Benny's coins. I might as well have killed him myself.'

Sam took her hands again. 'Devon, listen to me. I never want to hear you say those words again. I know what you meant, but someone else might not.' He glanced at Goddard and Devon paled.

'I know what she meant, too,' Goddard said wryly. 'But Dr Sam's right, Miss Jones. This was not your fault. Although I do have to ask – why didn't you tell Carla or Vanessa that Crawford had asked about the coins?'

'Because they would have told Miss Evans and it would have come back on me. They could leave, but I still had to work here, and I couldn't cross him.'

'It's all right,' Sam said softly. 'Crawford was an authority figure, and it sounds like you had every reason to fear him.'

Devon looked up at them, misery in her eyes. 'One of the nursing assistants reported him to Miss Evans for touching her – you know – inappropriately. Evans said she'd take care of it, but then the girl got let go. I can't lose this job. It's feeding my daughter. Please don't tell Miss Evans that I said anything about Mr Crawford. *Please.*'

Sam found himself glad that Crawford was dead. The man was a grade-A asshole. Sounded like Miss Evans wasn't any better. Sam had thought her cold, but not complicit.

Maybe I don't read people as well as I thought. 'I'll make a note of our conversation, Devon. If Miss Evans tries to retaliate, I'll speak on your behalf.'

'I'll also record this in my report,' Goddard said. 'But back to Crawford's question about the coins. Which day last week and what time? Details could be important.'

She took out her phone, scrolled for a moment, then said,

'Wednesday. My mom took Mila to the pediatrician because I had to work. I remember being so scared, because if I lost my job . . .' She shuddered, then sighed. 'I'm sorry. That's not what you asked. Mr Crawford talked to me in the afternoon, after my break. So . . . three thirty or so.' Her shoulders drooped, her lips tilting in a sad smile. 'I ran outside to . . . I don't know. Get away. Try to calm down. Try to figure out what I could do – if anything. And I ran into Mr Frankie. He was coming back inside from the parking lot. He stopped and asked me if I was okay. If Mila was sick again, but I was so upset that I couldn't answer him. He . . . He put his hands on my shoulders and told me to breathe. He breathed with me until the world stopped spinning around. Then he asked if he could call anyone for me.'

'Did you tell him about what Crawford said?' Sam asked gently.

'No. I should have.' Her eyes filled with tears. 'If I'd told him, maybe he would still be alive.'

Goddard's frown had returned. 'Did Mr Frankie normally leave during the week?'

'Sometimes, but usually he left on the weekends.' Her gaze sharpened. 'Why? Is this related to his murder?'

'We don't know,' Sam said honestly. *But maybe.* He wondered if Kit and Connor had finally gained access to the server with all the entry gate records on it. They'd be able to see when Frankie had left the property and when he'd returned. He made a mental note to share this information with them in the event the IT guy hadn't been able to break through the server's encryption. Wherever Frankie had gone could be a critical clue.

'Thank you for your help, Miss Jones.' Goddard gave Devon one of his cards. 'If you remember anything else that might help, please call me.'

She took the card hesitantly. 'So you believe me?'

'I can't say,' Goddard said. 'It doesn't mean that I don't,' he stressed when Devon's eyes widened in resurrected fear. 'It just means that I can't comment right now. Do you plan to go out of town anytime soon?'

'I have a two-year-old who catches every germ at daycare and I don't have an extra penny. I'd be deep in debt if it weren't for Miss

Georgia helping me with the doctor bills. I'm disclosing that so you don't think I stole from her, too.' Her shoulders sagged. 'But to answer your question, no, I'm not going anywhere. I can't.'

'Well, if you do,' Goddard said quietly, 'just let me know, okay?'

She nodded, looking so fragile that Sam needed to give her a hug. He put his arm around her shoulder for a quick one before releasing her. 'You know, I think you should ask Miss Georgia about those bills. She told you that it wasn't her.'

'Well, yeah, but who else would –' She covered her mouth, her eyes filling with new tears. 'Mr Frankie. Oh. He did that for me? Why?'

Sam patted her shoulder. 'He liked you a lot, and he did not suffer fools. I think that he knew you'd go on to do great things and hated to see you stressed out. I didn't know about the bills, but Georgia mentioned it. I think it's okay now for you to know who really helped. So just keep calm about all this coin business, and if you need to talk to someone, you have my number, right?'

She wiped at her eyes. 'Thank you, Dr Sam. Thank you so much.'

'Go take your break,' Sam said kindly.

She left Sam and Goddard in Nurse Janice's office, pulling the door closed behind her.

'I don't think she did it,' Goddard said bluntly. 'But we can't eliminate her yet.'

'I know,' Sam said, because he knew what Goddard's priorities were. But Sam had priorities, too, and looking after Devon Jones was one of them. 'Crawford knew about the coins. That was definitely interesting. I need to look up that article.'

Goddard took out his phone, tapped at his screen. 'Just sent you the link. I'm going back to the precinct – I want to see that video of the thief leaving the facility with the box of coins. I also want to go over those key-card logs. I want to know who entered where and when from Friday at sunset until now.'

'*I* want to know where Frankie went on Wednesday.'

Goddard nodded. 'So do I. It could have been an innocent shopping trip, but I'm not counting on that. Would any of the residents know where he went and why?'

'Maybe. Frankie kept to himself, so it's possible he told no one. I'm coming back tonight to stay with Georgia. If she doesn't know, I can ask around then.'

'Thank you. Be careful, Doc. There could still be a killer walking around this place.'

A chill ran down Sam's back. 'I know.'

University City, San Diego, California
Tuesday, 8 November, 7.30 P.M.

'We should have grabbed Adler yesterday morning,' Connor grumbled, standing in front of the door to Archie Adler's third-floor walk-up apartment.

'Yep. I didn't see his car out front, so I don't think we'll be any luckier this time.' Kit knocked on Adler's front door for the second time that day. They'd come by once before, straight from the meeting in Navarro's office, but had gotten no answer. 'Mr Adler, this is San Diego PD,' she called. 'We need to talk to you.'

'He's not there,' a voice said.

Kit and Connor turned to find a young man coming out of the apartment across the hall. He carried a motorcycle helmet in one hand and a very full backpack in the other. His red hair was unruly and he had a smattering of freckles across his nose, which made him look a lot younger than he probably was.

'Do you know where Archie is?' Kit asked.

'No, I sure don't. I don't think he'll be back, though. I saw him loading up his car. Looked like he was moving out.'

'Shit,' Connor muttered. 'When was this?'

'Around four o'clock, maybe four thirty,' the young man said.

He could be in Mexico by now, Kit thought sourly. *Dammit.*

'I'll put out a BOLO on his car,' Connor said. He turned to the neighbor. 'Does he drive a Kia Sorento? White 2015?'

It was the car registered to him and had given them pause. If he was dipping into the till at Shady Oaks, he should have been able to drive a better car than that. But now that he'd run? Yeah, he was involved somehow.

'He does,' the man said warily. 'Why? What's he done?'

'We need a warrant for Archie's apartment,' Kit murmured to Connor.

'I'll get one started.' Connor headed back down the stairs for the car, while Kit focused on the young man.

'I'm Detective McKittrick, San Diego PD. That was my partner, Detective Robinson. Can I get your name?'

'Roger McNichol. What's going on? Has something happened to Archie?'

Kit hoped not. They needed Archie Adler alive. 'We just need to talk to him. What can you tell me about Mr Adler?'

Roger looked apprehensive. 'He's a grad student. Works a lot.'

She looked around. The apartment building was clean. Not lavish, but she'd seen far, far worse. 'Does he have visitors?' She was hoping to establish that he'd met with either Crawford or Evans or both.

'Not really. Only his mom, and she doesn't come all the way up here often. He usually goes downstairs and sits in her car to talk to her.'

That was a little unusual. Maybe Adler had been doing something in his apartment that he didn't want his adoring mother to see.

Kit remembered the Mercedes they'd seen in Mrs Adler's driveway. 'She has a nice car.'

'Yeah. Archie's a good guy. He bought his mom that car, y'know. His Kia was on its last leg, but he fixed it somehow and used the money he'd been saving for a car to buy her a new one.'

Isn't that nice. A probable criminal with a soft spot for his mother.

She sent Connor a text. *Request a unit be sent to Adler's mom's house. He might go there.*

Will do was Connor's reply.

Kit gave Roger her card. 'Please call me if you see him. He could be in danger.' Which was true. Assuming Adler was involved, he could end up like Crawford.

Roger paled as he took the business card. 'I will. Am I in danger, too?'

'Were you working with him?' Kit asked bluntly.

Roger's eyes went wide. 'No. I live with my mom and go to school. I work at the In-N-Out. I haven't done anything wrong.'

'Good. If you see anything out of the ordinary, call me. You'll most likely be fine, but if Archie was involved in what we're investigating, he's associating with some dangerous people.' She turned to go but turned back when Roger made a strangled sound. He was staring at her business card, having gone even paler, making his freckles stand out in stark relief. 'Roger? Are you okay?'

'You're *Homicide*. Archie's involved in *murder*?' His tone hitched higher and higher with every word. 'He might have brought a *killer* into our building?'

'That's what we're trying to find out. Do you know anything else that might help us?'

'Um . . . he's got a boat. I think.'

Wonderful. He could be anywhere. 'What kind of boat, Roger?'

'I don't know, but I heard him on the phone once. He was coming up the stairs and I was going down. He'd caught this huge fish.' Roger spread his hands wide, easily three feet apart. 'I stopped to look at the fish because it was really gorgeous. He told whoever he was talking to that he'd caught a lingcod. He was laughing, really excited. Said something like, "And you said I shouldn't buy a boat. It'll pay for itself if I keep catching fish like this one." The other person must have disagreed because Archie laughed and said that, fine, it might take a couple hundred lingcod, but it'd pay for itself eventually.'

'Did you ever see the boat or a photo of it?'

Roger shook his head. 'But I think it's in his mother's name, because he said that he'd been paying the taxes on it and his mother was none the wiser.'

'Thank you, Roger. You've been a big help.' She got the young man's phone number, then called Navarro as she jogged down the stairs. 'Can you run a deeper check on Archie Adler's mother?' she asked when her boss picked up. 'I think Archie bought a boat in her name, but it didn't come up in our original search.'

'Shit. He could be anywhere by now.'

'He left his apartment around four or four thirty. That gives him at least a three-hour head start. He might have taken the contents of his apartment to his mother's house, but that still gives him plenty of time to get far away. If you can get a make and model on the boat, we can ask the Coast Guard to aid in the search.'

That was one of the duties Kit had had while she served.

'Give me a minute,' Navarro said.

She could hear him typing as she got to the bottom of the stairs and ran to the department sedan. She slid into the passenger seat, put the phone on speaker, and quickly brought Connor up to speed.

'A lingcod that size is worth about three hundred bucks,' Kit said. 'So a couple hundred means he could have paid as much as fifty or sixty grand. Not bad for a college student working a night job.'

'I've got uniforms en route to Mrs Adler's house,' Connor said. 'They're going to sit outside until we get there.'

'I've got my clerk working on the warrant.' Navarro made a pleased sound. 'Found the boat under his mother's name. He's got a Grady White Marlin. You know that boat, Kit?'

Kit whistled. 'My sister looked at those. They go for eighty to a hundred grand, used. Importantly, they can go way out offshore. He could definitely be in Mexico by now. Dammit.'

'I'll put in the call for assistance,' Navarro said. 'You two head back to the mother's house. I'll have your warrant by then.'

Connor brought up the map to Mrs Adler's house on his phone. 'We also need his phone records. It may have been the same friend who Georgia Shearer overheard him talking to. Sounds like that friend is privy to Archie's secrets. Okay, we're heading out, boss.'

He put the car in drive, but Kit saw motion from the corner of her eye. It was Roger. 'Hold on a minute, boss. The neighbor is running toward us like he's on fire.' He'd burst out of the building and was now waving them down. Keeping her call to Navarro open and on speaker, she got out just as the young man reached the car, breathing heavily.

'Roger, what's wrong?'

'Nothing.' He panted, then sucked in a deep breath. 'My mom says that he has a visitor sometimes, but it's usually when I'm not home, so I never saw him. Guy's about five-ten, one-fifty. Brown hair, kind of scruffy. That's my mom's description. She said Archie called the guy Dominic.'

Connor got out of the car, and they shared a glance over its roof. *I knew Stanza was lying.*

'The teaching assistant,' Connor said. 'Who said he hadn't seen Archie since Friday and didn't hang out with him anymore.'

'The very same,' Kit said grimly. 'Roger, did your mom remember the last time she saw Dominic with Archie?'

'Sunday night. I'd left for work at seven and Mom always goes to bed by ten, so it was sometime between those times. Do you need to talk to her?'

'We probably will at some point,' Connor said. 'Thanks, Roger.'

'Yes, Roger, we appreciate it,' Kit added. 'Please thank your mom for us. And call 911 if you see anything that alarms you. And then call either one of us.'

'I will. Thank you.' Roger ran back into the building, and Kit and Connor returned to the car. 'So which way do we go, Lieutenant?' she asked Navarro. 'Revisit Mrs Adler or Dominic Stanza the teaching assistant?'

'The TA. I'll pull Marshall and his partner off their case to execute the warrant on Mrs Adler's house and have the mother brought in. Between the two of them, maybe we can get a straight answer as to where Adler was going.'

'I've got Stanza's home address,' Kit said. 'He was heading out of his office at the college when we saw him, so hopefully he's at home. Head for University City.'

Connor stepped on the gas. 'You got it.'

Twelve

Shady Oaks Retirement Village
Scripps Ranch, San Diego, California
Tuesday, 8 November, 7.30 P.M.

'Siggy!' Miss Eloise opened her arms and, tail wagging, Siggy ran into the common room for pats and love. The Lab mix was a frequent visitor to Shady Oaks and even had his own ID badge. It was studded with rhinestones, so Sam figured Eloise had made it.

Eloise and Georgia sat at one of the card tables, looking sad despite Siggy's grand entrance. Sam understood. This was where they'd played cards with Benny and Frankie for years.

'You're back,' Georgia said, relief evident in both her voice and her posture.

Sam kissed them on the cheek, first Eloise, then Georgia. 'I told you I was coming back. I'll sleep on your couch tonight, Georgia. But first, we're going to have a movie night.'

Eloise smiled, but it was forced. 'That sounds lovely, Sammy. You're such a good boy.'

Sam joined them at the table, putting the bag of groceries he'd brought on the floor. 'I try. I brought ten different movies. I figured you could pick which one you like. Fair warning: I raided my parents' DVD cabinet, so I had to pick from what they had there. I always stream movies to my computer.'

Georgia sniffed. 'So do we. We are not Luddites, Sam.'

He grinned. 'Excellent. I didn't want to watch *Steel Magnolias* again.'

'That one always makes me cry,' Eloise complained.

'And it's got death in it,' Georgia added, her lips thinning in disapproval.

'I know,' Sam said, putting his hands up in surrender. 'But my mom said I should bring it anyway. Blame her.'

'I shall,' Georgia said, then looked at the bag of groceries. 'Did you bring snacks?'

'I sure did. All your favorites. Lots of chocolate.'

Eloise whispered, 'Don't say that too loudly. Everyone will show up in our room and we'll have to share.'

He chuckled. 'Mum's the word.' He pointed to the deck of cards on the table. 'Are you playing?'

'No,' Eloise said with a sad sigh. 'Just reminiscing. Everything changed so fast. Last week we were all here. Now . . .'

'Do you want to play a game with me?' Sam asked.

Both women shook their heads.

'I can't,' Georgia said, her voice trembling. 'Not yet. Maybe in a few weeks.'

'I understand.'

She patted his hand. 'I know you do. Maybe we should go upstairs and start this movie night. Sitting here at this table is bad for my joints anyway.' She pushed herself to her feet, grabbing the cane she used only when she was in a lot of pain.

'I keep telling you to smoke some weed,' Eloise said with a shake of her bright blue head. She gripped her rhinestone-studded walker and clicked her tongue at Siggy. Obediently, Siggy followed her. 'I do miss a good bowl,' she added with a sigh.

Sam choked on a laugh. 'You don't smoke here, do you, Miss Eloise?'

'Oh no, not here. No smoking allowed here, plus my lungs can't take it anymore. But in my youth? I *was* at Haight-Ashbury, you know.'

Sam grabbed the grocery bag. 'I did not know that. But I can't say that I'm surprised.'

Georgia sniffed again. 'Hippies. In your case, old hippies.'

Eloise frowned. 'I was twenty-five in sixty-four. Not exactly an old maid. There were all ages there, not just teenagers. It was quite a time. The summer of love in sixty-seven and all that. I got married and moved to San Diego before it got really crowded and the police started cracking down. But I'd learned to like weed and wasn't going to give it up.'

Sam loved these women. 'Did you grow your own?'

'Yes. Never got caught, either.' Eloise plodded along to the elevator, her step noticeably slower, but she kept the chatter up. Sam thought it was mostly a show for Georgia, who kept giving her haughty glares.

'I take it that you didn't smoke weed in your youth, Miss Georgia.'

Georgia lifted her chin. 'I most certainly did not.'

'I do edibles now,' Eloise said as they entered the elevator. 'I keep telling Georgie that she should try them, but she's a prude.'

'I am not a prude, Eloise. You take that back.'

'I'm no liar, Georgia Shearer.'

'You shouldn't pressure Georgia, Miss Eloise,' Sam said gently, trying to deescalate the argument. He was also very glad that he'd never accepted one of Miss Eloise's homemade brownies. 'It's her business what she tries.'

Eloise pouted. 'I know. But Frankie used to do edibles with me and now I have no one to share with.'

Sam gaped at her, ignoring the elevator doors which had just opened. 'Frankie used pot?' It was legal, of course, but Frankie had always seemed so straitlaced. Ever the cop, Sam now realized.

'He did.' Eloise's expression saddened again as she left the elevator, turning left toward Georgia's apartment, Siggy at her side. 'He learned to use it when Ryan was sick with cancer. Helped him sleep.'

'They didn't find any in his apartment,' Sam said.

'No, they wouldn't. He'd come to my place for his nighttime brownie.'

'Every night?' Sam asked.

'No, not every night. Only when he was stressed. He was pretty stressed the past few weeks.'

Sam nodded to the officer standing in the hallway outside

Georgia's room. True to his word, Navarro had given a guard to the people who'd been closest to Frankie and Benny.

Eloise stopped to bat her eyelashes at the man. 'Aren't you handsome?' she cooed.

Georgia rolled her eyes, but her smile was affectionate. 'Leave him alone, Eloise. Officer Stern's got a wife and a new baby.'

'Pics or it didn't happen!' Eloise demanded.

With a smile, the cop took out his wallet and proudly showed them a photo of a woman with curly red hair. The child she held had hair just as red and just as curly. 'My wife, Savannah, and our daughter, Kristen.'

'They're lovely,' Georgia said quietly. 'I hope guarding us isn't keeping you from them for too long.'

'They're out of town at the moment,' Stern said. 'Visiting family in Chicago. So I'm all yours, ladies.'

'But you're married,' Eloise said with a dramatic sigh. 'Too bad for us. I don't poach.'

'Anymore,' Georgia added under her breath, earning her a scalding glare from Eloise.

'For that unwarranted dig, I get to pick the first movie,' Eloise declared.

'Oh God,' Georgia moaned. 'Not *Magic Mike* again.'

Officer Stern coughed to hide a laugh. Sam opened his mouth to challenge Eloise's movie choice, then shrugged. It wasn't worth it.

Stern cleared his throat, crouching to pet Siggy. 'Nice dog.'

'He's Sigmund,' Sam said. 'Siggy for short.'

'You're a good boy.' Stern straightened. 'Why does he have two collars?'

'One is a GPS collar,' Eloise told him, because they'd had this discussion before. 'Siggy escapes.'

'Only if someone doesn't close the front door all the way,' Sam explained. 'But he got out a few months ago and went exploring. Made it all the way to the lobby of my apartment building. So I got the tracking collar.'

'I've got a dog like that,' Stern said. 'Good to know about the collar. I'll have to get one for Mugsy. Enjoy the movie,' he added, coughing again to hide another laugh.

It's going to be a long night.

Sam got the ladies into Georgia's apartment, then unpacked the snacks while they got themselves comfortable. 'Can I get you ladies anything to drink?'

Eloise pulled a hip flask from the pocket of her walker. 'I'm good. You want some, Sammy?'

Sam wasn't even shocked. 'You ladies are going to corrupt me.'

Eloise cackled. 'We'll leave that to Detective McKittrick.'

Sam blushed. 'Miss Eloise.'

'Leave him alone, El,' Georgia said. 'I'll take a soda, Sam.' She patted the sofa, next to where Marmaduke snoozed. 'Up here, Siggy.'

Siggy climbed onto the sofa and made himself at home. Sam took the other chair and gave Georgia the remote. 'If you can manage not to find *Magic Mike*, I will owe you dinner.'

'Frankie liked it,' Eloise said slyly.

Sam laughed. 'I'll bet he did.' He sobered, thinking of the other reason he was with them tonight. 'Eloise, you said that Frankie was stressed the past few weeks. Did he tell you why? I'm sorry to ask, but it could be important.'

Eloise shook her head, becoming very serious. 'No, Sammy, he didn't, and I asked him. So did Georgia.'

'Did you know he went somewhere on Wednesday?'

Both women looked surprised. 'No,' Georgia said immediately. 'Where did he go?'

Sam studied Eloise, because her surprise had quickly morphed to something else. It looked like guilt. 'We don't know yet. Miss Eloise? What's wrong?'

'He'd been coming to get edibles every night before bed for a few weeks, but he didn't on Tuesday night. I asked him why on Wednesday at breakfast and he said that he'd fallen asleep on his own. He never took them the night before he drove back to San Francisco. I should have realized he planned to go out.'

'But he didn't go to San Francisco last week,' Georgia said. 'That trip he only did on the weekends and he ate dinner with us on Wednesday evening.'

Sam frowned. 'I thought he didn't eat in the dining room often.'

'He didn't.' Eloise sighed quietly. 'I could be wrong, but I think it was because he and Benny had been arguing. It was like he was keeping an eye on him or something.'

'Arguing?' Sam asked. 'About what?'

'I don't know. I point-blank asked him, because I figured that was why he was stressed, but Frankie was a closemouthed kind of guy. Unless he was yelling at me for cheating at cribbage,' she added with a fond smile, which quickly faded. 'Benny had been acting withdrawn, but he got like that sometimes. He'd miss Martha and get melancholy.'

'That's true,' Georgia agreed. 'Where do you think Frankie went, Sam?'

'I have no idea, but I'm betting it was important. Give me a minute to text Kit and then we can watch the movie.'

'Kit,' Eloise stage-whispered to Georgia.

Georgia's sigh was long-suffering. 'Eloise. Leave the boy alone. He can romance Detective McKittrick without our help.'

Eloise snickered. 'It'll be more fun if we help.'

Georgia shook her head. 'He might not give you any chocolate.'

Eloise gasped. 'He would never be so mean.'

Sam tuned them out, crafting a group text to Kit, Connor, and Goddard. *Frankie went somewhere last Wednesday, but Georgia and Eloise don't know where. He was at Shady Oaks for breakfast and dinner so he couldn't have gone far. Eloise says that Frankie was stressed for the past two weeks and thinks it was because Frankie and Benny were having some kind of argument. That's consistent with what Benny told me yesterday, that he should have listened to Frankie and that Frankie had called him naive and lonely. No other details now but will let you know if they remember anything more.*

Goddard's text was the only reply. *Thx Doc. Keep us up to speed.*

Sam waited for Kit to answer, but after a minute she hadn't, so he put his phone down and looked at the TV screen.

Thankfully, *Magic Mike* was not queued up. '*The Lincoln Lawyer*? I like this one.'

'She always picks legal dramas,' Eloise complained.

'You still get Matthew McConaughey,' Georgia fired back. 'So stop griping.'

'But he keeps his clothes on in this one,' Eloise wailed. 'You're harshing my vibe, Georgia.'

Saying nothing more, Sam passed out the chocolate and sat back to enjoy the movie.

La Jolla, San Diego, California
Tuesday, 8 November, 8.45 P.M.

'Is this the place?' Connor asked, slowing the department sedan.

Kit peered up at the mini mansion and checked the address. 'It is. The residence of Chadwick Redford, president of the company that owns Mrs Adler's house. Hopefully he can tell us who pays her rent without requiring a warrant.'

'Don't count on it,' Connor said glumly. 'The way our luck is running tonight.'

They'd gone to Dominic Stanza's apartment, looking for information on Archie Adler, but no one had answered Stanza's door and a neighbor had said that Dominic hadn't been home in weeks.

Weeks. Dammit. Kit had known that Dominic had been lying, but they hadn't had cause to arrest him or even to bring him in for questioning. They'd put out a BOLO on him, listing him as a person of interest. Navarro had already put out a BOLO on Archie Adler and the Coast Guard was actively searching for him.

Their final lead of the evening was the man who owned the house that Mrs Adler rented. *Follow the money.* It was an adage for a good reason.

They'd talk to Chadwick Redford, then call it a night. They'd been going since four a.m. and needed some rest.

Kit yawned. 'I haven't been this tired in a long time.'

Connor's yawn followed a few beats later. 'Don't yawn.'

Kit got out of the car. 'Sorry. Let's get this done so we can sleep.'

'That's a plan.' Connor jogged around the sedan, meeting her on the sidewalk. 'Chadwick Redford sounds like a fake name.'

'It might be. I ran a background on him and found his social security number, work history, and driver's license, but he doesn't have a passport, which is a little unusual these days for a businessperson.' She breathed deeply, the brisk night air helping to wake her up. 'Let's do this.'

Connor knocked on the door a little louder than usual. 'Hoping the neighbors hear,' he whispered. 'Then they'll ask us in so the neighbors don't snoop.'

It was a good plan. Except no one answered.

Connor knocked again, louder this time. They could see a portion of the stairs through the small windows at the top of the door. For another minute the stairs were empty, and then a woman came downstairs. They saw her bare legs first, then the white of a towel.

'Oh dear,' Kit muttered.

The door opened and a woman in her midtwenties glared at them, clutching at the towel around her body while the towel on her head slid sideways to perch at a dangerous angle. 'Yes?' the woman asked impatiently.

Kit gently edged Connor aside because he was still blinking owlishly. It wasn't often they were greeted at a door by half-naked people. 'We're looking for Mr Redford. Is he in?'

The woman blinked. 'He doesn't live here.'

Wonderful, Kit wanted to snarl, but kept her smile in place. 'Can you tell us where we can find him?'

'No, because I don't know him, but my boyfriend might.' She turned and yelled up the stairs in a surprisingly powerful voice. 'Honey! Someone's looking for a Mr Redford.'

Connor winced, giving his head a little shake.

'What?' a male voice asked. A very familiar male voice.

'Motherfucker,' Kit muttered. It was Dominic fucking Stanza.

Stanza came into view, took one look at them, and started to run. Connor grabbed Stanza's shirt, holding him in place.

The towel-clad woman shrieked, demanding to know what was going on.

'Care to tell her, Mr Stanza?' Connor asked silkily.

Dominic swallowed hard. 'Let me go. You have nothing on me.'

'We can start with trespassing,' Kit said. Then she noticed the suitcases stacked in the foyer. 'Considering that you were running from the police, I think we can keep you behind bars for a little while.'

They probably couldn't, but Stanza might not know that.

'We're not trespassing,' Stanza said defiantly. 'My friend owns this house and lets us live here.'

The woman in the towel blinked at him. 'You said that *you* owned this house. That your parents gave it to you.'

'He lied, ma'am,' Kit said helpfully. 'May we come in?'

'No,' Stanza snapped.

But the woman nodded. 'I live here, too, and I say yes.'

'Thank you. Go get dressed, please. I'll wait upstairs for you. Detective Robinson, please escort Mr Stanza back into the house.'

'With pleasure,' Connor said darkly, and gave Stanza a small shove. 'Move it.'

The woman was still blinking. 'Detective? What's going on?'

'That's what we'd like to know.' Kit gestured to the stairs, one hand on the service weapon holstered at her hip. 'Don't think about running. I will catch you.'

'I'm not a criminal,' the woman protested. 'I'll get dressed. No running.'

Kit followed her up the stairs, all the while listening to Stanza trying to convince Connor to let him go.

Ha. Fat chance.

Kit searched the upstairs rooms for Archie Adler while the woman was getting dressed, just in case Archie hadn't taken off in his boat after all. The woman emerged from a bedroom within two minutes wearing jeans and a T-shirt, her hair lying wet and tangled around her shoulders.

'I didn't want you to think I was hiding a weapon in my towel,' she said earnestly.

'Thank you,' Kit said. 'What is your name?'

'Brittney Shay. I've only known Dominic for a few months.

I don't know about anything illegal. I swear it. I'm getting my law degree. I can't get arrested.'

'Well, let's see what Mr Stanza has to say.' They started down the stairs, Kit still on her guard in case Brittney made a run for it. But Brittney was wearing no shoes, which made her less of an escape risk. 'Did you meet him at the university?'

'I did. He was my TA when I took a computer course last summer. We started dating when the fall semester started.' She walked into the living room, arms crossed tightly over her chest. 'What the fuck, Dominic? You're going to get me disbarred before I ever take the damn exam!'

'Have a seat, Miss Shay,' Kit said calmly, following her into the room.

Stanza was sitting in a chair, his hands cuffed in front of him.

'He tried to run,' Connor said. 'He didn't get far.'

'Upstairs is clear. Let me check down here.' Kit searched the lower level, then returned to the living room. 'Adler's not here. Where is he, Stanza?'

Stanza glared at them both, then turned his attention to Brittney. 'I'm sorry I lied about my parents owning this place, but I didn't lie to the cops. My friend does own this house.'

'Archie Adler,' Kit said.

Brittney's eyes widened. 'Archie? What did he do, rob a bank? Oh my God.'

Kit smiled her most threatening smile at Stanza. 'How did he get the money for this place, Mr Stanza?'

'I don't know.'

Brittney slumped into another chair. 'Did you steal, too?' she demanded of Stanza.

'No!'

'You just covered for Archie when he was off running his scam?' Kit guessed, and Stanza winced.

'You don't even lie well,' Brittney muttered. 'Just tell them. It'll go easier for you. They can put in a good word with the DA and my father can recommend a lawyer.'

Stanza's shoulders sagged. 'I didn't steal anything.'

'I don't care,' Kit said coldly. 'Archie did, and he's the fish we're after. Where is he?'

'I don't know.'

Brittney rubbed her forehead. 'This is so ridiculous. I can't believe this is happening to me. I heard them talking tonight, Detectives. I didn't know what I was hearing at the time, but now it makes sense. Archie's taken his boat.'

'We figured that,' Connor said. 'Where did he go?'

Stanza glared daggers at his girlfriend. 'I do not know,' he said slowly, his expression daring Brittney to say a word.

'Catalina Island,' Brittney said, glaring back at Stanza. 'Buddy, the sex isn't good enough for me to cover your ass. I'm going home to a house just as nice as this one. In case you missed it, we are done.' She turned to Kit. 'I only heard part of the conversation, but Dominic said, "Why the hell are you going to Catalina? Why not south?" Then he looked up something on his phone and told Archie that he could charter a flight with a private plane on Catalina and fly to LAX, where he could transfer. Then he hung up and told me to pack my bags, that we were meeting Archie on his boat for a vacation. I needed to get myself ready. If you'd been a little later, we would have been gone.'

'If you hadn't been so damn vain, we'd have been out of here by now,' Stanza snapped, then realized what he'd said and blanched. 'I was taking her to see my mother,' he added weakly.

'Your mother's dead,' Brittney said, her fury barely controlled. 'Do I need to come downtown to give a statement, Detective? I'll have my family's lawyer meet me there. I'm happy to cooperate with San Diego's finest,' she added through clenched teeth.

Kit's lips twitched. 'Thank you. Do you know who we think Archie was stealing from, Dominic?'

Dominic turned his face away and said nothing.

'From elderly people in a retirement home,' Kit said.

Brittney's mouth fell open. 'You're stealing from old people? What kind of asshole are you?'

'I never stole anything!' Dominic shouted.

'You just profited,' Brittney said with a sneer. 'And dragged me into it. If you mess up my chances with the bar, I will ruin you.' She glanced at Kit. 'Legally, of course.'

'Of course. How long ago did this conversation happen?'

Brittney glanced at the time on her phone. 'Maybe three hours ago.'

'Which is when you should have been ready to go,' Stanza snarled. 'But *no*. You had to take a *bath* and pack your *bags* and paint your fucking *toenails*. Bitch!'

'Shut up,' Brittney snapped. 'You're a pig. Stealing from old people.'

'I did not steal!'

Ignoring their arguing, Kit pulled out her phone and dialed Navarro. 'The Coast Guard can intercept him at Catalina Island. He's got a three-hour head start. The boat he owns has a top speed of about thirty miles per hour, so he'll be close to the island by now.'

'What?' Her boss was stunned. 'He went north? I thought he was a boy genius or something.'

'He's going to Catalina and booking a charter flight. He'll probably use the name Chadwick Redford. I don't think Redford actually exists. I think that Adler built up an identity for the guy, including a driver's license, so that he could build his real estate empire. Assuming he was stealing from Shady Oaks, too, it's a reasonable way to invest his ill-gotten gains.'

'Money laundering 101,' Navarro grumbled. His keyboard clacked loudly in the background as he typed. 'Coast Guard acknowledges the request and will keep us informed. How do you know this?'

She told him about finding Stanza in the house owned by Chadwick Redford.

Navarro made a sound of disbelief. 'Wow. Why didn't Adler just go to Mexico?'

'Probably because he didn't have a passport as Redford, so he wouldn't be able to get out of Mexico. He knew we'd be looking for him under his real name.' Kit turned to Stanza. 'Sound right, Dominic?'

Dominic shook his head and said nothing.

'You are in such big trouble,' Brittney said, still glaring at her former boyfriend.

'Who was that?' Navarro asked.

'Stanza's girlfriend. Law student by the name of Brittney Shay.'

Navarro whistled. 'The daughter of Judge Shay?'

'I don't know.' Kit turned to Brittney. 'Is your dad a judge?'

Brittney nodded. 'He is. And he's going to be very unhappy.' She pointed at Stanza. 'I'll make sure he turns all that unhappiness on you, dickwad. I'm *not* going to jail for you.'

Stanza swallowed hard and remained silent. Maybe he was smarter than they'd thought.

'We'll bring him in, sir, then we're taking a break,' Kit said.

'I'll have someone ready to book him. Nicely done, McKittrick. Tell Robinson, too.'

'I will. Sir, what about—' Kit cut herself off, not wanting to mention Faye Evans's possible involvement in front of Dominic. If they had to play one against the other, Kit wanted to be able to control the flow of information. 'What about the other person you're having watched?'

'So far she's driven from Shady Oaks to the grocery store, and then home, where she's been all evening.'

'Good. Have a good night, sir.' Kit pocketed her phone. 'Brittney, get a pair of shoes and a jacket. I'll have a police officer bring you back to pack your things as soon as we get your statement.' She looked around. 'Did Archie live here, too?'

Brittney gave an unladylike snort as she went up the stairs. 'Sometimes. But most of the time he lived with his mommy, two blocks over. Did he buy her house, too?'

Kit didn't answer her and Brittney seemed okay with that. A minute later she was coming down the stairs, shoes on her feet, a jacket on her body, a purse over her shoulder, and a hairbrush in one hand.

'You can search my purse if you need to.'

Kit did a cursory search. 'Thank you.'

'Please tell everyone how cooperative I've been.'

'I will,' Kit promised. 'Next time, maybe do a little more due diligence on your boyfriends.'

'Oh, I will. You can be sure of that. Asshole,' she muttered as Connor took Stanza to their car. 'Do I have to ride in back?'

'No. I'll ride in back with Stanza.'

She looked up at Kit, her eyes vulnerable and scared for the first time since the altercation had begun. 'Thank you. I won't forget this.'

'Just be more careful. I don't know if these guys are violent and I don't know exactly what they've done, but I've got at least two murder victims in the morgue. I'd have hated for you to be their next victim if you learned too much.'

Brittney paled. 'Murder? Holy shit. Can I make a call to my father? I'll need him to pick me up.'

'Make the call in the car,' Kit said gently. 'Let's go.'

Carmel Valley, California
Tuesday, 8 November, 10.30 P.M.

Every muscle in Kit's body ached as she pulled into the driveway at McKittrick House. She'd been closer to her boat in the marina on Shelter Island after leaving the precinct, Dominic Stanza having been handed off to the officers who'd book him. She'd even turned her car toward the marina.

But then she'd crumpled inside, not that she'd admit that to anyone. She'd been stopped at a red light and realized that she'd been clutching the cat-bird carving that Harlan had made for her six months before.

She didn't want to go to her boat tonight. It was cold and empty and she had no food in the fridge.

She was hungry and she needed . . . something. Her parents. Her dog. A good meal, a snuggle with Snickerdoodle, and maybe even a hug.

From Sam Reeves? *Maybe.* That she didn't instantly deny it was telling.

He'd held her once, six months ago, and he'd felt so . . . solid. So

214

safe. Like he wasn't going anywhere. But then he had because she'd pushed him away, then run like she'd been chased by the hounds of hell.

She'd questioned that decision too many times, usually when she was tired like this. *Not tonight.* She couldn't think about Sam tonight. Not about his compassion, nor his calming persona, and especially not the way he stared at her when he thought she wasn't looking.

He was lonely, too. Lonely and sad, and she hated that. He was too nice a man to be lonely and sad, grieving the loss of his friends.

She could help with that, at least. She couldn't bring his friends back, but she could bring whoever killed them to justice.

But not tonight. Tonight she needed to sleep. And she really needed that hug, so she'd headed north. To the only real home she'd ever known.

She got out of her car and just drank in the sight of the house. There were lights in the windows, despite the time. Betsy might be asleep already, but Harlan would be awake.

She should nag him to get more sleep, but she'd do it after she got that hug.

The front door opened and the familiar sight of her father filled the doorway, all big and broad-shouldered. Safety. And unconditional love.

Her eyes burned and she hated that. She was just tired.

'Hey, Pop,' she called, relieved that her voice didn't crack.

'Hey, Kitty-Cat,' he called back. 'Everything okay?'

No. It wasn't. 'Of course.'

Harlan wasn't fooled. He waited until she was within hugging distance and dragged her to him, kissing the top of her head, as was his way. 'Kit.'

She swallowed hard, taking the comfort he so freely offered. 'Hey, Pop.' Normally she would have pulled away by now, prickly both by nature and by personal experience. But tonight she needed a little more.

He rubbed her back in slow, big circles. 'Rough day?'

'Just a long one.'

'Still working on the retirement home case?'

She breathed him in, the scent of Old Spice, wood shavings, and horses, with a little hint of cinnamon. *Mom must be baking.*

Betsy was always baking.

It was grounding, coming home. So little changed here. It was . . . safe.

She pulled away, patting Harlan's cheek gently. 'Thank you. I think I'm good now.'

'You're always good, but I'm happy to hug you anytime.'

She smiled up at him. 'Love you. I should say it more often.' Because even when a man lived to be eighty-five like Frankie Flynn or eighty-nine like Benny Dreyfus, life could still be too short.

His eyes softened. 'Love you, too, Kitty-Cat. Come on in. It's cold out here.'

She let him draw her into the house, drawing in another deep breath. 'What's Mom making?'

'Cookies for the new girls.' His eyes twinkled, his lips curving up in a smile. 'They're having a bedtime snack. Come on.'

The kitchen was a beehive of activity, and Betsy was in her element. There were cookies in the oven, cookies cooling on racks, and cookies on the table – surrounded by three smiling teenage girls. Jane and Janey – Tiffany and Emma – were busily decorating cookies with Rita.

'Kit!' Rita exclaimed. 'We didn't know you were coming.'

'I didn't know I was, either,' Kit said, and Snickerdoodle jumped to her feet and ran over, too polite to jump but clearly wanting some love. Kit knelt to hug her dog, scrunching her face when Snick licked her cheek. 'Gross, Snick.' She rose and examined the table. 'Nice job, ladies. They look almost too good to eat. Hey, Mom.' She wrapped Betsy in a hug, smiling when Betsy held her a little too hard, a little too long.

'We've missed you,' Betsy said. 'It's been too long.'

Kit laughed. 'It's been one day. I just saw you last night at Mateo's. And the day before that at Sunday dinner.' She looked at the oven hopefully. 'Is there any dinner left? I've been running ragged since four this morning.'

Betsy tutted. 'You sit and I'll make you a plate.'

Kit settled in and studied the new girls. 'You two are looking better.'

Tiffany, the leader, nodded cautiously. 'It's been wild. Mr and Mrs McK have been really good to us.'

'They're good to everyone,' Rita said loyally.

'It's nice to have a comfy bed again,' Emma said softly. 'Thank you, Detective.'

Kit smiled at her. 'I didn't do a thing, Emma. You are Emma, right? Or should I call you Janey?'

Emma rolled her eyes. 'Tiffany wasn't very original. Jane and Janey.'

'I panicked,' Tiffany said with a careless shrug. 'Why have you been running ragged since four a.m.?'

'I'm on a case and that's the way they go sometimes.'

Rita handed Kit a decorated cookie shaped like a turkey. 'Sometimes it's run, run, run, and sometimes it's hurry up and wait.'

Kit's lips twitched because Rita was cute. 'That is the honest truth.'

Rita raised a blond brow. 'You laugh now, but one day I'll be a cop.'

'You can do whatever you want to do, Rita McKittrick,' Kit said simply. 'I believe in you.'

Rita's smile made a little of the hard day fade away.

Yes, Kit had needed to come home.

'So . . . ,' Tiffany said casually, pretending to focus on the cookie she was icing, but she was really studying Kit. 'How is Dr Sam?'

Rita and Emma exchanged a look of suppressed laughter.

Kit shook her head at their obvious attempts at matchmaking. 'Last I saw him, he was fine. We had a meeting at the precinct about the case. He's my colleague.'

'Uh-huh,' Tiffany said. 'He's also very nice.'

Kit drew a breath, needing to cut this off. 'He is. Tell me about this placement, girls. Are you going to go to school or homeschool? What's the plan?'

'Dr Sam recommended we go to school when he dropped us off at New Horizons last night,' Emma said shyly, but there was a persistent gleam in her eye.

Rita nodded. 'He said I should go back to school, too, since I'll have wingmen now.' She giggled when Emma gave her a good-natured nudge of her elbow. 'Or wing-girls.'

Rita had refused to go to school the spring before because bullies had taunted her when her mother's killer had been arrested and details of the crime had been made public. Asshole bullies. Kit had wanted to knock some heads together because Rita had been crushed. That Rita was entertaining the idea of returning to the classroom was good news.

That Sam had been the instigator was no surprise.

That the girls sought to bring up the psychologist's name at every opportunity was no surprise, either. Kit had revealed a lot about herself on the street the night before, but she couldn't be sorry. It was likely that the girls would have bolted had she not earned their trust, and then who knew where they'd be?

'He's right.' Kit took a bite of the cookie, nearly moaning at the buttery taste. 'When do you re-enroll?'

Rita drew a deep breath. 'Tomorrow. I'm going in with Tiff and Em and we're all going to sign up together.'

'That is very good news. I'm proud of you, kid.' Kit reached across the table and ruffled Rita's pink-and-blue-streaked curls, making the teenager scowl and abandon the cookie she was icing to smooth her hair.

'Kiiiiit,' she whined. 'Stopppppp.'

'Okaaaaay,' Kit whined back, then laughed. 'Mom, do you need any help?'

'Pfft. Of course not.' Betsy put a plate in front of her.

Kit's mouth watered at the aroma coming off the fried chicken. 'So hungry.' She dug in, listening to the girls' chatter as they returned to their cookie decorating.

'We're going to take the cookies to the retirement home,' Tiffany said. 'The one Dr Sam volunteers at.'

Kit thought of the residents and staff of Shady Oaks, so saddened by both Frankie's and Benny's deaths. 'They'll appreciate that. They're missing their friends right now and some of them have no family to give them comfort.'

'We know how that is,' Emma said, then clamped her lips together, as if she'd already said too much about her background.

Rita gave her a hug, and the girls went back to cookie decorating. Their conversation resumed with lighter topics, like what they'd wear and who could borrow whose clothes for school next week.

Kit just ate her dinner. The girls would talk about their backgrounds and the families they'd run from – or those who'd abandoned them – when they were ready.

I did. She looked over at Harlan, who was sitting in one of the chairs off to the side, thoughtfully regarding the block of wood in his hands. She recognized his expression. He was trying to decide what to carve next. Every foster kid who came through McKittrick House got a carving that was special and unique. He'd started the practice sixteen years before when he'd carved a small bird for Kit, putting it in her hands the night they'd buried Wren. She'd received another carved bird every year on the anniversary of Wren's murder.

So she wouldn't forget her sister. *As if I could.*

'I'm off to bed,' Kit said. 'You girls need to go to sleep soon, too. Mom and Pop won't sleep until you do.'

The teenagers turned to look at Betsy, who was wiping down the stovetop, her movements a bit slower than usual.

'I'm sorry, Mrs McK,' Emma said, her eyes going wide and fearful, as if she expected to be slapped at any moment.

Kit laid a gentle hand on the girl's shoulder. 'You don't have to be sorry here, Emma. Mom and Pop won't tell you to go to sleep tonight because you're new here and they know you're just finding your way. But this is a farm, and they've got to get up early to feed chickens and milk the cow. If they don't go to sleep soon, they'll be falling face-first in the cookie icing.'

Emma's smile was tentative. 'Thanks, Detective.'

'Kit,' Kit said. 'Here, I'm Kit. And I hope you never meet me in a place where you have to call me "Detective." '

Emma nodded, understanding exactly what Kit meant. 'I won't. I promise. This place is too nice to get thrown out of.'

'I know. I remember rediscovering how nice a soft pillow felt under my head and how nice it was to be warm and dry, my belly full. This is a good place and Mom and Pop are the best. We all want you to be happy here. Now, I've got to sleep before *I* fall face-first in the icing.'

'Say hi to Dr Sam for us,' Tiffany said earnestly. 'Tell him thank you again.'

Rita smirked. 'Yeah, Kit. Tell him hi. And tell him good night. Like right now.'

'I'll give him your messages when I see him *at work*,' Kit said with as much dignity as she could muster, considering all of them were grinning at her, even Harlan and Betsy.

Kit snapped her fingers for Snickerdoodle, who dutifully followed her up the stairs to the room she'd once shared with Wren. It was Rita's room now, but Kit slept in her old bed whenever she stayed overnight.

'They're all insane, Snick,' she told her dog as she dug her pajamas out of the drawer Betsy kept for her things. 'I'm not calling Sam right now.'

She sat on the edge of the bed, her thoughts focusing in on the psychologist despite her best intentions. She wondered if he'd gone to Shady Oaks for the night.

Wondered if he was okay. If he was still sad.

Of course he is. He'd lost two friends. One didn't just get over that. People like Sam especially. His heart was too big and he was too easily hurt.

Kit should know. She'd hurt him herself, but still he waited. *For me.*

Restless, she switched her mind to work, checking her phone for new messages. She'd seen the text Sam had sent earlier that evening saying that Frankie had gone somewhere the Wednesday before his death. They'd have to track down where he'd gone. It felt important. She made a mental note to check with Jeff from IT in the morning to see if he'd unearthed the parking lot gate records from Shady Oaks.

She kept scrolling, then felt some of the tension leave her body when she read a message that Navarro had sent while she'd been eating dinner.

CG picked up Archie Adler. He'll be here by morning for you to interview. Brass will be observing. Be here by 8.

Connor had already replied in the affirmative and Kit added her acknowledgment. *Good news. See you tomorrow at 8.*

She wondered if Sam knew, if anyone had told him. She opened a text window to Sam, then stared at the blank screen. She could simply convey the case status. Or she could reach out. Maybe call him. Return some of the kindness that he showed everyone else. It didn't have to mean anything.

Which was stupid. Of course it would mean something.

'I'm stupid, Snick,' she muttered. 'I shouldn't even be thinking about calling him. He'll probably be asleep anyway.'

Snickerdoodle licked Kit's hand, then let out an immense doggy sigh.

'Yeah, yeah, I know that you like him, too. Everyone does.' Blinking back a burgeoning headache, she typed: *You awake? Have news.*

The reply was immediate. *Awake. What's happened?*

Kit stared at her phone for a long moment, then tapped Sam's name in her contact list and hit the call button. It didn't even ring once.

'Kit? Are you all right?'

'I'm fine. I'm at Mom and Pop's and everything's fine. Just wanted you to know that we've tracked down Archie Adler. He'd headed up to Catalina on his boat.'

'His boat, huh? Purchased with Shady Oaks money?'

'Money he'd stolen, yeah. He's set up quite a real estate empire under an assumed name. Owns several pricey homes and has his mom living in one, a friend in the other. Rented out a few others. Coast Guard is bringing him in, and we're going to question him in the morning. We start at eight if you want to observe.'

'I'll be there,' Sam said, steel in his tone. 'Do you think he stole Benny's coins?'

Kit had hoped so. 'He might have, but I think he's too tall to be the man leaving Shady Oaks in the surveillance video. According to his driver's license, Adler's about six-two and the man in the video can't be more than five-ten.'

'He still could have killed Crawford and taken the coins from the motel room.'

'That's possible. Maybe even likely.' The lipstick on Crawford's genitals bothered her, though. They needed to find whoever had been in his room. Even if Archie had killed Crawford, the lipstick-wearer was still a loose end. Kit hoped it was Faye Evans. At least they knew where she was. 'Detective Goddard told us that Crawford knew about the coins.'

'Yes. Crawford told Devon Jones that he'd read about them in a magazine. You're still thinking Crawford took the coins?'

'He's the right size. The question is, if he took them, where are they now? We're assuming his killer took them.'

'Then you'll find them,' Sam said with simple confidence. 'Because you'll find who killed him.'

His faith meant a lot. 'Thank you, Sam.'

'You're welcome.' He hesitated. 'Devon also said that Crawford had been harassing some of the staff at Shady Oaks. They knew not to let him get them alone.'

'Crawford was a real piece of work, wasn't he? That could be another possible motive for Crawford's murder.' Sam didn't say any more, but Kit felt his distress. 'Sam? What's wrong?'

He sighed quietly. 'Am I a bad person if I'm glad Crawford's no longer breathing?'

'No. You're human, Sam. A very kind human, so don't give that concern another thought.' She was aware that her tone had softened. She cleared her throat. 'Where are you tonight? Did you go back to Shady Oaks?'

'I did. Had movie night with Georgia and Eloise.'

The notion made Kit smile. 'Did they give you a makeover and paint your nails?'

His chuckle warmed her to the core. 'No, but Eloise nearly had me watching *Magic Mike*.'

Kit laughed. 'I can see her trying that. What did you watch instead?'

'Georgia picked a legal thriller. It was fine. I . . . just don't want anything to happen to them. They're nice old ladies. Eloise is bunking with Georgia.'

'Where are you sleeping?'

'On Georgia's sofa bed. It's not all *that* uncomfortable. Why did you go home? To McKittrick House? Why not go to your boat?'

It took her a beat to find an answer she was comfortable giving. 'I needed to see my dog.'

'And your folks, too?' He paused, the silence warm and . . . sweet. 'It's okay to need someone, Kit.'

That he'd hit the nail so squarely on the head should have made her squirm, but it didn't. It made her feel seen. Known. Understood.

Cared for.

'Have a good night, Sam. Be careful. We don't know who's snipping off loose ends. Call if you need me. I'll talk to you soon.' She ended the call before he could say another word and she sat staring at her phone for a long time before realizing that she'd forgotten to pass on the greetings from the girls.

No problem. I'll see him tomorrow.

And the thought didn't scare her the way it should have. No, it wasn't fear that she was feeling.

It was anticipation.

And that *did* scare her.

Thirteen

Shady Oaks Retirement Village
Scripps Ranch, San Diego, California
Tuesday, 8 November, 11.45 P.M.

Sam punched the pillow under his head, trying to get comfortable on Georgia's sofa bed. He'd lied to Kit. He'd told her that the bed wasn't that uncomfortable, but it was like a torture device. But Georgia and Eloise had gone to sleep feeling safe, so it was worth a few sore muscles.

He rolled to his back, staring up at the ceiling.

Kit had called. She'd reached out. *Without any prompting from me.*

It wasn't the declaration of affection for which he'd been waiting for six months, but it was a start. *Have a good night, Sam. I'll talk to you soon.* The words loosened the tightness in his chest. There was also the requisite *be careful* in there, too, but he figured she couldn't help that. It was how she was wired.

He reached down to pet Siggy, who was stretched out on the floor beside him, then stilled, his hand in Siggy's fur.

Siggy was growling. It was a low, barely audible sound that Sam felt more than heard. Sam's pulse began to race and he slowly sat up on the sofa bed, wishing he'd brought his gun.

But weapons weren't allowed here in Shady Oaks, and his gun had gotten him into trouble once before because it hadn't been registered. It was now, of course, but he didn't have a concealed carry permit, so he'd left it back in his apartment.

He looked around Georgia's living room for something he could use to protect them, if necessary, his gaze falling on an iron sculpture on the entry table.

He threw the blankets back when Siggy slowly rose, the growl becoming louder. There was a scraping at the door and Sam leapt from the bed, stumbling for the entry table.

He hefted the iron statue in one hand, testing its weight. It would do, if he had to use it. He took a step back, drawing a deep breath.

The hum of the electronic lock releasing had his shoulders tensing. He lifted the statue, backing up against the wall as the door eased open. The intruder was tall, only a few inches shorter than Sam.

I can take him.

Unless he was armed. Then who would protect Georgia and Eloise?

A second later, he released the breath he held with a whoosh. It was a woman wearing blue scrubs. A nurse. Nurse Roxanne, specifically.

She crept into the room, then turned to see him, letting out a small shriek that she stifled behind the hand she slapped across her mouth. Her other hand was pressed to her heart.

Off-kilter from the fright, Sam put the statue back on the table and backed away, his hands up, palms out. 'I'm sorry,' he whispered. 'I didn't know it was you.'

She stared at him, her eyes wide and wild. 'Dr Sam! What are you doing here?'

'Just staying with Georgia and Eloise for the night. They were missing Benny.' He didn't need to tell her that he was afraid for their safety. The cops didn't want anyone disclosing that they suspected someone on the staff. It would cause undue stress to the residents and their families.

And to the innocent members of the staff. Which was nearly all of them.

Heavy footsteps thudded down the hallway, Officer Stern appearing in the still-open doorway. 'Everything okay in here?'

'Just a misunderstanding,' Sam said. 'Nurse Roxanne didn't know that I was here and I startled her.'

Roxanne pointed to the iron statue. 'He was going to hit me with that.'

'Not you,' Sam said, torn between wanting to comfort her and berate her reaction. 'A prowler. I was asleep and heard a noise. I woke up unsure of where I was and I . . . panicked.'

He hated the lie, but he didn't want to alert the staff to how afraid he was for his friends.

'But everything's okay?' Stern asked again.

'Yes,' Roxanne said, still holding her hand to her heart. 'I'm just here to check on Miss Georgia. She had a sedative today and I always check on my patients after they've been sedated for any reason.'

'I'm fine.' Georgia eased her bedroom door closed behind her. 'I wish I were sedated now because Eloise snores like a freaking freight train. I'm going to make some tea. Anyone want a cup?'

'I'll take one,' Sam said. 'Nurse Roxanne?'

'Sure,' she said faintly. 'I'd ask for something stronger, but I'm on duty.'

'Then I'll leave you all to it,' Stern said, closing the door.

Roxanne sat at Georgia's dinette table and rubbed her temples. 'Dr Sam, you scared the life out of me.'

'I'm sorry. You scared me, too, if it's any consolation. Georgia, can I get anything for you?'

'Some of those cookies we were eating during the movie,' Georgia said. 'I think tea with cookies is in order.'

Her shoulders relaxing a fraction, Roxanne folded her hands on the table. 'What movie did you see?'

'*The Lincoln Lawyer*,' Sam said. 'Miss Georgia liked the plot. Miss Eloise liked Matthew McConaughey.'

Roxanne smiled fondly. 'At least it wasn't *Magic Mike* again. I got an eyeful the night I checked on her and she was watching that movie. She was dancing to the music. I was afraid she'd snap her hip. She told me that she'd done belly dancing back in the day and that she had core muscles of steel.'

Chuckling, Sam put the cookies on a plate. He'd have eaten them straight from the box, but Miss Georgia liked things just so. 'Miss Eloise is a treasure.'

'She is at that,' Roxanne agreed. 'Can I get the tea for you, Miss Georgia?'

'No, thank you. I need to move so that I don't snap *my* hip. I was *not* a belly dancer back in the day.'

Within minutes, they were enjoying tea and cookies in companionable silence, Georgia slipping Siggy a cookie when she thought Sam wasn't looking.

Sam frowned at her. 'Miss Georgia. You know cookies aren't good for him. I'd expect that from Eloise, but not you.'

Georgia sniffed. 'Now you're just being mean.'

Sam's lips twitched. 'Roxanne, I've been meaning to ask how you like being a traveling nurse. One of my clients is considering it.' The young woman, experiencing PTSD after an armed break-in at her home, needed a change of venue. She was considering going on the road.

'I like it. I get to meet new people every few months. And I can refuse assignments if I want to.'

'Which assignments do you like?' he asked.

'I love the retirement and nursing homes. I love older people. I was raised by an elderly grandmother who had a lot of very spry friends, so I suppose I'm looking for someone like my grandmother every time I move on to a new place. Her best friend was a lot like Miss Eloise – quirky, but very smart and funny. Those are happy memories. Tell your client that it can be a solitary life, though. Not many partners are willing to share a nomadic life.'

Sam nodded. It was the primary concern he'd had for his client – having no support system nearby as she traveled from place to place. 'I'll tell her. Thank you.'

Georgia turned to Roxanne. 'I wanted to thank you for taking such good care of Benny over the last few weeks. We're going to miss you when you're gone.'

Sam lifted his brows. 'You're leaving? When?' He hadn't realized her contract was winding down.

'This is my last week. I'm taking a few days' vacation in Monterey to see the otters and then I'm off to my next contract. Thank you, Miss Georgia. Mr Benny was a joy to care for.' Her smile was sad. 'I'm going to miss him.'

'We all will,' Georgia murmured.

Sam's chest squeezed as he thought again about the loss they'd suffered. Frankie and Benny in the same week. It was going to take them all a while to heal. He lifted his teacup. 'To Frankie and Benny. May you be at peace.'

Georgia lifted her cup as well. 'May you be reunited with the loves of your lives.'

Roxanne lifted her cup with a sigh. 'May their memory be a blessing.'

They finished their tea in what was now a subdued silence. Nurse Roxanne rinsed her cup and set it in the sink. 'Call me when you want the dishes done, Miss Georgia. I'll come and do them for you or I'll send Devon to help.'

'Thank you,' Georgia said graciously.

Sam hid a smile behind his cup, knowing that Georgia's tone meant that she'd ask for help on a cold day in hell.

Roxanne pulled a blood pressure cuff from the pocket of her scrubs. 'Let me take your BP and then I'll be on my way.'

Georgia obediently stuck out her arm, patiently waiting as Roxanne took her vitals, then pouring herself another cup of tea when her numbers proved good.

'Good night,' Roxanne said. 'I'll see you Thursday or Friday. I'm on days for the rest of the week.'

'I hope your next assignment is less chaotic than this one has been,' Georgia said, and Roxanne smiled ruefully.

'I have to say this is the most drama I've ever experienced on a job. But I still enjoyed being here and meeting you all. Thank you for the tea.'

She closed the door and Sam sighed. 'I was ready to smack her on the head with that ugly statue on your table.'

Georgia rolled her eyes. 'Would have been fitting. Roxanne turned up her nose at my statue when she thought I wasn't looking.'

Ah. There was the snarky Georgia he knew and loved. He'd been a little worried because she'd been so polite all evening. She'd even let

Eloise watch an abbreviated version of *Magic Mike*, fast-forwarding through most of the movie until she got to the 'good parts.'

Sam looked over his shoulder at the statue. 'It *is* ugly, Miss Georgia.'

It was a fertility statue of some kind, with overly exaggerated genitalia.

'I know, but I love it and it comes with a good memory. I got that on a photo safari in Africa. It's not real, of course. Just a replica. But I think Roxanne was appalled by the exposed dangly bits.'

Sam choked on his tea. 'You can't make me laugh like that.'

She pounded his back. 'You'll survive.'

'I don't know about that. Dangly bits?' Shaking his head, Sam drained his cup, then gathered the dishes, loading them into the dishwasher before putting the rest of the cookies away.

'You don't have to do that, Sam.'

Sam got a dog treat for Siggy from his overnight bag. 'I didn't want you giving Siggy any more cookies. It'll bother his gut and nobody wants that.'

She made a face. 'On that note, I'm going back to bed. I hate to take sleeping pills, but I need something. I'll never fall asleep with Eloise's snoring.' One silver brow lifted. 'I'm going to record her with my phone for future use.'

Sam lifted a brow. 'Blackmail, Georgia? Really?'

Georgia grinned a little evilly. 'Really. We don't become nice just because we become old, Sam.'

'Good night, Georgia.'

Sam turned off the lights and went back to the sofa bed, Siggy on his heels. He was sure he wouldn't sleep a wink on that uncomfortable bed, but that was all right.

He could sleep soundly when everyone was safe.

San Diego PD, San Diego, California
Wednesday, 9 November, 7.45 A.M.

Kit slid a cup of coffee in front of Jeff Mansfield, who looked as if he'd been working all night. 'Any luck getting through that encryption?'

Jeff looked up, his eyes bloodshot. 'No. You're going to question Adler, right?'

'I'm headed to the interview rooms as soon as I'm done nagging you.'

He sighed as he accepted the coffee. 'It's okay. I understand. I have to say I didn't expect to be on such a high-profile case so quickly, you know? I only got promoted into this role a few months ago. I wish I had better news.'

'I get it,' she said. 'Luckily we caught Adler running. We have leverage, so I'm hoping we can convince him to assist us quickly. Can you join us? You can sit behind the glass and watch. If there are specific questions we need to ask about passwords and such, you can feed them to us.'

Jeff jumped to his feet. 'I'd like that.' He grabbed his phone and laptop. 'Let's go.'

Kit moved the thick folder she held under one arm so that she could carry her own coffee. 'Have you ever observed before?'

'Yes, but not a case of this magnitude. What's in the folder?'

'Kent Crawford's offshore bank information. We got the electronic file this morning.' Dave, Crawford's financial advisor, had been as forthcoming as he'd promised – once he'd had a signed warrant in his hands.

'And you printed it out?' Jeff asked, frowning. 'Why?'

'Because I need to see the figures spread out and I can't do that on my screen. It's hard for me to follow the numbers unless I can run my fingers over them.'

Jeff shook his head, as if that made no sense to him, which was the usual reaction she got from computer types. 'Did you find anything?' he asked.

'Not really. Not yet, anyway. I've only been looking for an hour. What I do know is that two years ago, Kent's deposits into his offshore account and into his investment portfolio shrank by fifty percent, then started to rebound a few months later. He hadn't reached the earlier deposit levels, but he was getting there. Then they dipped again a year ago and are just going up again.'

'Two years ago was when Chadwick Redford started buying real

230

estate,' Jeff said thoughtfully. 'And a year ago was when Miss Evans was hired.'

Kit smiled, pleased that he'd come to the same conclusion that she and Connor had. 'Good job. I think two years ago was when Adler found out what Crawford was doing and horned in. Then together, they managed to increase their take so that they were bringing in nearly twice as much together.'

'Then Miss Evans entered the mix?'

'Exactly. We have to look into what happened to her predecessor, Selma Waite. I'm hoping Adler can shed some light on her accident. Dr Batra checked the autopsy report and the break was clean, but there weren't a lot of other bumps and bruises consistent with a fall, which was suspicious. But there was no sign of forced entry into the house and no evidence anyone else had been there, so they declared it an accidental death.'

'You think she found out about Crawford's shenanigans?'

Kit nodded. 'That's exactly what I think. But let's see if we can get some actual evidence.'

They hurried to the observation room, which wasn't nearly as full as Navarro's office had been the day before. Alicia Batra was in her office at the morgue, and CSU's Ryland was up in San Francisco with his team, searching Frankie Flynn's house in Russian Hill. The captain was in the observation room, but the assistant chief had another commitment.

Detective Goddard was also there, talking to Connor.

And Sam was there. He smiled at her tentatively when she entered the observation room, then schooled his features to a detached, professional expression.

'Can we get started?' the captain asked. 'I have a full schedule today.'

Kit readied her tablet, bringing up the notes she'd taken earlier that morning when she and Connor had met at their desks for breakfast and brainstorming.

Breakfast had been a box of Betsy's baked goods, of course. Connor never turned down a treat made by Betsy McKittrick.

'I'm ready,' she said. 'Connor?'

He rolled his shoulders and shook out his fingers. 'Showtime. I'll wait for your signal before I jump in.'

They'd choreographed their approach. Kit would be the good cop this morning and Connor would loom menacingly.

They entered the interview room and Kit got her first look at Archie Adler. He appeared younger than twenty-five, although at the moment he looked like he hadn't slept a wink.

Good, Kit thought irritably. He could sleep in jail.

She sat at the table, nodding to Adler's lawyer before turning a sweet smile on Adler himself. 'Mr Adler, we're so sorry to have interrupted your trip to Catalina Island last night, but we have some questions for you.'

Adler's lawyer cleared his throat. 'I've advised my client to say nothing.'

'I figured as much,' Kit said. 'Although we are talking a murder charge, so . . .'

Adler's head jerked up, his eyes wide. 'I did not kill anyone.'

'Archie,' his lawyer said quietly. 'Say nothing. We agreed.'

Kit recognized Adler's defense attorney. She'd tangled with him before. He was smart and didn't seem as sleazy as some she'd met. 'Mr Adler, where were you Saturday night between six thirty and nine o'clock?'

Adler paled. 'Why?'

She smiled. 'Just answer the question, please.'

The attorney stepped in. 'My client was on his boat all day Saturday. He left Friday evening at five, dropped anchor about five miles out in the Pacific, and slept on board. He spent Saturday on the water, then returned Sunday afternoon.'

'Who can verify this, Archie?' Kit asked. 'Did you have anyone with you?'

Archie swallowed. 'I was alone.'

Kit had expected this. Dominic Stanza and his girlfriend had said the same thing, that Archie had gone out alone, and Roger – Archie's apartment neighbor – had said that his mother had witnessed Dominic and Archie together on Sunday evening. So that all fit together.

'That's really too bad,' she said with a heavy sigh. 'That means you have no one to verify your alibi for midnight to eight a.m. on Saturday, either. Do you know the significance of these times, Mr Adler?'

Archie said nothing. Kit cleared her throat, the signal for Connor to do his thing.

'Oh, for God's sake,' Connor snarled, playing the bad cop with gusto. He opened his folder and spilled photos on the table – photos of both Frankie Flynn's and Kent Crawford's bodies. 'Don't give me your lame excuses. We have two dead bodies, and you not only have no alibi, you have motive and opportunity.'

Archie looked green. 'Stop,' he said hoarsely, pushing the photos away. 'I didn't kill anyone. And Crawford killed himself. I read it online.'

'Well, Frankie Flynn didn't kill himself,' Kit said, tapping the photo. 'And we don't think Crawford did, either. How did you find out that Crawford was stealing money from Shady Oaks?'

Archie's lawyer turned the photos facedown, patting Archie's shoulder. 'We want a deal.'

Kit shrugged. 'Depends on what he tells us. I can put together a lot of the pieces myself. Like . . . Archie became suspicious when he noticed that Crawford was driving a nice car, nicer than he should've been able to afford. Archie had broken into the personnel files, so he knew Crawford's salary and realized that Crawford was embezzling.'

'You can't know that,' the lawyer said.

Kit smiled. 'I can.'

'How?' Archie demanded.

'You were overheard on the phone one night about two years ago telling a friend that you needed to hire Crawford's investment guy. But then you wondered how Crawford had money to invest, considering his pay.'

Archie's eyes had widened. 'How did you—'

'Archie,' his attorney interrupted, but it was too late.

Got you, you little bastard. 'Did you know that your mother's house was searched last night? Totally legit, the officers had a warrant and

233

everything.' Navarro himself had presided over that search, emptying out the boxes Archie had stored in his mother's garage. 'We found evidence of your offshore accounts. In the same bank that Crawford used, interestingly enough.'

'Having an offshore account is not a crime,' the lawyer interjected, but Archie had grown even paler.

'No,' Kit agreed, 'but stealing from old people and depositing it in that offshore account is a crime. You're a grad student, Archie. And, according to your advisor, not a very good one. You skip classes and TA sessions. You're flunking out, which is a shame because Professor Chen says you have a brilliant mind. Too bad you use it so selfishly. Where did you get your money, Archie, if you didn't steal it? You have a lot for a twenty-five-year-old fuckup.'

Archie flinched. 'I'm not a fuckup.'

'No, you're a criminal mastermind,' Kit said sarcastically.

Connor pulled a chair away from the table and straddled it. 'We have your mother in custody.' It was a lie, but Archie didn't know that.

Archie's color rose and he started to rise from his chair. 'No. She had nothing to do—'

His lawyer yanked him back into the chair. 'Shut up, Archie.'

'No. My mom worked hard to put me through school. I'm not letting her go to jail for something—' He cut himself off that time, glaring at Connor.

'For something you did?' Kit asked. 'Look, we've dug into Chadwick Redford and found that he doesn't exist. We can proceed with a murder charge against you at full speed, but we may drag our feet on your mom's case. I mean, she had the records in her house. She had to have known that the house had not been bought legitimately. But that might take a while to prove, so she might be in jail for a long time.'

'She can get out on bail,' the lawyer told Archie.

Connor scoffed. 'Did you know that Frankie Flynn was a cop, Archie?'

Archie sucked in a harsh breath. 'No, he wasn't. He ran an antique shop in San Francisco before he retired to Shady Oaks.'

Kit slid another photo across the table. 'This is Frank Wilson at the time of his retirement from SDPD. He was a homicide lieutenant who later changed his name to Flynn. Do you know what happens when a decorated cop is murdered, Archie? Even a retired one?'

Archie closed his eyes, visibly sagging. 'I didn't kill him.'

'Then who did?' Kit asked.

'Crawford. He hated Flynn because Flynn was gay.'

Kit shook her head. 'He didn't kill Mr Flynn, Archie. He was already dead by the time Mr Flynn was killed. Start telling me what I need to know or we're going to assume you killed them both.'

'Why would I kill Flynn?' Archie cried. 'I didn't kill Crawford, and I didn't have a single reason to kill Flynn.'

Kit shrugged. 'Maybe he'd caught on to what you and Crawford were doing. It could be that simple.'

Archie slapped the table in frustration. 'I didn't kill Flynn!'

'Then who did?' Kit asked again.

'Evans,' Archie spat. 'It had to be Evans.'

Kit sat back in her chair. 'Why would she kill him?'

'Like you said, Flynn found out about the money.'

The lawyer closed his eyes. 'Archie. Shut up.'

'No. They can't pin any murders on me because I didn't kill anybody!' He turned to Kit. 'We stole money, fine, but I didn't kill anyone.'

'How was Miss Evans involved?' Connor asked coldly. 'She says you're a "nice young man," but you throw her under the bus. Why should we believe you?'

'There's proof on the server,' Archie said. 'I know you took it. Evans called me all upset because she was afraid that you'd find evidence on it.'

'Why would you leave evidence on Shady Oaks's company server?' Kit asked, genuinely puzzled. 'Doesn't seem very secure.'

'It's very secure,' Archie said through clenched teeth. 'Nobody's cracking that encryption except for me. You can tell your pet monkeys to stop trying. You'll all be in a retirement home before your IT wannabes figure it out.'

'Or we can hire Professor Chen,' Connor said coldly.

Archie paled once again, then rallied, lifting his chin. 'He won't be able to, either.'

'Again, that's fine,' Kit said. 'We'll pursue the murder charges while we wait. Your mom and Dominic might be able to get out on bail, but we're going to do everything we can to see that doesn't happen.'

Archie huffed impatiently. 'I didn't kill anybody.'

'What about Selma Waite?' Connor asked.

Archie's head rocked back as if they'd slapped him.

'Who is Selma Waite?' the lawyer asked.

'Miss Evans's predecessor,' Connor said, keeping his gaze fastened to Archie's face. 'She died under very mysterious conditions. Fell down a flight of stairs and broke her neck, but there were no other major injuries. No other broken bones, and only minor bruises.'

'I didn't kill her, either,' Archie whispered. 'That was Crawford.'

Kit shrugged. 'Too bad he's not here to confirm or deny. You're on your own, kid. And it doesn't look good. You stole money from old people. Even if we can't pin a murder charge on you – and we will work very hard to make that happen, by the way – you'll have to hope a jury believes that you did not commit grand larceny.'

Archie leaned over to whisper in his attorney's ear. He must have asked what the sentence was for larceny. The young man's lips curved in relief when he heard the answer. 'Three years? That's all?'

'Per count,' Connor said. 'And we'll make sure that we charge you for every time you dipped into Shady Oaks's money. We've got your financials from the boxes in your mom's garage, remember? You made deposits into your offshore account every month for two years. How many years in prison did we figure, Detective McKittrick?'

'Twenty-four counts,' Kit said. 'Times three years each. I might not be a genius like you, but even I can calculate that that's seventy-two years. You'll never make it to Shady Oaks, Archie. You'll die in prison. And even if it's half that, that's still thirty-six years. And don't forget, there's a dead cop in the middle of all this. Juries don't generally like entitled young men who own fancy boats they bought by stealing from retired people they murder. So, what are you gonna do?'

236

Kit and Connor had no idea if the prosecutors would take that approach to charging and sentencing, but it had been done before and Archie's lawyer seemed to know this.

'What do you want from him?' the lawyer asked.

'We want access to that server, for starters,' Kit said. 'We want a signed statement detailing how the theft occurred, and how Crawford figured out how to steal the money to begin with. We want to know about the death of Selma Waite and we want to know where Archie hid the coins.'

Archie frowned, appearing confused. 'What coins?'

'The coins that were stolen from Benny Dreyfus's room,' Connor snapped. 'Four million dollars' worth. Crawford was the last to have them.'

Archie shook his head vehemently. 'I do not know *anything* about coins and I *didn't* kill Kent Crawford. I'll admit to the rest – for a deal. But not murder, because I didn't do it. Crawford was the killer, not me.'

Kit stood up. 'Give us a minute. We'll be back.'

She and Connor went back to the observation room, where Navarro was pacing. 'I don't know,' the lieutenant said. 'Do you believe him?'

'I do,' Sam said quietly. 'I don't think he killed anyone. You didn't find the coins in any of his things, did you?'

'No,' Goddard said. 'We searched his apartment, his mother's house, and all the boxes he'd moved into her garage. We searched the house his friend was living in, all their cars, and the boat. If Adler's hidden them, he's done a good job.'

'I think his confusion concerning the coins was genuine,' Kit said slowly. 'But I don't know about Crawford's murder. He might have done it.'

'I think it's more likely that Crawford would have killed Adler,' Connor said. 'Crawford was pulling in a lot of money before Adler came along and then they had to split it. And then they had to split it again when Evans came into the picture.'

Kit sighed. Connor was probably right. 'Adler's the best option we have for Crawford's murder right now, although he's too tall to have been the person who took the coins out of Shady Oaks early Saturday morning. Let's get his statement on the money theft and let him believe murder is still on the table. Mainly because he's an arrogant ass.'

'He is that,' Sam agreed. 'Where is Miss Evans?'

'We picked her up as she was leaving for work this morning,' Navarro said. 'She's waiting in the next interview room. She thinks she's here to answer questions about Crawford. Get Adler's statement about how she came into the picture. I want her to roll on Adler. I also want to know when Crawford started stealing – and if the director before Selma Waite knew anything about it.'

'What about Crawford's killer?' Kit asked, frustrated with herself because she'd dropped the ball on Waite's predecessor, JoAnne Tremblay.

'We need to beef up our search for whoever he was banging,' Navarro said bluntly.

'He was with someone?' Sam asked.

Kit nodded. '*With* someone in the motel room where he was found, sometime before he died.'

Sam nodded once. 'Okay. Got it. Maybe Adler knows who they are.'

'Can't hurt to ask.' Kit turned to Jeff. 'What do we need Adler to provide for server access?'

Jeff handed her a sheet of paper where he'd neatly printed exactly what he needed. 'This. I may need more to get to the files we're interested in, but this is a start. Would he know about Devon Jones? Because I searched the key-card logs and her key card was used at several entry points the night Mr Dreyfus died.'

Goddard shook his head. 'We verified her alibi. Devon Jones was at the ER with her daughter all night.'

'So,' Kit said, relieved that the young woman could be eliminated from the suspect list, 'someone either had her key card or a copy. Is that possible?'

Jeff nodded. 'It is. All of the ID numbers attached to the key cards are in the personnel file, which I haven't been able to access yet. But once I have that info, I can tell you which card was used – her assigned card or a copy.'

'Go back in there,' Navarro said wearily. 'At least make him tell you how to access the information on the server.'

Kit suddenly felt as drained as Navarro sounded, despite getting a full night's sleep. 'Will do.'

Fourteen

San Diego PD, San Diego, California
Wednesday, 9 November, 12.30 P.M.

Sam settled into a chair in the observation room adjacent to where they'd watched Adler's interrogation, readying himself for the interrogation of Faye Evans. The woman was sitting at a table in the interview room on the other side of the glass, clearly irate. They'd kept her waiting since eight a.m.

Sam had hoped she wasn't guilty, but Adler's confession had left little doubt. The man had photos and recorded messages, all of which he'd eventually shared.

It had taken quite a while to wheedle the confession and necessary server passwords out of Archie Adler. The young man's lawyer had proven savvy enough to demand that a deal be drafted first, so they'd had to call the prosecutor's office.

Sam had been relieved when the prosecutor who'd turned up was his best friend, Joel Haley. The other prosecutors were good, of course, but Sam trusted Joel to treat this case right. Joel had been thorough, but eventually he and Adler's lawyer had come to an acceptable deal and Adler had spilled everything he knew about the thefts.

Crawford had been stealing from the Shady Oaks operating fund for years before Adler had figured out his scheme and wanted in. It was less money for Crawford, but he'd had little choice.

Joel dropped into the chair beside him. 'Pretty interesting, huh?'

'Much better to be on this side of the glass,' Sam said wryly. He'd been questioned as a possible suspect during Kit's big serial killer

240

case six months ago. It had been how they'd met and, while he was glad to have met Kit McKittrick, he didn't want to be on the other side of the glass ever again.

'I guess so. So I take it that everyone was surprised about JoAnne Tremblay.'

'Oh yeah.' One of the biggest bombshells of Adler's disclosure was that Crawford had started his stealing after catching JoAnne Tremblay, the director before Selma Waite, dipping into the facility's money on a regular basis. Crawford had demanded a cut and the previous director had been forced to agree. 'I knew Mrs Tremblay. She was the one who signed off on my volunteering. I never would have expected a woman whose favorite song was "Love Letters in the Sand" to be an embezzler.'

'What's "Love Letters in the Sand"?' Joel asked.

Detective Goddard took the chair on the other side of Sam. 'Pat Boone. One of my great-aunts had the album.'

Joel huffed a laugh. 'Wow. Still waters.'

'Exactly.' Goddard smoothed his tie. 'I'm hoping that Evans knows more about the stolen coins than she's let on. Adler didn't seem to think so, but he also didn't know that Evans and Crawford had been meeting up.'

They hadn't proven that yet, but the emails Jeff Mansfield had uncovered were so bizarrely written that they had to be some kind of private code between the two. There were the reminders to bring an umbrella on a sunny day, but also reminders to avoid construction traffic on a certain street downtown that had no construction – and hadn't for the past year. There were a number of inquiries about the state of the roses in Evans's front yard, but there were no roses there. So something was going on.

'Fingers crossed,' Goddard said. 'I don't know that Evans killed Crawford, though. Her alibi checks out for his TOD. She was caught by traffic cams exiting the freeway at midnight near her mother's residence in Temecula. Ironically, her mother lives in a continuing care facility there. Not as high-priced as Shady Oaks, but it's still a hefty monthly payment.'

'A motive for robbery,' Joel mused. 'She could have driven back, killed Crawford, taken the coins, then returned to Temecula, avoiding the traffic cams.'

'Possibly,' Goddard agreed, 'but she's also too short to have been the person to leave Shady Oaks with the coins. She could have killed Crawford, though, then taken the coins. That's more likely.'

'She could have been the woman in his motel room,' Sam said, 'but I swear that if they were lovers, they were good actors. Just watching them, they were consistently irritated with each other. I can't see them stopping snarling at each other long enough to do anything.'

'Crawford did successfully lie to his friends for ten years,' Connor said as he joined them, brushing a few crumbs from his tie. They'd broken for lunch after Adler's interview, which had left Evans waiting in the adjacent interview room for another forty-five minutes. She'd been there since eight a.m. and had to be hungry.

Kit had suggested the delay. She wanted Evans mad enough to slip and say something incriminating. From the look on Evans's face at the moment, Kit had achieved at least part of her goal. Evans was pissed off.

'That's true,' Sam conceded. 'But even though I was only there a few times a month, I never heard a peep from the residents about them being together. If there had been even a spark, it would have been all over Shady Oaks in a single day. I love the residents, but they are among the worst gossips I've ever met.'

Connor grinned slyly. 'They're already whispering about a certain shrink and a certain detective.'

Sam gave Connor a sharp look of reproof. 'Detective.' Because that wasn't okay. Connor was discussing Kit's private life like it was nothing more than a football game.

Connor sighed. 'Sorry. You're right.'

Goddard shrugged. 'He didn't need to say a word, Doc. It's clear to anyone who bothers to look.'

Joel looked delighted. The bastard. 'What's this?'

'Nothing,' Sam said, shutting down the conversation. 'Where is Detective McKittrick?'

Connor sighed again. 'Skipping lunch to do a background on

JoAnne Tremblay. She wanted to find out how well the woman is living. Tremblay hasn't answered our calls.'

Sam made a face. 'Hell, maybe Crawford and Evans were doing the horizontal tango and I just missed it. I missed Tremblay being an embezzler.' The older woman had been stealing from Shady Oaks long before Crawford had been hired.

'I'm sure if you'd known to look, you would have seen it,' Joel said loyally. 'Ah, here she is. Hey, Kit.'

Kit came into the room, her tablet and a thick folder in one hand, a plastic sack in the other, and a triumphant gleam in her blue eyes. 'Got it.' She put everything she held onto a chair, then showed them her tablet, on which was a photo of a very nice house on a beach. 'JoAnne Tremblay lives in a one-point-four-million-dollar house on Anna Maria Island in Florida. It was bought by an LLC – whose ownership isn't exactly clear yet – two years ago. Cash.'

Connor perked up. 'Is Chadwick Redford involved?'

'Nope. But that's not to say that Adler didn't get tips from Mrs Tremblay.'

Sam shook his head, stunned. 'She was such a sweet lady.'

'I don't know, Doc,' Goddard said. 'Being a Pat Boone fan should have been your first clue. That's so wrong.'

Sam chuckled. 'Maybe. Wow. I wonder how long she was skimming.'

'We'll find out,' Kit vowed. 'I'm going to come at Evans with the murder of both Crawford and Frankie Flynn. We've assumed that one person was involved and Adler was fairly convincing in his denial, but Adler has no verifiable alibi and the two of them could have done it together. Sounds like no one liked Crawford. If they got rid of him, they could have both kept more of the money. Navarro started search warrants for Evans's home and bank accounts last night. Hopefully, we'll be able to dig into her life today.' She glanced at the glass. 'She still doesn't know she's here as a suspect?'

'Not unless she's figured it out while she sits here and stews,' Connor said cheerfully. 'So ask me what I found during lunch.'

Kit frowned. 'You ate lunch during lunch.'

'I can eat and work at the same time. *I* don't skip meals,' Connor said loftily, then grinned when her frown became a scowl. 'I contacted the chairman of the board of directors for Shady Oaks. He was very interested to hear that money was being stolen. He'd been suspicious for some time, but he'd been assured by Miss Evans that she was having an audit done. He's been waiting for the results.'

'So this might have come to light without Frankie's murder,' Sam murmured.

Connor shot him a look of sympathy. 'Probably not. I don't think Evans would have allowed a legit audit. But that's not all. I asked the chairman who recommended Miss Evans after the death of Selma Waite and he said her name was suggested by . . .' He drummed his fingers on his knee. 'Kent Crawford. Crawford had met Evans while she worked for the doctor who'd been treating his wife's lupus.'

'Sonofabitch,' Kit muttered. 'He couldn't even go to his wife's appointments and support her without running his own angle.'

'Looks like,' Connor said.

The door opened and Navarro entered the observation room. 'Sorry I was delayed. We just got the warrants for Evans's home and bank accounts. I sent Detective Marshall and his partner to oversee the search of Evans's house. We'll get the bank information sometime this afternoon.' He nodded at the glass. 'Let's get moving on this, Detectives.'

Connor stood up and smoothed his tie. 'We ready, Kit?'

'Oh yeah,' Kit said menacingly. 'I want her begging for mercy.'

Sam wasn't ashamed to admit that he found that totally hot.

San Diego PD, San Diego, California
Wednesday, 9 November, 12.45 P.M.

Connor sat next to Evans while Kit took the same chair she'd used when questioning Adler, the smile on her face belying any ill intent. Kit McKittrick was fresh-faced and cute, her blond ponytail adding to the girl-next-door persona that Sam thought she cultivated on purpose. It often disarmed her opponents until it was too late and she had them in her clutches.

244

'I'm so sorry, Miss Evans,' Kit began sincerely. 'We've been running like chickens all morning. Please accept our apology.'

Evans glared. 'It is *not* okay, Detective. I have a job, too, and you're keeping me from doing it. Plus, I'm starving.'

'Oh, I can fix that.' Kit put the plastic sack on the table in front of Evans. 'I brought you a sandwich and a bottle of water. Please help yourself.'

Sam sighed. 'I bet that was Kit's lunch.'

'Probably,' Navarro said with a shake of his head.

'Thank you.' Only very slightly mollified, Evans took a bite from the sandwich. 'What do you want to know, Detective?' she asked once she'd swallowed.

'Well, for starters, why did you kill Frankie Flynn?'

Evans's mouth dropped open in shock. *'What?'*

'Why did you kill Frankie Flynn?' Kit repeated patiently.

'I . . . I didn't.' Evans lurched to her feet. 'I'm not sitting here and listening to this for another second.'

'Sit down, Miss Evans,' Kit commanded, her sweet demeanor gone. *'Now.* Because we know you've been stealing from Shady Oaks's operating fund. We know you've been meeting Kent Crawford. We know that he was stealing from Shady Oaks, and we know he's dead. Connect the dots, ma'am, and you get a picture of you killing both Flynn and Crawford.'

Miss Evans paled, sinking back on the chair. 'I didn't kill anyone,' she whispered.

'But you did steal,' Connor said kindly.

Sam guessed Kit got to be the bad cop this time. It suited her better.

Evans shook her head, but it was unconvincing. 'You don't have evidence. If you did, you'd have already arrested me.'

'Were you having an affair with Crawford?' Kit demanded, ignoring Evans's very rational point. Adler's word alone wasn't good enough. They didn't have enough to arrest her. Yet.

Sam hoped the search of Evans's home would yield something immediately useful.

Beside him, Navarro glanced at his phone. 'Detective Marshall found a printed copy of that article about Benny Dreyfus's coins in Evans's home office, dated last Wednesday.'

'The same day Devon said that Crawford asked about the coins,' Sam murmured.

Navarro nodded. 'Exactly. Marshall also woke her computer up and looked at her browser history.'

Goddard sniffed. 'She didn't have it password protected? Amateurs. What had she been checking?'

'How to sell coins,' Navarro said dryly.

'This is almost too easy,' Goddard complained.

'Hush,' Joel admonished. 'I can't hear.'

'– was *not* having an affair with Kent Crawford,' Evans was insisting shrilly.

Kit tapped her tablet, then turned it so that Evans could see. 'This you standing in the lobby of the Excelsior Hotel with Kent Crawford last month?'

Evans's mouth opened again, then closed. She shook her head mutely.

Kit leaned in. 'It's not you? Do you have an evil twin, Miss Evans? And that wasn't a serious question. You have no sister. I checked. This *is* you. You used your own credit card to pay for incidentals. Crawford paid for the room with the credit card attached to his offshore account.'

Sam smiled. 'She was busy while we were eating lunch.'

'She was,' Navarro agreed. 'But to be fair, I assigned a few of the other detectives to cross-check the dates of those weird emails between Evans and Crawford with Crawford's offshore bank account. One of them turned up the photo from the hotel.'

That didn't matter. The photo was now in Kit's hands and she was very good at interrogating. Sam knew that from personal experience.

'You and Crawford had a standing appointment,' Kit went on. 'First Tuesday of every month.'

'We were *not* having an affair,' Evans said firmly. 'We were talking business.'

'What kind of business?' Connor asked mildly. 'We're all ears, Miss Evans.'

Kit glanced at her phone, then at the glass, nodding impercept-ibly. Connor followed her lead, a Cheshire cat grin spreading across his face.

'I just forwarded them the message from Marshall about the search of Evans's home,' Navarro explained.

Connor leaned closer to Evans to murmur, 'You wouldn't have been talking about how to fence Benny Dreyfus's stolen coins, would you? You had been searching the internet for how to sell valuable coins, and you did know about the collection. You printed an article about them seven days ago.'

Evans gasped. 'You've been in my house? You had no right!'

'We have a search warrant,' Kit said coldly. 'Based on the infor-mation provided by Archie Adler. I wonder what he'll add to his statement when he finds out that you and Crawford were planning on stealing the coins and cutting him out?'

Evans's skin went gray and Sam feared they'd need to pause the interview to get her medical assistance.

Evans closed her eyes for a long moment. When she opened them, she looked resigned. 'We planned to steal them, but we didn't. I was as shocked as anyone else to hear that they'd been taken. I guessed that Crawford had stolen them himself.'

'She did seem shocked at the news,' Sam said. 'But she and Craw-ford put up a nice act about their relationship, so her reaction to the stolen coins could have been bogus, too.'

In the interview room, Kit sat back, her expression stony. 'Con-sidering you've lied about so many other things, why should we believe you?'

'Because I was out of town when they were stolen. I was in Temecula, visiting my mother.'

'Whose monthly fees for assisted living were costing you five grand a month,' Connor said with sympathy. 'Four million dollars would buy a lot of care for her.'

Evans huffed in frustration. 'I did *not* steal the coins. I wanted to, but I didn't. Someone else got to them first.'

'You did steal from Shady Oaks, though,' Kit said.

Evans looked away.

'We'll find the money,' Connor said, his tone still mild. 'I promise you that. We'll tell you the same thing we told Archie Adler – we're going to ask the prosecutor to charge you for every time you took even a dime. Separate occurrences. Even if you've only been at it for the year you've been at Shady Oaks, that's more than thirty years in prison.'

'So start talking,' Kit snapped. 'Because I'm still inclined to believe that you killed Crawford. I know what your alibi is *and* what it is not. You still could have driven back from Temecula, killed Crawford after he stole the coins, then killed Frankie Flynn when he threatened to expose you.'

Evans covered her face with her hands. 'I didn't kill anyone. That was Kent.'

'Who did he kill?' Connor asked. 'Besides Selma Waite, your predecessor? Because we figure that she caught Crawford in the act, so he killed her and brought you in. You were in the know from day one, weren't you?'

Evans swayed, then propped her elbows on the table, steadying herself. 'Crawford killed her. Told me that I'd get the same if I told anyone what we were up to. Told me to look the other way and he'd pay me.'

'So you weren't actually stealing from Shady Oaks,' Connor said. 'You were just accepting money Crawford had stolen.'

Evans nodded miserably. 'Yes. But I didn't kill him. I didn't kill anyone.'

'Then who did?' Kit asked, her face unsmiling. 'I want answers, Miss Evans. Because you and Adler are still alive. You'll bear the brunt of both the theft *and* the murder.'

'I don't know who killed Kent or Frankie Flynn!' Evans cried loudly. Tears began to stream down her cheeks. 'I don't know!'

Connor pushed a box of tissues in front of her. 'Then tell us what you do know. The sooner we find the real killer, the sooner you're not a suspect. You were meeting Crawford once a month. Why?'

'For sex,' Evans admitted quietly. 'But it wasn't an affair. It was . . . payment.'

Kit tilted her head, studying the older woman. 'For what, exactly?'

'When the board came to me asking if I'd like the job as director of Shady Oaks, I didn't know that Kent was involved. I jumped at the chance to change jobs. It was a big step up and more salary. My mom needed the care and I'd gone through my savings. Then I showed up for my first day and there was Kent, looking smug.' Her expression hardened. 'I'd had an affair with him a year before and regretted it. His wife is nice and . . . I don't know why I started with him. I was in a bad place then, and he was charming when he wanted to be.'

'So you took the job at Shady Oaks,' Kit said. 'Then?'

'Then he took me out to lunch my first day, told me that he was the reason I'd gotten the job. Told me that he'd picked me specially and that he expected me not to rock the boat. I didn't know what that meant for another week, not until Archie brought me the invoice to sign for the purchase of the new security system. I knew how much it should have cost and the invoice was twice the right price. I said something to Archie and the next thing I knew, Kent was in my office. Told me to sign the invoice or I'd end up like my predecessor. Who I knew was dead. I still didn't want to sign it, but then he showed me an offshore account he'd opened – in my name. It already had twenty thousand dollars in it. He told me to sign the invoice for the overpriced security system or he'd go to the board and accuse me of theft. I . . . signed it.' She sighed. 'After that, he had me. He and Archie were skimming everything from the operating fund to the supplies to payments to vendors.'

'When did the sex start?' Connor asked quietly.

'My second week. Kent knew that my mother needed continuing care and that I couldn't afford it. So he added . . . stipulations to my continued employment. It was disgusting,' Evans said bitterly. 'I'd scrub and scrub after we were done, but I haven't felt clean since I started at Shady Oaks.' She lifted her chin and met Kit's unflinching gaze. 'I wanted to kill him so many times, Detective, but I never did. I had the opportunity several times – every time he rolled off me and took a nap – but I never did. I'm not a killer. I'm not really even a thief. Just . . . weak.'

'What about the coins?' Kit asked.

'I knew about them. Janice, the head nurse, had told me that Devon Jones had reported it, but I wasn't about to tell Kent. He found out anyway. I asked how he'd found out, but he . . . Well, he wasn't a nice man. When he hit, it hurt. He told me that he'd checked the browser history of my home computer when he . . .' She closed her eyes.

'You weren't just meeting him at the hotel, were you?' Connor asked.

Evans shook her head. 'No,' she whispered, then cleared her throat. 'Kent came and went as he pleased. He owned me. Which he was pleased to tell me every chance he got. He taunted me with emails "reminding" me of our standing appointment. Sometimes they were reminding me to bring my umbrella. That was code for condoms. But then he'd ask how my roses were doing. That's my mother's name. Rose. He knew I'd do whatever I had to do to keep her safe and healthy.

'Anyway, he found the article about Benny's coins on my computer. He printed it out and shoved it in my face. I'd googled the coins when Janice told me about them. I don't know how Kent zeroed in on that one article in my history, but he was good at ferreting out secrets. Security was his job. Kent told me to find out where Benny was keeping the coins. I told him that the Dreyfus family would never allow Benny to keep something so valuable in his apartment and he laughed. Said I was a terrible liar.'

She really is, Sam had to agree.

'Kent told me that I better find out how to get my hands on the coins or I'd be sorry. My mother would be sorry. So I made up a reason to visit Benny and found the safe inside the cabinet. But we needed the combination to the safe in addition to Benny's fingerprint. The fingerprint was easy, especially since Benny took sleeping pills at night, but the combination would be harder. So Kent gave me a camera to put in Benny's room. It was one of those that records directly to a memory card, no internet involved, because he didn't want Archie to know about it. Kent had hidden it in a vase, like a nanny-cam.'

'We didn't find a vase like that in his room,' Kit said, but Sam could tell she was interested.

'It was gone when he died. I was surprised, too, Detective.

250

I figured that Kent had taken it and stolen the coins.' Evans narrowed her eyes. 'You think he stole them, too.'

Kit shrugged. 'Maybe. But he's dead, so we can't ask him. Convenient.'

Evans shook her head. 'I did *not* kill him. I didn't want to help him. That I did was on me, but I did not kill him, and nothing you say will get me to tell you otherwise.'

'When did Crawford give you the vase? Date and time, please?' Connor asked. 'And when did you plant it in Mr Dreyfus's apartment?'

'He gave it to me on Wednesday. It was at the end of the workday, so sometime around five. I put the vase in Benny's living room when he was at dinner. So around six o'clock.' She studied Kit, then glanced at Connor. 'You're searching my house right now?'

'Yes,' Connor said simply. 'Your financials, too.'

'You won't find the coins there. Or the camera vase. I guarantee it. But Kent had a storage unit. I saw a receipt for it once when I went through his briefcase.'

Connor lifted a brow. 'When he was sleeping after sex?'

Evans flushed. 'Yes. I was hoping to find something incriminating on him, but I'm not that lucky or devious. I don't remember where it is, but maybe he hid the coins there.'

Kit flipped through the pages in the folder she'd been carrying, nodding. 'All right. We'll check it out. Did you ever meet Mr Crawford anywhere else?'

'Other than my own house whenever he felt like barging in? No. He liked the Excelsior Hotel. I think he met all his lovers there. I don't know that he was ever faithful to his wife. I don't know why he stayed married to her.'

Kit was still studying the pages in the folder. 'Did you meet at the hotel any other day besides Tuesday?'

'No. I got the impression he was meeting someone else there, though. One of the women behind the front desk said something like, "Welcome back, sir, I trust your and Mrs Crawford's stay last week was satisfactory?" Kent told her that it was and we went on to our room.'

Kit closed the folder and gave Evans a notepad. 'All right. I want you to write out your statement. Include anything that you think will help you steer clear of a murder charge. And "I could have done it at any time but didn't" isn't a great defense, just so you know.'

She and Connor rose and left the room while Evans silently began to write.

Kit entered the observation room, her frustration palpable. 'We are no closer to knowing who killed Crawford and Flynn,' she complained.

'Did you find charges for a storage unit in Crawford's financials?' Connor asked as he closed the door behind them.

'Yes,' Navarro said, holding up his phone. 'I just texted the other detectives I put on the case and one of them had noticed it. It's a place not too far from Crawford's house.'

'We can cut the lock off to search the unit,' Connor said, 'since we didn't find a key. Both Evans and Adler could have killed both Crawford and Flynn. We'll keep digging, Kit. We'll find something.'

'I know,' she said grudgingly. 'All we know is that Crawford is still the most likely to have stolen the coins. Evans is too short and Adler is too tall to be the figure exiting Shady Oaks at four fifteen on Saturday morning.'

Sam frowned. 'If either Adler or Evans could have killed Frankie, where did they enter the building? The camera on Frankie's floor was disabled the night he died, but the exterior cameras were working, weren't they? Neither Adler or Evans should have been on-site Saturday night. Neither was invited to Eloise's party, and they didn't usually work weekends unless there was a problem. Did you catch one of them on camera somewhere?'

Kit nodded, looking annoyed with herself. 'You're right. We should have thought of that. I think we need to go back to the beginning. Connor, let's have another look at all the cameras and recheck alibis. Assuming that the camera feeds haven't been tampered with by either Adler or Crawford, we'll hopefully find something that sticks out. Thank you, Sam.' She looked back at Faye Evans, who was bent over the notepad, scribbling her confession. 'What about Shady Oaks? Who will take over?'

Because Evans was not leaving custody. Not unless she made bail at her arraignment.

'Probably the head nurse, Janice Lenski,' Sam said. 'Janice covered for Evans when she had to take off time for her mother's surgery a few months back. Everything was fine then. Evans's assistant Lily doesn't have any computer knowledge and Evans was only keeping her on until she retires. Which is next month.'

'We should check Lily's financials, too,' Navarro said. 'If the woman two directors ago fooled everyone, this woman might, too.'

'We already did,' Connor said, 'but we'll give her bank accounts a deeper look.'

Navarro nodded. 'Sounds good. Go eat, McKittrick. We've had this conversation before. Take care of yourself or I'll catch holy hell from your mother.'

Kit sighed. 'Yes, sir.'

San Diego PD, San Diego, California
Wednesday, 9 November, 5.00 P.M.

'This doesn't make sense,' Connor complained, leaning back until the chair in which he sat was balanced on two legs.

Kit considered giving the chair a little shove but decided it wouldn't be in her best interest. She didn't have time to train a new partner right now.

They'd been holed up in one of Homicide's conference rooms all afternoon, viewing footage from Shady Oaks's security cameras. They'd examined each entrance, first for the four-hour period around Frankie Flynn's death, then expanding it to eight, then to twelve. Finally, they'd examined the entire twenty-four hours that encompassed both Crawford's and Flynn's deaths.

So far, they'd seen no one who hadn't been on the duty roster for that day – the roster that Jeff had pulled from the server, once he'd finally gotten in.

'It only makes sense if a staff member on duty that night killed

Flynn,' Kit said, looking at the list of personnel they'd been tracking via a combination of the key-card system and the camera footage.

'And Benny,' Connor added. Because they'd checked the camera on Benny's floor – thankfully reset by Jeff Mansfield in time to capture the footage from the morning that Benny had died.

Just as the key-card logs had reported, Nurse Roxanne had entered Benny's apartment twice before ten p.m. on Monday evening, staying for a few minutes each time. Nurse Janice had entered twice between midnight and four a.m. Nurse Janice had confirmed all four visits as legitimate.

Then, at five a.m. on Tuesday, someone dressed in baggy blue scrubs and shoes with platform soles had entered Benny's room using Devon Jones's key card. The intruder had worn a puffy jacket that obscured the size and shape of their torso. They'd also worn gloves so that their hands were hidden. Their head, hair, and face were also hidden by a cheap wig and a baseball cap, because of course they were. Kit and Connor couldn't even see how high the intruder's platform soles were, as their pants covered most of the heel, but the figure appeared to be between five-eight and five-eleven, similar to the thief seen leaving Shady Oaks early Saturday morning.

The person stayed in Benny's apartment for ten minutes, then crept out and down the nearest staircase. But the intruder hadn't exited the building. Not through any of the exits.

Kit didn't need the results of Mr Dreyfus's blood test to tell her that Benny had been murdered at five a.m. Tuesday morning.

So now they were looking at every member of the Shady Oaks staff. Including Miss Evans and Archie Adler, even though neither of them had come close to the facility the whole weekend. Either one – or both – could have been calling the shots. Perhaps paying or extorting a staff member to commit the crimes. So they were still suspects in the murders.

Kit stared at the list of staff. 'We can eliminate anyone under about five-four.' It was an educated guess, as it was difficult to tell exactly how tall the intruder was because they'd slumped their shoulders and back but had also increased their height with the thick wig on their head and platform soles on their feet. 'They knew they were being watched.'

'Yeah, they did. I wish we could at least figure out the body type of Benny's intruder. That jacket hides everything.'

'This sucks,' Kit muttered. 'Now we have to check the financials of nearly everyone here. Only twenty percent of the staff are too short. I wish we had a look at the intruder's face. I wish the camera angle was better. I wish the killer had left something behind we can work with.'

Because, so far, they had nothing. No fingerprints, no hair, no nothing.

Connor sighed. 'We have video of Evans entering Benny's room, carrying a large shopping bag. The bag would have been big enough for the vase she claimed to have planted a camera in to capture Benny putting his combination into the safe's lock. Evans leaves a few minutes later with the folded bag tucked under her arm.' He paused, thinking. 'Which is odd on its own. I mean, Crawford – or someone – turned off the camera the night that Flynn was killed. Why leave the video of Evans entering Benny's room? Unless Crawford meant to set Evans up to take the fall for the theft.'

'Sounds like something he'd do,' Kit agreed. 'He was going to let Evans take the fall, but someone killed him first. And got the coins. And the vase, because nobody's seen it.'

Connor nodded. 'It's fair to assume that whoever stole the coins took the vase, too. Maybe we search the staff lockers for the vase? If we can get a warrant. All of the lockers might be too broad a search.'

Kit sat up straighter. 'That's a good angle, actually, even though I doubt the vase is still around. The thief would have to have taken the vase *before* Saturday morning when they took the collection. Evans said the camera wasn't connected to the Wi-Fi so that Adler wouldn't know about it. The thief would have needed to view the video on the memory card to see what the combination was before breaking in. They could have viewed it on a laptop in a break room or even in Benny's apartment, but nobody else going in and out of Benny's was carrying a vase or a laptop.' She sorted through the key-card logs once again. 'Here's the master key card used by Evans the Wednesday before the coins were taken – at six o'clock, just as she said.'

Connor frowned. 'Crawford gave Evans the vase right after Devon told him that she didn't know about the coins. That Crawford specifically asked Devon meant that he knew that she knew. How? How did he know that Devon had seen them?'

'That's a good question. It's possible that Evans lied about that, and she did tell Crawford that Devon knew. But just about every-thing she said in her interview checks out. She placed the vase in the room, but she didn't go back to get it, at least not with a key card that could be traced to her.'

'So she either had one of the fake key cards or someone else was involved, because Crawford himself isn't on any of the camera feeds inside the residence areas. So maybe Crawford had another accom-plice on the staff?'

Kit scanned the key-card log for what felt like the millionth time that day. 'Nobody entered Benny's room except for the nursing staff until the night the coins were stolen, and *that* entry could have been Crawford.'

The camera hadn't been working that night, so they had no feed from the corridor.

Connor made a groaning sound. 'And his killer still could have taken the collection from his hotel room.'

'Unless Crawford went straight to his storage unit from Shady Oaks,' Kit said. 'He could have done that and still made it back to his motel in time to have sex with the mystery woman and then get murdered.' She placed a call to the forensics team that had taken custody of the contents of Crawford's storage unit. 'Hey, this is Mc-Kittrick. You didn't happen to find any coins in that storage unit of Crawford's, did you?'

'Sorry, Detective,' the team leader told her. 'No coins. But we did find a second set of key cards, one for each current employee and a few from former employees.'

'Like Devon Jones?' she asked.

'No, hers isn't in there.'

No, it wouldn't be, she thought. 'Because Benny's killer used it.

You'll call if you find anything else important?' They promised they would, and she ended the call and scowled. 'Still no coins, so Crawford didn't put them in his storage unit. Crawford's killer has to have them, and chances are that Crawford's killer also killed Benny Dreyfus.'

'Let's go back to the videos, then.' Connor reran the video of the figure entering Benny's room the morning of his death, then brought up the video of the coin thief leaving Shady Oaks early Friday morning, running the two side by side. 'They *could* be the same person,' he said.

Kit blinked hard and viewed the videos again. 'The gait is a little different because of the platform shoes the person wore into Benny's apartment.' Or she might be seeing things after viewing the videos so many times. 'But you could be right.'

'And if I am,' Connor said heavily, 'if they are the same person, Crawford didn't take the coins, either, because he was long dead by Tuesday morning.'

'Then we're back to looking at a staff member,' Kit said, rubbing her forehead. 'We don't have video from the night Frankie was murdered, just from the night Benny died. It has to be one of the nurses or nursing assistants who went into Benny's room, because we know that no one else did.' They'd viewed all the videos and could at least be sure of that fact. 'We can eliminate anyone under about five-four.' She culled out those nurses. 'Crossreferencing these names with the key-card log shows four possibilities: Janice Lenski, Roxanne Beaton, Amy Norwood, and Kaley Cross. One of them used Devon's key card to enter Benny's room, but we know that Devon was in the ER with her daughter the whole night Benny died, so it couldn't have been her, even if she weren't only five-two. We need to get the movements of the other four. We also need complete background checks on these four nurses to see if any of them had a pressing motive for the theft, but I'm going to do that after we take a break.'

'Oh, thank God,' Connor muttered. 'I've needed a break for an hour, but I was trying to keep up with you.'

She frowned at him. 'If you need a break, call for one. Is the cafeteria all right?'

'It is, but we have incoming,' Connor said, holding up his phone. 'Check your phone. Goddard just texted us. He's got something to share and is on his way up.' He opened the door to the conference room and a minute later Goddard walked in.

From the huge grin on his face, he'd had better luck than they'd had.

'You found the coins?' Connor asked.

'Not yet, but remember I said yesterday that we watch the online chatter about the sale of stolen antiquities and other treasures? Online fences use code. Not all are the same, but there are recognizable phrases. Today one of our guys saw a listing for "old money."'

'Coins,' Kit murmured. 'Are you sure they're the coins we're looking for?'

'Not one hundred percent, but reasonably sure. There was talk of previous owners like "Julius," "Aristotle," and "George Washington," which we assumed meant Greek, Roman, and early American, which are the most valuable coins in Dreyfus's collection.'

'Where will they be sold?' Connor asked. 'At an auction?'

Goddard shook his head. 'No, they seemed to be in a hurry to sell. One of our undercover operators has a collector persona online. We've planted high-value items in the past and have had him purchase them, giving him a good rating.'

Connor grimaced. 'Like Amazon Marketplace on the dark web?'

'Pretty much. Our operative has an appointment to view the coins tomorrow evening at six p.m. in San Ysidro.'

The suburb of San Diego was about twenty miles away and right on the border with Mexico. 'Quick hop-skip into Mexico if things go wrong?' Kit asked.

'Basically, but we've done this before and we know how to block the escape routes. We even had one thief try to escape in a helicopter. It was very James Bond. But we caught him.' But he frowned, just slightly enough that she knew she'd irked him. 'We know what we're doing, Kit.'

'I know. I'm sorry. This case has my head spinning in circles. What can we do to help?'

His frown changed abruptly to a supercharged grin. 'Was gonna ask if you two wanted to come with?'

'Yes,' Connor said before Goddard was finished asking.

Kit chuckled. 'Yes, please. You'll brief us ahead of time as to what we should and shouldn't do?' Robbery division were the experts here. If there were no dead bodies, Kit and Connor would be ordinary backup.

Goddard nodded, and it seemed her unintended dig was forgiven. 'I will. I have to admit that I was surprised to see the coins hit the web so quickly. Usually, the thieves hold on to the merchandise for a few weeks to a few months.'

'They know we're looking for them,' Kit said. 'We've put uniformed officers outside the apartments on Flynn's floor and in the office and at the major exits. Everyone at Shady Oaks has to know by now that we're suspicious, and we're thinking that includes the thief.'

Goddard blinked. 'You're not looking at Crawford?'

'We don't know anymore,' Kit grumbled. 'Look at those two videos side by side and tell us what you think.'

Connor restarted the video of the coin thief alongside the intruder the morning of Benny's death and Goddard's gaze fixed to the screens.

'Play them again, please,' was all he said when the videos ended. He ended up watching four times before turning to Kit and Connor. 'You think it's the same person?'

'We can't say that it isn't,' Connor said, his tone heavy with disgust. 'What do your eyes tell you?'

'Seventy-five percent sure that it's the same person, but there's enough doubt. Have you asked the guys in IT to take a look? Maybe they can analyze something we can't see.'

'That's our next step,' Kit said. 'Also, no coins in Crawford's storage locker, but that would make sense since you have a seller looking to get rid of them.'

'True enough. What's next?'

'We're taking a break,' Connor said. 'Then I've got plans. It's my girlfriend's birthday today and I don't want to cancel on her if I don't have to.'

'Oh, that reminds me.' Kit emptied the contents of her pants pocket onto the table, separating a new carving from her cat-bird. The new figurine included three small children hugging a woman, because CeCe was a kindergarten teacher. 'For CeCe from Pop. He says you can tell her that it was your idea for him to carve it.'

Connor took the carving, clearly delighted. 'She's gonna love this, but I won't tell her that I asked for it. Knowing that Harlan thought to make it for her on his own will make her so happy.'

'He says that he likes CeCe and that you shouldn't screw it up.'

'I'm doing my best.'

Goddard held out his hand for CeCe's carving. 'May I?' He took the carving and held it up to the light. 'This is exquisite. Your father made this, Kit?'

'He did. Made this one for me, too.' She showed him the cat-bird. 'For luck.'

'It's amazing,' Goddard said. 'Make sure you have it in your pocket tomorrow night. I hope we don't need luck, but I'll take all I can get. Are you free for dinner, Kit?'

Kit pocketed the cat-bird, reading between the lines to know what he was really asking. *Free for dinner* usually meant *Wanna go on a date*. And she didn't want to, at least not with him.

If she were being truly honest with herself, she'd admit that she wanted to see Sam Reeves again.

'Not tonight,' she said with what she hoped was a kind smile. 'I'm going home for dinner at my parents' house. They have new fosters that need attention. And after dinner, I'm going to Shady Oaks for the night. I want to keep an eye on the nursing staff since we're almost certain that one of them stole the coins or killed Benny and may even have killed Frankie Flynn. They're all walking around with master key cards. One of the residents should have a sofa bed I can use.'

'Sam's going to be there, too,' Goddard observed.

She felt her cheeks heat. 'I know. I worry that he's there alone. If the killer thinks Sam suspects the staff, he could be a target.'

'Didn't Navarro say that he'd put a uniform on the floor where the friends of Benny and Frankie live?' Goddard asked.

'He did, but I want to watch the nurses. I have a feeling we won't get a warrant for searching their homes and finances very easily. We don't have enough direct evidence, only circumstantial.'

'Call if you need me,' Connor said with uncharacteristic urgency. 'You might worry about Sam, but I'm going to worry about you, too, if you're there all night.'

She smiled at her partner. 'Don't worry. I'll be fine.'

Fifteen

Carmel Valley, California
Wednesday, 9 November, 6.30 P.M.

'Mom?' Kit called as she walked through the living room of Mc-Kittrick House. The furniture was newly dusted and the room smelled like lemon Pledge. It smelled like home. 'Pop?'

'In the kitchen, Kit,' Betsy called.

Snickerdoodle bounded into the living room, tail wagging. Kit dropped to one knee, hugging her dog. 'I missed you,' she murmured into Snick's curly coat.

'She always misses you,' Harlan said from the doorway into the kitchen. 'Two nights in a row? You okay, Kitty-Cat?'

It was said lightly, but Kit could see the concern in his eyes.

'I'm okay, Pop. Just have a squirrelly case and I needed a break before I jumped back into it.' She rose and walked into his arms, letting out a small sigh of relief. 'I've been staring at data all day and my eyeballs hurt.' She pulled away to look up at him. 'I bet some of Mom's pie would help the eyeball pain.'

He smiled down at her. 'Apple okay?'

'Absolutely yes.' She fell into step with him as they walked to the kitchen, where Betsy was bustling around as usual, and everything felt right in Kit's world.

Betsy shoved a bowl of potatoes into Kit's arms. 'Peel.'

Kit laughed. 'I love you, too, Mom.'

Betsy patted her cheek. 'We have five of our girls here tonight. And Akiko loves potatoes, so we need extra.'

Kit sat at the table, Harlan in the chair across from her and Snick

262

at their feet. 'Where is Akiko?' Her foster sister Akiko had been adopted by Harlan and Betsy about the same time Kit had been – four full years after Kit had hidden with Wren in the McKittricks' barn.

'She took Rita, Tiffany, and Emma out on the boat this afternoon,' Harlan explained, 'to celebrate the three of them registering for school today. Tiff and Emma had never been fishing. They're out back, cleaning their catch. All three girls caught a rockfish and Akiko brought in a halibut.'

Kit licked her lips. 'We're going to eat well tonight.' She eyed the huge bowl of potatoes doubtfully. 'You sure you need this many, Mom? This looks like twice as many as we'll need, even with seven people here tonight.'

'Just peel,' Betsy said. 'After all this time, you question me?'

Kit chuckled and began to peel. 'No, ma'am.'

Across from her, Harlan laid a piece of newspaper on the table and began to carve the piece of wood he'd been examining the night before. The curls from the block of wood joined the potato peels, both of them working in companionable silence while Betsy hummed to herself.

This was . . . perfect. Kit's mind began to relax as she methodically peeled.

'You can think out loud if you need to,' Harlan murmured. 'We're the vault.'

They were. She was safer in this kitchen than anyplace in the entire world.

'I'm looking at four of the nurses in this retirement center for at least two murders,' Kit said, keeping her gaze fixed to the potato in her hand. 'Maybe three murders.'

'The former cop is one,' Harlan said. 'Who are the others?'

'The head of security for the facility is another. The cop's best friend is still a maybe-murder, because it looks like he died in his sleep of a heart attack, but my gut says he was killed. Sweet old guy, by all reports. Had early-stage dementia. I think he knew something that someone didn't want him to tell.'

Like who killed Frankie or who stole his coins or both. Especially if the same person was responsible for all of it.

263

Betsy made a hurt sound. 'Poor man.' She put a glass of iced tea at Kit's elbow and an empty pot for the peeled potatoes on the table, running her hand over Kit's hair before returning to the stove.

'I know. Everyone is mourning him. Like I said, it looks like he had a heart attack, but I'm not so sure. The nurses had access to him every day, long before either he or the former cop died. The cop had lived independently, but someone had been in Benny's room every day, making sure he took his meds and caring for him in other ways.'

'So you think one of the nurses did it?' Harlan asked.

'Maybe.' Kit tossed the peeled potato in the pot and grabbed another. 'The nursing assistant, Devon Jones, was on the list of nurses with access, but she has an airtight alibi for the night of the most recent death.' Which relieved Kit. She hadn't wanted Devon to be a murderer. Or a thief. 'The head nurse, Janice Lenski, has been at Shady Oaks for years.' But so had Kent Crawford. 'Amy Norwood is another nursing assistant. I haven't met her yet, but I'm going to look for her tonight when I go back to Shady Oaks. Kaley Cross was normally in the nursing ward but was assigned to Benny's floor the night he'd died because the duty roster got all confused when the cop's body was discovered Monday morning.'

'So she wasn't well acquainted with the men who died,' Harlan commented.

'I don't know. It's a relatively small place as continuing care facilities go, maybe three hundred residents total. That includes the independent residents, those in assisted living, those under full-time nursing care, and those in the memory ward. So I don't know. I'll figure out who had access and motive.'

Unfortunately, the only people with clear motive – Archie Adler and Faye Evans – didn't have access during the times that Frankie and Benny had died.

'Of course you will,' Harlan said, turning the wood in his hands. 'You always figure it out.'

Kit looked up from the potatoes and pointed to the block of wood with her peeler. 'What's it going to be?'

'It's for Tiffany. I found a photo of a dragonfly chandelier online, made by Tiffany. I'm hoping I can achieve the look I want without any color.'

'It'll be beautiful. You always make things beautiful.'

'I hope so. I haven't decided what Emma's should be yet.'

'Connor's giving the teacher-and-kids figurine to CeCe tonight. He was so touched that you thought of them.'

Harlan just smiled and returned to his carving. 'Who's the fourth nurse?'

'A traveling nurse. Name's Roxanne Beaton. She's been there less than three months.'

Harlan looked up. 'What would she have against a retired cop and a nice old man? She would have barely known them.'

'A four-million-dollar coin collection,' Kit said dryly. 'It was stolen from the nice old man's apartment a few days before he died.'

'Peel,' Betsy commanded. 'And four million does change things, doesn't it?'

Kit obediently returned to her task. 'It does. I think the retired cop suspected something or someone was interested in his friend's coins, and it cost him his life. This whole case is just muddled in my mind. Every time I turn around, something else happens to change my focus.'

'I'd say you focus on the first victim again,' Harlan said. 'Seems like he's key.'

Frankie Flynn was the key. He had been killed for a reason – it *had* to have something to do with the stolen collection. Benny hadn't died until three days later, so clearly the thief hadn't meant him harm initially.

What Frankie had known – or suspected – was the key. She'd go back to Frankie and his interactions with the staff.

'You're right, Pop. As usual.'

'All part of the service, Kitty-Cat,' Harlan said mildly.

Kit laughed, resumed peeling, and was putting the last peeled potato in the pot when Akiko and the three fosters stormed the kitchen, laughing like loons.

'Kit!' Rita held up a bag of mangled fish meat. 'I filleted it myself!'

'So did we,' Tiffany declared as she and Emma showed off their bags of fish. 'We are legit fisherwomen now.'

Akiko made a so-so motion with her hand and Kit bit back a smile.

Rita made a face. 'Our fillets might not be as pretty as Akiko's, but they'll still taste good. Right, Mom?'

Betsy took the bags of fish from the three girls, kissing each of them on top of the head. She had to go up on her tiptoes to kiss Tiffany, since she was taller than the others. 'It will be fabulous when I fry it up. You just wait.'

Akiko presented her fish, a beautifully filleted halibut. 'I can sauté this, Mom.'

Betsy waved them away. 'Nonsense. You girls go clean up. I've got this. Kit, please set the table for ten.'

Kit's brows lifted, then her eyes narrowed when the three teenagers giggled. 'What's going on?' Kit demanded.

'We didn't know you were coming, Kit,' Rita said. 'And we had all this fish, so Mom invited a friend and he's bringing two friends. So ten.'

With that, the giggling girls left with a smug Akiko, and Kit sighed. 'You invited Sam Reeves, didn't you?'

Harlan chuckled. 'We did. It wasn't an ambush, honestly. Nobody knew you were coming home tonight.' He tilted his head at the same moment that Snickerdoodle ran from the kitchen to the front door, barking. 'I think they're here.'

Kit sighed again. 'I'll help Sam. Miss Eloise is going to need help getting up the porch steps, Pop.' That Sam's two friends were Georgia and Eloise was not in doubt. 'The ramp was wobbly last time I checked it.'

Harlan wrapped up the potato peels and wood shavings to put into the compost pile. 'I made sure the ramp was secure right after Sam called to ask if he could bring his friends.' He met Kit's gaze. 'You aren't the only one worried about what's going on in that place, Kitty-Cat. Sam's worried, too.'

Betsy put a stack of plates on the table as Harlan left the room. 'Let your father help the women in, Kit. It soothes his need for chivalry. I need you to wipe down the table, if you don't mind. Tiffany and Emma asked if Sam could come, so they can thank him for recommending that they get placed with us. He didn't want to leave his friends there alone, so I suggested he bring them, too. It'll be good for them to get out of the home.'

Kit nodded. 'You're right.'

'I always am,' Betsy said lightly.

Still seated, Kit leaned her head against Betsy's soft middle for a quick hug. 'You really are.' Then she rose and cleaned the table, setting it for ten as requested.

She was smiling when Miss Eloise breezed through the doorway, her rhinestone-studded walker sparkling in the overhead lights. 'Miss Eloise. Welcome.'

Eloise beamed. 'Thank you, Detective. I didn't know you'd be here.'

'Neither did Sam,' Georgia said dryly. 'You should have heard him sputter when we saw your vehicle in the driveway, Detective.' She held out a box to Betsy. 'Thank you for inviting us, Mrs McKittrick. I'm Georgia and this is Eloise.'

'You will call me Betsy,' Betsy said firmly as she dried her hands on her apron and opened the box. 'Oh my. How lovely.' She drew a piece of art glass from the box, holding it to the light. 'Look at it shimmer. Thank you, Georgia.'

'It was made by a glassblower in Ireland,' Georgia said. 'I've been waiting for the right person to gift it to. Please enjoy it.'

Betsy beamed. 'Oh, I will. Kit, please put it on the mantel, where the sun will hit it in the morning.'

Kit complied, ignoring the smirk on Harlan's face as she brushed past him in the doorway to the living room. Where Sam stood, looking a little uncertain and a lot guilty. Butterflies took flight in Kit's chest and she had to remember to breathe.

'I didn't know you'd be here,' Sam said. 'I'm not trying to crowd you or intrude on your family time.'

Kit placed the glass on the mantel, taking longer than she needed to straighten it. 'Sam, it's all right. It's more than all right.' She turned to meet his gaze directly. 'You're welcome here. So are Georgia and Eloise.'

'Okay,' he said. 'For the record, I am glad you're here.'

She wanted to smile at him. She really did. But the butterflies had become bats and, once again, she was struggling to breathe. 'I'm glad you're here, too,' she managed to say, but it sounded stilted and insincere. 'Let's join the others. Mom will have dinner ready soon.'

Grimacing, Sam followed her and she hated that she was so uncomfortable in her own skin. Abruptly she stopped and turned.

Sam's eyes widened as he looked down at her, closer than she'd expected he'd be. 'Kit? I . . . I can leave.'

'No,' she said too quickly. 'I'm sorry. I . . .' She closed her eyes, her cheeks heating in humiliation. 'I'm no good with this,' she confessed.

'With what?' he asked so softly that she almost couldn't hear him.

'With what you want from me,' she blurted out, too embarrassed to look at him. 'And I'm truly sorry for that.' More than she could say.

She was simply not relationship material, and the sooner Sam Reeves accepted that, the sooner he could find someone else and be happy.

But the thought of him with someone else made her stomach curdle.

His warm hand cradled her cheek and she leaned into it, unable to stop herself. Her eyes burned and she had to bite the inside of her cheek to keep the stupid tears at bay.

'I'm not in a hurry,' Sam whispered. 'I can wait until you're ready.'

She drew a breath that hurt. 'And if I'm never ready?'

'Let's not worry about that just yet.' His voice was as warm as his hand, and both did things to her insides. 'For tonight, let's just be friends enjoying a fish dinner, okay?'

She nodded jerkily, breaking the contact between them. 'Okay. Go on into the kitchen. I'm going to take Snick outside for a few minutes.'

She whistled, Snick came running, and she took the dog outside without looking back.

Cheater

Carmel Valley, California
Wednesday, 9 November, 7.30 P.M.

Sam hated that he'd put Kit in an awkward position. She'd returned from walking the dog, but she was far too quiet as she ate her fish. The girls made up for Kit's silence, though, chattering about their day and drawing Georgia and Eloise into their conversation.

'We saw a yacht while we were coming back in,' Rita said. 'It was huge.' She looked at Sam, her eyes widening. 'Sam, why are you making that face?'

He hadn't realized that he was making a face. 'Not a big fan of boats. I don't have a phobia, exactly, but going out far enough to see a yacht makes my skin itch. I'm more of a fan of the desert. It doesn't move when you walk on it.'

Rita grimaced in sympathy. 'You wouldn't mind Akiko's boat, though. She's an amazing captain. She got us all to wave to the people on the yacht and they waved back to us when we passed each other.'

'I certainly am an amazing captain,' Akiko preened, and Sam laughed.

'Then we played "where are they going,"' Tiffany said. 'That was fun.'

'And we talked about all the places we'd go,' Rita added wistfully.

Akiko smiled. 'Remember when we used to do that, Kit?'

Kit smiled back, but it was a shade brittle. 'I do. You always wanted to go to Japan.'

Akiko leaned into Kit for a moment before drawing away. That was the way everyone seemed to touch Kit, Sam noticed. No one held her for any length of time. Except Harlan. He'd seen the two hug each other and Kit seemed most comfortable in his presence.

Sam thought about the anguish on her face as she confessed the fear that she'd never be ready, and his chest physically hurt. He had no idea how to help her.

Or if he should even try.

'You never wanted to go anywhere,' Akiko said, still talking about Kit. 'You got to sail the sea with the Coast Guard but you always wanted to be here.'

Kit's smile became more genuine. 'Still do. This house is home.'

'Where did you go, Kit?' Emma asked. She was less shy today, which Sam was glad to see.

Eloise had taken the two new fosters under her brightly colored wings, placing one on either side of her. She'd quickly established a bond with Rita, who'd loved that the elderly woman had dyed her hair blue.

Georgia was her usual taciturn self, sitting closer to Kit and watching, but she was enjoying the conversation.

I should have taken them out around other people a long time ago.

Sam was seated next to Betsy, who kept patting his hand in a motherly way, but Kit hadn't looked at him since that moment in the living room. He wished he could leave, but Georgia and Eloise were having a good time so he stayed put, enduring Betsy's encouraging pats.

'I was stationed off the coast of Texas when I finished boot camp,' Kit said. 'I was with the Guard's police unit and we caught all kinds of traffickers, smugglers, and general seafaring criminals. Luckily for me, I was transferred back to Coronado toward the end of my tour of service. I had friends who wanted to go to Asia and Europe and do all the traveling, but I just wanted to come home. The Guard was a way to pay for college, and college was a way to join the San Diego police force. I never wanted to be anything but a cop.'

'I've traveled a good deal,' Georgia said. 'All over the world. And you're right, Kit. I enjoyed the sights I saw, but I really loved coming home.'

Eloise smiled. 'Remember when we went to Rome, Georgia?' She glanced at Sam. 'That was back when Frankie's Ryan and Benny's Martha were still alive. It was an amazing trip.' Her grin was wicked. 'I met this Italian hottie with his own yacht and—'

Georgia cleared her throat. 'Eloise.'

Eloise tried to look demure, but it was an impossible task, and Sam's heart swelled with affection. 'Where did you go, Miss Eloise?' he asked.

'We toured the Greek islands and sailed around Sicily on his yacht. Then I rejoined the others in Rome and we flew home. It was a nice trip. A nice memory.'

'And I got to have the hotel room in Rome all to myself,' Georgia added tartly. 'Because Eloise snores.'

Eloise bristled. 'I do not.'

Georgia started to argue, but Sam shot her a look and she settled, grumbling under her breath.

'I traveled a lot,' Emma said quietly. 'All over the country with my mom and dad. I didn't like it.'

Eloise immediately sobered because she, like everyone at the table, recognized the importance of Emma's statement. 'Why not, honey?'

'My dad didn't travel to see the country. He . . . well, he'd borrow money, then we'd have to leave in the middle of the night because his debt would come due.'

'Where did you go to school?' Rita asked, concerned.

'I didn't.'

Betsy tilted her head in confusion. 'But you scored so well on your entry tests this morning. You said you'd been homeschooled.'

'I was. My mom taught me, but I never had an actual . . . what do you call it? The program at school?'

'A curriculum?' Sam offered, and Emma nodded.

'Yeah, that. I saw kids on TV going to school – you know, the reruns – but I don't think *Saved by the Bell* is much like real life.' She made a face. 'Next week will be my first time at a real school.'

Tiffany reached across Eloise to grip Emma's hand. 'We'll be with you.'

Rita put her hand atop the others'. 'We got your back, girl.'

Emma's smile was wistful. 'I'm not afraid, not really. I'm kind of excited. I just wish I'd been able to go before. It'll be easier having you guys, though.'

'How did you two meet?' Eloise asked, placing her gnarled old hand atop the three teenagers' hands.

Emma drew a breath and looked around the table. Tiffany pursed her lips, like she was trying not to let the explanation spill from her mouth. No one said a word or even breathed until Emma exhaled.

'My dad didn't just borrow money. He stole all the time – usually

jewelry – and he'd sell it for cheap, you know? He'd steal a necklace
or a bracelet and hold on to it for a while, until our money ran out,
and then he'd pawn it. We'd usually moved twice by then, so no one
suspected him. He said the police would have forgotten about the
theft by the time he pawned whatever it was. But one day he stole a
diamond ring from the woman who my mother was working for.
She cleaned the lady's house. The lady's husband caught up to us.
He recognized me because I'd played with his dog while Mom
cleaned. He said he was calling the cops, so my dad claimed that
he'd been covering up for my stealing for years, but it was time for
me to answer to the law.'

'What an asshole,' Eloise muttered.

'What did your mother do, Emma?' Kit asked.

'Nothing. She never told him no. She never took up for me, so I
knew she wouldn't that time, either.' Emma shrugged. 'So I ran. We
were just outside Bakersfield, so I ran to the downtown. It's not a big
city like LA or even San Diego, but I figured I could still get lost in
all the people. I wanted to hitch a ride to LA, but I kept chickening
out. I found a place to sleep in an alley, but it was already claimed by
some other kids. They threw me out, but one of the kids took up for
me.' She looked at Tiffany with a grateful smile. 'The next morning
Tiff and I started hitchhiking. Tails was LA and heads was San
Diego. It was heads, and about a month later we ended up here.' She
glanced at Betsy, then Harlan. 'I didn't do anything wrong, I swear.'

'We believe you, child,' Harlan said gruffly.

'We do,' Betsy confirmed. 'You don't have anything to fear here.'

'I'll make some calls to the Bakersfield police tomorrow,' Kit
promised. 'I'll make sure the police know to charge your father.' She
propped her elbows on the table. 'But I'm curious. How did he pick
who he'd steal from?'

Emma shrugged again. 'He'd search online for the rich people's
houses, then he'd send Mom to apply for a job there, usually as a
cleaning lady. She'd get established and figure out what they had
that was worth stealing and where all the cameras were. Then Dad
would plan to steal it when Mom had a solid alibi – usually her
second job at another rich person's house. It worked for them for a

long time. My whole life, actually. It might still be working for them. Why?'

Kit's eyes had narrowed, her expression becoming faraway, and then she blinked and nodded once like she'd decided on something, and Sam was intrigued. 'Thank you, Emma,' she said. 'I'll get this cleared up with Bakersfield PD as soon as I can. I want you to write down anything you can remember – places, dates, names your parents used. All that.'

'Okay,' Emma said tentatively.

'You won't get her into more trouble?' Tiffany demanded.

'No,' Kit said firmly. 'She won't get into any trouble. I'll make sure of it. Mom, do you want me to make the coffee?'

Betsy was frowning at Kit. 'Yes, dear. Thank you.'

'I'll clear the table, Betsy.' Sam wagged his finger at Mrs Mc-Kittrick when she opened her mouth to argue. 'Please, let me help. My mother raised me right.' He gathered all the plates, put them in the sink, then joined Kit at the coffeemaker. 'What was that about?' he whispered.

Kit looked over her shoulder. 'Come with me.'

He followed her out the kitchen door onto the back porch, shivering at the chilly wind. He hadn't brought a coat outside, but Kit seemed impervious to the cold so he said nothing.

'Connor and I have narrowed our suspects to four of the nurses or nursing assistants at Shady Oaks,' she said.

Sam knew he should be surprised that one of the nurses was involved, but he really wasn't. 'For which crime?'

'All of them. Crawford couldn't have killed Frankie. He was dead before noon on Saturday and Frankie was killed Saturday night. Crawford could have stolen the coins, but he couldn't have killed Benny, again, because he was already dead. Remember the vase that Evans mentioned in the interview this morning?'

'Of course.'

'Where is it?' she asked. 'Because it wasn't in Benny's room at the time of his death.'

He opened his mouth, then closed it, considering her question while she patiently waited. 'Someone took it, presumably to watch whatever video the camera had captured so they could get the combination to Benny's safe. Crawford?'

'Maybe, but I don't think so. He would have needed to watch the video in Benny's room, and no one was in there long enough to do that prior to Saturday at four fifteen a.m., when the coins were taken out of the building. The vase was planted on Wednesday and we never saw anyone on video removing it. It could have been removed after the camera was disabled sometime Friday afternoon, a few hours before Frankie was killed, but Crawford had checked into that cheap motel by then. He could have left the motel and returned to Shady Oaks, but we've examined the camera feeds from every entry and exit point and Crawford doesn't show up in any of them. I'm assuming whoever stole the coins had to have viewed the video from the nanny-cam vase. They wouldn't have known exactly when Benny would open the safe, so they'd be fast-forwarding until they found it. They could have been searching through days of tape.'

Clearly, she'd thought this out.

Sam let the logistics play out in his own mind. 'So they removed the memory card from the vase, took it with them and viewed it somewhere else, then came back early Saturday morning to steal the coins. Why not just steal the coins directly after killing Frankie? Why did they come back?'

'Good question. I don't think Frankie was a target for murder. I think Frankie surprised his killer. His killer was rattled enough to risk going into Georgia's apartment to steal a knife to cover up what they had done.'

Sam played through the scenario in his mind. 'That makes sense. His killer suspected that Frankie knew something about the planned theft, had maybe hidden some kind of evidence in his apartment, so they ransacked it. But how would they know that Frankie suspected? What would have made them think he had evidence that they needed to find?'

'Good questions. Maybe Frankie confronted them? Or maybe Frankie said something to Benny, and word got to the thief? They were upset with each other, Benny and Frankie. Benny might have let something slip to the wrong person. Like I said, I don't think

274

Frankie's killer intended to kill him when they entered his apartment. They picked the time during Eloise's birthday party for their search. Frankie discovered them and . . .'

Sam sighed. 'If it was a staff member on duty, they would have had someplace they were supposed to be. They either used their break or slipped away to search Frankie's place. They couldn't risk discovery or have anyone notice they weren't at their duty station. So that might be why they came back later to steal the coins from Benny.'

'And then Benny got agitated on Monday when Frankie was found and started saying that it was all his fault.'

Sam swallowed. 'He wasn't thinking clearly.'

'Or maybe he was. He might have known that Frankie suspected someone was after the coins. Someone that Benny didn't want to distrust. Frankie and Benny had argued the week before they died, right?'

'Eloise said that, yes. Benny said it, too, in his own way.'

'I read Goddard's report of his interview with Georgia. She didn't believe that Benny was aware that the coins were missing.'

'I think he would have said something if they had been. He would have called his daughter or granddaughter right away. So Benny didn't know his coins were already gone, but he might have known who it was that Frankie had suspected?'

'Maybe. Lots of maybes, but that makes a lot of sense, doesn't it?'

Sam closed his eyes. 'It does. That means Benny was killed to shut him up?'

'I think so,' she said so gently that his eyes burned.

'Who?' he asked hoarsely. 'Who are you looking at?'

'Someone entered his room at five a.m. yesterday, but they'd disguised themselves and used Devon Jones's key card. Devon has an alibi, though – she was at the ER with her daughter. Whoever entered Benny's room was around five-ten, but they wore platform shoes, so they could have been a few inches shorter. The nurses on duty that night were Janice, Roxanne, Amy, and Kaley. I'm starting to think it was Roxanne.'

He tried to consider it logically, shoving his emotion aside. 'She had opportunity, for sure. You're thinking that she's been stealing for a while, like Emma's father. Traveling and stealing.'

'That's exactly what I'm thinking. Her surface background check came back clean, but I'll dig deeper into her history and check with her former assignments. I can do that from Shady Oaks tonight.'

Sam lifted his brows. 'Shady Oaks?'

'I'm staying with you tonight. I don't want you alone.'

Sam felt a chill go down his back that had nothing to do with the cold night air. 'Roxanne came into Georgia's apartment last night. Nearly scared me to death. She said she was checking on Georgia because she'd sedated her that day.'

Kit went still. 'What did you do?'

'Nearly beaned her with an iron statue, then apologized when I realized it was her and not an evil villain.' He shrugged. 'Georgia was still awake because Eloise *does* snore, thank you very much, and she made tea. I served cookies and Roxanne joined us. We chatted a bit, then Roxanne left. That's all.'

Kit bit her lip. 'She could have been legitimately checking on Georgia.'

'She could have been. But you don't think so.'

'I truly don't know. But Roxanne was the one with Benny the day Frankie's body was found. She's the one who had him sedated, and we couldn't talk to him until the next day.'

'I saw him that day, though – after Frankie's body was found. I talked to him. He was agitated, and she called his doctor to approve the sedative.'

Kit frowned. 'True. I wonder why Benny wouldn't just tell you what had him so upset.'

'He was . . . scattered.' Sam closed his eyes, trying to remember every detail. He opened his eyes and met Kit's concerned gaze. 'He said that it was his fault and Roxanne said that it wasn't. Benny yelled, "She lies." I thought he meant about it not being his fault. I didn't even think of it till now.'

'It was a chaotic moment, Sam. Don't beat yourself up. What else do you remember?'

Sam nodded at her attempt to make him feel better, but he still felt like shit for not seeing it sooner. 'His pupils were super dilated and he was slurring his words. He was repeating himself. When I

276

first got there, he was beating his fists against Roxanne, but when I drew him into a hug, he was slower. He hit me but it was weak. Then Roxanne gave him a shot and he just wound down. Really quickly.'

'His pupils were dilated *before* she sedated him by injection?'

Sam nodded. 'You think she gave him something before the shot?'

'Maybe. Maybe she needed to quiet him for a while.'

'But then he died.' Grief mixed with blinding fury. 'She might have done that, too.'

'Come on. Let's clean the kitchen and head back to Shady Oaks.'

'You'll have your gun?'

She never broke eye contact. 'I will. And if you or any of the others are in danger, I'll use it. But I'm hoping to take her in quietly. If she's guilty.'

Now that Sam thought about it, he was sure that she was. 'Let's go clean the kitchen.'

Shady Oaks Retirement Village
Scripps Ranch, San Diego, California
Thursday, 10 November, 1.25 A.M.

Sam couldn't sleep. Part of it was Georgia's uncomfortable sofa bed and part of it was the knowledge that one of the nurses had probably killed both Frankie and Benny.

For money. *Goddammit.*

Another reason for his sleeplessness was sitting at Georgia's dinette behind him, quietly typing on her laptop. Kit had claimed she'd sleep in Georgia's recliner, but she'd been on her laptop ever since they'd returned from McKittrick House and didn't show any signs of stopping.

'You need to sleep, Kit,' he said quietly.

The typing ceased. 'I'm sorry,' she whispered. 'I didn't know I was keeping you awake. I'll turn down the light on my screen.'

'It's not that.' He levered to a sitting position and fixed his gaze on her. He could see her plainly, her face bathed in the blue light of her laptop screen. She probably couldn't see him, and that made it easier. 'It's everything else that's keeping me awake. It's knowing

277

that someone killed my friends and that it's probably someone I know. Or thought that I knew. It's wondering if someone's going to come in here tonight and try again.'

'I doubt she'll come in tonight. Officer Stern is outside.'

'He was outside last night when Roxanne broke in.' That he wasn't sure if Roxanne really had wanted to check on Georgia or hurt her was messing with his head. He didn't want to suspect someone for simply doing their job. At the same time, he didn't want Georgia to die.

Kit regarded him soberly. 'But I wasn't here last night.'

'True. If she finds out you're here, will she run?'

'She's not on duty tonight, so she'll only know I'm here if she's watching the entrance. She's due back in in the morning. She has day shifts for the rest of the week. Try to act naturally around her. We don't want to spook her into bolting before we have enough to detain her. Navarro sent a black-and-white to sit outside the house she's renting, so we'll know if she leaves. Go ahead and try to sleep. I'll be quieter.'

'No, that's okay.' He threw back the covers and got up, wincing at the pain in his back. 'The main reason I can't sleep is that bed.'

Which was a lie. The real reason for his insomnia was that she was sitting not twenty feet away. So close, yet so far away. But he'd promised to give her time, that they could be friends for now. He'd keep his word.

'Last night you said it wasn't that bad,' she said.

'I lied. You want some tea?' he asked.

'Yes, that would be nice.' She cocked her head, listening to the rumble coming from the bedroom. 'How is Georgia sleeping through that?'

'I bought her some earplugs and she took a sleeping pill.' Sam reached up to get the teapot from where he'd stored it that morning. 'Georgia has a soothing mint or a strong black tea that will keep you up all night.'

'The black tea, please.'

He set about making the tea, peeking over his shoulder at her. She was staring at him, but quickly averted her gaze when he caught her at it, a blush tinting her cheeks.

At least there was that.

He prepared the tea and poured it at the table. 'Sugar?'

'Only a few pounds, please.'

Wide-eyed, he watched her add four heaping spoonfuls of sugar. 'Wow. Your dentist must have a thriving business.'

She chuckled. 'He's always fussing at me.'

'I'm surprised you take the time to go.'

'Akiko makes me. It's not worth hearing her bitch about it, so I go.' She sipped the tea and winced. 'That is strong tea.'

'I warned you.'

'Yes, you did.'

They sat in silence as the minutes ticked past, and then Sam frowned. 'What happened to the vase?'

'The one in Benny's apartment? I don't know.'

'You didn't see anyone walk out with it?'

'No. And that's a loose end that bothers me.'

'It should. The thief could have pocketed an SD card. They're the size of a thumbnail. But what about the vase?'

She sat back, her gaze intent on his face. 'What do you think?'

'Did you check Benny's apartment again?'

'I did. Tonight, while you were getting the ladies settled in front of the TV.'

Georgia had planned to write Frankie's eulogy, but Eloise had put the kibosh on that, saying they needed to laugh, so he, Georgia, and Eloise had watched *Legally Blonde*. Georgia had wanted another legal movie and Eloise had complained that she hadn't gotten her choice the night before so Georgia owed her. Georgia had cracked a smile or two during the movie, so Eloise had considered her job done.

Tomorrow would be soon enough for Frankie's eulogy. SDPD had planned a special funeral with honors that weekend, but the memorial service itself would be here at Shady Oaks, with Frankie's friends in attendance.

No family. Because Frankie's son hated him. Why? How could Gerald hate his father? Sam had loved the old man.

It took him a moment to realize that Kit was studying him over her cup. 'You okay?' she asked.

'Yeah. I just got to thinking about Frankie's memorial service and wondering why he and his son were estranged.'

'We checked out the son,' she said, surprising him.

'You did? You never said.'

'We needed to cross him off the suspect list, so Navarro found him. He was with his mother in a hospice in Lincoln Park.'

'Hospice?'

'Yes. Cancer. The staff there verified that he hasn't left the facility in a week.'

Oh. Sam wondered if Frankie had known. He wondered if Frankie had cared. *Yes, he would have,* he decided. The Frankie Flynn who Sam had known would have cared. It didn't matter now, though. The Frankie Flynn he'd known was gone. So was Benny.

He realized that he was staring at his tea and lifted his eyes to Kit's, rewinding his brain to what they'd been discussing. The vase. Benny's apartment. The killer who'd taken Frankie and Benny from them.

'So you searched Benny's apartment and found no vase,' Sam said.

'And it's bugging the hell out of me.'

Sam shrugged. 'Maybe the thief broke it. It would be easier to hide fragments of a vase in pockets or to toss them into the trash. Especially if they threw the pieces in a biowaste container. Nobody'd look in there.'

Kit stared for a moment, then grinned, the smile lighting up her whole face, and he felt the familiar pang in his chest. She was so pretty all the time, but when she smiled . . . It was like an electric shock.

'You are very smart, Dr Reeves,' she said, and somehow the formality didn't hurt like it had before. It felt more like an endearment than a title meant to push him away.

'I have my moments,' he said lightly. 'I might even solve this case before you do.'

She laughed, a merry sound that held no derision or spite. 'You just might at that.'

'I did before, you know,' he said, referring to the case they'd shared six months ago.

Her eyes narrowed. 'You did not.'

'I think if you'll check your reports and your cell phone logs, you'll find that I did.'

She frowned, her lips parting, then pursing. Her eyes flared wide in surprise for a moment before narrowing again. 'Okay, fine. Beginner's luck.'

He chuckled. 'I bet I can do it again.' He had no such inclination, but it was fun to tease her. 'What if we make a small wager?'

She regarded him suspiciously. 'Like what?'

The words were on the tip of his tongue and for a moment they hovered in the air, waiting to be claimed.

She might get mad. Or she might not. Be brave, Sam. Life is too short.

He lifted his chin. 'If I win, you'll go out to dinner with me.'

Her mouth pinched on one side. 'And if you lose?'

He shrugged. 'It'd be your win. You get to decide.'

She hesitated so long that he felt his stomach lurch. *She's going to tell you to leave her alone. She's going to tell you to go away. To stop bothering her.*

Time seemed suspended as he waited.

Then she nodded once. 'If I win – and I will – you'll go fishing with me on my sister's boat. We'll get rid of that phobia of yours.'

'It's *not* a phobia. It's an . . . intense dislike.' He hated boats. He hated water. But he *really* liked Kit McKittrick, so his answer was a no-brainer. 'But it's a deal.'

She extended her hand and he shook it, holding on longer than he should have. Her throat worked as she swallowed, and then she gently pulled her hand free. 'It's a deal. Now go to sleep and let me work.'

Sam returned to the sofa bed, his heart lighter than it had been in a very long time. He might not sleep, but insomnia suddenly didn't seem so bad.

Sixteen

'Thank you for breakfast, Miss Georgia,' Kit said.

Georgia shot her a disapproving look. 'Least I could do considering you didn't sleep a wink last night. That's dangerous, Detective. I can send you off with a nutritious breakfast, but what if you need good reflexes today and you're too tired? You could get hurt. Or worse. And how would your lovely parents endure that?'

Sam, the traitor, swallowed a smile and made no move to change the subject for her.

Eloise, the troublemaker, didn't even try to hide the gleam in her eyes. 'They would be despondent, Detective. And what about poor Sam? He'd be devastated.'

Sam narrowed his eyes at the old woman. 'Leave me out of this, Miss Eloise.'

Kit sighed. 'I caught a catnap in your recliner,' she said for the third time. 'I slept enough. I will be fine.'

Georgia sniffed. 'That's what they always say. What are you going to do next, Detective?'

'I have a million calls to make.' To every retirement home, nursing home, and hospital on Roxanne Beaton's résumé. And to check the other three nurses' finances, to see who had the biggest motive to steal four million dollars' worth of coins. None of the four had criminal records. They were all squeaky clean. But one of them had to be the thief. And the thief was most likely the killer. 'So I'll be at my desk all day long. No excitement, no car chases. Just boring paperwork.'

Georgia skewered Kit with a gimlet eye. 'You were up all night and all you came up with is *phone calls*?'

Kit smiled brightly. '*Lots* of phone calls. I'll talk to you all later.' She grabbed her cup, plate, and silverware to put into the dishwasher, but hesitated, sobering. 'Be careful, ladies. I don't know who's responsible for all this, but I have a feeling that they're close. Don't wander off without letting the officer outside know where you're going, and stick together.'

Eloise scoffed. 'We're octogenarians, Detective. What would we do if someone did come after us?'

'We'll shoot them,' Georgia said grimly.

Kit's eyes widened. 'With what? I thought weapons weren't allowed here.'

Georgia shrugged nonchalantly. 'Neither was recreational weed up till 2016, but that didn't stop Eloise from smuggling it in.'

'Georgia,' Sam gasped. 'You have a gun?'

'Shh,' Georgia hissed. 'Tell the whole world, why don't you?'

Sam closed his eyes. 'Oh my God. You don't have one, do you, Eloise?'

Eloise patted his hand with her misshapen one. 'Like I could pull a trigger if I wanted to. No, dear boy. I do not have a gun. But now I'm getting one. Can't have Georgia being the biggest badass in Shady Oaks, can I?'

Sam groaned.

Kit dropped her chin to her chest. 'Is it at least registered, Georgia?'

'Of course it is. I've practiced with it, too.' Georgia sighed quietly. 'I was mugged shortly after I moved here, Detective. I'd gone to the grocery store alone and some little asshole pushed me down and stole my purse. I was scared. Frankie took me to a shooting range and taught me to shoot. Which made sense later when I found out that Frankie had been a cop.'

Kit rubbed her forehead. 'Don't carry it with you, okay? You don't have a concealed carry permit.' She hesitated. 'Do you?'

'No, I don't, so I won't carry it.'

Kit stilled, a thought suddenly occurring to her. 'Georgia, did Frankie have a gun in his apartment?'

Georgia drew in a sharp breath. 'He did. His killer took it, didn't he?'

She, Kit corrected to herself. 'Probably. I'll add that to my list of things to check today.' She turned for the door and noticed the iron statue on the entry table. 'Ladies, did either of you notice a vase in Benny's apartment any time in the last week or so?'

The two elderly women looked at each other, then both nodded slowly. 'It was tacky looking,' Eloise said. 'Benny used to have a jade carving on one of his living room tables, but about a week ago the carving was gone and the vase was in its place.'

'We thought,' Georgia said faintly, 'that Carla – Benny's daughter – had taken the jade and put the vase in its place, hoping that Benny wouldn't notice. Why? What's the significance of the vase?'

Kit glanced at Sam. He was watching her, his green eyes sharp. 'Tell them,' he said quietly. 'You owe them that much.'

'All right. What I'm going to tell you doesn't leave this room.' Both women nodded, so Kit said, 'One of the participants in this crime put the vase in Benny's room. It had a hidden camera.'

Georgia glared. 'To capture the combination to his safe.'

'One of the staff did it,' Eloise said softly. 'That's what you meant by "they're close."'

'I'm not sure,' Kit hedged.

Georgia's jaw tightened. 'But you think so.'

Kit nodded. 'Yes, I think so. I don't know who.'

Georgia narrowed her eyes. 'But you have a good idea.'

'I can't tell you that. Not yet.'

Georgia huffed impatiently. 'I *hate* this. I hate that someone targeted Benny's collection, I hate that someone killed Frankie because he probably suspected it, and I hate that Benny's gone, too. However it happened.' Her lips trembled, her voice breaking. 'I *hate* this.'

Kit gently squeezed Georgia's hand. 'I know. I'm sorry.'

'Not your fault,' Georgia whispered, two tears rolling down her wrinkled cheeks. 'You're just doing your job.'

The crusty woman's tears made Kit want to cry herself. 'Sometimes I hate that I have a job to do. I'll do my best to solve this quickly. Then . . .' She sighed. 'Then you'll get on with the process of finding the new normal.'

'I *hate* that phrase,' Eloise spat.

'So do I,' Kit said. 'So, the vase. You didn't see anyone carrying it around later?'

Both women shook their heads.

'It was too big to fit into a pocket,' Eloise said.

Georgia lifted a silver brow. 'Not if it was in pieces.'

Kit looked at Sam ruefully. 'I figured you were right about that last night, but I wanted to ask. I should have thought of it sooner, that the vase had been broken.'

'You might have,' Georgia said tartly, 'if you'd ever get a decent night's sleep.'

Kit's lips twitched. 'You're probably right, Miss Georgia. I'll do better.' Once again, she gathered her cup, plate, and silverware. 'I really need to—'

The buzz of the phone in her pocket interrupted her. The caller ID made her pulse kick up. She put the dishes down because it was Alicia Batra.

'Good morning,' Kit answered, getting up and walking toward the door to keep the ladies from overhearing. Eloise was a little hard of hearing, but Georgia had told her once that her hearing was just fine. 'Whatcha got for me?'

'Murder,' Alicia said grimly. 'Benny Dreyfus's blood test came back positive for diltiazem and digoxin and two different sedatives.'

Yes. She looked over her shoulder. Three sets of eyes stared at her, making no pretense of giving her privacy. 'I thought that might be the case.'

'You were right. Are you with other people right now?'

'I sure am. Would any of those have been prescribed?'

'The diltiazem might have been. Digoxin used to be a popular drug, but it's not used as much anymore. There are newer, more efficient ways to treat heart issues. There was a lot of both drugs in his system, though. It had to have been deliberate. I'm ruling Mr Drey-fus's death a homicide.'

Dammit. Kit had known it would be true but hated that it actually was. 'How would one have gotten them?'

'He may have been taking the diltiazem. That's a pretty common treatment for certain heart issues, and he had a history. The digoxin is harder to say. It can last years in tablet form, so someone didn't have to obtain it recently. I'm betting someone in that retirement home takes it. Or did a while back.'

Or someone in another retirement home where Roxanne had once worked. 'Do you need to do any further procedures?' *Such as a full autopsy.*

'No. This is more than sufficient. And, to be clear, I had to specif-ically ask for this test. If I'd just done a general blood test, this would have gone unnoticed. Whoever killed Mr Dreyfus would have gotten away with it. So, good instincts as usual, Kit.'

'Thanks, Alicia. What about the sedatives?'

'Two different kinds. One is usually administered as a tablet. It can be crushed and put in water or applesauce, that kind of thing. The other is injectable. Why?'

'I can't tell you right now, but it explains a lot.' Like how Roxanne had kept Benny Dreyfus too sedated to make any sense when Sam had come to calm him down. 'Thank you again.'

'You're welcome. Please tell the Dreyfus family that I'm here to answer any medical questions they might have.'

'I will.' Kit ended the call and suddenly wished she *had* gotten a decent night's sleep. She was so tired.

A warm presence behind her startled her at first, and then she smelled Sam's aftershave, even though its intensity had faded during the night. Strong hands settled on her shoulders, giving her a quick massage that felt entirely too good.

'It was about Benny, wasn't it?' Sam murmured.

She nodded. 'I'm sorry.'

'I know.' His hands dropped away and he stepped back, taking all that delicious warmth with him. 'I'll stay with the ladies for a while. You need to inform his family.'

Kit turned to look up into his eyes. *So green.* 'Yes. How long is a while? I'm going to get an additional uniform to sit in here with them when you leave. Can you stay another hour or so?'

'Yes, I can.' Relief flooded Sam's eyes. 'I have client sessions I can't reschedule today, but I can stay for an hour. I'll be back this afternoon.'

'Keep in touch with me. Call and leave voice mails if I don't pick up. I want to hear voices, not receive texts.'

One side of his mouth lifted. It was a nice mouth. He was a nice man. 'I think you're worried about me.'

'I am. Don't be a hero, Sam.'

The one-sided smile became a full smirk. 'I won't have to. Georgia's got me covered.'

Kit couldn't stop her own smile. 'You're impossible.' She went back to the table, sobering at the sight of tears streaking down the faces of both women. 'I'm sorry. Can you both stay here for the morning? I want you safe until we've ID'd whoever killed Frankie and Benny.'

'You were right,' Georgia said hoarsely. 'Someone did kill Benny. I didn't want to believe it was true.'

Eloise looked shocked. 'I didn't know it was a possibility. I thought he had a heart attack.'

'He did,' Kit said. 'But he had help. You can't say anything until I inform his family. Okay? Please?' The two women clutched each other's hands and Kit's heart broke a little more. 'Please,' she repeated.

'We won't say anything,' Georgia promised. 'Right, El?'

'No. I know everyone thinks I'm flighty, Detective, but I can keep a secret.'

Kit bent down so that she was eye to eye with Eloise. 'You are *not* flighty, Miss Eloise. You're as sharp as a tack. You use the flightiness act to make people underestimate you, but I have your number now. I think you run this joint.'

Eloise's chuckle was watery. 'Takes a sharp tack to know one. Don't get yourself killed, Detective. We like you.'

It was a pleasant jolt, a shot in the arm. She normally didn't care who liked her, but she'd grown to like these ladies, too.

'I don't plan to, ma'am.' Kit grabbed her plate, silverware, and coffee cup for a third time, heading for the dishwasher. Her brain was a tumble of thoughts, the main one of which was how to prove that Roxanne was the killer. Because now she was sure of it.

She opened the dishwasher and put the coffee cup in the top rack, then stopped, staring at the contents. One of the cups had a dark red lipstick stain on the rim. It was wine-colored and Kit knew she'd seen that color before – on the autopsy photos Alicia had shown her of Kent Crawford's penis. Someone with this same color lipstick had performed oral sex on him shortly before his death.

'Who drank from the light blue mug?' she asked, even though she thought she already knew.

Georgia got up to look. 'Roxanne did. Two nights ago, when we had tea.' Her eyes widened as Kit's words sank in. '*Roxanne* did it? Are you *serious*?'

'Shh,' Kit cautioned. 'Don't say a word.'

Georgia's scowl was rather terrifying. 'That bitch.'

Sam put his arm around Georgia's shoulders and led her back to the table. 'Detective McKittrick will take care of this. We're going to sit here, finish our coffee, and let her work.'

Eloise was nodding as the two sat. 'You said she'd figure it out that very first day, Sammy. I didn't expect her to work so fast, but you were right.'

Kit gave Sam a look of gratitude. Even when she pushed him away, he still supported her.

And I can't think about him right now. I have work to do.

She bagged the mug for evidence. 'I have to go, but I'll make sure the uniform outside knows to stick close to your apartment. I think everyone else here is safe, but you two were close to both Frankie and Benny. You're probably safe, too,' she added hastily when both women stared at her in fear, 'but I'm not taking chances. According to the duty roster, Roxanne is on shift today, so just . . . stay here. Don't go anywhere. Please.'

If she couldn't get another uniform here fast enough, she'd have them picked up and put in a safe house. Georgia would balk, but Miss Eloise would probably like the excitement.

She opened Georgia's front door, taking one last look at them. The three of them held hands, their expressions identically grim.

She needed to work fast – before the three of them did something they'd all regret.

Claremont, San Diego, California
Thursday, 10 November, 10.15 A.M.

Kit got into the department sedan with a frustrated huff. She glared at the little Craftsman bungalow as if it had been the one to have committed the offense. 'She lied.'

Sliding behind the steering wheel, Connor fastened his seat belt. 'A murderer lied? Say it ain't so.'

Kit double-checked the address listed on Roxanne's personnel file. They were at the right address – except that it wasn't her rental house.

A very large, heavily muscled and tattooed man who hadn't yet had enough caffeine had answered their knock, glaring at the black-and-white that had been sitting in front of his house all night before turning his glare on Kit and Connor. He had *not* been happy to see them.

His name was Shaun Blanchard and he was the homeowner. That was easily verified. After that, it had gone downhill.

Roxanne Beaton did not rent a room from him. He'd never heard of her, in fact. He didn't know why she'd listed his address as her temporary home while completing her contract with Shady Oaks.

After he'd guzzled down the full mug of coffee in his hand, he'd softened his tone, even allowing them to come in and look for Roxanne.

That had surprised the hell out of Kit until she'd seen the framed photo of the homeowner wearing a Coast Guard uniform. They hadn't known each other in the Guard, but Blanchard had recognized her name from the online news articles written about the big serial killer case she and Connor had closed six months before.

The articles invariably cited her service and, as a favor to a fellow

Coastie, Blanchard had said that he wanted to help Kit cross a lead off her list.

There was no sign of Roxanne, which by then they'd expected. This was a major problem, because she hadn't shown up for her shift today, calling in sick instead.

They had no idea where she was. They'd immediately called in a BOLO, but she'd had at least a twelve-hour head start.

'We wasted the black-and-white's night watching the wrong house,' she grumbled. 'Motherfucking Roxanne.'

'At least we know where she's not,' Connor said mildly, tapping something into his phone.

A woman's voice proclaimed, 'Starting route to Starbucks.'

'I think you need caffeine as much as Mr Blanchard did,' Connor said. 'How much sleep did you get last night? You know how cranky you get without sleep.'

Kit narrowed her eyes at him. 'I was going to apologize for being cranky until you called me cranky.'

'If the shoe fits,' Connor said cheerfully, starting the car. 'So Roxanne isn't here, she lied, and we don't know where she is. Let's get coffee and regroup.'

Kit sighed. He was right. She was cranky and it wasn't fair to take it out on him. 'I've got the list of places Roxanne worked at over the last five years. Last night, I checked for reports of lost or stolen items at all of them. I called two of the places who'd reported thefts on my way into the station, but I had to leave messages at both. And then I got the call from Janice Lenski saying that Roxanne hadn't shown up for her shift this morning.'

Roxanne's shift had started at seven. When she hadn't shown up by eight, Lenski had started calling the traveling nurse to find out if she was okay. But when she hadn't reached Roxanne by nine, Lenski had called Kit. Which had prompted them to go to Roxanne's home to bring her in for questioning. Kit had expected Roxanne to have run, but not to have never been there at all.

'What was reported stolen at the two retirement homes you called?' Connor asked.

'One was a small painting. The family found that it was missing after the resident of the assisted living center passed away. None of the relatives had been to visit in quite some time, so they had no idea when the painting disappeared. They accused the staff, but the investigation showed no leads.'

'How long had Roxanne been gone from the facility?'

'Eighteen months.'

Connor frowned. 'The family had no contact with the old guy for eighteen months?'

'Old lady,' Kit corrected, 'and no, nobody had visited in that long.' Which was incredibly sad. 'The painting had been appraised at nearly a hundred thousand dollars. It hasn't turned up in any legit auctions. I passed it and all the others I found on to Goddard. Hopefully his crew can find some online breadcrumbs to follow.'

'And the other retirement home you called?'

'A man, early seventies. Family visited once a month since they lived out of state. He and his wife had moved into the continuing care facility when she began losing mobility to rheumatoid arthritis. He owned a diamond-and-emerald-studded brooch made in the 1920s, valued at over twenty-five grand. Roxanne had moved on from the facility a full year before it was reported missing after the man died. The family was stunned because it was an heirloom that their father treasured. He had to have noticed it was missing.'

'That is weird. How many total theft reports did you find?'

'Six,' Kit said. 'I wonder how many others were never reported?'

'Or reported outside of California,' Connor said thoughtfully. 'Can the traveling nurses cross state lines?'

'Good point. I don't know. Let's find out.' Kit googled it. 'They have to be licensed in every state. There's a consortium that accepts licenses from different states, but California, Oregon, Washington, and Nevada don't participate. Neither do Alaska, Hawaii, Minnesota, or Connecticut. Others are pending, but those states would be the ones she'd need an individual license to work in.'

Connor turned when his phone told him to, bringing the coffee shop into view. 'At least the consortium cuts down a lot of checking. We can split the work and get a scope of this woman's scheme.' He shook his head. 'Stealing from old people is really low.'

Kit thought of Benny. She'd never met him, but she had the impression of a kind, good-hearted soul. Not just a victim of the nurse's greed.

'I wonder what exactly Benny knew that caused Roxanne to kill him?' she wondered as Connor guided the sedan into the drive-through. 'It must have had something to do with the fight he and Frankie had before they died.'

'Sad that they both died while still angry with their best friend,' Connor said quietly. 'Maybe Frankie warned him and Benny didn't believe him. Or didn't want to, anyway.'

'But when Benny saw the knife in Frankie's chest, he was forced to believe him. Sam talked to him that day. Said Benny was confused but insistent that Frankie's death was his fault. That he should have listened. He said that Frankie was wrong, but then he was right, so the theory that seeing Frankie dead made Benny believe him rings true. You talked to him that first day before I arrived. Did you see any kind of guilt or regret?'

'I wasn't looking for it. I was just trying to keep him quiet and not throwing punches at . . .' He sighed. 'At Roxanne. He was so frail, but he got a few good hits in before she calmed him down.'

'How? How could she have calmed him down on Monday if Benny knew what she'd done?'

Connor placed their order, rolled up his window, then turned to her. 'Maybe Benny didn't know that she'd done it. Everyone said how good Roxanne was with him. Who knows what she was whispering into his ear? If you know what I mean.'

Kit made a face. 'You're suggesting that Roxanne used sex to get Benny to cooperate?'

'He was old, Kit,' Connor said wryly. 'Not dead at that point. It could have even been simple companionship. He'd been lonely since his wife died. Friends like Georgia and Eloise are different than a woman whispering sweet nothings into his ear.'

'Frankie did accuse Benny of being naive and lonely. That's what Benny told Sam. That all makes sense, unfortunately. He loved his wife, though. Maybe Roxanne did offer him simple companionship, the kind that Georgia and Eloise couldn't offer.'

'Well, all we know is that she got him calm for a little while, he got agitated again, and she had him sedated with a doctor's permission. "For his own good," ' he added with air quotes.

'She was giving him sedatives orally even before she injected him,' Kit reminded him. She'd shared what she'd learned in the call with Alicia Batra.

'Right,' he allowed. 'Slipping him a mickey would have helped her control him. I wonder if she planned to kill him all along. Or at least after she killed Frankie. She wasn't on duty the Sunday that Frankie was supposed to have died. She had an alibi.'

'Which was why she pulled Frankie's I'm-okay cord on Sunday morning. To give herself that alibi. She was on duty until eight a.m. that morning, but off for the rest of the day. She had the opportunity to use the master key card on Frankie's door one more time, to misdirect his time of death until after she was no longer at Shady Oaks.'

'She had to have worried that Frankie had warned Benny,' he said. 'But killing Benny so close to Frankie's death would have been suspicious.'

'So she waited and faked his heart attack,' Kit murmured. 'Benny was taking diltiazem. I took a photo of the meds on his bedside table before I left this morning.' By her request, the family had left the old man's bedroom as it was. 'Roxanne would have had to have brought the digoxin with her. Alicia says it's rarely used anymore. I meant to ask Nurse Janice if anyone at Shady Oaks was currently prescribed it, but I got distracted when she said Roxanne hadn't come in this morning. Roxanne didn't leave Shady Oaks after she had Benny sedated, remember? She said she'd crashed in the staff quarters. So if no one at Shady Oaks took digoxin, Roxanne had to have planned to kill Benny before she left for work Monday morning. Damn. Killing Frankie was unplanned, but Benny was premeditated.'

They got to the window and Connor flashed a cordial smile at the very attractive server as he took their coffee from her, when before CeCe, he'd have turned his flirt on high.

'How did CeCe like her carving?' Kit asked, once they'd gotten their coffee.

Connor's face lit up. 'She cried, she was so happy. She's putting it on her desk at school. I think she's going to have the kids make an art project for Harlan.'

'He'll *love* that.' Kit took a large sip of coffee, not caring when it burned her tongue. 'Thank you for the caffeine. I needed it.'

'No big. So did anything happen last night at Shady Oaks?'

'Nope, no Roxanne. It was a quiet night.'

Connor pulled back into traffic, heading for the precinct. 'I wasn't talking about Roxanne. You spent the night with Sam.'

Kit glared at him. 'I did not "spend the night" with Sam. I worked and he slept on the sofa. Don't you go spreading rumors, Connor Robinson.'

'Yes, ma'am, Kit McKittrick.' But Connor's wicked grin belied his promise.

Kit rolled her eyes, prepared to deliver a diatribe on personal boundaries when her cell phone rang.

'It's one of the retirement homes I called this morning.' She answered the phone on speaker. 'This is Detective McKittrick.'

'Hello, Detective. This is Nora Gregson, returning your call. I'm the director at Serenity Retirement Village.'

'Thank you for calling me back. I'm with my partner, Detective Robinson, and I've got you on speaker. Is that okay?'

'Of course, Detective McKittrick. I understand that you're interested in a police report filed by the Brighton family after their grandfather passed.'

'Yes, ma'am,' Kit said as Connor pulled into a parking lot so that he could safely listen. 'According to the police report, a brooch worth about twenty-five thousand dollars had gone missing. Was there ever any resolution?'

'No. The family actually sued the facility, but our lawyers got it dismissed. We have a clearly stated policy that residents keep valuables in their units at their own risk. We warned the family to take it home with them, but they didn't do it.'

'What can you tell us about Roxanne Beaton?' Kit asked.

There was a moment of silence, followed by the clacking of a keyboard. 'Oh. I'd forgotten her after all this time. I do remember her now, though. She was a traveling nurse who completed a twelve-week contract with us. Why do you want to know about Nurse Beaton, Detective?'

Kit proceeded carefully. 'We're looking at anyone who had access to a valuable coin collection that was stolen within the last week. The circumstances of our theft seem similar to the theft of the brooch from your facility. But, unfortunately, we have several murder victims connected as well.'

Gregson gasped. 'Is this about Shady Oaks? I read about the murder in the paper. There's been more than one victim?'

'Possibly,' Kit hedged, regretting the slip of information. Miss Georgia was right. She should have slept more. 'We're still investigating. We think one of our murder victims was an accomplice of some sort to the killer. Did Roxanne socialize when she was working with you?'

Another gasp. 'Is Roxanne one of the victims?'

'No, she's alive,' Kit said, wishing she could just ask what she really wanted to know.

Gregson grew very quiet. When she spoke, it was in a low, angry tone. 'Are you accusing a nurse of killing a patient? Because if you are, you'd better be very, *very* sure.'

'Becoming very, *very* sure is what we're trying to do, ma'am,' Kit said, understanding the woman's ire. No one wanted to believe that a colleague was capable of murder, particularly a medical professional. 'We'd really like to be upfront with you, but there are things we can't share until we *are* very sure. And right now, we're trying to figure things out. We'd appreciate your help.'

'All right,' the woman said, her warning clear. 'What do you want to know?'

'Did Nurse Beaton attend to the resident in your facility who was robbed of his brooch?' Kit asked.

Another moment of quiet. 'I don't remember, and that's the truth, Detective. I'd have to go back into his patient files. Can you give me a few minutes to check?'

'Of course. I'll wait.'

'When she comes back ask her if she had an address for

Roxanne,' Connor said softly. 'We can follow up and see if she gave fake addresses everywhere she worked, or just here.'

'I will.'

Kit muted the phone, just in case Miss Gregson hadn't put them on hold and was listening to their conversation. 'Does Roxanne even have a real nursing license?'

'I'll check.' Connor googled the state licensing board, showing Kit his phone screen before stepping out of the car to make the call.

Kit reviewed the rest of the retirement facilities on Roxanne's résumé while she waited for Nora Gregson to come back on the line. Roxanne had been a traveling nurse for more than fifteen years, working in twenty-nine facilities during that time. Kit had identified only six thefts so far from the police reports. There had to have been more.

They were going to have to call all twenty-nine retirement facilities. Kit had started an email to Navarro asking for a support person when Connor got back into the car.

'Roxanne's legit,' he said. 'She got her nursing degree from the University of Tennessee, just like her résumé says. Her continuing education credits are up-to-date. The interesting thing is that they also have a Roxie Moynahan, an Anna Dupree, and a Rocki Davidson. All under the same license number.'

Kit blinked and took another gulp of coffee because that wasn't computing. 'Didn't they realize that four people were claiming the same license?'

'They're all Roxanne. Apparently, she's been married a number of times.' He tilted his head, his expression meaningful. 'I had our clerk run a quick check. All four husbands have died. Roxanne was widowed, every time. Poor Roxanne,' he added sarcastically. 'How unlucky she is.'

Kit caught his drift and nearly choked on her coffee. 'She's a black widow? Marrying the men and killing them? For money?'

'I don't know that, but we're going to find out. We also need to find out if any of her husbands were patients in the retirement homes where she worked. For now, we know that Beaton is her given surname.'

Kit's mind was spinning. 'Our background check didn't bring this up.'

'We ran a criminal check. Prior marriages slip through, sometimes.'

'Fucking hell,' Kit muttered. 'She's worked in twenty-nine places as Roxanne Beaton. How many others has she worked at under the other names?'

'Fifty-three in total over fifteen years.'

'Oh my God. Fifty-three?' Kit revised her request to Navarro with the new details, requesting two support people to help them make calls instead of only one. She sent the email and regarded Connor grimly. 'We definitely need to find out if she inherited money from those deceased husbands. They are all husbands, yes? No wives?'

'No wives.'

Kit drained her coffee and pinched the bridge of her nose. 'I thought we were finally on top of this case and the sand just shifted. Again.'

'We'll roll with it,' Connor said. 'We always do.'

Gregson came back on the line. 'Detectives?'

Kit unmuted the phone. 'We're still here.'

'She did attend to Mr Brighton. She was his favorite nurse. She spent a great deal of time in his apartment.'

'So she would have had access to the brooch that was stolen,' Kit said.

Gregson sighed. 'Yes. Look, you didn't ask for more, but I asked one of Roxanne's colleagues from that time if she'd be willing to talk to you and she said yes. She's here with me now. Would you like to speak with her?'

Kit glanced at Connor and saw that they were on the same page. 'Yes, please.'

'This is Nurse LaVerne Dempsey,' Gregson said. 'Nurse Dempsey, these are Detectives McKittrick and Robinson from San Diego PD.'

'Detectives.' LaVerne Dempsey had a deep, rich voice. 'I knew Roxanne better than anyone for the short time she was here. She worked here for three months, but that was more than two years ago.'

297

'Was she very social?' Kit asked, because she hadn't been at Shady Oaks. Not unfriendly, but she didn't go out of her way to socialize with the other care providers.

'No, not really. I only knew her better because one night I passed her truck pulled off on the shoulder on a lonely stretch of highway. She'd blown a timing belt and wasn't going to be able to get it towed until morning. I offered to drive her home and initially she declined, but she was coming down with a cold and feeling downright miserable, so she eventually said yes.'

'Where did she live?'

'In an RV park. She had one of those tiny houses and she hauled it from place to place. She was off the grid, Detectives. It didn't seem too weird to me then, because she said she did a lot of personal travel between contracts. She said that she had a goal of visiting all forty-eight contiguous states before she died. Said that so far she'd only driven around in California.'

'Did you believe her?' Connor asked.

'I did,' LaVerne said. 'I didn't have a reason not to.'

'The thing is,' Gregson cut in, 'the address of the RV park doesn't match the address she gave on her personnel forms.'

Bingo, Kit thought. She'd lied about her address there, too.

'Can you give us both addresses?' Connor asked aloud. 'The RV park and the address she provided?'

Gregson did, then sighed. 'We never even suspected Roxanne of the theft. She'd been gone for over a year when Mr Brighton passed. There had been three other traveling nurses in the meantime.'

'We don't know for sure that she has done anything,' Connor cautioned. 'We're putting the puzzle together right now, so we'd appreciate your discretion.'

'We won't say anything,' Gregson promised.

'Nurse Dempsey,' Kit said, 'were you able to see the license plate on the truck?'

'No,' LaVerne said, 'but I know where she took the truck to have the timing belt fixed, if that helps. They'd have the info on the truck's registration and VIN.'

'That would be a big help,' Connor said. 'Thank you.'

'We'll email you with all the information you've asked for, Detectives,' Gregson said. 'Is there anything else we can do to help you?'

'Only to call us if you—' Kit started.

'Wait,' LaVerne interrupted. 'There is one more thing. The day after I took her home, I picked her up to take her to work. The tow truck was going to pick up her truck during the day. She had a package with her. I asked about it – because I'm nosy and not afraid to admit it – and she said she had to mail a package to her sister. I peeked at the name.'

Kit sat up straighter. 'Which was?'

'Jackie Beaton. The address was somewhere in Tennessee. I don't remember the town. When I asked her about it, she was annoyed that I'd pried, so I shut up. She asked me to come to dinner at her tiny house the next day to thank me for helping her out, and I brought my husband. She didn't seem happy that I'd done that, either. She made up an excuse about having burned dinner, but there was no burned smell. We ended up going out for dinner instead and after that, Roxanne was even less social than before. Not impolite, just remote. We threw her a bon voyage party when she left, but that was mostly because we like to party. Not because we considered her a friend.'

Kit wondered what Roxanne had been planning to do to LaVerne at that dinner. 'Thank you, Nurse Dempsey. You've been extremely helpful. Miss Gregson, if you could send us that email right away, we'd be grateful.' Kit gave them her email address, then ended the call. 'We need to adjust the BOLO to include Roxanne's tiny house. The cameras at Shady Oaks got a picture of her truck, so we know she's driving a Ford F-250. A tiny house being hauled by a truck can't be that hard to find.'

'Your mouth, God's ears,' Connor muttered, already dialing Navarro. They updated the BOLO, then Connor ended the call. 'Where to next?'

Kit sighed. 'To Benny's daughter's house. We need to tell her that her father was murdered.'

Seventeen

Sam locked his desk drawer, all his session notes secured. He hoped he'd done right by his clients, but his mind had been on Georgia and Eloise. And Kit, of course. Always on Kit.

He'd put on his jacket when his cell phone buzzed. Heart suddenly racing at the caller ID, he lurched for his phone. 'Georgia? Are you all right?'

'I'm fine,' she assured him. 'So is Eloise. Detective McKittrick has two new officers on our floor in addition to that nice Officer Stern.'

'Aw shucks, ma'am,' a deep voice said in the background.

'Stern's in your apartment?'

'Been sitting at my kitchen table all day, showing us photos of his family. Eloise has adopted him.'

'So have you!' Eloise shouted.

'And have you?' Sam asked, amused.

'Maybe. Look, I've been working on Frankie's eulogy today.'

Sam's little bubble of happiness abruptly popped. 'Oh.'

Georgia sighed. 'Yeah, I know. The ME has released his body to the funeral home and his memorial service is Sunday. I want to do his eulogy right, just in case some of his old colleagues from SDPD show up to our service. I've written about the Frankie we knew – the husband of Ryan and purveyor of antiques who had a gruff exterior and a marshmallow heart, but it feels . . . incomplete. I was hoping to talk to some of those colleagues, to maybe get a feel for the man he was when he was a cop.' She hesitated. 'Maybe even speak to his ex-wife.'

Sam thought about Frankie's ex in the hospice. 'Do you think she'd talk to you?'

'Frankie only mentioned her a few times, but he spoke fondly of her. Her name is Sharon. He said she'd remarried, but I don't know her new last name. I tried googling her, but I didn't get anywhere. She's not attached to Frankie in any of the people-finder databases. I was hoping you'd know how to dig deeper.'

'Let me make some calls.'

'You are a good boy, Sam. Thank you.'

'Bye, Sam!' Eloise called.

'Tell Miss Eloise goodbye and that I'll be there soon. Can I bring you two anything?'

'Eloise, he wants to know if you want anything,' Georgia said.

'Wine,' Eloise said plaintively. 'Lots of wine.'

Georgia's sigh was long-suffering, which was a common occurrence around Eloise. 'If you bring wine, you might as well bring some chocolate, too. Thank you, Sam.'

'No problem. I'll call you if I find anything out.' He ended the call with Georgia, then looked at the contact list on his phone. Kit had said the woman was in a hospice, her son a constant presence at her side. She'd know the ex-wife's name and her location.

And, he could admit to himself, he wanted to hear her voice.

He hit her name and waited to be sent to her voice mail, but she answered. 'Are you all right?' she asked without even saying hello.

'I'm fine. So are the ladies. Are you?'

'Yes, of course.' Then she hesitated before saying quietly, 'Not really. We had to notify Benny's family that he'd been murdered. Never a pleasant task, but this one was rough.'

'Why?' Sam asked gently.

'I don't know. I never met the man, but he seemed like such a gentle soul. Murder is never fair. Or hardly ever, anyway. This one was so unnecessary. And for what? Greed? It's just . . . well, it's difficult.'

Part of him wanted to shout from the rooftops that she'd trusted him with something so personal. The other part of him wanted to help. To soothe.

'It's okay to feel, Kit.'

Her laugh was a touch bitter. 'No, it's really not. I won't be able to do my job if I feel too much.'

'I get that. I really do.' Because he often felt the same way about his clients. It was on the tip of his tongue to suggest she speak to a therapist, but he knew that would have her hanging up on him. 'Look, I was hoping you could help me help Miss Georgia. She's writing Frankie's eulogy.'

'Oh.'

Sam smiled sadly. 'Yeah. She wants to be thorough, especially if anyone from SDPD attends. She wants to speak to some of his former colleagues. Maybe even his ex-wife. I didn't promise her anything because I remembered you said that the ex-wife was in a hospice. I haven't tried to find her yet. I didn't think I'd be interfering with your investigation because you already crossed Frankie's son off your suspect list, but I wanted to be sure.'

'Thank you,' she said, seeming a little surprised. 'I have the name of Frankie's former police partner, but Baz said the man is rather homophobic. Or was, anyway. He might not have nice things to say. I haven't talked to him yet.'

'I'll contact him. See if Georgia and I can arrange a visit.'

'By yourselves?' Kit asked anxiously.

Sam frowned. 'We're not in danger outside of Shady Oaks, are we?'

'No.' Again she hesitated. 'But if you see a Ford F-250 truck following you, avoid it. And if you can't, call 911, then me. Especially if the truck is hauling a tiny house.'

That told him what Roxanne was driving and where she was living. *All right, then.* 'I will. I promise.'

'Thank you.'

'What about his ex-wife and son?'

She blew out a breath. 'Mrs White is close to the end of her life, and her son hasn't left her side. The son changed his name, by the way. Shady Oaks had him listed as Gerald Wilson, but he's gone by Gerald White since he was a teenager. His stepfather adopted him.'

Ouch. Seemed like the rift between Frankie and his son went deep. 'Should Georgia and I not call them?'

Another brief hesitation. 'The charge nurse said Mrs White has periods of lucidity, so you might be able to speak with her. Her son may say no, though, and that's his right.'

Sam stared at the framed photo of his grandfather Del on his desk. 'Frankie was like my grandfather, you know. Gruff exterior, soft heart. It's what drew me to him in the beginning. They shared a name – Franklin Delano. It felt like fate, me walking into Shady Oaks and meeting him that first day. Frankie made me feel like I had a little more time with my own grandfather. I don't want to distress Mrs White at this time, but Georgia said that when Frankie spoke of her, it was fondly. Maybe she'd like to know that.'

'Maybe. Just . . . be prepared for the son to be hostile. He was estranged from his father for most of his life. He might react poorly to his father's friends.'

'Okay, we'll start with the former partner and, depending on how tired Georgia gets, we'll try the hospice center. Can you text me the information?'

'I will. And, Sam? Be careful. I'm serious.'

'I will if you will. Thanks, Kit.' Sam ended the call and waited until his phone buzzed with her incoming text.

Frankie Flynn's former partner – Henry Whitfield. There was a phone number and an address in La Mesa.

His phone buzzed again with a second text. *Sharon White – Restful Heart Hospice, Lincoln Park.*

He'd call the former cop partner first. If Henry Whitfield was overly hostile, Sam wouldn't subject Miss Georgia to him.

Although Georgia could hold her own. If Whitfield was abusive, Sam would let Georgia have at him. The old cop would definitely be schooled by the end of that confrontation.

Cheered, Sam had started to dial Whitfield's number when he received a third text from Kit.

Be careful. Please.

It was a small thing, but it made him smile. She cared. Sam knew that she did. He just needed to be patient. For how much longer, he didn't know. But it would be worth it. *She* was worth it.

He finished dialing Henry Whitfield, who answered with a snarl. 'If you're a telemarketer—'

'I'm not,' Sam interrupted before the older man could launch into whatever diatribe he'd planned. 'My name is Sam Reeves. I'm a friend of Frankie Flynn's. You knew him as Frank Wilson.'

A long, long silence. 'How did you get my number, son?'

The question was asked warily, but without the anger that Sam had anticipated.

'From SDPD Homicide. A mutual friend of Frankie's and mine is writing his eulogy. She was hoping to talk to some people who knew him well when he was still a cop.'

'I clearly didn't know him that well,' Henry said wryly. 'I had no idea he was gay until this week. But I'll talk to your friend. Frank Wilson was a good cop. I wasn't crazy about him divorcing his wife, but she never said a bad word about him. Almost defended him, even. She's a good woman, so her defense of him's gotta count for something.'

There was something unsaid in his tone. Something personal. 'You were fond of Sharon?'

The old man chuffed a laugh. 'You some kind of shrink?'

Sam blinked. 'Actually, yes. Was I that obvious?'

Henry cackled. 'No. I looked you up on the computer while you were talking. I don't just talk to anyone, you know. Who's Frank's friend? The one writing the eulogy?'

'Georgia Shearer. She was his neighbor at Shady Oaks, the retirement center.'

'Well, she can call. Or visit. I don't much care.'

Henry cared. It was clear in his voice. He wanted company. 'If you'd trust me with your address, I'll drive her over.'

'Who in SDPD gave you my name?'

'Kit McKittrick.'

'Baz Constantine's protégé. She's making quite a name for herself.'

304

'She is.' Sam winced a bit at the pride in his own voice and hoped the old man hadn't heard it. No such luck.

'And you're fond of her,' Henry said slyly.

'Are you a shrink, sir?' Sam asked mildly.

'Nope. Just a cop for forty-five years. You learn a thing or two about people. What time will you be here?'

Sam calculated the time it would take to pick up Georgia and get to La Mesa. 'Four, four fifteen. Is that okay?'

'It is.' His tone changed, becoming sadly weary. 'I'll drag out some photos I have of Frank.'

'Thank you, sir. Can I bring you anything?'

'I wouldn't say no to an In-N-Out animal style.'

Sam lifted his brows. The burger loaded with extra spread and onions might not be the healthiest choice. 'But would your doctor say no?'

Henry laughed. 'Not if he doesn't know. I'm eighty-four years old, Dr Reeves. Let me have one vice.'

'If there's one on the way, I'll stop.'

'There is. I'll text you In-N-Out's address when I text you mine.'

Sam figured it was best to stay on the old cop's good side. 'All right. See you soon.' Then he remembered Siggy. 'I've left my dog with my friend. If I have to go home to drop him off, I'll hit downtown traffic. Do you have a yard where I can put him while we talk?'

'I do, but if he's a good dog, he can come in the house. That makes the burger more of a requirement than a request.'

Sam smiled. 'Deal. See you soon.' He hung up and called Georgia back. 'I'll pick you up in thirty minutes. We're going to see an old cop and probably break his dietary restrictions with In-N-Out.'

'We're old, Sam. Let us have a few vices.'

Sam chuckled. 'That's what he said. Stay put in your apartment. I'll come up to get you.'

A pause. 'Roxanne didn't show up for her shift today.'

Sam's smile faded. That was why Kit had been so nervous. 'Even more reason for you to be careful. She might have run, but if she didn't, I'm not letting anything happen to you. See you soon.'

San Diego PD, San Diego, California
Thursday, 10 November, 3.30 P.M.

'Oh my God,' Kit breathed, staring at the painting on her computer screen. 'I think I found one. Finally.'

She and Connor had spent the early afternoon calling retirement homes, asking about items that had gone missing from patients whom Roxanne had cared for – under all her names. They'd compiled a list of twenty items, including five paintings, four coin collections, two stamp collections, three sculptures, and six rare first-edition books. The items had a total insurance value of over twelve million dollars. And that didn't include Benny Dreyfus's coin collection.

They'd begun searching for the items online, to see if anything came up regarding their current location or a past sale. They hadn't really expected to find anything, thinking that most of the stolen items would be sold in private dark-web auctions, like the one Goddard had discovered was selling Benny's collection. But the internet was a place to start.

Kit had been about to give up when one of her searches hit pay dirt.

Connor slid his chair from his desk to Kit's to study the painting on her screen. *'Woman on a Summer Night.* It's in a museum? Really?'

'Yep. A small art museum in Denver. The caption on the picture of the painting said it's on temporary loan from an anonymous donor.'

Woman on a Summer Night was a seventeenth-century painting by an artist of the Dutch Golden Age. Or so the museum's description said.

Kit split her screen, one side showing a photo of the painting reported missing by the retirement home in LA and the other showing the photo from the museum's temporary exhibit.

'Denver's only an hour ahead of us,' Connor said, 'so the museum should still be open. Let's find out who the anonymous donor is.'

Trying not to get her hopes up, Kit dialed the museum's office, relieved when she got a live human on the line. 'Can you connect me with the director's office, please?' she asked. 'My name is Detective McKittrick. I'm calling from the San Diego Police Department.'

'All right,' the woman on the line said warily. 'I'll see if Dr Stevens is in.'

Kit clicked on About Us and found a photo of Thomas Stevens, PhD. He looked a bit forbidding, in a my-family-came-over-on-the-*Mayflower* kind of way. 'I hope he doesn't think we're accusing him of anything. The museum has a stellar reputation and has been around for over fifty years.'

'Then they'll want to cooperate,' Connor said confidently. 'You found the painting, so you should take point, but signal if you want me to jump in.'

Because Connor was better at communicating with the rich, elite types. Like those who managed museums featuring four-hundred-year-old paintings.

She nodded, saying nothing more to him because a male voice came on the line.

'Hello, this is Dr Stevens. With whom am I speaking?'

'I'm Detective McKittrick, San Diego PD. I'm here with my partner, Detective Robinson. A painting on temporary loan to your museum has come up in one of our investigations and we were hoping to get some information on it.'

'An investigation?' he asked sharply. 'What kind of investigation?'

'We're Homicide, sir,' she said quietly. 'This is a murder investigation.'

'I . . . I see. What do you want to know?'

'We're tracing collections or items of art that were reported stolen—'

'Our paintings are *not* stolen,' he interrupted stiffly. 'We have documentation. We double and triple check for authenticity and legal ownership. We do our due diligence, Detective.'

'I'm not suggesting that you don't, sir,' Kit said respectfully. 'But a painting matching the one in your exhibit was reported stolen. We're not investigating the theft. We're trying to trace the ownership.'

'The owners are respected members of our community.' Stevens's tone had become downright frosty. 'I will not have you maligning their name or legacy.'

'I'm not suggesting they did anything wrong,' Kit said calmly. 'If they had, they'd be foolish to loan it to a museum who'd put it on display, wouldn't they?'

'They would indeed. So what exactly *are* you suggesting, Detective?'

'Honestly, I'm not sure. We're not even sure that this particular painting connects to our murder investigation. Right now, we're exploring leads. I'd appreciate it if you could answer just a few questions, sir.'

'You may ask.'

Kit grimaced. She'd expected attitude, but this guy . . . 'The painting is *Woman on a Summer Night*. Who is the anonymous donor?'

'I'm not at liberty to say.'

Kit wanted to tell him where to shove his liberty. Connor pointed to himself and she nodded. It wouldn't do to irritate a source before they got the information.

'Dr Stevens, this is Detective Robinson. We need to trace this painting's provenance and, not to sound threatening, we are prepared to get a subpoena for the information. I really don't think the anonymous donor would like all the dust a subpoena is likely to kick up.'

A long silence. 'No, they probably would not. Let me call you back.'

There was a click and then empty air.

'That was fun,' Kit said.

Connor chuckled. 'He'll call back. He's just giving the donor a heads-up.'

'And if the painting disappears?'

He shrugged. 'Screenshot that museum page. Just because the painting is no longer in their possession means nothing. Goddard will want the painting if it's part of Roxanne's theft. We want the donor and that won't change.'

'You're right.' Kit stood up and stretched her back. Her sleepless night was catching up to her. 'I need coffee. You want some?'

Connor made a face. 'From that pot in the bullpen? No, thank you. Hurry up, I expect Dr Museum to call back soon.'

Kit did hurry to the bullpen coffee machine, the movement helping her to wake up. By the time she returned to where Connor waited, she was almost fully awake.

She sat down at the table, making a face identical to the one Connor had made when she took her first sip. 'Who made this? It was better when Baz was here. He'd make a fresh pot after lunch every day.'

'I'm not going to do that,' Connor said dryly. 'No matter how sad you are that Baz isn't still here. I'm here now and I'm not making coffee.'

She grinned. 'It was worth a try. Did you feel a little sorry for me?'

'Not even a little. Did that "poor me" routine work with Baz?'

'Usually, yes. He—'

Her phone rang and Connor smiled smugly. 'Told you he'd call you back.'

She answered and put the call on speaker. 'This is Detective McKittrick.'

'This is Dr Stevens of the Kensington Museum of Art.'

'Dr Stevens, thank you so much for calling us back.' Kit hoped she sounded humble, but Connor's rolling eyes told her that she'd laid it on too thick.

Stevens harrumphed. 'The donor is Judge Emil Barrington of the lower circuit court. He lives in Denver. He says you may call him at any time. He has proper documentation of the purchase of the painting from a reputable source. His father, Emil Senior, purchased the painting ten years ago. It remained in his private collection until he died last year. We've only received the temporary loan this month.'

'I see,' Kit said, because it made sense that it had only been on loan a short time. Otherwise the robbery department of LAPD would have found it long ago. 'Can I get the number for Judge Barrington?'

Dr Stevens recited the number. 'Let me know if I can be of further service.'

'We will. Thank you.' She hung up and googled Judge Emil

Barrington. 'He's been a judge for twenty years. We'll need to tread lightly with him.'

'It's possible that the painting wasn't part of Roxanne's thefts.'

'Entirely possible.' She pulled up the police report. 'The family of William Freeman reported it missing after his death, ten years ago. Roxanne worked at William Freeman's retirement home two years before that, for three months. We don't know if Roxanne took care of him or not. The director at the time retired five years ago and the new director couldn't find any records in the files.'

'When was the last time the family had visited William Freeman?'

'They visited frequently, according to the police report. The officer noted that the family kept tight control over the old man's finances, which, according to the family, made the old man angry. They hadn't let him keep the painting in the retirement home. It was kept in a vault in the family's bank.' She rolled her eyes. 'They apparently had so much art that they stored the "lesser pieces" in the vault.'

Connor's lips twitched. 'Just so you know, my family is nowhere near their level. My father collects pipes and he has one that supposedly belonged to Abe Lincoln, but that fact is in high dispute. I think his most valuable pipe set him back a few thousand dollars. So don't go thinking that the Robinsons have a family vault with "lesser" paintings shoved inside.'

Kit chuckled. 'Understood. One of Pop's carvings went for two thousand dollars at a charity auction last year, so maybe my carved birds are worth something.'

'Those birds are priceless, Kit.'

Kit's hand automatically sought the cat-bird figurine in her pocket. It was one of seventeen carvings Harlan had made for her over the years. Sixteen were simple wrens, and those she kept on a shelf in her bedroom where she could see them when she woke up.

'Yes, they are.' She held the cat-bird on her palm, as astonished by its delicate beauty as she'd been the first day Harlan had given it to her. *Priceless.*

She'd take her father's handmade treasures over million-dollar paintings any day of the week.

Carefully slipping the cat-bird back into her pocket and giving it a quick pat for luck, she dialed the number for Judge Barrington. The call was answered by an office administrator, who put them through to the judge.

'Detectives McKittrick and Robinson?' the judge said, forgoing a polite greeting.

'Yes, sir,' Kit said. 'I don't know what Dr Stevens told you when he called, so I'm not sure where to begin.'

'He said my painting was stolen,' the judge said bluntly. 'I can assure you that it was not.'

'We didn't say that it was stolen,' she said. 'We said it was *reported* stolen. We're tracking items that were reported missing from retirement homes over the past fifteen years.'

'I thought you were homicide detectives.'

'We are,' Connor said. 'The murder of a retired SDPD homicide lieutenant started us on this path. We believe his murderer stole items from senior citizens in nursing homes. Your painting was one of those reported missing by surviving family members when the previous owner passed away.'

There was a pause. 'I see,' the judge finally said. 'You're talking about Frank Flynn, who retired as Lieutenant Frank Wilson. I just ran a search online.' He sighed. 'My father loved that painting. He was well into his eighties when he bought it, but still sharp. He told me that he'd checked the certification carefully. I have all the documentation that was sent with the painting. I found it in his files after he passed. I'll have my assistant scan and email it to you.'

'Thank you, sir,' Connor said. 'We appreciate it.'

There was a moment of silence followed by another of the judge's sighs. 'Like I said, my father loved that painting. He'd been an amateur painter himself and had always wanted a Dutch Master. He'd tried to buy several in the past at auctions and was always outbid. He grew more and more determined. And then one day he brought home *Woman on a Summer Night*.'

There was something the judge was not saying, Kit was certain. 'How badly did he want it, sir?'

'He would never allow the painting to be loaned out, not in the ten years he owned it. I told him that a painting like that one should be enjoyed by everyone, but he outright refused to allow anyone else to even see it. No one outside the immediate family.'

Kit shared a glance with Connor and he grimaced. 'Do you think he had an idea that it might have been stolen at some point, Judge Barrington?' he asked.

'I'd like to say that my father would never own something that was stolen, but . . . well, I don't know. I don't want to think it, but he was very determined. I was the one who offered it for loan to the museum. I've actually broken the terms of my father's will by loaning it out, but I sold his house after he died and I couldn't stand to see it collecting dust on the wall of my study. My father is probably spinning in his grave. But he does have documentation.'

The final sentence was said like the judge was trying to convince himself as well as Kit and Connor.

'We'll investigate it, sir,' Connor promised.

'And if it was stolen at some point?' the judge asked.

Kit and Connor looked at each other. Connor shrugged.

'I think we'd pass that part of the case to Detective Goddard,' Kit said. 'He's our colleague in the robbery division. We're truly just interested in catching a killer. Three people have been killed here so far.'

In San Diego, she thought grimly.

There was still the matter of Roxanne's many marriages, through which she'd inherited millions after her husbands had died. Two had been residents of retirement homes just like Shady Oaks. Two had lived independently in their own homes but had visited friends in other retirement homes, which might have been how Roxanne had met them. Whether the husbands had died of natural causes hadn't been determined and might not ever be, given the amount of time that had passed since their deaths. But that was an investigation that would have to wait until they found Roxanne and charged her for the three homicides they had in San Diego.

'I see,' the judge said quietly. 'Well, I won't delay. You'll have my documentation within the next fifteen minutes.'

'Thank you,' Kit said sincerely, and gave him her email address.

'I wish you good luck in catching your murderer.' With that, Judge Barrington ended the call.

'What do you think?' Connor asked.

'I think he figured his dad knew all along that the painting was stolen. Whether the judge knew ten years ago or just figured it out, I don't know. But he is a judge. I can't imagine something like this would look good for him if it came out. It's possible that he's cooperating to head off bad press before it becomes a scandal.'

'I thought the same. It's all about optics at his level. He can't get voted out, because judges in Colorado are appointed, not elected. But it would cause him embarrassment, for sure.'

'Do you think he'll really send the documents?'

Connor smirked. 'I think he will after he reads them.'

Eighteen

Connor was right. Fifteen minutes after their call with Judge Barrington, an email was delivered to Kit's inbox. She downloaded the attached documents immediately.

'We should ask Goddard to check these documents out,' she murmured as she examined the certificate of authenticity. She tabbed to the next document and froze. 'What is this?'

Connor frowned. 'He bought it from a broker, who bought it from a . . . charity?'

'Who got it from William Freeman by way of donation to the charity.' Kit enlarged the signature line. 'Here's Freeman's signature.'

'We need to find out if the signature's been forged,' Connor said, still frowning.

Kit leaned back in her chair, thinking. So many thefts had been discovered well after the owners' deaths. *Why?* Why hadn't the senior citizens reported their things stolen? Benny might not have known his coins had been taken, but surely *some* of the seniors had noticed before they'd died.

'What if it's not forged?' she asked slowly.

'You mean it was actually given to a charity and Roxanne didn't steal it? Then we're back to square one and that would suck.'

'I'm not saying that Roxanne didn't steal them. I'm asking what if she got her victims to sign over their treasures?'

Connor's frown deepened. 'What?'

'Hear me out. We have twenty instances of missing items. *Twenty*, Connor. And not *one* was reported by the senior citizen owner.'

'Only by their families after their deaths.'

She nodded. 'Exactly. I mean, I get that a number of them had memory problems, but we have instances where the thefts went unreported for *years*.'

'Because she didn't steal the stuff,' Connor murmured. 'They gave it to her.'

'Donated, maybe. She's been at this for fifteen years and has never been caught or even suspected – at least as far as we know.'

'And the black widow business . . .' Connor pursed his lips as he considered. 'If she married them legally and they happened to die, it would be a legal inheritance. If someone pushed for an investigation, the ME would have to know what to look for. Like with Mr Dreyfus.'

'Yeah, Alicia said if she hadn't specifically asked about digoxin and diltiazem, the lab would have missed it. They would have assumed a heart attack.'

Connor sighed. 'I wonder which scheme Frankie Flynn found out about – the theft-by-donation or that she was a black widow?'

'We might not find out. Frankie didn't leave anything with anyone.'

Connor held up a finger. 'Maybe he did. He went out the Wednesday before he was killed, remember?'

Kit drew in a sharp breath. 'Where the *hell* did he go? He wasn't gone long enough to go to San Francisco, and Ryland's CSU team searched the house top to bottom anyway. He didn't leave information there.'

'And he didn't leave it in his car, because Ryland checked that, too.'

They sat for a full minute in silence, and then Connor nudged Kit's mouse, waking up her screen. 'Was William Freeman a veteran?' he asked.

'I don't know. Why?'

'The charity he signed the painting to is Warriors with Wounds.'

He pulled Kit's keyboard within reach and began typing. 'Here. Wounded Warriors is the famous charity. The name is close enough that William Freeman could have been fooled.'

'Look up Warriors with Wounds,' Kit said. 'If she faked a veterans' charity, she's a real piece of work.'

Connor's hands paused on the keyboard. 'She *is* a killer, Kit.'

She scowled. 'I know, but defrauding veterans is a really shitty thing to do.'

Connor pursed his lips again, this time to bite back a smile. 'Fine.'

'Shut up. I know it sounds ridiculous, but stealing from a charity is low. Even for killers.'

Connor gave up trying to hide his smile. 'The very nerve.'

She sighed. 'Just look up the fake charity.'

'It's not registered in California.'

Kit tapped her desk. 'Check Tennessee. That's where Roxanne went to college and where she was sending that package to her sister, right? That's what the nurse from Serenity Retirement Village said. LaVerne Dempsey.'

'She did.' He searched for the Tennessee business database and typed in *Warriors with Wounds*. 'Bingo. It's an LLC. Not a charity. If any of her victims wanted to check on the existence of her so-called charity, it's right here if they look it up. The names are the same, but the charity itself doesn't exist.'

'All profit, all day,' Kit said grimly. 'The puzzle pieces are starting to fit. Roxanne *did* steal valuable coins from Benny Dreyfus and she *did* steal *Woman on a Summer Night* from William Freeman. She just made her victims – William Freeman, anyway – believe they were donating to charity. And William wasn't going to tell because he didn't want his family to know he was giving anything away. If Roxanne had talked with William and he'd told her this, she'd know he was a safe bet. By the time the family found out that the painting was missing, it was too late. She'd already sold it to Emil Barrington Senior, who wasn't going to let anyone else see it. Barrington Senior even made that a requirement in his will – that the painting was never to be loaned out or shown to anyone outside the family.'

Connor nodded thoughtfully. 'So there was no risk to Roxanne of anyone seeing it. And if the other nineteen thefts were the same way and anyone did find out that their senior citizen had given her something, she could deny any knowledge. The person she'd tricked into donation was dead. They'd died thinking they'd made a legit charitable contribution. And her name is on none of the paperwork. She's guilty of theft, but all the evidence is circumstantial.'

'Exactly. Until Benny Dreyfus. Both Georgia Shearer and Devon Jones said that even in his confusion, Benny knew that the coins needed to be hidden. Protected. He wore gloves. He called his daughter when he couldn't remember the combination. I don't think he was willing to give them to Roxanne despite her attention, and I think she figured that out.'

'So she flat-out stole them,' Connor said. 'And somehow got Kent Crawford to turn off the camera that could identify her. How did she know Crawford would help her? He didn't find out about the coins until later.'

Kit shrugged. 'Maybe Roxanne recognized a fellow thief. Georgia said that Frankie suspected Crawford was stealing.'

'If Roxanne did her homework before arriving at each assignment, she might have seen that Crawford drove a fancy car.'

'She was most likely the woman in his motel room,' Kit said. 'The lipstick on that cup was the same color as the lipstick on Crawford's autopsy photo.'

'So Roxanne does a little flirting, gets on Crawford's good side, gives him sex, and then . . . what? He tells her how to turn off the cameras?'

Kit shrugged again. 'He had to have turned them off on Friday, before Roxanne was able to steal the coins. I think she killed Crawford because she didn't want to share the loot, but he could have threatened to expose her as well. So she's in Crawford's motel room sometime after midnight on Saturday and she drugs him. The oral sex happened shortly before he died.'

'Maybe the oral was to distract him from noticing that he'd been drugged. He finishes and feels tired. According to Faye Evans, that was his usual. He "rolled off" her and "went to sleep" when he was done.'

'Sounds right. Once he was dead, Roxanne took his laptop, his cell phone, and enough clothes that she would look like Crawford on the surveillance tape when she left Shady Oaks after stealing the coins.'

'But somehow she knew that Frankie Flynn suspected her,' Connor said, 'so she waited until Eloise's birthday party on Saturday evening to search his place. Frankie comes back early from the party because he dislikes duck confit and wants a real meal. He surprises Roxanne, who kills him with a thin stiletto.'

'And then she panicked and staged the butcher knife scene – we still need to figure out why she did that, by the way. There's got to be something about that stiletto that we don't know yet.' Kit noted it for later. 'Like you said earlier, she probably knew that she'd have to kill Benny once she'd killed Frankie, but she waited until after Frankie's body was found. Which brings us to now. It still bugs me that we don't know how she and Crawford knew they could work together.'

'I guess we'll have to ask her when we find her.'

Kit scowled. 'Trouble is, we're no closer to knowing where she is.'

Connor checked his phone for the time. 'We're going with Goddard to check out that dark-web private sale in less than two hours. If Roxanne did steal those coins, we'll catch her there.'

'I hope so.' Because they had no other leads.

She blinked hard, fatigue suddenly bearing down on her, and a gallon of coffee wouldn't be enough to pep her up. She needed to sleep before they backed up Goddard and his team. 'I'm going to—'

She was interrupted by the ringing of her phone. 'It's Ryland.' She hit accept and put it on speaker. 'Hey, what do you know?'

'The lipstick from the cup you brought me matches the lipstick the ME pulled from Kent Crawford's . . .' Ryland hesitated. 'Uh, his body.'

She was too tired to laugh at the man's inability to say 'penis.' 'Confirmation, then. Roxanne Beaton was in Kent Crawford's hotel room shortly before he died. Even if he didn't steal the coins, she killed him.'

'Probably didn't want to share her loot,' Ryland speculated.

'You're probably right. Thank you.' Ending the call, she pulled the scrunchie from her hair and massaged her scalp. 'I didn't sleep much last night. I'm going to crash in the break room for an hour.'

'Do that. I'll bring Navarro and Goddard up to speed.'

'Thanks, Connor.' She started for the bullpen's double doors, then looked over her shoulder. 'I'm glad you're here, even if you refuse to make me coffee.'

He laughed. 'Go to sleep. Sam will have my hide if anything happens to you.'

Kit walked away, looking at the floor. Her hair, let loose of the scrunchie, fell forward to hide her cheeks that she absolutely knew were burning.

Because Sam did care about her. And she still wasn't sure what she planned to do about it.

La Mesa, San Diego, California
Thursday, 10 November, 4.30 P.M.

Georgia sat in the passenger seat of Sam's RAV4, staring up at Frankie's old partner's house. 'Henry Whitfield still lives alone. Good for him.'

Sam glanced at the bag containing the In-N-Out burger, animal style. 'I don't think he drives anymore, if it's any consolation. If he did, he'd go get his own burger.'

'I don't know if this is a good idea, Sam. What if he's hateful toward Frankie?'

'I don't think he will be. He admired Frankie as a cop, and that's what you want to know about, right?'

She nodded once. 'Right. Let's do this.'

Sam got Siggy out of the cargo hold and, leash in hand, went around to Georgia's side of the car and offered his arm.

'Thank you, Sam.'

'I'm a good boy,' he said dryly. 'Everybody says so.'

Georgia chuckled as they made their way up to Henry Whitfield's front door. The house's paint was a little chipped, the bushes

319

in the front a little overgrown, but other than that, the place was in good shape.

'You're thinking about all the fixes you can do to his house, aren't you?' Georgia asked.

'Busted.'

'I should write your mother a thank-you note. She raised you right.' She stopped at Henry's doormat, then choked on a laugh. ' "Go away," ' she read. 'I might like this guy if he's nice to Frankie's memory.'

Sam knocked on the door, listening for a response. He heard the shuffle of footsteps before the door opened, revealing Henry Whitfield, age eighty-four. Sam had looked him up.

The old man was a decorated cop and had been Frankie Flynn's SDPD partner for years before Frankie had been promoted to lieutenant of the homicide department. Together, the two had closed a record number of cases.

'Detective Whitfield,' Sam said. 'I'm Sam Reeves and this is my friend, Georgia Shearer.'

'Just Henry,' Whitfield said. He lowered his hand to let Siggy sniff it. 'And who is this?'

'This is Siggy, short for Sigmund.' Sam handed the older man the bag of In-N-Out, earning a quick grin for his efforts.

'Thank you, Sam. And if it makes you feel better, my grandson brings me one of these every week when he visits with his kids. You're not killing me faster.'

Sam huffed a relieved breath. 'I'm really glad to know that. I'd feel guilty.'

Whitfield opened the door wider. 'Come in. Please.'

The inside of the house was vintage bachelor pad, complete with a BarcaLounger recliner held together with what looked like an entire roll of duct tape. The sofa was neat and clean, though, so Sam eased Georgia onto it while Whitfield settled into his recliner with a mild groan.

Siggy sat by the arm of the man's chair, accurately identifying a new person who would pet him. Whitfield complied and Siggy wagged his tail in pleasure.

Henry sighed. 'Frank.'

'He was my friend,' Georgia said quietly.

'Mine too. Although we weren't as close as I thought. I never knew he was gay.'

'Would you have been okay with it?' Georgia asked baldly.

Sam resisted the urge to wince. He supposed that Georgia wanted to know where she stood right away.

'The gloves come off,' Whitfield said mildly.

Georgia lifted a brow. 'They were never on.'

Sam cleared his throat. 'She's kind of a barracuda, Henry. Answer her question, please, so we can get to remembering Frankie.'

Whitfield sighed again. 'At the time? I probably wouldn't have been okay with Frank being gay. I would have been wrong. People change and . . . learn.'

'Who in your family is gay?' Georgia asked perceptively.

'My grandson. I love that boy with all my heart. So I learned to be a better man. I wish I'd known Frank was here in San Diego. I would have liked to have told him that. It stung when he left us and never looked back, but I get it now. What would you like to know, Georgia?'

'I guess I want to know what he was like back then. The Frankie I knew was gruff and could be standoffish, but he had a heart of gold. He loved his husband with all his heart.'

Whitfield drew a long breath and wheezed it out. 'I'm glad he was happy. His husband died four years ago.'

Again her silver brow rose. 'How did you know that?'

'Looked him up. I still dabble in researching people every now and then. Not much else to do other than watch television.'

'You could join us at Shady Oaks,' Georgia said without any sarcasm at all.

Sam wanted to stare at her in shock, but he controlled himself. The Georgia he knew would never invite a stranger anywhere.

'My grandson and his husband live on the next block. My great-grandkids come over almost every day. I'm good here, but thank you.' Whitfield grew quiet, stroking Siggy's head. 'I don't think Frank was that much different when he was a cop. We used to call

321

him Joe Friday because he was kind of stiff.' He glanced at Sam. 'That's from *Dragnet*, an old TV show. Friday was a cop.'

'I know who Joe Friday is,' Sam said dryly. 'Reruns, you know.'

Georgia patted Sam's hand. 'Sam's a good boy, even though he's young. We like him. Frankie liked him, too.' She chuckled. 'I remember the first day Sam came to play the piano for us at Shady Oaks. Frankie asked him to play some heavy metal, so Sam did.'

Whitfield laughed. 'That sounds like Frank. What did he say when you fulfilled his request?'

'Flipped me a double bird,' Sam said.

Whitfield laughed harder, then wheezed again as he sobered. 'He was . . . kind. He was wicked smart and a great judge of character. He could size a person up with a look. "He's guilty," he'd say after meeting a suspect. Nine times out of ten he was right. And when he wasn't, he worked that much harder to find the right perpetrator. He was methodical and had a memory like a steel trap. But he was kind. I can't count the number of times he gave money to bums on the street. Or to women leaving abusive husbands.'

Georgia sucked in a suspiciously wet breath. 'He and Ryan were foster parents. They took in gay teenagers. And just a few months ago, he paid off the medical bills of one of our nursing assistants. Her baby was sick. He was one of the best men I ever knew.'

'I think every cop you'll talk to would say the same thing. He was loyal to his people and everyone was loyal to him. I would have taken a bullet for him and I wasn't the only one. That's why we were all so stunned when he turned fifty-five and walked away.'

'He'd promised Ryan,' Georgia said simply.

'He kept his promises. Always.' Whitfield unwrapped the burger and took a bite, sighing happily. Siggy sniffed hopefully, then settled onto the floor when Whitfield told him no. 'Thank you, Sam. I appreciate this. Georgia, I figured I'd just tell you about some of our cases and let you ask questions. Will there be a private memorial service at Shady Oaks?'

'There will be, but you're all welcome,' Georgia said. 'That's why I wanted to talk to someone who knew him back then. I hoped some of you would come.'

'Then I'll spread the word.' Whitfield hesitated. 'He did love his wife. I'm sure of that. We were all shocked at their divorce, but now it makes more sense.'

'He did love her,' Georgia agreed. 'He told me so. He didn't speak of her often, but it was always fondly.'

'She'd like to hear that.' Another sigh. 'I remember when they split up. It was forty-five years ago, but I remember it like it was yesterday. Like I said, we were all in shock. Especially me. We'd been partners in Homicide for two years by then. I thought they had the perfect marriage. My wife and I had divorced already and . . . well, I didn't want that for Sharon. Frank's wife, you know.' Whitfield glanced at Sam. 'I really liked her.'

'Made a move on her, did you?' Georgia asked wryly.

'I did. She told me that she was done with cops. But she never spoke ill of Frank. She loved him. Told me that they'd agreed that it was time for them to part and that she loved him like her best friend.'

'He met Ryan forty-five years ago,' Georgia said thoughtfully.

Whitfield nodded. 'Again, that makes sense. Frank would never have cheated on Sharon. I know that like I know my own name. I think Sharon must have known. You know, that he was gay. She didn't seem surprised at the divorce. She even seemed happy for him, which I didn't understand back then. So . . . a mystery solved. Anyway, they were good friends for the next few years, until Sharon remarried. Up until then, he would come by the house to fix things whenever something broke and he always remembered her birthday, up until the day he retired. Maybe even after that, I don't know. You should talk to her.'

'She's in hospice,' Sam said gently, hoping to soften the blow.

Whitfield's eyes grew sad. 'I know. I've visited her a few times, whenever my grandson is free to drive me over.' He hesitated. 'I think Frank may have visited as well.'

Sam's eyes widened at that. 'When?'

'Every so often for the last three months. I'd see white roses in a vase in her room. Those were Frank's flowers. He said he'd brought them to her on their first date. Always sent her white roses on her birthday. I think if you want to know who Frank was back then, you should pay her a visit. But do it quickly. Today, even. She likes dogs, so you can take the pooch.'

'We'll go over there when we're done here,' Sam said, wondering if that was where Frankie had gone the Wednesday before he'd been killed. 'So . . . stories about Frankie?'

Whitfield pointed to a scrapbook on the coffee table. 'Photos. Frank's in some of them. Help yourself.' He applied himself to the burger in earnest as Georgia picked up the scrapbook.

'Oh!' she said in a happy voice. 'Look at Frankie, Sam. He had to have been in his thirties in this photo.' Sam looked over her shoulder as she went page to page, hungrily absorbing the details, asking the occasional question which Whitfield readily answered. Then she laughed when she came to the photo of an amused Frankie holding a clearly fake police ID.

Sam chuckled. 'The photo's of you and Frankie and he's holding up a police ID. The photo below it is an enlargement of the ID that says "Joe Friday." Did you make that for him?'

Whitfield laughed. 'We did. That was his retirement present.' His smile faded. 'That was the last time I saw him.'

'He kept the ID,' Georgia told him with an unsteady smile.

Whitfield's eyes grew suddenly shiny. 'He did? Really?'

'Really. I found it in a shoebox when I was helping him clean out Ryan's things after he died. I'd already found Frankie's actual old badge and was shocked that he'd been a cop. He never talked about those days. It was his "other life," he said. But he kept the Joe Friday badge. It was with some mementos of his time on the force. A few certificates of appreciation, that kind of thing. I remember him laughing when he saw the badge. It was only the second time he'd laughed since Ryan passed. The first time was when Sam played Iron Maiden on Shady Oaks's baby grand.' She glanced at Sam, then looked back at Whitfield. 'If no one in his family claims the badge, would you like to have it?'

Whitfield wiped at his eyes. 'Yes,' he said gruffly. 'I would. Thank you.'

Sam checked the time. They'd been there an hour and Georgia

was growing visibly tired, as was Whitfield. 'I think it's time we head out.'

Georgia met Sam's gaze. 'Can you bring me back sometime for a visit?'

'Of course.'

Whitfield struggled to get out of the recliner and Sam lent him a hand.

'Thank you for coming,' Whitfield said, his voice still rough. 'I didn't know how much I needed to talk about him. Come back soon.'

'I will,' Georgia promised.

Sam shook Whitfield's hand when they left the house, then waved to a pair of twin boys running from a car that had just parked in the driveway as Sam was putting Siggy in the cargo hold. A final look as he drove away revealed Whitfield still standing on his front porch, holding a hand of each boy.

'That was nice,' Sam said quietly. 'I'm glad we visited.'

'Me too,' Georgia agreed. 'Thank you, Sam.'

'You're more than welcome. I should be taking you girls out more often.'

'Eloise would get such a kick out of that. Can we go to the hospice now? I want to talk to Sharon.'

Sam hesitated, because she looked exhausted. 'If you're sure you're up to it.'

Georgia nodded once. 'I'm sure.'

'Then that's where we'll go.'

Restful Heart Hospice, Lincoln Park, San Diego, California
Thursday, 10 November, 6.00 P.M.

'You're sure you're up for this?' Sam asked one more time as he helped a visibly weary Georgia into the hospice facility. As if understanding that Georgia needed to go slowly, Siggy paced them, not pulling even a little bit.

Such a good dog.

He hoped the hospice would permit Siggy to come in. It wasn't too warm for him to stay in the car, but Sam didn't like to risk it. 'I can drive you back here tomorrow if you're too tired.'

Georgia clutched his arm a little tighter. 'No, I need to do it now. But thank you for asking, Sam.'

The lobby of the hospice was decorated for Thanksgiving, which lent a little cheer to what was an otherwise sad place. There was no one at the desk, but there was a bell with a small sign saying to ring for help.

Sam guided Georgia to the desk where there was a visitor sign-in book filled with scrawled signatures accompanied by dates and times in and out. Curious, Sam paged through the sign-in book, smiling when he saw Henry Whitfield's spiky scrawl. Henry had visited this past Saturday afternoon. Beneath Henry's name was the name of his grandson. Sam was glad the old man was being well cared for.

He paged back to Wednesday's guests and caught his breath. 'Georgia, look.'

She did and she exhaled quietly. 'Joe Friday. That's Frankie's handwriting. I'd know it anywhere.'

'So he was here. I'm glad.' Taking out his phone, Sam typed out a quick text to Kit. *At the hospice visiting Frankie's ex-wife. Frankie was here on Wednesday. Used the name of Joe Friday – his old partner said that was his nickname on the force.* He hit send, then flipped the book back to today's entries when the receptionist returned.

'I'm so sorry. I hope you two weren't waiting long. May I see your IDs?'

'Of course,' Georgia said and signed her name to the book. 'We're here to see Sharon White.'

Sam signed the book next. 'Is it okay to visit her now?'

The receptionist's smile was generous and kind. 'You can certainly try. I know she loves visitors. It's room 406. Her son is in there with her now. He'll know best if she's up to a visit.'

Oh dear, Sam thought, hoping the son who hated Frankie wouldn't make them leave. 'We brought our dog,' he said. 'Sharon likes dogs.' Or so Henry had said. 'He's a regular at the continuing care center where I volunteer. Is it okay if he visits, too?'

'Of course. But if he gets aggressive at all, you'll have to take him outside.'

'I understand. Thank you.' He guided Georgia to Sharon's room, frowning when he felt her trembling. 'Are you okay, Georgia?'

'I'm fine. Just . . . nervous.'

'Me too. If the son says no, we'll come back, okay?'

'Okay.'

Sharon's room was bright and sunny with a half-dozen vases overflowing with colorful flowers. And one vase with white roses that were a bit past their peak.

A man in his midfifties smiled warily when they entered. He looked so much like Frankie that Sam's throat closed. This would be Gerald Wilson. Who'd changed his name to White.

'Can I help you?' Gerald asked.

Sam waited for Georgia to say something, but her gaze was fixed on the woman in the bed. Sharon was thin, but alert. She was even wearing a bit of lipstick. That was a good sign. Now they had to get the son to let them stay.

'I hope so,' Sam said. 'My name is Sam Reeves. This is my friend, Georgia Shearer. We were friends of Frankie. I mean Frank.' He didn't say Flynn. If the son hated his father, Sam didn't want to pour gas on the flame.

The man's gaze hardened. 'No. This is not a good time.'

'Gerald,' Sharon said, her voice crackling like paper. 'I want to see them.'

'Mom.'

She lifted brows that were a tad too dark for her ashen skin. Her cheeks, however, had been colored a perfect shade of pale pink. 'These are the visitors I've been expecting. Oh, and they brought a dog. I love dogs.'

Siggy wagged his tail but didn't make a move to run or jump. *Good dog.*

Gerald's jaw clenched. 'Do not upset her.'

'We don't plan to,' Georgia said, then swallowed hard. 'You look like him.'

Gerald's cheeks flushed a hot red. 'Please don't say that.'

327

This is not starting well.

Sam helped Georgia into the chair beside the bed, then stood behind her, his hands resting lightly on her shoulders. He'd be her guardian, if need be. Siggy curled up at his feet, and Georgia reached back and patted Sam's hand. 'Sam's a good boy,' she told Sharon.

'I don't know about that,' Sharon said with a weak smile. 'He didn't bring *me* an In-N-Out animal style.'

Sam sagged in relief. 'Henry Whitfield called you.'

'Yes, he did. Said you wanted to talk about Frank.' Her smile disappeared. 'I didn't know that he'd died. Not until Henry called me.' She glanced at her son, who was watching with a mutinous expression. 'Gerald is shielding me from news. Normally, I appreciate it, but I wanted to know about Frank. I still can't believe he's gone. Murdered.' She reached for Georgia's hand. 'You knew him?'

'I did. I was his friend. He spoke of you. Quite warmly.'

Gerald snorted rudely.

'Gerald,' Sharon rebuked. 'Stop it. I've told you over and over again that your father and I both decided to divorce. I've told you this for forty-five years. If you can't at least be respectful, I'm going to ask you to take a break for coffee.'

Gerald swallowed. 'I'm sorry, Mom.'

Sharon shook her head, the movement slight. 'Son, I don't know what more to tell you. Your father was not at fault for our divorce.'

Gerald's jaw bulged. 'Fine, Mom.'

Sharon turned her attention to Georgia. 'Henry said that you're writing Frank's eulogy and wanted to know about him before he met Ryan.'

Gerald's gasp was loud and harsh. 'What?'

Sharon frowned. 'What do you mean, what?'

Gerald approached the foot of the bed and gripped the railing so tightly that his knuckles turned white. 'You knew about his . . . affair?'

'I knew about Ryan, yes. I told you that your father had met someone else.'

Gerald cast a panicked look at Sam and Georgia. 'But I thought you were talking about a woman. Not a man.'

'Does it matter?' Sharon asked gently. Then she sighed. 'Excuse me, Georgia and Sam. I'm getting the distinct impression that my son has been mistaken for a very long time. Gerald, I knew your father was gay. I knew almost from the beginning. Certainly before we got married. His parents were pressuring us to marry and . . . well, it was a different time. He didn't feel like he could be honest with them, but he *was* honest with me. It was okay. He was against our marrying. He didn't want to "use" me, but I was all for it. I told him that we'd be friends. That if we could have a child, I'd be grateful, but that I wanted to keep my career. I'd worked hard to get my PhD and I was on a path to tenure at the university. I wasn't ready to settle down and be a housewife. Not many men would have allowed me to continue working back then, but Frank was supportive of my work. We were friends, Gerald. Best friends. And, a few times, we were lovers.' She lifted a thin hand and waved up and down, taking Gerald in. 'Thus, you. He never lied to me.'

Gerald's mouth was open in shock. 'Why didn't you tell me?'

'Because at the time, you were too young to know. Later, I tried, but every time I brought him up, you told me that you didn't want to talk about him.' She sighed. 'Gerald, I was instrumental in his meeting Ryan. I was a professor at the university and so was Ryan's brother-in-law Benny.' She glanced at Georgia and Sam, then paled further at what Sam was certain were their stricken expressions. 'Benny isn't . . . Oh no.'

'Tuesday morning,' Georgia said quietly. 'He had a bad heart.'

Sam was grateful that Georgia had obscured the truth. Benny *had* had a bad heart. Sharon didn't need to know that the sweet old man had also been murdered.

A tear ran down Sharon's cheek, and Gerald came to her side, a tissue in his hand. 'Mom?'

She sighed. 'Benny was a nice man. So smart. A physics professor. Frank had escorted me to a faculty party at Benny's house. This was forty-five years ago. Benny's wife Martha was mingling and her brother Ryan was tending bar. As soon as Frank saw Ryan . . . Well, I knew it was time for us to part. We'd always agreed that whenever one of us found true love, we'd go our separate ways, so we divorced that same year. Frank and Ryan were together after that, but they had to hide. Frank's job wouldn't let them live together openly. Ryan had to wait fifteen years. But once your father retired, they were free.' Her smile bloomed. 'I met your stepfather a few years after the divorce and your father was so happy for me. Frank loved you, Gerald. I wish I'd made you listen.' More tears trickled down her thin cheeks. 'So much wasted time.'

Gerald was in shock. 'Mom, I . . . I'm sorry.'

'No, it's on me. I should have told you. I didn't tell you he was gay at the time we divorced because you were so young. And so angry. I was afraid that you'd tell people, and that would have put Frank in danger at his job. Gay cops couldn't be out then.' She took his hand and pressed it to her cheek. 'I went to their wedding, Gerald. They finally were able to get married thirty years after they met. I took their wedding photo. I still have a copy at home. I imagine you'll find it when you go through my things.'

'Mom,' Gerald said hoarsely. He was crying, too. 'I found out. I followed him on my bicycle one night and saw him kiss a man. I was afraid to tell you. I thought you'd be hurt. I was angry at him for cheating on you. For leaving you all alone. And he had this secret life. I didn't want you to know. All this time I thought I was protecting you.'

'And all this time I thought I was protecting Frank. I knew you were angry, Gerald, and I thought you'd expose his secrets. And then, once he'd retired, you didn't want to hear the truth. I suppose that I was selfish, too. By then we had a nice life and I didn't want to upset the apple cart by telling you the truth. I was wrong and I'm sorry.' Sharon sighed. 'Secrets suck, Gerald. Promise me you won't keep secrets from your children. They're still young and shouldn't know everything, but they'll grow up soon enough. Don't keep secrets.'

Gerald nodded woodenly. 'I won't. I promise.'

Sam felt like he should leave. This was a family moment. A private moment. Even Siggy sensed the tension, moving restlessly at Sam's feet.

But then Sharon turned back to them. 'I have something for you,

Georgia. Gerald, please get me the envelopes that are in my night-stand drawer.'

Gerald did, a puzzled frown on his face. 'Who gave you these?'

Georgia's indrawn breath was sharp. 'Frankie. That's his hand-writing.'

The envelope on top had Henry Whitfield's name written on it. Sharon took the other letter and held it up for them to see. It said: *Georgia Shearer.*

Nineteen

Sharon handed Georgia the letter addressed to her. 'Frank came to see me last week.'

Gerald gasped. 'I didn't know that, Mom.'

'I know. I told him to come when you weren't here. When I made you go home and spend time with the children. I figured you'd fuss and I didn't have the energy for that.'

She didn't have the energy to be talking to them now. She was flagging, her voice growing weaker with each breath, but Sam couldn't bring himself to go. Not just yet.

'He came here on Wednesday, a week ago,' Sam said.

'He did.' Sharon looked at the fading white roses. 'He always brought me white roses.'

Gerald's expression crumpled. 'I never knew they were from him.'

She lifted a bony shoulder. 'If I'd told you, you wouldn't have taken care of them. I should have told you, though. I should have told you so many things.'

From the turbulence in Gerald's eyes, he heartily agreed.

Sam's heart hurt for them – for Gerald for losing out on a father like Frankie, for Frankie for never knowing his son, and for Sharon, knowing the truth and being afraid to share it. But Sharon should have made sure that her son had known the truth. Because secrets did suck.

Sam told himself that he was going to call his folks as soon as he got Georgia back to Shady Oaks. They could be pains in his butt sometimes, but they loved him with everything they were. *And I love them.* His adolescence had been far from idyllic. He'd had his fair share of trauma and loss, but to his knowledge, his parents had always been truthful with him.

'Frank told me that if something happened to him, I was to give you that envelope,' Sharon said to Georgia. 'I knew something was very wrong. I knew him for too many years not to be able to tell. I asked him if he needed the police. He said that he might, but he didn't want to make a formal report in case he was wrong. I told him that he could trust Henry Whitfield, that Henry came to visit me regularly. So he sat down where you're sitting now and wrote a second letter longhand.' She sighed. 'Frank always had a gut feeling for danger. It kept him alive for thirty-seven years on the force. I guess his luck ran out,' she finished sadly. 'I wish I'd known earlier that Frank had been killed. I would have made sure you and Henry got the letters sooner. Would you open yours? And read it if you can?'

Georgia opened the envelope and pulled out the letter. It was typed, having come from a printer. Sam scanned the letter over Georgia's shoulder, his heart beating faster with every word.

'"Dear Georgia,"' Georgia read in a voice that trembled. '"If you're reading this, I'm dead. I always thought people who wrote those words were overly dramatic, but here we are. Cutting to the chase, if I've been murdered, Roxanne Beaton is my killer. She's been cozying up to Benny and I got suspicious. No woman in her late forties is going to cozy up to a man in his eighties unless money's involved. At first, I thought she wanted Benny's coin collection. Benny slipped and told me that she'd seen it. He thinks that she loves him. When I told him that I suspected her, he got angry with me. I know you noticed that Benny and I have been arguing. I figured I'd prove it to him, so I've set out to woo the bitch. I have more money than Benny, so I figured she'd be more interested in me. I did some investigating and discovered that she's worse than a coin thief. I believe that she's a black widow.

'"I considered going to SDPD with my theory, but there is a small chance that I might be wrong. And if I am wrong and word gets back to Benny, he'll be even more upset with me. I don't want to hurt him any more than I already have.

' "Anyway, Roxanne's been married four times and all four of her husbands met a quick end. Could have been natural causes, but nobody is that unlucky – or lucky, as the case might be. I've listed the names of each of her husbands below. It'll give SDPD a place to start, because there might be more.

' "I figured that if Roxanne thought I was interested, she'd drop Benny and he'd be safe. I was married once before to a woman, so I've let it slip to Roxanne that I'm bi. For the record, that's not true. She's starting to take the bait. She's been visiting me in my apartment, bringing me baked goods and wine, even offering me sexual favors. But last night Benny saw her leaving my place, and now he thinks I'm stealing her from him. I let him think it, because I wanted him to get angry enough to cut ties with her. But Roxanne is far from stupid. I think she's checking me out, too.

' "I know that I'm walking a fine line, but I have to admit, it's exhilarating. Like I'm a cop again. I didn't realize how much I missed it.

' "I'm planning to ask her to marry me soon. It will be a hush-hush wedding, and then I'll start checking my food for poison or drugs. In my experience, that's how these black widows kill. Once I have the evidence needed to put her away for good, I'll share it with SDPD and let them take it from there.

' "However, if you're reading this, everything's gone from sugar to shit, as we used to say on the force. Be well, dear friend, and take care of yourself and the others for me. Tell Eloise to keep cheating at cards. Tell Benny that he'll always be my brother and that I know he didn't mean the things he said, because I know his words are haunting him right now. Yours always, Frankie Flynn." '

Georgia lowered the letter to her lap, her hands shaking. 'Sam.'

'I know,' Sam murmured. 'Kit doesn't know about the dead husbands.' Or if she did, she hadn't yet shared it with him. 'But Frankie was also right about the coins.'

Sharon and Gerald were staring at them, mouths agape. 'That's the woman who killed him?' Sharon asked. 'Do you know who he's talking about?'

'We do,' Georgia said. 'And the detective on this case has her suspicions about Roxanne, too.' She looked up at Sam. 'Please send this to Detective McKittrick's email, right now. I don't want to wait until Henry Whitfield reads his letter and shares it with SDPD. I want that dreadful woman to be arrested *now*.'

Agreeing wholeheartedly, Sam took the letter from her hands and photographed it, emailing it to Kit and cc'ing himself and Georgia. He then placed it back into the envelope and slipped it into Georgia's hand.

Georgia's focus was on Sharon. 'Thank you. This will help the police punish the woman who took him from us.'

Sharon sighed. 'At least he and Ryan are together again. And Benny,' she added sadly. 'I'd like to come to their funerals, but I can't leave here.'

Gerald met his mother's gaze and held it for several heartbeats. 'I'd like to come to his funeral,' he finally said. 'If you're okay with that, Mom.'

'Record it,' she said, her voice now only a whisper. 'Sorry. I'm tired. I need to sleep now.'

Georgia rose from the chair, grimacing in pain. She held Sam's arm so tightly that he thought he'd have bruises, but he never said a word of protest.

Sam smiled at Gerald. 'I hope to see you on Sunday for his service.'

Sam escorted Georgia to the lobby, where he helped her to a chair. 'Siggy, sit. I need to call Kit.'

Georgia opened the envelope and read the letter again. 'Yes, you do.'

He got Kit's voice mail and left a terse message. 'Check your email. Frankie left your evidence with his ex-wife. I've sent you a photo of the letter.' He ended the call and checked the time. It was only six forty-five. Someone had to still be in the office.

He first called Connor's cell phone, then Navarro's, getting voice mails on both. He left them messages. He called Kit's cell once more, but there was still no answer, so he put his phone away.

'Let's get you back, Georgia. You look like you need a nap.'

Georgia slid the letter back into the envelope and put it into her purse. 'I think I need better earplugs because Eloise has been keeping me awake.'

'I can borrow a wheelchair to get you to the car.'

Her chin lifted. 'You will do no such thing.'

Sam sighed. 'Fine. Let's go.' He helped her to the car and buckled her into the passenger seat before opening the hatch. 'Siggy, in.' The dog jumped in and curled up to sleep. Sam leaned against his car wearily, pulling out his phone to try Kit one more time.

He waited while her cell rang, grimacing when he got her short, no-nonsense request to leave a message. 'Kit, it's Sam. Call me. It's . . . more than important.'

Sliding his phone into his pocket, he closed the hatch and got behind the wheel. He buckled his own seat belt and headed out of the hospice parking lot onto the busy street. Then his heart stopped cold.

As cold as the barrel of the gun that was now pressed to his head.

He heard Siggy growling, but only barely because his head was filled with the sound of his own heart, which was suddenly pounding. His vision started to go wavy. He blinked hard and began pulling over, but the gun was jammed harder into his head.

'Drive, Dr Reeves,' Roxanne said. 'And don't even think of calling for help or you'll watch your friend die. Call off your dog.'

Because Siggy was growling loudly now.

Sam swallowed. 'Down, boy. Down. Good boy,' he added when Siggy's head disappeared behind the back seat. Where Roxanne had been hiding.

Dammit.

'Give me the letter, Georgia,' Roxanne demanded. 'I was watching you through the lobby window. I saw you put it in your purse.'

Georgia drew a deep breath. 'Roxanne?' she asked, her voice trembling. 'What are you doing?'

Roxanne huffed impatiently. 'Don't even try to look confused. Eloise could pull it off, but you can't. Give me the letter.'

'Give it to her,' Sam murmured.

Georgia handed it over without further argument.

Sam kept driving, looking around for any possible way to signal for help. But no one was looking at them. Everyone was busy tending to their own lives.

'How did you know about the letter?' Sam asked evenly, even though he thought he might throw up.

'I found the file on Flynn's laptop,' she answered, her tone managing to be bored, smug, and irritated, all at once. ' "Dear Georgia," ' she mocked. ' "If you're reading this, I'm dead." '

'When did you find the file?' Sam asked. 'Before or after you killed him?'

'After. He . . . interrupted my search.'

'He caught you stealing his computer that night, didn't he?' Georgia asked coldly. 'The night of Eloise's birthday party.'

'That he did.' Roxanne snorted. 'I actually believed him, you know? I thought he had the hots for me. But then Kent Crawford told me to be careful, that he was a retired cop, so I stole his laptop and imagine my surprise. Is this the only copy?'

'Yes,' Georgia lied without hesitation.

Go, Georgia. Sam nearly laughed, but it would have been entirely hysterical and he managed to hold it in. He was not going to show Roxanne any weakness.

'Why were you following us?' Sam demanded with more courage than he actually felt.

'To get the letter. Flynn hadn't emailed it to Georgia, so I knew he must have printed out a copy. But he couldn't have given it to Georgia yet, or McKittrick would have arrested me days ago. So I followed you all. Georgia never left the home anymore. Only to go out to McKittrick's parents' house for dinner that night, but again McKittrick didn't arrest me, so I knew Georgia still hadn't read it. Then the two of you left today and . . .' She laughed quietly. 'I guess I just got lucky.'

'That's why you came into my apartment that night,' Georgia said. 'You were looking for the letter.'

'Well, it wasn't for the tea,' Roxanne said sarcastically. 'I knew you hadn't read it yet because neither of you two can hide what you're feeling. You're better than he is, though,' she said to Georgia. 'The good doctor wears his emotions on his face.'

'You won't be able to just walk away,' Sam said, attempting to reason with the woman. 'McKittrick suspects you.'

'No shit,' Roxanne snapped. 'But without this letter, she has nothing on me. Just a lot of what-ifs.'

No, Sam thought. *Kit took that coffee cup with your lipstick print for a reason. She knows something.* That was hard evidence. Sam didn't know why it was important, but Kit did. It was a comforting thought. Even if Roxanne managed to kill him and Georgia, Kit would make her pay.

'How did you break into Frankie's laptop?' Sam asked.

In the mirror, Roxanne rolled her eyes. 'His password was Ryan-ten-thirty-one-oh-eight.'

'Their wedding date,' Georgia murmured.

Damn, Frankie. Ryan plus your wedding date? Really?

But that was the last thing he should be thinking about.

Ask more questions. Because if they managed to survive, Kit would want the facts. 'Did you kill Crawford?'

'Yes. He'd outlived his usefulness. Dr Reeves, get on the 5 going south.'

Shady Oaks was north on I-5. The only thing south was Mexico.

Maybe she only wants to escape.

No, she has to kill you because you know.

Dammit. At least he still had his phone. Someone could track them.

'Toss your phone, too, Dr Reeves. I don't want anyone tracking us.'

Dammit.

Sam fumbled with his phone, holding it in front of his face briefly to unlock it. He tapped the last call he'd made – to Kit. She'd know what to do.

If she ever gets my message. Where were they?

He tossed the phone before Roxanne could hear Kit's line ringing. It landed on a patch of grass in the median strip.

'Now yours, bitch,' Roxanne said to Georgia.

Slowly Georgia complied. 'Where are you taking us?'

'Shut up. And shut your dog *up*, Dr Reeves. Or I'll shoot him, too.'

Sam swallowed back his fear. 'It's okay, Siggy. She's a bad lady, but you can't growl at her. Siggy, down.'

Siggy's head disappeared behind the back seat and Sam forced himself to breathe.

Kit, where are you?

San Ysidro, California
Thursday, 10 November, 6.30 P.M.

'That's him,' Detective Goddard said. 'Perry Dunst. In the Bentley.'

Kit shifted sideways in Goddard's plain black sedan so that she could peer through her night-vision binoculars at the undercover detective getting out of the Bentley. Goddard's car was across the street from where the luxury car had been parked in the shadows of a strip mall's deserted parking lot.

She might have been nervous for Detective Dunst, but she knew that there were sharpshooters positioned on the roofs of every empty storefront of the strip mall, as well as a van full of cops waiting behind one of the stores. The van could rush to Dunst's aid in seconds. And, as Goddard said, this was not Dunst's first rodeo.

Connor whistled softly. 'Where did the department get a Bentley?'

'An impound from a case we closed five years ago,' Goddard said. 'It's now registered in the name of the alias Dunst has been developing for about that long. We've used him to orchestrate several buys, usually jewelry or artifacts, like the Roman coins. His alias is well-known by fencing operations all over the world. Most of the buys were set up by us. We put up certain items recovered after their thefts and he bought them. We involved known fences who thought they were watching a real transaction. They told two friends and so on, giving Dunst's cover five gold stars. He's also done some legit purchases of stolen goods with actual cash. Mostly low-level, relatively inexpensive stuff, but that's a necessary evil in this business. He's known in the industry as being meticulous, knowledgeable, and careful. Under his cover, he doesn't buy for himself, but for private clients who don't want to get their hands dirty.'

'How many times have you used him?' Connor asked.

'This is the first time doing a big takedown. Every other time he was building his cover. We've been saving this persona for a long time, because once word gets out that the cops made a bust, this cover will be pretty much useless. Seemed like solving the murder of a retired homicide lieutenant was as good an occasion to use it as any.'

'Thank you,' Kit murmured as she watched Detective Dunst get out of the Bentley, a briefcase in his hand. The case was handcuffed to his wrist. A precaution, Goddard had said. Dunst leaned against his car, casually lighting a cigarette and blowing smoke into the night. 'He looks bored.'

'He's not. He's alert as hell, but being bored is a good way to distract the sellers. He's done this for years, remember. Or his cover has. As transactions go, four million is a small one. We've orchestrated individual fake buys of well over ten million.'

'Does he have other covers?' Connor asked.

'Yep. At least four others. Part of being a UC is developing the backstory of your covers. Every one of his covers looks different. He once walked past his own mother in disguise and she didn't notice him. Perry Dunst is very good at this.'

'And if Roxanne brings backup, your sharpshooters will neutralize them,' Kit said, because she had a bad feeling about this situation. Roxanne was late.

If Kit had been selling four million dollars' worth of stolen coins, she'd have had someone watching the area for just this scenario – cops posing as real buyers. But this was Goddard's area of expertise, so she kept her concerns to herself.

Goddard grimaced. 'I hope it doesn't come to that, but yeah. They will. They've had to do it before, but it's more likely that we'll make the arrest before they start shooting. But if bullets start flying, the sharpshooters' mission is to protect Dunst and to keep the targets from escaping.'

'Did you expect Roxanne to be so late?' Connor asked. 'And are we even sure the coins Dunst is buying are the ones stolen from Benny Dreyfus?'

'They're the same. Dunst got the documentation on all of the coins. Your killer took photos on a black background. No identifying characteristics that way. This bitch is smart, but she's off her normal MO.'

'Selling the merchandise right away,' Kit said.

Goddard nodded. 'Exactly. If your theory holds – and it sounds right to me – she's always waited at least a year before selling the stolen items. But now we know she's stolen Dreyfus's coins, so she has to get rid of them quickly. Plus, if what she did with William Freeman's Dutch Master painting is her norm, she has paperwork proving she was the actual owner by way of donation. We'll have to find out if those donation documents are legit. I have a feeling she forged most, if not all, of them. How did the family not know Freeman had donated the painting?'

'I called William Freeman's son,' Connor said, 'to get the full background.'

Connor had made the call when Kit had been asleep and while she wished she'd heard the conversation, she was grateful for being able to get some rest. She was truly alert. For now. She'd crash later.

'His son confirmed that William was independent about his charitable giving,' Connor went on. 'His family tried to stop him, but William found ways to do what he wanted. He also wasn't happy that they'd put him in a home. He wanted to be in his own home, but his son had a limited power of attorney that William had signed when he was going in for quadruple bypass surgery. The son didn't want William living alone after the surgery, so he sold William's house, and William was forced into a retirement home when he got out of the hospital. He was angry and determined to leave his family with as little as possible.'

'I'd be pissed off, too,' Goddard said, sounding horrified.

Connor sighed. 'Same. William was also very passionate about supporting veterans. His oldest son had come back from Vietnam with critical injuries. Lost both legs. Had terrible PTSD. He took his own life, and William never recovered.'

'So appealing to William's need to help vets was a good way to get him to agree to donate something valuable,' Kit murmured. 'Roxanne did her homework. Just like with Benny's coins. She might have waited to sell Benny's coins for another year had Frankie Flynn not become involved. She killed Frankie, then had to kill Benny before he could say whatever it was that he knew. She called in sick today, so I think she knows we suspect her.'

'Do you know how Frankie knew about her?' Goddard asked.

'Not yet, but we'll figure it out,' Kit vowed. 'Frank had to have suspected something because he's dead.'

'What about Roxanne's sister?' Goddard asked.

'We're looking for her,' Connor said. 'Jackie Beaton's address is in Tennessee, just outside Knoxville. We requested that local law enforcement check her house, but she wasn't home. The neighbors said that Jackie lives there with her boyfriend, Neil Fogarty, but they haven't seen them in a day or two. She's an accountant who works out of her home, so she's usually there. Knoxville PD offered to keep an eye on her property, doing drive-bys until Jackie comes back. We have no idea if Jackie has anything to do with Roxanne's crimes, but she lives in the same town where Warriors with Wounds is based. If Jackie isn't involved, she might know where her sister would run to.'

'Who owns this fake charity?' Goddard asked.

'We don't know yet,' Connor said with a frustrated edge to his voice. 'I started checking this afternoon, but so far all I've found is a tangle of shell companies.'

'We can help with that—'

'Guys,' Kit interrupted, pointing to the Chevy SUV slowly approaching the Bentley in the parking lot across the street. She peered through her binoculars to get a good look at the license plates. She read out the plate numbers and Connor called it in.

The Chevy continued its slow approach, driving in a circle around the Bentley. 'There's a man in the passenger seat,' Kit said. 'A woman in the driver's seat.' Disappointment lanced through her, because the woman appeared petite, sitting low behind the steering wheel. Roxanne was five-eight at least. 'It's not Roxanne Beaton.'

Connor put his cell phone on speaker and used his own binoculars. 'That,' he said with satisfaction, 'is Jackie Beaton.'

Connor's cell phone crackled when Dispatch came back on the line. 'Detective Robinson? The vehicle is a rental from Endeavor Rental Cars.'

'Thank you.' Connor ended the call just as Jackie stopped her SUV next to the Bentley. The man in the passenger seat got out.

'That looks like Jackie's boyfriend, Neil Fogarty,' Connor commented.

Kit noted the bulge at the man's back. 'He's got a gun.'

Goddard communicated that to Dunst through his earpiece, then got on his radio to inform the sharpshooters in case they hadn't spied the gun through their scopes.

Goddard started the engine of their department sedan but left the lights off. He used the radio again to speak to the van full of cops waiting for his signal. 'The subject has an accomplice. White male, approximately five feet ten, fifty years old. He has a handgun. Be ready for the takedown. On my signal.'

Neil Fogarty was frisking Dunst, who was frowning in a very calm and dignified kind of way, his comments audible via the microphone hidden in the pen poking out of the breast pocket of his suit.

'Is this really necessary?' Dunst asked, affronted.

'Yeah.' Seemingly satisfied, Fogarty pointed to the suitcase, obviously cuffed to Dunst's arm. 'Open it or I'll cut it off your arm,' the man growled.

Dunst took a step back. 'I want to see the coins.'

Fogarty looked around suspiciously. 'We discussed this. Money first.'

Dunst huffed out an impatient breath. 'Very well.' He set the briefcase on the trunk of the Bentley and pressed his thumb to the print reader and the briefcase popped open.

'Whoa,' Kit whispered, knowing the briefcase was full of cash, but startled at the sight of it nonetheless.

That was a lot of money.

'Three million, five hundred thousand,' Dunst said, quickly closing the briefcase. 'As we discussed. Now let me see the coins.'

Through her binoculars, Kit saw Jackie's man smile. 'Goddard,' she hissed. Because that was an evil smile if ever she'd seen one.

'Move!' Goddard shouted into his radio. 'Snipers, be ready!'

Fogarty pulled the gun from his waistband and pressed it to Dunst's temple.

And then a shot cracked the air. One of the snipers had fired. Fogarty's gun flew out of his hand and dropped to the pavement. His left hand gripped his right wrist, which was now bleeding profusely.

A shocked look on his face, Fogarty backed away, looking around and finally up. 'Motherfuckers,' he screamed. 'Cops, Jackie. Go!'

Fogarty dropped to his knees to grab his gun, but Dunst swung the briefcase and clocked the bastard upside his head. Fogarty rolled to his side, groaning.

Goddard had their car in drive and was crossing the street to the parking lot as Jackie's SUV took off like a rocket. Kit thought they might lose her, but the police van and several cruisers came around the last store in the strip mall, blocking Jackie's path. Her tires squealed as she hit the brakes.

Goddard pulled up beside the van as the SWAT team poured out, ten rifles aimed at Jackie.

Goddard jumped from the car, Kit and Connor following. Dunst had already locked the briefcase full of cash in the Bentley's trunk. He now stood rubbing his wrist where the cuff had cut into his skin when he'd used the briefcase as a weapon. One of the SWAT members had cuffed Neil Fogarty.

Goddard cuffed Jackie Beaton, then came over to check on Dunst. 'You okay, Perry?'

'I'm fine. Minor abrasions.' He glared at the man on the ground. 'Asshole. Did you get the coins?'

'Let's go find out.' Goddard led them back to the SUV and popped the hatch. There, sitting in an old Amazon shipping carton, was the small trunk that Roxanne had taken from Benny's apartment.

'They didn't even put it in a lockbox.' Pulling on a pair of gloves, Kit lifted the lid, quickly counted the coins, and exhaled with relief. 'They seem to all be here. Can I chat with Jackie?'

'Let me read her her rights first.' Goddard Mirandized Jackie, then stepped back. 'She's all yours.'

Kit crouched next to Jackie, who lay on the pavement, her hands cuffed behind her back. Connor crouched on the other side of the woman.

'Jackie Beaton, I'm Detective McKittrick, Homicide. This is my partner, Detective Robinson. Detective Goddard has questions for you regarding the stolen items in your possession. But we have only one question. Where is your sister?'

Jackie's lips pursed and she said nothing.

'Theft is one thing,' Connor said quietly. 'Murder is something else. Roxanne killed three people this week. One was a retired cop. We *will* find her and she *will* go down for the crimes. Right now, we only have you on possessing stolen merchandise. I don't think you want to add three homicides to that. Especially not that of a cop.'

'Tell her, Jackie,' Fogarty spat. 'Roxie's not worth it. She fucked up. I'm not protecting her.'

'You shut up,' Jackie ordered, then pursed her lips again.

They had Neil Fogarty on attempted murder of Detective Perry Dunst, which should give them some leverage when they interrogated him. Kit had the feeling that Neil would be more open once Jackie was no longer in his presence.

'Well, Jackie?' Kit asked, but the woman still said nothing. Kit gestured to Connor. 'Let's check out the SUV.'

'You can't search my phone!' Jackie shouted. 'I know my rights!'

Unfortunately, she was right. They'd need a warrant for that.

Leaning against the SWAT van, Kit called Navarro, telling him that they'd apprehended Roxanne's sister but still needed to find Roxanne. 'Can we get a warrant for this woman's phone?'

'Oh yeah. The judge who's on call tonight already told me to call him on his personal cell if something came up on this case.'

Because Lieutenant Frank Wilson was dead and everyone wanted to bring a cop killer to justice. Fortunately, that would get justice for Benny, too. 'Thanks. You'll call me when we have the warrant?'

'Of course.'

'We're going to search the sister's rental while we wait. Thanks, boss.'

'Wait, Kit. I got a voice mail from Sam Reeves. He said he'd sent a document to your email that Frank had written. I was in a meeting with the brass, so I only got the message a few minutes before you called. I tried calling him back, but it goes straight to voice mail.'

She quickly checked her phone and a spear of panic stabbed her heart. 'Oh shit. He's called me four times and sent a text. Let me check them out and I'll call you right back.' She ended the call and brought up Sam's text message.

At the hospice visiting Frankie's ex-wife. Frankie was here on *Wednesday. Used the name of Joe Friday – his old partner said* *that was his nickname on the force.*

And then she knew. That was where Frankie had taken whatever evidence he'd gathered.

Sam's first voice mail confirmed it. *'Check your email. Frankie left your evidence with his ex-wife. I've sent you a photo of the letter.'*

He'd left no voice mail with his second call. The message he'd left with the third call sounded both weary and frantic, begging her to call him. It was 'more than important.'

His fourth call, though . . . She held the phone to her ear, trying to hear something. But there was nothing. Only the sound of traffic. She waited, her heart beating faster with every second that passed. She waited the full length of the message, but there was only the same sound of traffic.

She dialed Sam back, but the call rang and rang before going to voice mail.

Something's wrong.

Twenty

San Ysidro, California
Thursday, 10 November, 7.00 P.M.

Hands shaking, Kit opened the email from Sam and quickly read the letter that Frankie Flynn had written to Georgia. 'Connor!'

Connor straightened from where he'd been searching Jackie's SUV. 'What's wrong?'

'Sam found it. He found what Frankie suspected before he was killed.'

Connor read the letter with grim satisfaction. 'He found out about the dead husbands. This is good, Kit. Why are you as white as a sheet?'

She drew a breath and forced herself to calm down. 'Sam told me that he was taking Georgia to visit with Frankie's ex-wife. His last voice mail is nothing but the sound of traffic.'

Connor shrugged. 'He butt-dialed you.'

'No. Navarro's called him and so did I just now. Goes straight to voice mail. He was with Georgia. I'm going to call her.' She tapped Georgia's name in her contact list, but the call went to voice mail once again. 'Dammit. This letter was written on a computer. Most likely Frankie's computer.'

'Which Roxanne stole when she killed him,' Connor said, finally understanding Kit's fear. 'She knows he wrote the letter to Georgia.'

'She let herself into Georgia's room two nights ago.'

'She was looking for the letter? Or she wanted to kill Georgia, too?'

Kit swallowed. 'Either. Maybe both.' She stalked over to Jackie

347

Beaton and crouched down, getting in the woman's face. 'Did Roxanne find a letter from Frankie Flynn to Georgia Shearer?'

Jackie's eye twitched, but she said nothing. Kit took that as a yes. 'She's going to kill Georgia Shearer, isn't she?'

This time Jackie couldn't hide her reaction. One side of her mouth tipped up in a vile little smirk. But she still said nothing.

She didn't have to.

Kit rubbed her forehead. *Think.*

Goddard crouched beside her. 'How can I help?'

'I don't know.' She leaned close to Jackie again. 'If she hurts that old lady and the man with her, there won't be anywhere she can hide. I will find her.'

Needing to move, Kit got up and paced back to Connor, who was on his phone. Goddard followed.

'You don't know when they'll be back?' Connor asked, then climbed into the SWAT van and beckoned Kit and Goddard to join him.

Goddard closed the doors, giving the three of them privacy.

Connor put his phone on speaker. 'Miss Eloise, I've got Detectives McKittrick and Goddard with me. We need to find Sam and Georgia. Can you track Georgia's phone?'

'No. I wouldn't know how, even if she'd allow it.' Eloise's voice cracked with worry. 'Are they all right? Is it Roxanne? Has she hurt them?'

Kit injected a smile into her voice for Eloise's benefit. This stress couldn't be good for the elderly woman. 'We're looking for them now.'

Eloise's gulp was audible. 'She's after them, isn't she?'

'We don't know that,' Kit said, trying to soothe. 'They went to visit Frankie's ex-wife. They could still be there.'

Connor shook his head. *I checked*, he mouthed. *They signed out at six forty-five.*

So in between the second and third calls, Kit thought. Those sounds of traffic on the fourth call were even more ominous now. But Sam's fourth call had come through at six fifty-five, less than fifteen minutes before. They couldn't have gotten too far.

'They went to a hospice center,' Eloise was saying sadly. 'I know. They asked if I wanted to go, but . . . I don't like those places. I stayed here with Officer Stern.'

'I'm here, Detective,' Stern said. 'I might have a suggestion. This is a total long shot, but . . . Dr Reeves has his dog with him.'

'Siggy,' Kit said. 'How does that help?'

'Oh!' Eloise said. 'I get it! Siggy's a runner and Sammy was worried that he'd run away and get lost. He got him one of those GPS collars.'

'If we could track that . . . ,' Stern said with a note of hope in his voice.

'Okay,' Kit said again. 'Let me make some calls. Stern, please stay with Miss Eloise. And make sure the officer in the front lobby knows to watch for Roxanne Beaton.'

'Yes, ma'am. Will do.'

Kit ended the call and stared at Connor, her thoughts whirling.

Connor's jaw tightened. 'We'd need to find Sam's phone to track the dog's collar.'

'Does he have a dog walker?' Goddard suggested. 'Maybe they'd have access to the tracker.'

Kit shook her head. 'I don't think so. His old dog walker was killed, and it hit him hard. He could have found a new one, but I don't know for sure.'

Connor closed his eyes and began taking measured breaths. He'd taken up meditation with his girlfriend CeCe and he often used it to calm himself. When his eyes opened, they were sharp and confident. 'Call Joel. He dogsits Siggy sometimes. Sam mentioned it when we went bowling one night.'

Kit blinked at him. They went bowling together? How had Kit not known that?

Focus. Joel was Sam's best friend. He'd be able to help.

Willing her hands to still, Kit found Joel in her contacts. A city prosecutor, he was a friend of Kit's as well. He'd even come to Thanksgiving at McKittrick House in the past.

She dialed and held her breath, praying he'd answer.

'Kit. This is a surprise. How can—'

She put him on speaker. 'Joel, I'm sorry, but I need your help. I don't have time for the full explanation. I think Sam's in trouble and he doesn't have his phone. But he has Siggy. Can you track his collar?'

'Um, yeah? I think so? Give me a second. Here's the app. And . . . here's Siggy. Right now he's on the 5 heading south. No, wait. The app isn't exactly real time. It jumps. Now they're on Tocayo Avenue, heading west.'

That was close. Very close. Less than ten minutes. Less than five if they drove like a bat out of hell with lights flashing.

'Let's go,' Goddard said. 'I'll drive, you give me directions.'

They ran from the van to Goddard's car, Goddard barking out last-minute directions to the SWAT team and the detectives from the robbery division to hold the scene.

'I'll call Navarro, get backup,' Connor said.

Goddard stepped on the gas and flipped on the flashers. 'We'll get to him in time, Kit.'

'You still there, Joel?' Kit asked.

'I am. I won't hang up. Is he okay?'

'I don't know,' she answered honestly, and this time she couldn't control the tremble in her voice.

'Well, my map app says that there's slow traffic where Tocayo meets Hollister, so that might buy you some time. What are they doing there?'

'Good question.' She opened her own map app and then she understood. 'There's an RV campground at Tijuana River Park.'

'I don't understand,' Joel said. 'Who's with you?'

'Connor Robinson and Bruce Goddard. He's a detective in the robbery division.'

'Ah. Frankie Flynn – a.k.a. Frank Wilson – and the missing coins. I've heard about it. You think Flynn's killer has Sam?'

'Yeah. I do.'

'Shit. Hurry, Kit.'

Cheater

Tijuana River Valley, San Diego, California
Thursday, 10 November, 7.30 P.M.

They were going to die. Roxanne was going to shoot them with her gun and they were going to die. Sam knew he should do something, but he didn't know what that something was.

So he kept driving, hoping for a miracle.

Siggy had popped his head up every five minutes to check things out. He had to be feeling the tension in the car. The silence was heavy. But he hadn't growled again and every time Sam had told him to lie down, his sweet pup had obeyed.

Maybe Roxanne would let Siggy go and some nice person would find him and give him a home. Or read his dog tags, then contact Sam's parents or Joel.

Or Kit. One of the kids at McKittrick House surely would love his dog.

She'd probably won their bet. She'd probably proven Roxanne was responsible already. She hadn't said why she'd grabbed Roxanne's cup out of the dishwasher, but Sam knew the woman didn't do anything without a good reason.

The letter he'd emailed her would be icing on the cake.

But he would miss their date. Going out on a boat filled him with trepidation, but he would have happily spent the day with her anywhere.

'Let my dog go, please,' Sam said quietly. 'He didn't do anything wrong.'

'He's seen me,' Roxanne replied. 'Gotten my scent. If they try to use him to prove I've been around you, he could be used against me.'

'He's seen you at Shady Oaks several times. I sometimes bring him with me when I come to play the piano. Tell them he knows you from that.'

In the rearview mirror, he could see her hesitate before she shook her head. 'Too risky. I'm sorry.'

'But you're not sorry to kill us,' Georgia said, acid dripping from her tone. 'And you a nurse. Shame on you.'

351

Roxanne shrugged. 'You got in my way. I don't leave loose ends.'

Sam exhaled. They were going to die.

No. No, you will not *let her win. You'll figure something out.*

But what?

Roxanne directed him off I-5 and onto Tocayo Avenue, then south on Hollister. Right now, it was a crowded subdivision with houses and businesses, but he knew that the area would soon become wild open spaces.

'Turn here. Right onto Monument.'

I know the way, Sam wanted to say, but he remained silent and did as she commanded. They were headed toward the Tijuana River Valley Regional Park, and Sam felt a spark of hope. He knew this place, had hiked it with Siggy dozens of times in the four years he'd lived in San Diego.

If he could figure out a way to get the gun from Roxanne, they could get away. Find a park ranger. Get help.

If. For now, he was helpless, the woman's gun pressed to the back of his neck in a way that no one casually glancing into their car would see. Especially now that the roads were becoming less crowded.

It was dark and the park would be closed.

No one knew where they were. No one would be coming to help.

'I wish I'd called my parents,' Sam murmured.

Georgia hummed in sympathy. 'I'd ask her to just kill me, but . . .'

'Georgia, no.'

'I'm sorry, Sam,' Georgia whispered. 'I shouldn't have asked you to take me out today.'

'No, you should have. If making Henry Whitfield and Sharon White happy was the last thing we did, I'd say we did okay.'

No, that will not be the last thing you do. You're going to fight.

Georgia sighed. 'Plus, Gerald now knows the truth about his father.'

'Who's Gerald?' Roxanne asked sharply.

Sam tensed. The woman wasn't stupid. If they lied, she'd still figure out that Gerald was related to Frankie. So he told the truth. 'Frankie's son. For forty-five years, he thought his father had cheated on his mother. He never spoke to his father again. Today he learned the truth – that his mother had known all along that Frankie was gay and that he never cheated. That his mother had a hand in introducing Frankie to his husband, Ryan. They didn't see the letter. Gerald would have torn it up had he known his father had left it.'

Which was true. Mother and son hadn't seen the letter. Georgia had unsealed it and read it aloud.

Gerald would be all right. Kit knew he and Georgia had been at the hospice. She had the letter. She'd put two and two together and protect the son. The mother wasn't long for this world as it was.

Roxanne made an angry noise. 'Pull over here. Take your SUV over the brush and behind those trees.

This is it.

Sam guided his RAV4 over the bumpy road. He'd driven over similar terrain hundreds of times, so he knew his vehicle could handle it.

They weren't far from the campground, but not so close that anyone would see them. Especially since darkness had fallen. The campground was primitive – no electrical hookups – so the only light came from the area around the shower building.

No one was going to see them.

Sam pulled behind the trees as instructed. His SUV couldn't even be seen from the road. *Goddammit.* 'What are you going to do to us?'

'Well,' Roxanne said slowly, like he was a child, 'you're going to leave your keys in the ignition and then we're all going to get out of the SUV, walk into the trees, and . . . *pow*. I'll take care of the dog afterward so you don't have to watch. If it makes you feel better, none of you will feel any pain.'

'That does *not* make me feel better,' Georgia snapped.

'And if we refuse?' Sam asked. 'If we stay put?'

Which I should have done all along. At least she would have had to shoot me in a busy neighborhood, versus out here in the middle of nowhere.

What had he been thinking?

He hadn't been. He'd had a gun to his head. So he'd have to cut himself a little slack. *I'd be dead either way.*

'I'll make it hurt,' Roxanne said steadily, 'and trust me, I know how to do that. I'll make Georgia suffer a lot and your dog, too. So get out. Now.'

He did trust her on that, so he got out of the car, managing to get to Georgia's door despite his knees buckling with every step.

'I'm sorry,' he said, taking Georgia's hand. 'You don't deserve any of this.'

'Neither do you, my boy.' She took his hand, gripping it firmly. 'I wish I hadn't listened to your detective. I left my gun at Shady Oaks.'

Sam laughed, the sound more than a little hysterical.

'Move it,' Roxanne snapped. '*Now*. I don't have all night.'

Georgia slid from the SUV, grimacing when her feet hit the dirt. 'I'm moving as fast as I can. I'm eighty-two years old, for God's sake.'

The trees loomed before them, not so large but forbidding in the darkness. A park ranger would find their bodies eventually.

'Stop here,' Roxanne said.

So they did.

The nurse pulled her phone from her jacket pocket, while holding the gun steadily pointed at them. She'd added a silencer to the barrel, probably while Sam was getting Georgia out of the SUV.

'Don't move or it'll hurt,' Roxanne said coldly. 'I promise.'

'I believe you, you bitch,' Georgia muttered.

Roxanne smirked. 'Under the circumstances, I'll allow you one "bitch." But no more.' She dialed and lifted the phone to her ear, never taking her gaze from them. She waited, frowning. 'What the fuck?' she muttered, clearly upset.

'Who's she calling?' Georgia whispered.

Sam had no idea, so he said nothing.

'Where the fuck are you?' Roxanne demanded, after a long enough time that Sam assumed that she was leaving a voice mail. 'You'd better be at my rig. Come and get me. *Now*.'

Roxanne pocketed her phone and aimed her gun at Sam's head. 'You're first. The bitch gets to watch you die before she gets hers.'

He wanted to tell Georgia to run, to get into the SUV and drive, but she'd never be able to run far or fast enough.

So he released Georgia's hand, stepped in front of her, and studied the distance between him and Roxanne.

Five feet. He could leap five feet.

He could knock her down. Take the gun.

Or not. *She might shoot you.*

She's going to do that anyway. So move.

He drew a breath and took a running leap, charging headfirst into Roxanne's middle. He heard the soft pop of the silenced bullet and prayed that she hadn't hit Georgia.

He slammed Roxanne to the ground, gripping her wrists and pinning them over her head. But she was like a wild animal, snarling and bucking. He lost his grip on her left wrist, but it wasn't the one holding the gun.

Stay calm. Get the gun.

He could hear Georgia's anguished cries of 'Sam, Sam!' and Siggy's muted barking from the SUV. He could feel Roxanne's knee lifting and knew she'd be aiming for his crotch, so he swiveled, trying to simultaneously move his hips and grab her gun.

But Roxanne was faster – and had another weapon. Sam froze at the sound of metal sliding against metal. And the feel of the sharp point at his throat.

Drawing a breath through his nose, he looked down. Roxanne was holding a switchblade to his throat. A stiletto blade.

Just like the one that had actually killed Frankie.

But then, just when he thought he was dead, the barrel of a gun came into view, pressed to Roxanne's temple. Followed by the sweetest sound he'd ever heard.

'If you draw one drop of his blood,' Kit said with utter menace, 'I will blow your brains out.'

Sam hadn't heard Kit approach, the pounding of his heart filling his ears. He didn't dare move, because Roxanne's blade was still at his throat, but he could see the woman hesitate.

'You'll never find your precious coins,' Roxanne whispered hoarsely.

'Already did, along with Jackie,' Kit said. 'So drop the knife or die.'

Roxanne's lips curved and Sam stopped breathing. She didn't believe Kit was serious.

Panicked, he lurched out of Roxanne's hold, gasping at the sudden burning at his throat. On reflex, he slapped his hand to the wound as he rolled to the side.

But no blood gushed from his throat. The wound was small. *Just a nick.* Running on pure adrenaline, he grabbed the gun from Roxanne's hand and backed up, his ass dragging in the dirt.

Heart slamming against his ribs, he set the gun down, far away from the nurse who now closed her eyes in defeat.

Holy shit. I'm not dead.

Hysterical laughter filled his ears as a weight fell to the ground beside him. 'No, boy, you're not dead,' Georgia said. He must have said that part out loud. She pulled his hand from his throat. 'Let me see.'

'How bad is it, Georgia?' Kit asked as she cuffed a silently scowling Roxanne.

'Just a scratch,' Georgia said faintly. 'He rushed her. She was pointing a gun at his head and he rushed her. Goddammit, Sam. You nearly killed me with fright.'

'I saw him,' Kit said, breathing hard. 'I was running toward you and I saw him jump at her. Nearly killed me, too.'

Sam felt a slow grin stretch his face. 'But it worked.'

Georgia slumped beside him, leaning into him. 'It did, you cheeky boy. Never do it again.'

Sam put his arm around Georgia's shoulders. 'I promise.'

More feet pounded and Sam heard Connor calling to Kit.

'Over here!' Kit called back. 'Got 'em.'

Connor rushed toward them, his weapon drawn. 'Sam?'

'I'm okay,' Sam said, gingerly rising to his feet, bringing Georgia with him. It was too cold for her to be sitting on the ground. 'Maybe I'll need a butterfly bandage.'

'Stitches,' Georgia and Kit snapped at the same time.

Sam shuddered out a breath. 'We're not dead, Georgia. I'd say a few stitches are worth it. Let's get you into the SUV. You're shivering.'

'I'm scared, dammit. Not cold.'

'I've got her, Sam,' Connor said quietly. 'Let me help you, Miss Georgia.'

Still kneeling by the cuffed Roxanne, Kit was glaring up at Sam as Connor led Georgia to the waiting ambulance that had, apparently, followed them. When another officer arrived to take Roxanne, Kit shoved her gun in its holster and stalked toward him.

'What the hell were you thinking?' she demanded.

'That I didn't want to die!'

She stopped six inches away, her eyes turbulent with too many emotions for him to name. 'I was coming,' she insisted, but her voice shook.

'I know,' he said soberly. 'I knew you'd come.' Then, ignoring the small voice that was telling him not to rush her, he threw his arms around her and pressed his face against her neck. 'I knew you'd come.'

Slowly her arms came around him, her palms settling firmly on his back before giving him a few awkward pats. But she wasn't pushing him away.

Finally, her shoulders sagged and she rested her cheek against his. 'You scared me,' she whispered.

He pulled away enough to tip her chin up. She was biting her lips and he wanted to kiss them. But the small voice screamed for him to wait and he listened to it this time.

'How did you find us?' he asked instead.

'Siggy's GPS collar. Oh. I forgot about Joel.' She pulled her phone from her pocket and dialed. 'I have him, Joel. He's okay.' She answered a few of Joel's questions before ending the call. 'Come on, Danger Boy. Let's get you seen to.'

She led him back to Georgia, who was sitting in the back of an ambulance. An EMT rushed toward him, eyes fixed on the steadily bleeding cut on his throat.

The cut that was almost at his jugular. *But 'almost' only counts in horseshoes and hand grenades. I'm not dead.*

As his heart began to slow to a normal rhythm, he picked up the shrill, panicked sound of Siggy's barking.

'Can you check on him?' Sam asked Kit. 'He knows you.'

'Of course.' She handed him over to the EMT. 'We'll debrief you when you're patched up.'

Sam was more worried about Georgia. *That was too much excitement for me. Georgia's eighty-two.*

But she was sitting up straight, her jaw set in a way that Sam recognized. His friend was too stubborn to succumb to the stress of a near-death experience. She met his eyes and gave him a sharp nod and a thumbs-up.

Then he remembered Roxanne's phone call. 'Roxanne called someone,' he told Connor because Kit was tending to Siggy. 'They're supposed to be picking her up. She said something about a rig. I think they're close by.'

Connor nodded. 'The rig is Roxanne's tiny house. She's been parked at the campground down the road from here since Sunday morning. One of the park rangers recognized her tiny house from the BOLOs we put out this afternoon and called us when we were en route to save your ass.'

'And the people who were supposed to come for her?'

'I'm guessing that she was calling her sister, and she's too late. We picked the sister and her boyfriend up trying to sell the coins. We got the coins back, and both the sister and the boyfriend are in custody.'

Sam exhaled in relief. 'Good. Nobody was hurt?'

'Minor injuries,' Kit said, coming up from behind him. 'All our guys are okay. And so is Siggy.' She looked up at him. 'You took five years off my life.'

'I knew you'd come.'

'I couldn't lose you or I'd have to break in another profiler,' she said lightly, but the look in her eyes belied her tone. She had been scared for him, and he could see that she was processing that. 'Plus, I won the bet.'

Sam laughed. 'Yeah, you did. I can't wait to go fishing.'

Twenty-one

'Thank you,' Kit said, smiling tentatively at Sam when he put a cup of coffee on her desk. She'd already had three cups that morning, but she wasn't going to say no to a fourth. She and Connor had been working nonstop to pull all the remaining puzzle pieces together, and they were ready to debrief with Navarro.

Kit had asked Sam to join them. She figured he'd more than earned it.

Sam perched on the corner of her desk. 'You've already had a lot of caffeine this morning,' he observed. 'You're twitching.'

It was true, unfortunately. 'Connor and I burned the midnight oil last night. The brass wants this case closed up nice and tight before Frankie's service tomorrow morning.'

They'd have a double memorial service for Frankie and Benny at Shady Oaks, and then there'd be a police procession to the cemetery where Frankie Wilson Flynn would get a burial with full honors. Gerald had asked that Sam, Connor, and Goddard join him, one of Benny's grandsons, and Henry Whitfield's grandson as the pall-bearers for Frankie's casket. Frankie would be laid to rest next to Ryan, with Ryan's sister – and Benny's wife – Martha already in the adjacent plot.

Benny's funeral would be later on Sunday afternoon at a syna-gogue downtown. He'd be laid to rest with the others afterward. It was going to be a long and emotionally exhausting day for everyone.

359

'Did you get it all closed up?' Sam asked.

'I think so.' She glanced through the windows of Navarro's office, where he was finishing a phone call. 'We'll find out soon enough. How's Georgia?'

'She's okay, thank God. Your parents have adopted her. Your mom is making her and Eloise come home with them for a late dinner after the services tomorrow.'

Kit grinned. 'I know. And Rita, Tiffany, and Emma have claimed them as their honorary grandmas. Whether Georgia wants it or not. Eloise is tickled.'

'Georgia wants it, trust me. She's touched and excited, even if she won't admit it. She's also ready to smack Eloise, who's hovering over her like a mother hen.'

'Poor Eloise. She was so upset when she found out you and Georgia were missing. She's a sweet old girl.'

Sam nodded. 'They both are. And they're going to have a hard time for a while. Now that everything is over, losing Frankie and Benny is hitting them hard.'

'Mom and Pop will make sure they're kept busy,' Kit said, pushing away from her desk when Navarro hung up his phone. She picked up her coffee. 'I think it's time.'

'Where's Connor?'

'On his way up. He went for a bakery run.'

Because he'd been writing up reports on all of Roxanne's dead husbands and needed a break. It was a sad but necessary chore.

Kit led the way to Navarro's office, leaving the door open. 'Hey, boss.'

'Good morning. Dr Reeves, I'm glad you could join us.'

'Me too. I have questions.' Sam took one of the seats at the table, then raised his eyebrows meaningfully at Kit.

Feeling her cheeks heat because Navarro was avidly watching, Kit sat next to Sam. Fortunately, Connor arrived with the food and she didn't have to endure Navarro's amusement at her discomfort.

'We ready?' Navarro asked when everyone had their sugary breakfast of champions.

Connor opened his notebook. 'Yep. Where do we start?'

'With the timeline,' Navarro said. 'We know that Roxanne was working with her sister and the sister's boyfriend on the thefts, but let's save that. Review the timeline of the homicides.'

'Roxanne had been sleeping with Kent Crawford, the head of security at Shady Oaks, nearly the entire time she was working there,' Connor began. 'We found confirmation when we searched her cell phone.' They'd had a signed warrant, which had allowed them to hold the phone in front of Roxanne's eyes to unlock it.

Roxanne herself had been silent, as had her sister. But Neil Fogarty, the sister's boyfriend, was singing like a damn canary.

Funny how the charge of attempted murder of a cop could loosen a man's tongue.

'Roxanne and Crawford had been meeting at the same Excelsior Hotel he used to meet with Miss Evans,' Kit went on. Crawford had, apparently, been a regular. Evans and Roxanne hadn't been his only sex partners. 'We have security footage of Crawford and Roxanne entering a hotel room and signed affidavits from the hotel staff.'

'But they didn't use the same hotel the night Crawford was killed,' Navarro said. 'Why use the cheap motel?'

'No cameras,' Connor said. 'That's our best guess, anyway. He knew his affairs at the Excelsior would be caught on camera, but he wasn't worried about that. The worst that could happen was that his wife would divorce him. But he knew that he and Roxanne would be heisting the coins, so . . . no cameras.'

'Makes sense.' Navarro waved his hand. 'Please continue.'

Kit checked her notes. 'We recovered Frankie's, Crawford's, and Roxanne's laptops from her tiny house, and there are emails between Crawford and Roxanne detailing how Crawford would turn off the camera so that Roxanne could take the coins. These were private emails and not sent through the Shady Oaks server, otherwise Adler would have found out and Crawford didn't want to share.'

'How did they find out about Benny's coins?' Sam asked.

'Roxanne had found the article about Benny's collection before she'd arrived at Shady Oaks,' Kit said. 'Her sister's boyfriend, Neil Fogarty, investigated the staff to see if anyone was a particular concern. Frankie would have been a red flag if he'd dug any deeper.

Fogarty dug deep enough on Crawford to find that his spending patterns didn't match his salary. He also knew that Crawford was sleeping around, so Roxanne could get to him that way. She tricked Evans's assistant Lily into letting her use her computer. Lily confirmed this when we asked some pointed questions. She was afraid to say anything because she didn't want to lose her job before she could retire. But Roxanne was able to access personnel files from Lily's computer. She knew how much Crawford was earning and, all the while, the sister's boyfriend was following Crawford around town, tallying up his purchases. They figured if they had to, they could use him as a confederate.'

'Which they needed,' Connor said. 'Benny Dreyfus wouldn't donate his coins, but he did believe that Roxanne was . . . y'know, interested in him.'

'Which Frankie knew,' Kit added. 'He said as much in his letter to Georgia. It was the reason for his and Benny's argument.'

Sam sighed sadly. 'Roxanne knew that Benny wasn't going to hand over his coins, so she'd have to steal them. For that, she needed access to the cameras. So she risked an alliance with Crawford.'

Kit nodded. 'Exactly. Roxanne told Crawford in an email that the coins were in Shady Oaks. Neil Fogarty says that Roxanne picked times when Benny was more confused to press for details. Putting the nanny-cam vase in Benny's room to record him punching in his safe code was Fogarty's idea, but he said that Roxanne refused to place the vase in Benny's room herself. She didn't want to be caught on camera holding it, so Crawford forced Miss Evans to do it.'

'Also so that Evans could take the fall once the theft was discovered,' Navarro said.

Connor nodded. 'We asked Ryland to search Benny's room for the evidence that the vase had been there. He found dust that was consistent with the vase that Evans planted there.'

Kit smiled at Sam. 'You and Georgia were right. The vase was smashed to remove it from Benny's apartment.' She turned to Navarro. 'When Ryland examined a pair of scrubs in Roxanne's dirty clothes hamper in her tiny house, he found residual dust that appears to match the dust he found in Benny's living room. The lab's still testing to be absolutely sure, but Ryland says the dust is a match under the microscope.'

'That'll be good enough for the brass,' Navarro said. 'The prosecutor will want the lab confirmation, so keep me informed. Do we *know* that Roxanne killed Crawford?'

Kit frowned. 'Well, we have a lot of circumstantial evidence that says yes. The lipstick on Crawford's body matches that on the teacup that both Sam and Georgia will swear was used by Roxanne. Ryland says he got a DNA sample from the cup, and it's Roxanne's. Plus, we found Crawford's car in a chop shop. Recall, it had been missing from the parking lot. The chop shop identified Roxanne as the one who sold them the car. So we have her physically in Crawford's motel room and we have her in possession of his laptop and his car. We don't have video proof, but with everything else, Joel says it should be enough.'

She and Connor had spent hours with Joel Haley the evening before, detailing all their evidence. While each piece of evidence wasn't a slam dunk, all of it together painted a convincing picture.

'Good.' Navarro had been taking notes and scanned them. 'So she killed Crawford first – Saturday between midnight and probably three forty-five a.m. – then went back to Shady Oaks dressed in his clothes to steal Benny's coins at four fifteen a.m.?'

Kit nodded. 'Exactly. We don't have Roxanne going into Shady Oaks dressed in Crawford's clothes, though. She entered through the nursing ward using poor Devon Jones's ID.'

'Devon Jones is the young nursing assistant who saw Benny's coins, right?' Navarro asked.

Kit nodded again. 'Yes. That made Devon the best choice for a frame if something went wrong. Janice, the head nurse who Devon had told that she'd seen the coins, had reported it to Miss Evans. Evans told us that she hadn't shared that with Crawford, but the sister's boyfriend, Neil Fogarty, said that Evans did.'

'Poor Devon,' Navarro said. 'I'm glad she had an airtight alibi for that night.'

'Me too,' Kit agreed. 'Devon was on duty that night in the nursing ward, so the record of her key card being used to come and go didn't raise any immediate flags. Roxanne went through the nursing ward and disappeared into the stairwell where there was a camera blind spot. Crawford had told her about the blind spot in the stairwell. That was in their emails. She changed into his clothes, went up to Benny's apartment, and stole the coins, exiting through the closest rear door where we saw her on the camera.'

'She wanted the closest exit after stealing the coins because she didn't want to be caught with them,' Connor said. 'It also would have been a red flag had she used Devon Jones's card to get *in* via that door. One, because Devon's card wasn't keyed to that door, but also because Devon was working in the nursing ward that night on the other side of the facility.'

Navarro nodded his approval. 'Fine. So give me the rest of the timeline.'

'Crawford had turned off the cameras remotely from his laptop at five p.m. on Friday,' Connor said. 'We know that Archie Adler wasn't involved because, a, he didn't have remote access to the cameras and, b, he left on his boat at five on Friday afternoon. His defense attorney provided security camera footage from the marina where his boat was moored.'

'So Adler really wasn't involved in the murders. Just in stealing from the operating fund?' Navarro asked.

'Exactly,' Connor replied. 'Roxanne broke into Benny's apartment using Crawford's master key at four oh five on Saturday morning. Benny had taken a sleeping pill that night and was sound asleep. She'd already figured out the safe code and probably used the wheelchair in Benny's room to get him to the safe for his fingerprint. She steals the coins and, wearing Crawford's clothes, leaves Shady Oaks at four fifteen on Saturday morning.'

Sam nodded. 'And she came back Saturday evening during Eloise's party to search Frankie's room because he suspected her.'

'That's right,' Kit said. 'She went into Frankie's apartment during the party at seven thirty-five p.m. to search for whatever Frankie had against her. We found an email from Roxanne to Crawford saying that she "might have a bigger fish than BD" – Benny Dreyfus. Frankie had started to come on to her in the previous week, mentioning that he was bi, hoping to get her attention, and she knew about his fortune. We got that from the letter Frankie wrote to Georgia. And then Roxanne admitted to Sam and Georgia that she'd found out from Crawford that Frankie was a retired cop and not to trust his sudden advances.'

'When she was kidnapping you,' Navarro said to Sam.

'Yes,' Sam confirmed with a shudder.

Kit felt the same way. She wasn't sure she'd ever forget the sight of Roxanne holding a stiletto to Sam's throat.

'And,' she added, 'Georgia had overheard Crawford telling Frankie that he wasn't a homicide lieutenant anymore, that he – Crawford – was in charge at Shady Oaks, so that confirms that Crawford *did* know that Frankie was a retired cop. So Roxanne needed to find what Frankie knew.'

'He left the birthday dinner early and interrupted Roxanne's search,' Navarro recalled. 'She killed him. Why did she pull the stunt with the knives? Changing the wound and leaving a butcher knife in Frank's chest?'

Connor smiled triumphantly. 'Because some of the other Shady Oaks nurses had seen the stiletto. We asked around at Shady Oaks yesterday because that was a loose end for us. Two of the nurses identified it as the same blade they'd seen fall out of the bag that Roxanne kept in her locker. Roxanne told them that she'd been mugged once, and because she lived alone and traveled all the time, she kept it for protection. Neither nurse had thought any more about it until we showed them the stiletto.'

'Also, Roxanne knew she had to fake the real time of Frankie's death,' Kit said, 'because she didn't have an alibi for that hour on Saturday night. She was on her dinner break and we couldn't find her on any of the facility's surveillance cameras. She pulled Frankie's I'm-okay cord the next morning after her shift to give herself an airtight alibi. She wasn't on the schedule to work most of Sunday and she made sure she was seen by her neighbors at the RV campground at various times of the day.'

'What about Crawford's car?' Navarro asked. 'Did she take that also?'

'Yes,' Kit said, 'but not that night. She came back the next day and drove it to the chop shop. It's all on traffic cams and surveillance video. We didn't find that ourselves, by the way. The people you loaned us did all the footwork. We've noted who got what info in our formal report.'

'Thank you,' Navarro said. 'So we have evidence supporting Roxanne killing Frank, killing Crawford, and stealing the coins. What about Benny Dreyfus's murder?'

'We found a clone of Devon Jones's key card in Roxanne's pocket when we arrested her,' Kit said. 'That's how she got into Shady Oaks the night she stole the coins, then again when she killed Benny.'

'Plus, we found the bottle of digoxin hidden in her tiny house,' Connor said. 'She knew that Benny was on the diltiazem already. I don't know if we're going to be able to prove that she killed any of her elderly husbands that same way, but I think it's a fair assumption.'

Navarro nodded. 'I agree, and that segues nicely into the thefts. Talk to me about the thefts from the retirement homes first.'

'Goddard is formally handling all of that,' Connor began, 'but we have a lot of the high points. Roxanne would research the retirement facilities her agency scheduled for her to identify which elderly person made the easiest and most profitable mark. Goddard found some files on Roxanne's laptop, and Neil Fogarty – the sister's boyfriend – supplied some of the rest. She didn't steal from every job, only one in three or so. We thought that Frankie might have discovered this, but he didn't. He suspected something, but then found out about her four dead husbands and feared Benny would be next. We'll come back to the husbands later.'

'Roxanne and her sister Jackie had been stealing stuff from the elderly for more than fifteen years,' Kit said, 'according to Fogarty. That confirmed the pattern we found in the reported thefts from the retirement homes Roxanne had worked in – they started fifteen years ago. She'd do the schmoozing and the stealing. Sometimes her marks were men, others were women. She'd research what causes were important to them, then casually mention she was on the board of this or that charity. She'd get her mark to sign over something valuable – paintings, jewelry, collections, and other portable things – to her "charities." They weren't really charities, but they looked legit on the surface. They were shell companies set up by her sister Jackie, who – again according to the boyfriend – was the brains of the scheme. Jackie's an accountant and knew how to funnel the money and how to donate enough money to actual charities that they wouldn't raise suspicions.'

'Neil Fogarty was the broker,' Connor added. 'He came into the picture about ten years ago. On the surface, everything looks legit. When she could, Roxanne got the targets to legally sign the items over. She usually picked targets who either didn't have family who visited or who were angry with their families for putting them in a home.'

Navarro frowned. 'Benny Dreyfus wasn't either of those things.'

Kit sighed. 'But he had a four-million-dollar collection, and they couldn't pass that up. This was going to be Roxanne's last job. She was going to retire from being a traveling nurse. She'd already bought a beach house in Florida. Ironically, not too far from the previous Shady Oaks director who embezzled for years.'

'I'm missing something,' Navarro said, still frowning. 'Roxanne found out about Benny's coins because of the article, but that claimed they were in the family's bank vault. How did she originally expect to steal them?'

'The same way she stole the Dutch Master painting from William Freeman,' Connor answered. 'Freeman was angry that his son had put him in a home, even though medically speaking that was the safest place for him to be. We talked to the bank manager where William's painting was kept. It was ten years ago, but the manager remembered that William was brought to the bank in a wheelchair – during the time frame that Roxanne worked in William's retirement facility. He remembers because it was a valuable painting. He was concerned and asked William if his son knew he was taking it. William was very clear that the painting was his, not his son's, and if the son found out, William would have the bank manager's job. The manager respected William's wishes and never divulged his trip until the painting was reported stolen. When the police asked if it had been stolen, he said that William had taken it. There was no theft, as the painting belonged to him. He also remembered that William had been accompanied by a woman. It was probably Roxanne, but we can't prove it. She most likely thought she could get Benny to do the same thing. And then, according to Frankie's letter to Georgia, she found out the coins were in Shady Oaks, when she saw Benny looking at them. Having the coins at Shady Oaks made Roxanne's job a lot easier. Until it wasn't.'

'Because of Frank,' Navarro murmured. 'Does Goddard think they'll be able to recover any of the other stolen items?'

Kit shrugged because Goddard hadn't sounded hopeful. 'They're going to try, but most of those items went to people like Emil Barrington Senior – people who bought privately or illegally and who had no intention of showing their purchase to the world.'

'That sucks,' Sam muttered.

Navarro nodded. 'It does, indeed. I imagine the four dead husbands will also be hard to prove.'

Connor sighed. 'Yeah. I've written up what we know to pass on to the jurisdictions where the murders occurred. One of the husbands lived in California, one each in Nevada, Arizona, and Tennessee. The one in Tennessee was likely her first. The circumstances were the same. She met them through a retirement or nursing home – they were either residents or visited friends who were residents. She picked men who were close to death and who had pre-existing heart conditions, and who didn't have any families to contest the will once her victim died.'

'Why didn't she just get them to donate the money to her?' Navarro asked. 'Why marry them?'

'There was a lot of money at stake,' Kit said. 'More than she could get them to donate. It was easy money, especially with no one to contest the will. She didn't do it that often, but the marks she picked were very wealthy.'

'Frankie thought Benny was her next intended victim,' Sam murmured. 'But he did have a family to contest any inheritance, so she just intended to rob him.'

'If Roxanne used the same drugs on the dead husbands that she used on Benny Dreyfus,' Connor said, 'exhumation of their bodies won't show anything because the drugs are gone from the body in days. A week tops. And all the husbands were cremated anyway,' he finished sadly. 'At Roxanne's request. She was thorough.'

'Joel Haley wasn't optimistic that Roxanne could be charged for those crimes,' Kit finished. 'And none of the murders happened in our jurisdiction, so we're handing it off to the locals. We're going to make sure she goes down for the three murders she committed here.'

Navarro looked resigned at the notion of Roxanne skating on four additional murders. 'I agree. I think you've wrapped it up nicely. Is Joel our prosecutor?'

'He is,' Kit said. 'He knows everything you do.'

'Good. Thanks for coming in this morning to summarize. I've got a meeting with the brass in an hour to bring them up to speed. I hope Shady Oaks can seat a large group of people. I know of at least a hundred who'll be attending the memorial service tomorrow.'

'I think they're going to provide chairs for the residents and Frankie's older colleagues, like Henry Whitfield,' Sam said. 'The rest might have to stand, but there should be room.'

'Are you still playing for the service?' Connor asked.

Sam's nod was pensive. 'I am. Georgia's doing the eulogy and I'm going to play some of the expected standards, but also the song I played the day Frankie and I met. Georgia and I both agreed that he'd have appreciated that.'

'What song was it?' Navarro asked.

Sam smiled fondly. 'Iron Maiden's "The Number of the Beast." He requested a heavy metal song because all the other residents wanted Sinatra and Bing Crosby. He didn't expect me to know how to play it.'

Navarro laughed loudly. 'That's amazing. I think you should explain before you play it, though, or everyone will think you're insinuating that Frankie went to hell.'

'Frankie would like that, too, but I'll make sure to explain.' Sam sighed. 'I'll be glad when this is over. It's been hard for the residents.'

'And you,' Navarro observed. 'Thank you for your help. Now I have to prepare for my meeting. Go. Get some sunshine.'

Connor didn't have to be asked twice. 'CeCe's waiting for me.'

He was gone, leaving Kit and Sam to wander back to her desk alone.

Sam exhaled, then visibly braced himself. 'So . . . give it to me straight, Kit. Are we still having a day on your sister's boat, or do you plan to tell me that you can't see me for my own good again?'

Kit grimaced, because the thought had crossed her mind. 'I was going to tell you that you don't have to go on the boat,' she admitted. 'But mainly because I know you hate the water. We can go out for a meal.'

His slow smile sent shivers down her spine. 'No, I want the whole day. I'll take some Dramamine, just in case. But I want the whole day with you.'

She drew a deep, deep breath. 'I'll text you with the details after I set it up with my sister.'

He pushed a lock of hair away from her face, dropping his hand to his side after the brief touch. 'It's a date.'

They were the same words that had sent her scurrying for cover six months ago. Now . . . *I think I'm looking forward to it.* 'Yes, it's a date.'

Epilogue

Shelter Island Marina, San Diego, California
Tuesday, 22 November, 4.30 P.M.

'Did you really have a good time?' Kit asked for the third time as Sam walked her down the dock where the rented sailboat that she called home was moored.

She'd felt guilty since she'd made the dare, over a week ago. It had been the most outrageous thing she'd been able to think of to counter his demand for a date should he win their bet over who'd prove Roxanne Beaton guilty first.

Sam Reeves hated the water. He'd insisted it wasn't a phobia, but it had sure seemed like it when Kit's sister had set sail that morning. He'd gripped the rail until his knuckles had turned white and, for a little while, his skin had developed an alarming greenish tinge. Every few minutes he'd mutter something like *Deserts don't rock. Deserts stay still.*

But after an hour or so, he'd started having fun.

'I did,' Sam assured her for the third time. 'I caught the biggest fish, after all.'

She laughed. 'Yes, you did.'

'Twenty-eight inches and nearly nine pounds,' he boasted, his pride making Kit grin.

The California halibut had been well over the minimum keeper size. Akiko had excitedly told Sam that his fish was probably six or seven years old, and that was when Sam's excitement had begun to wane.

It had survived all that time, he'd said. He hadn't wanted to kill

371

it. So after getting a photo with it, Akiko had shown him how to safely return it to the water.

'You nearly made Akiko cry,' Kit said, chuckling at the memory.

He shrugged. 'I couldn't kill it.'

'It's okay. Really. It's just that grilled halibut is her favorite meal.'

They reached the edge of the dock and she paused to look up at him. She'd been anxious at the thought of spending an entire day with him, but her anxiety had been unfounded.

He'd been wonderful. The perfect companion.

Perfectly polite. Too polite, if she were being honest.

He hadn't touched her once, except to help her on and off the boat. As if she'd needed the help. She'd been boating since she was a teenager and her footing was sure. But she'd taken his hand anyway, which had made Akiko grin with a delight that her sister hadn't even tried to disguise.

Kit had held her breath for the second hour – he'd been busy clutching the rail during the first. She'd wondered when he'd make his move, but he hadn't. So she'd finally relaxed and had a good time, too.

'I still shouldn't have forced you to go,' she said quietly. 'I'm sorry for that.'

He smiled at her. 'You didn't force me to do anything. You gave me a choice. Dinner for two or a whole day on a fishing boat, chaperoned by your sister. Not that I realized Akiko would be there. But that was good, too.'

'I don't have a captain's license. I can only be first mate.'

'Kit, I get it. And I had a wonderful time.' He tipped her chin up. 'Because I was with you.'

She swallowed hard, her heart pounding in her chest. This was the moment she'd been both anticipating and fearing. The good-night kiss.

'You are a very nice man,' she murmured. 'A true gentle-man.'

He lifted his eyebrows over the rims of his nerdy Clark Kent glasses. 'On the outside, sure.'

She narrowed her eyes. 'And on the inside?'

He shrugged, but he was still smiling. 'Mine to know.'

'And mine to find out?'

'Maybe.' He winked. 'I guess we'll see.' He continued to smile down at her, patience personified.

She was starting to hate his patience. 'What are you doing tomorrow?' she blurted.

'Going to Shady Oaks in the morning.'

'Arts and crafts day?'

'No, I'm picking up Henry Whitfield from his house and taking him to see Georgia. His grandson's picking him up after lunch to take him home.'

Kit stared at him. 'Georgia and Frankie's old homicide partner? Our Georgia?'

His green eyes sparkled, his lips quirking up. 'Our Georgia. I think they're becoming friends. They seem well suited for each other.'

'Wow.'

Sam chuckled. 'I know. Eloise is green with jealousy but Georgia saw him first and Eloise doesn't poach.'

'Anymore,' Kit said wryly.

'True enough. But she loves Georgia and won't get in the way. It'll be good for all of them, I think. Meeting new people.'

'You're kind to pick him up.'

Another shrug. 'I'm a really nice guy.'

Kit laughed. 'You are.'

He took a step back. 'I'll call you soon.'

She stood there a moment, her mouth open. *What?* He was leaving? 'Sam?'

He stopped, tilting his head. 'Yes, Kit?'

'You're leaving? *Now?*'

'Our date is over.'

Kit blinked slowly. 'I figured . . .' *That you'd want to come into my place. That you'd want . . . more.*

'I promised I wouldn't push you. This bet was as close to breaking that promise as I'm willing to go.' But he didn't move another step. He was waiting.

She knew what he wanted. He wanted her to take the next step.

Suddenly her heart was pounding again, butterflies fluttering in her stomach. But it wasn't unpleasant. And she wasn't afraid because this was Sam Reeves and he was a patient man. A kind and gentle man.

A man who, for whatever reason, wants me.

So she took the next step, closing the distance between them, gingerly placing her hands on his chest where his heart thundered under her palm. She lifted onto her toes until their mouths were a whisper apart. 'I still don't know if I can be what you need.'

'And I still say you don't get to decide that.'

They were close now, so close that she could feel his answer on her lips. Tentatively, she slid one hand up, hooking it around his neck, pulling his head another millimeter closer.

His hands were still at his side, his body tense. Because he was still waiting.

'You're going to make *me* do this, aren't you?' she asked, her lips brushing his as she spoke.

He smirked. 'Yep.'

'I thought you were a nice man.'

'Growing less nice every second.' His voice was husky and sent shivers all over her skin. 'Kiss me, Kit, or let me go home. You're killing me here.'

She swallowed again, closed her eyes, and kissed him. Then gasped when his arms closed around her, pulling her tight against him. He took control of the kiss, pulling the scrunchie from her ponytail and threading his fingers through her hair.

She wound both hands around his neck and held on, letting it all go, losing herself in his warmth. His affection. His mastery of her mouth.

Sam Reeves is a damn good kisser.

She forgot where she was, every thought cleared from her mind as she allowed herself to simply feel for the first time in a long time.

Maybe ever.

He pulled away and she sucked in a breath. They were both panting. His lips were wet and his cheeks were flushed.

His eyes were hot and filled with all the things she wanted, too. Her mind stuttered back into gear, expecting that he'd walk her to her door, ask to come in, and they'd continue that kiss in her tiny living room.

Maybe even in her bed.

But he didn't. He gripped her hands gently, pulling them from around his neck to his lips, where he kissed one hand, then the other.

'Good night, Kit,' he said hoarsely.

She stared up at him. 'What? You're leaving? *Now?*'

'I am.' He lifted one brow. 'I don't put out on the first date.'

She stared for several heartbeats, then began to laugh. *'What?'*

He still held her hands. Kissing them one last time, he released them. 'I want more with you than one night. Call me. This date was because of my bet. Next time, it's your turn to ask me out on a date. No bet involved.'

She blinked a few times. 'Where? When?'

'You choose. I'll be waiting.'

Then he turned and walked down the pier toward where he'd parked his RAV4. Just before he would have turned the corner, he looked back and waved.

Fingertips of one hand pressed to her lips, she waved back automatically and watched him disappear out of her sight.

Wow.

She stepped onto her boat's deck, her feet almost floating, her heart still beating out of rhythm. Her body tingled. All over.

Wow.

She went down the short flight of stairs to her door and, hands trembling, she managed to unlock it.

Snickerdoodle leapt from the bed, bounding over to greet her, tail wagging. Muscle memory kicked in, and Kit grabbed Snick's leash and led her out onto the pier for her walk.

Kit had a lot to think about.

Next time. Six months ago, she'd sent Sam away. Now her mind was churning with thoughts of *next time.* What did he like? Where would he want to go?

How could she make him smile? Make his green eyes crinkle behind those nerdy glasses that she now just wanted to take off?

And then she knew what she needed to do.

Shelter Island Marina, San Diego, California
Tuesday, 22 November, 5.05 P.M.

Sam rested his head on the steering wheel of his RAV4, his hands clenched and his body shaking. Walking away from Kit McKittrick had been the hardest thing he'd ever done. His body ached with how tightly he'd held himself.

He'd kissed her. Finally.

She'd kissed him first. *Thank God.* He almost hadn't been able to make himself wait, but he was so glad that he had.

He had to chuckle, remembering her stunned expression when he told her that he didn't put out on the first date. Not that he'd had too many of those. Kit was his fifth first date.

He didn't date often, wasn't one for hookups. He wanted a relationship. He wanted everything.

He wanted Kit.

And, although the very thought made him ache, he'd make himself wait for her to call or text. This had to be her choice. Her move.

Opening his hand, he stared at the scrunchie that had held her ponytail. He should give it back to her, but not tonight. He'd told her that he'd be waiting, so he'd keep it for a while. A little souvenir of what he hoped would be the first date of many.

He started the engine and had put the SUV in reverse when his cell phone buzzed with an incoming text. The caller ID made him dizzy with relief. It was from Kit.

Next Saturday. Hiking up at Anza-Borrego. Dogs + picnic lunch. Show me why you like the desert more than the ocean. Pick me up at 9am.

Closing his eyes, he reined in his galloping pulse. He could do that. The state park was the closest desert to San Diego and he and Siggy knew it well.

He could absolutely do that.

When his head stopped spinning, he typed out his reply. *It's a date.*

Acknowledgments

The Starfish – Christine, Brian, Sheila, Cheryl, and Kathie – for the brainstorming. I love your deliciously devious minds.

Andrew Grey for being my daily word count partner and cheerleader.

Rita Kaufman Grindle for introducing me to the beautiful 'Mi Shebeirach.'

Martin Hafer for keeping me fed and bringing me tea.

Sarah Hafer for catching my mistakes.

James Lee for the computer lessons.

Beth Miller for the proofreading.

Margaret Taylor for the law enforcement insights.

Liz Sellers, Jen Doyle, and Robin Rue for your enthusiastic support for this new series!

As always, all mistakes are my own.